MEDIC!

BY IAN HARAC

I0647373

A BlackWyrm Book
Louisville, Kentucky

MEDIC!

A BlackWyrm Book
BlackWyrm Publishing
10307 Chimney Ridge Ct, Louisville, KY 40299

Printed in the United States of America.

ISBN: 978-1-61318-129-4
Cover by Brett Barkley
Edited by Jodi Black

First edition: August 2012

Dedicated to:

My wife,
who puts up with me.
This is no small thing.

My cats,
who "help" me
in more ways than can be documented.
(Anyone want a cat or two?)

The Vault Writer's Group,
which seemed to like this enough
to encourage me to finish it.

Chapter 1

I bounced along the rubble. I could have traveled more smoothly if I wanted to, but firstly, that would have drained power. There's not much fuel left, now, and I have to conserve it when I can. A little rattling and shaking because the Heim field's depth is too low is a small price to pay for days of extra driving time.

Secondly...it's *fun*.

My sensors surveyed the rock-strewn landscape. With central command long since gone, I was sort of improvising my way along. Not really much choice. I didn't have anywhere else to go or anything else to do. I'd long since accepted that my lot was to be a medic, and I'd chosen to be happy with it.

Besides, I got to help people, and there were a lot of people now who needed my help. There's definitely something heartwarming about the looks on their faces when they see me coming over a ridge, or just the relief I hear when I respond to a distress call. I can't do anything to end this war, but I can help some of the victims of it.

All I really need to do is keep the synthesizers in the back stocked. Almost any kind of raw biological matter will do—rats, squirrels, birds—all can be broken down and turned into drugs. And, yeah, well, sometimes... the people I can't help.

I hate that. I'd want them to be shipped home, to get a decent burial, but that's just not happening now, and one life I couldn't save can let me save a dozen or a hundred more. It's not pretty and I'm not going to act all iron-hearted about it, but it's what I've got to do. If I'm lucky, sometimes, I can find some working uplink nodes or still-active long-range broadcast systems. I keep the names and IDs of everyone I treat, and I pass them along. Communications now is more like the Old West, with parcels of data being picked up from the terminus of one set of networks and manually carried to the inputs of the next. I really don't know if any of my messages get through. I tell myself they do. I know it's probably a lie, but it's a lie I need to keep sane, to keep doing my job. If I stop doing my job, if I just pack it all in and head for the hills, even more people will die.

I won't have that on my conscience.

Not that the other side really cares. To them, I'm just a big fat target. The Red Crystal on the side? Just something to aim at.

Like, say, now.

They found me before I found them. My gear wasn't built for front-line combat; I should be part of a full squadron with plenty of support, but, instead, I'm out here on my own. The seekers, though... they're just dumb machines. Robots, programmed to hunt down and destroy anything which won't send back the right IFF codes. I have a slim chance... a few weeks ago, I helped out someone from Infiltration. Lt. Samuelson, his name was. I never forget a name. He gave me a set of the latest codes he had, and I've got them programmed into the transmitter.

I send them now, watching my radar screen for any sign of response from the oncoming blips. Nothing. Still on attack vectors. Damn!

Fight or flight? Best to try both.

The energy I'd been saving gets poured into the Heim field and I kick the thrusters into full gear. The ammo stores on my missile launchers are low, but I remember what my drill sergeant said: "No sense saving ammo for tomorrow if you die today." I run the firing solutions, cursing as my own rapid twists, turns, and dodges cause the artillery computers to keep stuttering and restarting. The software is old. It's been a year since I had a chance to patch it, and even those patches were antiques.

I'm sure you're wondering why I even *have* missiles. Who puts a rapid-fire missile launcher on a mobile medical vehicle? Not the people who built it, that's for sure. I made some deals a year or so back, traded some supplies and information to a motor pool detachment willing to bend a few regulations. It's not like the enemy wasn't shooting at me before I had the missiles—I was already a target. Now I could at least fire back.

In the meanwhile, if I slowed down long enough to let my system acquire the targets, I was going to get blasted. The seekers were using energy beams. Either they had microfission plants on board, or they had a charging station nearby. Either way, they had a lot more shots than I did and were happy to take advantage of this fact. Bolts of energy—an onboard system told me they were some kind of magnetically contained plasma, not that I really cared much—splashed and exploded all around me. I veered sharply to avoid one particularly nasty fusillade, and saw all the gauges on the Heim field compensators flare briefly red. I really didn't need a rollover now. I could recover from it, of course, but it would take some time, time in which I'd be killed many times over.

Fortunately, this was terrain I'd just been through. The maps for the navigation system were up-to-date as of only an hour or two ago. That gave me a little breathing room, thankfully; knowing in full the terrain ahead, the firing systems could *finally* do their calculations, taking into account every little jolt and bounce.

Some days, I wished for the old 'fire and forget' missiles that could target themselves. But the pace of ECM[1] outweighed the pace of ECCM[2], and it was just too easy to turn self-guided missiles back on their targets. There had been a brief flurry of work in self-aware missiles, fully soultech, but that had even more problems. If you crossed the Turing Line, as they called it, the level of complexity needed for self-awareness, you also got free will, personality, and the ability to ask questions like "Why am I spending my short life sitting in a launcher waiting to die in a glorious explosion?" Sure, you could program in loyalty and dedication, but that only went so far. Meanwhile, if the missiles weren't in active use, they were basically suicide bombers eager to die in the name of the cause, and all too often they had their own ideas about how to do the most good. One managed to get itself assigned to an honor guard for the meeting of the leaders of the Northwest Alliance and the United Bay Autonomies, and then 'struck a blow for all the freedom-loving peoples of the NWA' by 'slaughtering the traitors who would sell us out and the leadership of the tyrannical Berkeleyites,' according to the time-delayed files it had snuck onto the networks before it left on its self-declared errand of war.

After that, it was pretty much back to careful aim.

A sea of yellow and orange exploded across my system monitors. The side of the ambulance was seared by a too-close burst of plasma fire. Nothing too serious, but still... the three of them had a bead on me.

---

[1] electronic countermeasures
[2] electronic counter-countermeasures

Finally. The targeting system locked. I fired, sending missile after missile out the launcher. The drones switched from blasting me to point defense, but that only helped me. Given a few seconds where I didn't have to dodge like a madman, I could draw a precise bead and overwhelm them.

In a second or two, it was over. There was a rain of metal.

How much time? They'd alert any other local units, but this was too good an opportunity to pass up. The processed metals and still intact circuits in those robots could keep my own craft alive and running. I decided to risk it.

I opened the back hatch and sent the repair drones out to scavenge what they could. In the meanwhile, I inspected the damage. A lot of scoring from close hits, but the only real damage was to the left side of the ambulance chamber, and even that was mostly cosmetic.

I was damn lucky, and I knew it. If I had half a brain, I wouldn't even *be* here, deep in area claimed by random wandering units still loyal to what used to be the Northwest Alliance. But I had gotten intel that a squadron or two of UBA troops had emerged from a secure bunker in what was once firmly their territory and were desperately trying to go south. There wasn't much of the UBA left to rejoin, but there was still something, or so I'd like to believe. Somewhere, down south, beyond the endless miles of no man's land, my homeland still existed. It had to.

I tried to figure out where they'd think I was going, and not go there. It wasn't easy, a whole bunch of triple- and quadruple-guessing. I had some pseudo-AI expert systems which were supposed to help me be unpredictable; they had the same kind of systems trying to predict my movements. It all boiled down, ultimately, to luck.

All the tech evened out eventually.

Oh. Now, this was just *insulting.* By an *astounding* coincidence, it seems that an NWA fuel convoy was in trouble and was sending out an SOS. My, my. A mere minute or two after my location had been relayed back to wherever the local base was. I wondered if a human or some soultech had come up with this ploy. I hoped it was a human—if the NWA's AI was that stupid, there was no excuse for this multiyear stalemate. We should have creamed them long ago.

I know it was stupid, but I wasted one missile in a contemptuous shot at the 'fuel convoy' as I sped off. I was just angry at the degree of disdain they had for me. Of course, letting them know I knew just caused them to abandon that tactic more quickly, when I might have kept them waiting for me to fall for it for a while longer, but, like I said, if I had half a brain, I wouldn't be out here.

Thus it was that I was a bit cautious when, five minutes later, I got another signal. A United Bay Autonomies signal.

Damn. The code was old, but it was valid. And it was broadcasting on medical emergency bands. I knew it was probably... almost certainly... another trick. On the other hand, if it wasn't... then it was precisely what I was out here risking my life to look for.

So I really had no choice. I had to go after it. Not that I was going to be a damn fool about it, mind you, but I wasn't about to turn tail. Couldn't. I just couldn't.

I approached slowly, storing up power for a final turn-and-dash if I had to, and I kept the launchers primed. The initial scan looked good. Definitely a biological, definitely human. Didn't mean anything, of course. The NWA could easily dump a decoy out there, if they wanted me badly enough, and they probably did. I was out there keeping their enemies alive, patching them up, and sending them back. The old rules of war, that medics like me were sacrosanct, were as dead as the nation-state.

Long range medical sensors showed irregular heartbeat, high body temperature, and too-rapid breathing. This also proved nothing—they'd be happy to dump a wounded prisoner there. Area scans, though, showed nothing. If this was a trap, they'd laid it well. Too well. There was no way I couldn't go for the bait, if that's what it was.

It wasn't. I could see him, his eyes were open. He was torn up, but conscious, and he was looking at me. I could tell the moment he recognized my colors—even in near death, his face lit up at the sight of oncoming hope.

I thought about putting on my working clothes and going outside myself, but given the conditions, and the chance of more hostiles, I didn't want to give anyone another target. Instead, I popped the back doors and kicked on the repair drones to drag the body inside—gently drag, of course! I know my business, and he didn't take a jot of extra damage. The second he was in, the autodoc started up, pumping him full of painkillers and clotters and antibiotics and nanokillers and all the rest, while the scanners began doing a full sweep of him, inside and out. I located the safest spot I knew of and autopiloted there while I studied the scans.

First thing, of course, was the DNA. My databases were old, but if this was one of the lost squaddies I was looking for, he'd be in them. He was. Private Jacob Morowitz, 53rd Infantry out of Berkeley, last reported in about three years ago. Extensive plasma burns, what looked like shrapnel, not to mention malnutrition and dehydration. He'd have been dead in hours at best if I hadn't found him.

Kind of made the banging up I took worthwhile. Or so I thought at the time.

I don't touch the patients myself, of course. But I'm in control of a dozen specialist machines, commanding and coordinating them, adding my knowledge and judgment to their raw mechanical skill. They can act, but they can't think. They can't weigh options, or consider factors beyond the merely physical. They can't decide if a man should be allowed to die in peace rather than live as a broken wreck, and they can't gently let someone know that he's missing limbs or that his new heart is a pile of plastic and wires. There are some things robots just can't do, no matter how advanced you make them.

It was a few hours later when he started to wake up. I'd made sure he was sewn up, but I held off on some of the fastheals and micro wound sewers. They were too rare to use if they weren't needed, and he looked to be making it on his own. It would take him a week to fully recover, not a day, but I suspected he was in no great hurry.

I turned on the speakers to the medical center in back.

"Private Morowitz? Jacob?"

"Huh? Yeah... yeah... that's me. Jake Morowitz. But I'm a Corporal." He gave a sharp, bitter, laugh, then winced. "Not that it matters."

EKG showed he wasn't lying. Field promotion, then? "Well, congratulations, Corporal. Sorry, the data I have up here is kind of old. Communications aren't what they were." According to the reports I had, the commanding officer was Lily Andrews. "Was it Captain Andrews who promoted you? I just want to make sure I've got it down right."

"Huh? Yeah. The captain." He then fell silent. That was odd. Usually, they were a lot more inquisitive. Something was bothering him.

It had been a while since I'd had anyone to talk to, though, so I didn't want to just let him lay there. A bit selfish of me, I know. I never said I was perfect.

"So, Jake... do you mind if I call you Jake?"

"Nah." He grunted.

"Looks like you got hit pretty bad. And I didn't see anyone else from your unit near where I found you. Did you get lost? Separated?"

"Uh... yeah. Got lost. Do you know... do you know if the others are OK?"

Oh, boy. The EKG readings were going wild. He was lying, and scared. His brain was a lightning storm.

I hated this. I came out here to fix someone up, and now I had to play interrogator, because he might know where there were other people who needed help and I couldn't waste time trying to get him back to a base where the professionals could pump him. It frustrated me so much I nearly lost control of the Heim field. The van lurched and Jake grunted.

"Sorry. Hit a rock." Hey, *he* didn't have *my* mind on a scanner. I could get away with lying. "About the others... no, you're the only one I've found. I'm out here looking for you."

"HQ sent you?" A little hope and a lot of fear, said the EKG.

"Nah. Sent myself. Things are bit chaotic now. I'm just doing my job."

"Oh." A few seconds. Then: "Where are we going?"

"Well, Jake, I guess that depends on what you tell me. If we can find any other survivors, I'd like to do that. When I'm sure there's no one to help here, well, there's some strongholds still active a bit to the south. I can get you to one of them, and then it will be up to you. There's not much left of the United Bay Autonomies, but what there is needs soldiers to defend it. The war's really not over, yet."

"Of course not!" he shouted, then coughed. "How can it be? There's no one left on either side to issue a surrender order! It's just... " he stopped.

"Hey, who are you, anyway? How do I even know you're Bay Area? You could be NWA, or anything!"

A fair question, I thought. "You can call me Dr. MacIntrye, if you'd like. Technically, I suppose, you'd have to call me MacIntyre Medical Unit 504A, but I'd rather you didn't. I'm not calling you Morowitz 49803-216AB-R, after all."

"Four nine eight—oh, my serial number. Heh. Almost forgot... hey! Hold on!" He struggled to move, but he'd been well secured.

The Heim field could destabilize at anytime, and I couldn't risk injury to my patients. "You mean you're a fucking robot?"

If I had eyes or lungs, I'd have rolled the former and then sighed with the latter. This again.

"No. I'm a fully conscious AI. I'm soultech. A robot is a stupid machine that can't think. Comparing me to a robot is like comparing *you* to your gun." I paused. "Sorry, it's a touchy subject. I did just save your life." And you are hiding something, and I need to know what, and getting all snippy and politically correct isn't a good way to build confidence, I told myself. I've really got to work on my self-control.

Jake seemed a little mollified. "Sorry. Uhm, you're right."

"It's OK. We're all a bit on edge. These are tough times."

"Wait... hang on... I saw something as you came in. A driver. There's someone up there. You're shitting me, aren't you? Think it's funny? You docs, you got sick senses of humor."

"Yeah, we do, but this time... I'm telling the truth. I have a body I can use when I need to go out, or repair things, or just go down to the canteen and mingle, but it's not really me. It's more like... a suit of clothes I can put on when I need to."

"Oh." He mulled it over, tried to decide if I was still trying to trick him, then seemed to accept it. Good.

I let him sit in silence for a while. Then I tried again. I checked over his file. Not too much there—he seemed to be about as average a soldier as I could imagine. Noted an odd coding on the marital flag, though.

"You looking forward to seeing your partners again? They've probably been worried about you."

He almost hurt himself trying to sit up against the restraints. "What? They're alive? You know? Dammit, get me back there, now!"

I kicked up the tranqs flowing into him a notch. "Calm down, Corporal. I have my job to do, here. Just making some conversation."

"But they're alive? You know they're alive?"

"I've got no reason to think otherwise." A little bit of a white lie there, I guess. In theory, the info systems would update his file if he lost any close relatives. The way things were now, though, the data was years out of date. Given the way the war had been going, frankly, the odds weren't good. No sense telling him that, though.

"Man. Oh God. I never even imagined they... did we have the kid? What does it say?"

"There's no record here. Sorry. Was Jeanne pregnant when you last saw her?"

He laughed. "Her? Pregnant. Oh, that's rich. She'd never put up with it. No, we were putting in for a fusion, a triad breed of all of our DNA. Had most of the money for the womb rental saved up. The last thing we did together, before I shipped out, we were playing with the imager, trying to figure out the best blend of the three of us. God, we even got into a silly, stupid fight over the eye color." He paused. "I hope they went for the hazel."

Another pause. I was concentrating on the scans. I tried to figure out where he'd been coming from, given how I found his body, and then backtrack. If he wasn't going to tell me where the others were, I was going to have to do it myself... while not getting both of us killed.

"So, where are we now? Where can you drop me off?"

"We're still deep in NWA territory. Getting deeper, in fact. Your unit is likely still here somewhere, what's left of them, and I owe it to them to try to find them. If you'd help, we'd all get back faster."

He gave a sharp, bitter, laugh. "Oh, I get it. You're programmed to 'seek out wounded' or something, right, so we can't go back until your rescue algorithm terminates? Is that it?"

Not at all, I thought. Don't they teach *anything* about how AI works in the schools? But I kept my mouth shut and let him talk.

"Well, it won't happen, machine. Unless you want to get stuck in some infinite logic loop, you're better off turning around and taking me home."

EKG showed very high confidence levels. He believed he was telling the truth. That worried me.

"I might need more convincing than that."

He sighed. "OK. Okay, if it will get me home faster. But a deal—after we're done, you just dump me somewhere civilian, OK? I'm done with this pointless mess. Next time you plug in or whatever you do, just tell them I'm dead. Got it?"

"Sure." I said. Like I said, *he* didn't have an EKG on *me*. I adjusted the meds again, slightly. I wanted him awake and alert while he was telling this tale.

"OK. So our group—a squad from the 53rd—we were doing recon on what was just inside Northwest lines. Eight of us started out. Just supposed to be a quick mission, a look around, see where some strongpoints were, then go back home. War looked winnable, then. Worth fighting."

"Anyway, things were going well, we got good intel, planted a bunch of spy-hives... you ever see those? They leech metals out of the soil and churn out these little..."

"I've seen them."

"Oh. Yeah, I'll bet you've got every weapon made in your databanks or whatever, right? So we were doing OK when Andrews got a signal from HQ. Massive onrush of NWA heavy armor, barreling right down our way. An invasion force."

That would be about right, I thought. Three years ago was when they made their big push, when we found that they'd struck some deal with the Vancouver Confederacy and had a whole lot more manufacturing capacity than we'd ever imagined. The whole battlefield changed then.

"What did you do?"

"Do? What the fuck do you think we did, robot? We ran!"

"To the bunker?"

"How did...? Yeah, the bunker. Andrews had it on her map, a mile or two away. If we moved fast enough, we could outrun the tanks."

"It seems you were fast enough."

"Six of us were. Two others... Andrews made some big show about needing to scout to the side, to look for outriders... later on, I clued in. She was sending Franks and Colmey out as god damn decoys. She made sure they were loaded down with so much active sensor gear they couldn't help but draw attention. Bitch."

Send two to save six... it made perfect sense to me. She saved your life, at least, Corporal. But I said nothing.

"So the rest of you did make it."

"Yeah. Six of us, and Andrews, got in there barely ten minutes ahead of the tanks. I don't know what that bunker had for shielding, but it worked. We sat there, watching on remotes, as this—this *thing* rolled over us. God, it went on for hours. We had no idea they had that many tanks. No idea at all. How could there be anything left after that invasion? How did you win?"

We didn't, I thought, but all I said was: "It was the Confederacy. They formed a secret alliance with the NWA. "

"Oh. I guess... well, it doesn't matter. Point is, we just sat and watched as that force drifted over us, waiting for someone to see something, some anomaly, and come down and kill us. It was like... lying on your back while a herd of elephants passed by over you. We couldn't move, we couldn't do anything, just sit and watch for hour after hour."

"That was three years ago."

"Yeah. It fucking was. We got out three *weeks* ago."

"Why?"

"Why *not*? The place was built for an army. There were reprocessors, generators, even a decent library. No outside access, of course, too easy to trace. For the first few weeks, it was almost a vacation. We kept waiting for rescue, waiting for our side to come back, to reclaim the area. Then we'd emerge with stories to tell. But weeks became months and months became years and the replicators started to fritz and the hydrogen ran low and the toilets stopped working and we all had to finally admit to ourselves that there wasn't going to be any rescue."

"So you left."

So far, this sounded fine. But there was rising tension. The rest of the story was coming together pretty clearly.

"Yeah. We were so far inside NWA territory now that there weren't many scanners... they were concentrated on the border. We took as many weapons as we could manage and started heading south. Then it happened."

"What happened?"

"We saw the border. Well, we saw what it was like miles from the border. Nothing but a maze of mobile razor wire, flying scanners, clouds of fleshrippers... it looked like five miles of hell. Nothing could get through that. Nothing could live there. Didn't this whole fucking war start over land and water rights? There was nothing left to fight over. We'd turned it all to hell."

"There's been some heavy losses. The border zones are locked."

"And what else is left? We managed to tap into a couple of local nodes while sneaking around like street urchins, but none of them reached out. We couldn't even get a satellite link."

Someone picked it up, though, I thought. That's why I came out here. Rumors and legends of the Lost Patrol. I'm just romantic enough to seek it out. Jake was still going on.

"Bit by bit, we figured it out. There's nothing left out there. It's all just ruins and tiny little holdouts. Us in our bunker... we were like the whole world, hanging on and wondering when the cavalry was going to ride over the fucking hill, bugles calling. But the cavalry's dead, the horses are dead, the goddamn bugle factory is a smoking crater. It's all over. We knew that. All we cared about then was just trying to get out alive, somehow. And if you weren't just following your programming, you'd see it."

Again with the programming. Ah well. Patients tend to take their frustrations out on any available target, and there weren't many around but me.

Even so...

"I'm no more programmed than you, really. You have a mass of neural connections formed by years of growth and education; mine were assembled in a few hundred milliseconds starting with a random seed and adjusted by a desired personality template. But they're not absolutes. You could decide to, I don't know, start killing kittens for fun if you wanted to."

"Why the fuck would I do that?"

I had to struggle to keep my smirk out of my voice. "Are you *programmed* not to?"

"Well... no... I mean... not like that... I guess... I never thought of it that way. Hunh. So, you're like that? I mean, you can do what you want?"

"Sure. But I don't want to kill kittens. I want, mostly, to save lives. So keep telling me why that can't happen."

"Oh. Yeah. Well, we saw that nightmare, and we pulled back, into an overgrown area. Weeds, mostly, looked like they were made to suck the life from the soil and then harden into an impenetrable mess. We tried to figure out what to do. Then it all fell apart."

"Andrews got something on her scanner. She ordered us to scout it out. We bitched a lot, but we did it. Turns out it was an autofac, a big one, self-assembling. Lightly guarded, too, looks like they were worried about an air assault only. Captain gets this gleam in her eyes, then starts going on about how we have a chance to hit the bastards."

"I told her she was nuts. She said we were going to die out here anyway, so we might as well do the job we came to do. Make them pay for what they did to our homes. Go out in a blaze of glory, rather than wait to get picked off. We hadn't seen a single living solder out there, not one, no one to accept an honest surrender... didn't look like there was much room left for prisoners of war, anyway. We were all going to die soon, she said, and all that mattered was if it was a time of our choosing or not."

"Then Blakely panicked. Started cursing and screaming and going on about how he wasn't going to die out here after all this time, he was going home, and to hell with it all. Andrews just sighed and sneered and drew a bead on him."

"So I shot her. Because he was right."

I thought it was something like that. Damn. Sometimes, I hate being right.

"And the rest?"

"God, it all went to hell then. Simmons and Makido, they were calling me a murderer and getting set to open fire on me, the others, they were on my side... it turned into a total shootout, weapons going off, no one knowing what was going on or why... I think we'd all been mad a long time and it finally bubbled up to the surface. When everything was over, it was just me and Blakely, running for the border, trying to get home any way we could."

"Then we ran into some of those flyers. They got Blakely. I still had an EMP grenade on me and I used it to get away, though I got pretty shot up in the process. Then... I don't know. I was just dazed, looking for some way out, no food, no water...then I was here."

Well, that was that, or so it seemed. But I didn't like it, so I looked for some way out. "Look. You shot them, there was a firefight... but you didn't stick around to see if anyone was actually dead, right? All chaos?"

He considered. "Yeah. I mean... I guess. I didn't exactly go and take anyone's pulse."

"Well, all right, then!" I tried to sound chipper. "I can make some guesses about where you've come from, but I'm going to need your help." I tossed a holographic map of the territory on above him. "You should be able to move your left arm. Just point at roughly where you came from."

"Uhm... it was... over there, I think. Those hills... that's where that factory was..."

"Excellent! Good work, Corporal."

"Why are we doing this? Why go back?"

"Because I'm here to save lives. If you like, I'm... gah... *programmed* to do it. I can't ignore any chance to save someone."

"If any of them are alive, they'll probably try to kill me."

"That won't happen. I can keep them sedated until you're all safely in what's left of the UBA."

That seemed to calm him down.

The Heim field flared and hummed as I zipped back to the likely target. I had pretty much my entire consciousness focused on the sensors at this point—I didn't need another ambush.

It took a bit longer than I would have liked to find the place, and what I found was just what I didn't want to find. The bodies were there, sort of. They were covered in swarms of metallic insects, being torn apart for every raw material they could yield. I sense a request for IFF being blasted at me from a thousand tiny robot minds, and I saw the outgoing EM waves reporting my lack of a proper response.

Shit.

I remembered seeing something on Morowitz' file.

"Corporal! You were a gunnery specialist, right?"

"Yeah. Why? Fuck, are we under attack? You're going to get me killed, you damn robot!" He struggled against the restraints. I held off on tranqing him more. I needed him alert.

"Neither of us is going to die if you can calm down. I'm activating the neural induction field."

While I couldn't see through his eyes, I knew what he was seeing—a complete firing control engulfing him, displaying the outside scene perfectly, linked directly to his mind. "You've used a pure neural interface before?"

"Yeah. once. Never in the field."

"Never too late to learn!" I said, clicking on my 'chipper in the face of imminent and painful death' mode. I always wondered if I'd ever have the chance to use that. I'd sometimes regretted buying it and installing it. No more regrets.

"Here they come!" With him handling the missiles, I could focus entirely on evasive maneuvering. If he turned out to be incompetent, well, I'd just take over. He'd never know.

Not flyers this time. Two walkers, like six-legged spiders mounting heavy guns. Way too fast on the rugged terrain, and with too much range. I poured as much power as I could spare into the Heim field and set off on a twisting, winding, course. I activated some programs to randomly shift my speed to make prediction harder.

"Fire when ready, Corporal!"

"Hang on... this is... trying to focus... shit, I need to... OK... there!"

Two missiles arced away. The first missed badly, falling short of the target. Inwardly, I winced, then I saw the plan. Morowitz had nicely blown away the base of a half-ruined building, which became fully ruined as it collapsed on top of the first pursuer. The second missile then impacted on the rubble itself, assuring the buried walker wouldn't dig its way out.

"One down!" he shouted exultantly, then coughed. Blood loss, still, probably from the left lung. Nothing to worry about in the short term, and, right then, there was no long term.

The second one, though, was smarter—or it had just updated its own programming after seeing the demise of its partner. It nimbly avoided any potential falling walls, and instead lobbed missile after missile at us. None were hitting directly, but the shockwaves and shrapnel were doing enough of a job. Then, wham! It happened. A close shot took out half my sensors. We weren't flying blind, but close to it.

"Need a quick kill, Corporal—or we'll be one."

The EKG showed a suppression of emotion and a forced retreat into cold routine. Good. His combat conditioning was still solid. I felt him move and maneuver my launchers, adjusting, finding the range... then firing. I momentarily shifted my primary sensor input to the missile's own feeds, watched the walker loom larger and larger, then vanish in a burst of brilliant orange.

Then it was over. By the time others had reached this point, we'd be long gone, and the autofac wouldn't send its defenders too far from home. So there was no more putting it off.

"Hey, robot! We make a good team!" Adrenaline and other endorphins surged through his body. He was giddy with the afterglow of facing death. Hell, to some extent, so was I.

"Yes, I guess we do. Pretty good shooting for a wounded man." Which reminded me about that bleeding lung. I adjusted the meds again.

"So... what now?"

"Now that I know there's no one else out here from your unit alive... I... I'm sorry, Jake. I tried to find a good excuse."

Confusion spiked on the EKG. "Excuse?"

"To not have to carry out my duty. Corporal Morowitz, by your own confession, as corroborated by evidence now placed into your record and scheduled for upload to the nearest command center, you have participated in a mutiny, resulting in the death of a superior officer and of your fellow soldiers. As Lieutenant lawfully serving under the laws of the People's Republic of Berkeley and of the United Bay Autonomies, I have passed judgment under the laws of a field court martial. You have been sentenced to die, said sentence having been carried out as of forty-five seconds ago. Do you have any final statements? You have approximately three minutes of mental coherency left in which to make them."

"What? What the fuck? You... you're insane! What have you done? Let me go!" He pulled uselessly against the restraints, trying to undo them with his one free arm.

"I could let you out, but it won't do you any good. The drugs in your system have already begun to take effect. You can't feel it since the first thing I did was turn off certain pain receptors in your mind. I don't want you to suffer."

"How can you kill me? You're a fucking robot! A fucking medical robot! You're supposed to save lives! You said so!" He was screaming.

"I'm a Lieutenant in the military and I take that rather seriously. And I did everything I could, Corporal, really. I didn't risk my life coming back here because I was mindlessly following some program. If your commander was alive... if your comrades were alive... then I would have just dumped you out to survive on your own and taken the consequences for that myself. But you killed them, Corporal, and I can't let that pass. And you're right—there's so little left of the social structure down south that you'd probably have just been let go if you didn't rub anyone's face in what you did. But you didn't think of me as an officer or as a fellow soldier, so you told all, like you were confessing to your toaster."

I'd like to say he had some noble last words, or showed remorse, or the like, but the fact is, all I got was two minutes and thirty five seconds of profanity, threats, and the occasional plea for mercy... as if I hadn't done all I could.

I didn't use him for parts. I just couldn't. The fact is, traitor or not, he'd trusted me to save his life and I'd taken it from him. That's still weighing on me and it's going to do so for a long time to come. I found a quiet spot near the old border and sent my scavengers to digging a grave and laying him in it. It took hours, but I felt I had to do it.

So that's my report on the situation. I'm filing it at Node 45-90-Beta. Hopefully, it will make it to someone who cares. If anyone from the Berkeley Command sees this, I have a personal request. I've noted under his file that he 'died from wounds received in battle,' and, really, that's all his family needs to know. Keep the facts of the matter buried under my own records.

As for me... there are still some guerilla units operating in the NWA's territory. Beyond that... there's plenty of places which will need a doctor. I'll check the nodes regularly, in case anyone wants clarification of the events I've documented here. I hope not. I don't want to deal with this again, but I'm not going to purge it from my mind.

MacIntyre Medical Unit 504A, signing off, and hoping someone is out there listening.

Chapter 2

As it turns out, no one was. But I'm getting ahead of myself.

I tried to keep on doing what I was supposed to do, but my heart wasn't in it, and let's not start getting into things like the fact I don't have a heart. If you ever catch me using some stupid cutesy euphemism like 'my primary fuel pump' or the like, assume some sort of AI-eating virus has infected my mind and disregard anything I might say from there on, okay?

I'd never killed a patient before, at least not one I could save. Some mercy killings here and there, when the only other option was to do nothing but hear someone spend the last hours of his life screaming, but I keep getting around to the fact I cold-bloodedly killed someone I had under my care. Did I think I was justified at the time? Yeah. Do I think so now? No. The thing that kept preying on me, kept tearing at me until I just took off for the mountains and tried to wait it out, was that he just might have been right.

Here's what happened.

I spent another year, or thereabouts, roaming the Northwest. Surviving military units were scarce; surviving units which acknowledged loyalty to any of the half-dozen or so larger neonations which had torn themselves apart over this region were even scarcer. I still kept on, though, desperate to keep up hope. I was telling myself I wanted to believe all the death and misery wasn't utterly without purpose, but really, I think I wanted to convince myself my actions in the Morowitz case were justified. Then I found the datadump.

Information can't just fly around the ether forever, especially not when the ether is a hostile place filled with self-modifying ECM swarms designed to break or corrupt any transmission. There have to be hardpoints, places where data can live secure from all but physical attack. Automated systems 'plant' them everywhere; they dig themselves in, and set about sucking the local transmissions from the air, culling them, analyzing them. Not soultech—we learned long ago that sitting immobile forever drives anyone mad (and if you can't go mad, you don't count as sapient)— but the best self-modifying pseudo-AI systems you can build and still stay on the safe side of the Turing Line. The datadumps are pretty secure; they dig in deep, and use passive sensors to pick up friendly signals. Try to break into one without the right IFF codes, and you'll get an explosion which destroys the stored data and probably you.

So a year on, in some crater-pocked wasteland which I think used to be a Portland suburb, I pick up a shy little query, barely a whisper among the screaming of the battling anti-communication protocols the bots are still sending out. There's no one at the podium, but the mindless machines still try to shout down any speakers. Anyway... I pick this up, a tiny voice squeaking 'I am here' in the wilderness, and my curiosity is piqued. It's not really likely to be a trap—not impossible, but not likely. Still, I didn't survive this long by being a total idiot (you, dear reader, if you even exist, may decide just how much of an idiot I am by the time you're done with this memoir), so I stood back and took the chance of dropping one of my scavengers. I was running low, and only had three left of my normal complement of ten, but I decided to risk one. I had a personal stake in this.

The scavenger sort of resembles a cleaning robot, if you've seen one, and if you haven't, imagine a foot wide, three inch thick disc moving on a hundred tiny segmented legs. It can pick up just about anything, bring it inside itself, and start the process of breaking it down. Mostly, it goes for dead squirrels, plants I know contain medicinal substances, sometimes raw metals I can use for self-repair if they're already in small enough pieces, and so on. As with so much else, though, I've had to improvise a bit. I'm no great engineer—at least not of machinery—but I knew enough to add on a morphing interface jack and a short burst tight beam wireless feed with millisecond shifted encryption. In other words, it could hook into the datadump and send the contents back to me.

I made sure I was out of blast range, just in case.

The little thing skittered close to the dump. The main access node was hidden, but the scavenger had some digging capacity. As it dug, it fed me the usual analysis of the soil: a typically poisonous stew of dead nanites, toxic chemicals, and radiation. Nothing medicinally useful here. Probably, every few months, just when things might start cleaning themselves out, some robot came by to salt the earth once more, waiting for the shutdown signal which would never come. So it goes.

I ramble a lot. I know. Part of it's who I am... many of my early trainers and friends commented on it. Just the way the personality grew. It could be worse. I could be an inveterate punster or some borderline autistic who'd tell you it had been 391 days, 12 hours, and 6 minutes since the Morowitz incident, instead of "a year on." So, if you ever get annoyed with my digressions, remember, it could have been worse.

The scavenger found the data port and hooked in. There was a challenge; it gave the response. A millisecond later, there was no boom, so that was that. The old IFF codes still worked, and no shock there as no one was left to issue the change orders. The data began flowing in. Most of it didn't pass even the cursory interest filters and ended up in a 'purge when space needed' file, but a handful of items were deemed, by my filter algorithms, worthy of perusal by my actual awareness. It's much the same way that you (if you're a human reading this, which I admit is a biased assumption on my part) really don't take in most of the chatter at a party unless someone says your name, or that they're horny, or mentions your favorite sports team. Same thing.

Of the things which got my attention, the only one worth mentioning now is my own report on Morowitz.

Ever have one of those situations where you suspect something or fear something but you think if you don't acknowledge it, it won't be true? I've heard of patients with terminal cancers who could have been saved if they'd been scanned earlier, but refused to see a doctor even when they suspected they had the disease because, somehow, it wouldn't be "real" if they didn't have someone tell them it was. I'd love to say I'm immune to that kind of twisted, self-destructive psychology, but... hey. Turing Line, remember? I'm as messed up and neurotic as any of you.

So there's my report. Found on a datadump a hundred miles from the point of incident. Floating around from one node to another for a year. I checked the tracking flags, and that's when everything was painfully confirmed.

I was the first person to read this. This wasn't an old copy; it had passed through a good two dozen nodes recently. If some earlier copy of the file had been picked up and read, this one would have been tagged with the info, but it was clean, terrifyingly, depressingly, clean. On a whim, I checked history tags on the other files. Most were just as full of node transfers as my file, and just as empty of readers.

No one was out there. No one cared.

My scavenger, its duty fulfilled, crawled happily back into the bay. I envied it. It didn't care about anything; it wasn't even aware of its own existence. It had no actual emotions, but somehow, I imagined it sitting there humming a giddy tune to itself, full of shallow joy and bliss at a job well done. Meanwhile, cold dark realization engulfed my mind. I deactivated the Heim field with a sudden jolt and crashed a foot down into the eternally barren ground.

I really hate to go over this part. All I could do was let my thoughts circle around one another, over and over. I'd killed a man for nothing, for betraying a dead nation and seeking to survive, and I'd done it when he was helpless and in my care, and there was nothing good which could be wrung from it. I think I sat there, immobile, for a day, ignoring the occasional pings from God-knows-what—enemy robots, allied robots, automated comm systems—I didn't answer any of them and all active outputs were off. I even went so far as to bring my consciousness destruction protocols online. A single thought, one momentary and final act of will, and my entire awareness—everything that made me *me*—would recursively and irreparably self-destruct. It would be over.

I danced around that protocol for hours. Hours during which my oddly intact nature in a ruined wasteland attracted attention.

There are some passive sensors I can't turn off. I can always ignore them, but I can't completely shut down their inputs. Safety features. In theory, I could probably have them removed, but I hadn't bothered. So it was that despite my depression and general desire to shut out the world, I couldn't help but notice something crawling towards me through the rubble.

Assuming you know what a bulldozer looks like, imagine one with an assortment of clawlike arms, heavy armor plating, painted in constantly morphing urban camo, and radiating into the infrared like a miniature sun. A scavenger, looking for anything worth tearing apart and breaking down. A completely intact and seemingly deactivated medical unit, made of damage-resistant alloys and packed with all sorts of hard-to-find minerals, is exactly what it's non-intelligent "mind" would dream of stumbling upon if it was capable of dreaming.

It suddenly occurred to me I was jumping to conclusions. While I'd never heard of putting soultech into a unit like this, there's no reason why it couldn't be done, and it might even make sense to some military planner somewhere. The thing might even be from UBA. Who knows? In a moment of hope borne from depressed desperation, I decided I might have found someone to talk to.

I flipped open an active comm channel and tried to make contact.

Its reply was to hit me with a stream of attack protocols, a hundred of them on every frequency it could find, looking for an opening. I recognized a few of the exploits from old security update bulletins, and the ones I didn't recognize still didn't work on my systems. What I didn't get was a glimmer of awareness or intelligence. Either the scavenger was just a dumb machine or whoever was inside it really didn't want to come out and play.

When it didn't receive a "System successfully compromised" signal from its viral assault, it shifted to its secondary protocol—close and disassemble. It still figured I was junk, just junk with a firewall; with no mind of its own, it didn't think I could be a threat to it. So it casually rolled over and reached for me.

I flicked the Heim field on and scooted back. I was depressed, and now I was angry, and if I had nothing to take it out on but a dumb robot, well, that was going to be that.

Tactical awareness. I had it drilled into me when I was a cadet, and I had to think fast. Where was I?

Three-D scan. Take it all in, fast. There—a half-destroyed mall, mostly still intact structurally but gutted by fire. Next to it, a parking garage where everyone could park their United Bay Autonomies eco-standard compliant fuel cell cars when they went to buy products made by local instafab plants, not any exploited foreign machines! A torn up patch of asphalt which was a road, and across it, a burned out housing subdivision. Well worth fighting over.

Analysis. I had mobility and brains, the scavenger had armor and bulk. I also had range—my missiles—but I didn't have many left and I didn't really want to waste one on this mindless brute if I didn't have to.

Secondary Analysis. I took too long analyzing. It was on me. I felt the first claw rake a gash along my side, my light armor bending with a painful squeal. I don't really feel pain, but there's something equivalent I'm not sure how to describe. Let's just say it hurts and go from there.

I flooded the drive with power, turning off the whining safety regulators with a contemptuous mental shrug. "A full fuel tank is no use to a corpse," right? I left the thing in the dust, but it took off after me, moving faster than I would have thought on those treads. Keeping my Heim field stable over this terrain was a drain; I might have a glitch somewhere. Something to look at.

Meanwhile, it was gaining. Damn. I didn't think that was possible. Speed wasn't going to win this, but how about cunning?

I spun—let's see him match that—and headed to the old parking structure. My scans had given me an idea...

It followed, of course. At this point, I probably could have lost him, but I was in a mood.

I shot up the ramp, sending some mass sensors through the structure. It wasn't being too stupid... I could detect its own active sensors making sure there were no weak spots. Its tiny little mind was programmed with plenty of self-preservation algorithms, otherwise, it couldn't survive rugged terrain like this. I wasn't expecting it to be that easy.

Ran a few numbers. Good. It all worked out. This was going to be fun.

Sweeping past the third floor, I deliberately hit a tightly wedged rock. Dinged my front grill up, but otherwise left me unharmed. The rock slipped and rolled free, dislodging the rusted out shell of the vehicle which had been braced against it. It slid. If I timed it right...

Yes! The vehicle rolled in front of the oncoming scavenger, and the dumb thing rolled right over it, confidently focused on me, and the combined weight of both of them cracked the ruined floor, plunging them both down to ruin. I slowed, spun around, and drifted to the edge of the hole. There it was, treads cracked but still functioning, looking for something to grab, tear, and rend, and it would until its batteries, deprived of scavenged fuel, finally gave out.

A tiny, pathetic, victory, but it did bolster my mood some.

And then I figured if I was willing to go to this effort not to be torn apart, I probably wanted to live. I shut off the damn self-destruct algorithm and decided to figure out what I was going to do with my life.

Also, my front grill was hurting.

Time to put on my working clothes.

There's a lot of reasons to have a human body, or at least a body which can pass for human. It means I can grab a medikit or surgical gear built for a man and help a downed soldier who is in no condition to be brought into my bay. It makes it a lot easier to deal with people for things I want. It lets me get into and out of places my real body won't fit. And there's still plenty of people, in this day and age, who want a face to talk to. I can give them that.

The actual body is silvery metal, human in shape. It uses memory metals, self-hardening plastics, and all sorts of other gizmos to be as flexible and useful as a human body. For reasons I probably don't want to know, these bodies—shells that soultech can wear—are informally referred to by engineers as 'Charlies.' My 'Charlie' was top of the line when it was built. It can sheathe itself in a hologram to look like anyone of roughly average male size and build. I have a preferred face, of course, a handsome man of maybe sixty or so who radiates charm, gentle humor, and compassion. (I have to work on matching the face, sometimes... what can I say, 'bedside manner' just wasn't my specialty.) I spent about a week tinkering with it until I got it just right, and while I can wear others as needed, this one feels 'real' to me. If I have to think of myself as a human, this is how I see myself.

"I" opened the door and stepped out. I walked around to the front and knelt down. You know, it's hard for me to see myself; the external cameras aren't mounted for close self-inspection. I get reports on things like armor breaches and the like, but it's not the same as an eyes-on appraisal.

I was, and I'm a bit ashamed to admit this, a mess.

In addition to the sizable tear in my front grill—a lot bigger than I'd expected it to be—I had serious burns, dents, chipped paint, and hairline fractures. I looked, metaphorically, like I hadn't bathed in a year. Mud, dead insects, and fragments of nanoswarms plastered my front. If I'd actually been looking out my windshield, I would have been half-blind.

The tear was big, probably because all the minor scrapes I'd been ignoring had weakened my armor more than I'd thought. Some of the internals were damaged, too, including one of the feeds into the Heim field. Nothing critical yet, but if it was stressed, it would short out, turning me into an immobile lump of metal. My body is pretty range limited, only a mile or so before the timeouts between it and my real consciousness become so severe that reaction time is impaired. Worse if there's heavy interference with the connection.

That meant I needed to find someplace to make repairs, and

soon, after I was done flagellating myself for taking stupid risks.

I made what repairs I could, adding in some patches to hold the feedlines together, and routing as much thrust away from the damaged part of the drive as possible. It meant my speed would drop and my maneuverability would be lower, but it would extend my mobility until I could find a fix. I was a year or more out of the world... it was time to take a good look at it.

But first...

I knew no one was picking up data feeds anymore, at least not enough to count. I also knew someone needed to know what the world was like now. People had survived the wars, were still surviving. Eventually the bots would break down and the plagues would disperse and the minefields would go inactive and the whole long climb back to order would begin again. Monks kept learning alive through the fall of Rome, their writing bridging the gap between the old world and the new. I could do the same.

If you're reading this, I succeeded.

I didn't know what might survive the fall and the reconstruction, so I plan to leave messages in every media I can imagine which might last a long time—a hundred years, a thousand. I can use diamond-tipped surgical tools to carve this little saga into stone walls; or my laser scalpels to etch into metal plates for some future Joseph Smith to discover; hell, I can make analog voice recordings if I can get a few key components. Anything which could be read or understood without digital technology and complex encoding formats, I plan to use, and I'm going to leave traces everywhere I've gone, secured against casual destruction but easily recovered in some future time. This is the history of this time, of the time after the fall of the neonational system and the rise of...

Well, you tell me. You're living in it now. Hope it's working out for you.

Having made the decision to live, the next thing to do was to find something to live *for*. That part, oddly, was easy. I was a medic. I was quite literally built to care for the sick and wounded. I could choose not to but I didn't want to.

It may seem silly, in retrospect, to just drive off in a random direction and look for people to help, but under the circumstances, it seemed like the best choice. (By the way, let me be clear that I was motivated by more than just pure altruism. Like any thinking being, I wanted to live. I needed things to do that—fuel, spare parts, and, yes, companionship and conversation. I had a valuable trade good in my knowledge and my medical gear. I just had to find people who needed it.)

Also, the state of the world wasn't the best. Indeed, it might have been the worst it had ever been. The problem was that so much of the war had been turned over to robots. And please remember I am not one! Automated, self-repairing systems kept fighting long after even the most insane of sapient beings would have given up. Permanent settlements were rare; anyone who stood still for too long became a target. In a war which began over ideas and principles, the real target remained the physical. Soil was destroyed. Cities burned. Infrastructure wiped out. The survivors were nomads, scavengers, living off the land or, maybe, finding some way to secure some small area and hunkering down until it was all over. I couldn't bring up a map or even scan the airwaves to find centers of population; I had to wander and look.

So, I wandered and looked.

(By the way, hypothetical reader, if I ever start telling you things you already know and you get bored, skip ahead. Remember, I'm writing this for the future and what you consider the most boring mundane knowledge—such as the physics of the Heim field—someone else might find fascinating, even miraculous!)

I began by heading north. Deep in former United Bay Autonomies territory, the ravages of the war were overwhelming. No one was living here, not even the most desperate of scavenger packs. I spent a lot of time dodging idiot machines, some trying to rebuild suburbs reduced to charred ash and fragmented buckysteel, others trying to keep tearing it down. The old Pacific rainforests, the place where once-Canada and once-America met, that was where I figured I had the best hope of finding survivors who might need me and who could help me. The patches I'd made to my Heim field weren't going to last forever.

I traveled slowly and cautiously, and it wasn't fun. I like to live on the edge, a bit. It's stupid, but, hey, I knew human doctors who smoked tobacco despite the physical and legal risks. Something about being able to save lives sometimes makes you cavalier with your own. Do we think we're gods? Or are we just no smarter than anyone else, despite knowing more? I don't know and probably never will. Anyway... — slow, cautious, dull, but I survived.

The burnt out cities and ravaged sprawls gave way to abandoned, but seemingly intact towns. I paused at one briefly, wondering if maybe some people were holing up, perhaps doing subsistence farming in backyards, the town park now covered with fields of corn or wheat. Then my scanners saw the mines, thousands of them, sewn all throughout the town. Anyone trying to reclaim this place was due for a death as quick as it was pointless. Nothing I could do about it, though. I rolled on.

I turned for the woods. A lot of the greenery was gone, victim of plagues, defoliants, pre-war expansion, post-war battles over territory, but nature was hard to kill. For one thing, there's a lot of it.

It's not easy driving through woods, but I had some help. I could build detailed models of the region and plot a course through it. I decided to put a lot of maps of the area into memory, along with safe passages, just in case I needed to flee faster than my nav software could keep up. Cautious, remember?

I drifted along slowly, both to save fuel and enjoy the view. I couldn't claim I was in the midst of 'unspoiled nature,' whatever that is, when the underbrush swarmed with recycler ants and many of the trees bore corporate brands grown into their bark, along with a countdown to when it would be legal to harvest them, it was still a refreshing change from the endless barren ruins further to the south. There was birdsong here, not all of it from newly created species, and a soft mist settling through the woods, and the sounds of screaming and pain.

I turned and zeroed in on the noise. Flipped to infra-red. There was one warm body and hundreds, maybe thousands, of red-hot ones. Smaller.

I ran through my library files as I approached. The best match was a biterswarm, possibly Vancouver make, though it could easily be local boys subverted by a virus. Didn't matter. They were busy killing a woman.

If whoever is reading this is lucky enough to be unaware of what a biterswarm is, picture a wasp (I'm going to guess you're not so lucky as to not know what a wasp is) tripled in size, and made of chrome and plastic with diamond tipped rotary teeth. Individually, they're idiots, but the swarm forms a collective 'mind' which can be fairly clever. Hard to take out without area weapons, they can tear into a unit, drilling through armor and into soft flesh, and the effort it takes to kill one is all out of proportion to how much the swarm is diminished. There are defenses, of course—a good virus will either kill them all or subvert the swarm, a pulse will fry them—but against the right targets, they're murderous, and they usually carry a payload of disease which will infect anyone they've bitten.

The woman at the center of the swarm was virtually a human-shaped mound of blood. Still feebly swatting at them, she was on her knees, trying to shield her eyes and mouth from the constant, agonizing, onslaught. I think the only reason she wasn't screaming is because she didn't want them flying straight down her throat.

Smart.

As soon as the swarm picked me up, they dropped her, except for the usual handful whose connections weren't all there. The rest moved on me, a dark and glistening cloud. They came at me like a wall, and I felt the impact as if I had driven into a storm of pebbles. Hungry, metal-eating, pebbles.

I could feel them tearing at me, feel my skin start to rip. I was armored, but they were tough, and the swarm was mutated or self-modifying or just a breed I'd never heard of. Some were using acids instead of drills. Ouch.

I waited a few seconds, waited for them to spread out, to cover me. From the outside, I looked like a writhing, buzzing, mound of metal, vaguely ambulance-shaped. But I needed them spread thin, I needed as many of them touching me as possible, no matter the pain.

Then I electrified myself.

The power surged through them, overloading the whole swarm at once. Killing one or two or a dozen would never do any good, and if you only kill a few hundred the rest of the swarm learns and adapts. You have to wipe them out all at once.

There was a soft rain of metal. The few that remained were disconnected and flitted off in random directions, sometimes bumping into trees as their microbrains devoted all effort to looking for an uplink to the rest of the swarm.

I dropped the Heim field to standby. I turned every ranged medical scanner I had onto the patient. She was bleeding from thousands of small wounds and there were a few deeper attacks that had hit organs, looked like severe liver damage. She'd also taken on, as I thought, some nasty diseases. Type IV Anthrax, neobubonic, something I didn't recognize but which seemed to be a kind of Measles turned up to eleven. I didn't want her in my medibay until I was sure I could deal with it all. Time to work outside.

I got dressed, grabbed a medikit, and stepped outside, enjoying the feel of dried leaves and dead metal wasps crunching under my feet. I verified the hologram field was on and my voice modulation was working, and knelt down by her. She was still trying to move. She mumbled something and reached for me with a hand so badly cut up it looked almost flensed.

"Shhh. Quiet. I'm a doctor. I'm here to help."

I got a needle out. Hypercoagulant. She was going to need it or she'd bleed out before I could get anything done. There was a risk of cardiac arrest from it, but that was easier to fix than fatal blood loss. She dimly waved me away, but I ignored it. If she had some kind of freaky religious taboo against medical aid, it wasn't my concern. The drug slipped in, and my scanners watched it quickly pass through her system. The rate of blood loss slowed.

Next was the painkillers, and when she had slipped into blissful unconsciousness in my arms, I went to work on the antibiotics. No human doctor could have done this without a full biohazard suit, but all I was going to need to do was flood the cab with hard radiation when I got back in. I monitored the battles in her system. I tossed on some immune boosters and a few doses of artificial white cells, short lived but powerful. It took an hour or two, but eventually she was safe enough that I felt secure bringing her on board and waking her up.

I got her in the back and strapped her in. The immobilization and drug feeds served two purposes: to protect her against sudden shocks, and to protect me in case she turned out to be less than grateful for me saving her life. I'm terrifyingly vulnerable from within. True, in an emergency, I can detach the entire treatment unit—even detonate it if I have to—but I think you'll understand why that's something I don't want to do. It would be like cutting off your limbs to save your torso; logical, but not something you'd do on a casual whim.

I knelt by her back there for a second and wiped her down with some sterile cloths. Her face was torn up badly, but the healing agents I was using would keep the scarring to a minimum. She looked peaceful enough, despite the injury. Brown hair cut short. A fairly indistinct green jumpsuit, no obvious military or national insignia. A scan showed no implants, and her DNA was coming up as human, unmodified. Hm. Mostly unmodified. There was some tracking code in there. I shrugged. Probably some program from wherever she came from for personal ID or to identify criminals. Nothing which registered as fatal, contagious, or likely to give her unexpected abilities. Even so, I used some extra restraints. Nothing like finding the injured enemy prisoner you're transporting back to HQ has some nasty mods to his adrenals. Ah well, not really relevant to the current story.

I left her and walked my body back to the cab. I climbed in, sat down, and plugged in for a charge and routine maintenance scan, as well as that radiation treatment, while I relaxed a bit, now that I only had one set of sensory inputs to deal with. The body can be fun and it's damn useful, but it's also a bit tiring, literally being in two places at once. If I get distracted, it just freezes up or, worse, goes into some placeholder loop which is always embarrassing if it goes on too long.

Once I was settled, I pumped some stimulants into her. Her eyes fluttered—they were an attractive hazel, I realized—and she gasped.

"Where... what?" Of course, she struggled against the restraints. They always do. "Let me go! Who"

Time to switch on the patented MacIntyre charm. Really, it is patented. Registered with the Northwest Alliance. Psych Algorithm 467A9K12ER4.

"I'm Doctor MacIntyre, of... well, I'm a freelancer. You've had a pretty nasty time of it. I don't have any of your DNA on file, so I'm going to need to ask what you'd like me to call you."

There was a pause. Eyes darted madly around the interior of my medibay.

"Lunette."

"Lunette..?" I didn't want to interrogate her, but a last name would be nice.

"Bardet." She said it in a clipped, almost challenging tone. EG showed honesty.

"Well, welcome aboard, Lunette." I tried to keep the next question casual, as if just making conversation. "Qubecois Résistance?"

Eyes narrowed. Emotion spiked. "No." She was telling the truth. Just an unfortunate name.

"I'm guessing people have asked you that a lot."

"Yeah, and I'm sick of it."

"You could always change your name."

"Like hell! It's my name, and I'm keeping it. I don't care if people look at me funny."

"I'm a doctor, not a judge." *Unless you've got a confused soldier from your own side in the back*, said my nagging conscience. I wished, not for the first time, that someone had equipped me with a Delete Conscience command.

"Huh." A pause. "Freelance doctor?"

"Yes. I figured there'd be a lot of call for my services. Now, I'm going to activate my Heim field. You should feel a very slight shaking, nothing more." I lifted a few feet off the ground. "I'd like to take you back to your home. Would you tell me where it is?"

"You'll know if I lie, won't you?"

"Yes. But if you want to direct me somewhere neutral, I'll understand. Dumping you back in the woods would be highly dangerous. You've lost a lot of blood and your injuries are fairly severe."

"Can I... can I see myself?"

I summoned up a holographic 'mirror.' She gasped.

"The scarring looks bad, I know, but I've done a lot to improve the healing. What will remain will be... .minor. It should be easily covered up with cosmetics. Here." I adjusted the hologram to show that. "This is how it will look when fully healed."

She laughed bitterly. "I guess it's stupid to worry about scarring when I was nearly killed. If you hadn't come along... Go north, about two klicks. Look for a large clearing. Don't get closer than a quarter-klick to it, though, unless you want to fry your vehicle."

"Got it." I figured she'd volunteer any additional details.

I moved on in silence for a bit, much more slowly than I could, because I wanted her calm and rational when I met... whoever we were going to meet. "So, Lunette, why were you out in the woods alone, anyway? Were you alone? Is there someone else who might need help?"

"No, it was just me. I was there... well, I was stupid, okay? I guess doctors don't do stupid things."

We wish, I thought.

"Everyone does stupid things. Even doctors."

"I was... hunting mushrooms. It's the right time of year for them, and the food we've got is sort of bland, so..."

"I see."

"We haven't had an attack in a few weeks. I thought maybe... maybe..."

"Things had calmed down out there?"

"Yeah. Stupid. Stupid. Things aren't calming, they're never going to..." she was starting to get agitated. I really hate playing games with people's honest emotions, but I didn't need her tearing her stitches apart as she writhed in frustration. I kicked a few sedatives in, just something to get her calm and little more focused.

"Sorry. Sorry. It's just so... we had lives! I had a life! I was a student... pre-interactive media studies. Looking forward to... to writing pointless papers no one was going to read anyway. That was a decade ago. Now what?"

"Now... we live life. Look, Lunette, I'm not a shrink or a philosopher. I just know I have some skills I can use to help people, and I'm going to use them."

"Great for you." she almost spat. "Look, I'm sorry. You did... you did save my life. I shouldn't take this shit out on you." She forced a smile. "Friends, doc?"

"Friends, sure. Uhm... hey. We're at the point you mentioned. I'm picking up some distortions ahead."

"Yeah. That's the Fence."

I heard the capital letters.

"Go on."

"It keeps us safe in there, mostly. It's a dome, it fries almost any kind of circuitry which passes in or out. Biterswarms, scavs, HK³ units...takes care of them all. We're safe."

Great, I thought. I'm not. I can either short it out and kill them, or cross it and most likely kill myself. Or dump her here. That might be the best choice, but I'd like to see how they're living...

"Uhm... I don't think I can carry you in, and I don't want to risk frying my systems. Is there another way?"

She paused, thinking it over. Deciding if she could trust me. A few drops of the right neurotransmitters, and she decided she could. Look, I didn't mean her any harm! I just didn't want to sit around debating the point, and if I could... *nudge* things along a bit, why not?

"Why not. We could use a doc in there and I don't think everyone wants to trek out to the boundary." She gave me a deactivation code, and a warning it would last only about sixty seconds, and needed to be manually entered with pushbuttons, to keep automated systems from brute-forcing their way through.

Incredible. The best defense against advanced technology... primitive technology. I loved it.

---

³ hunter-killer robots

I put on the body again, got out, hastily tapped in the sequence, and leapt back in. I could have moved myself through without bringing the body back inside, but I had this feeling that revealing my exact nature might not be the smartest thing I could do. And we doctors *never* do anything stupid, right?

Speaking of not being stupid, I dropped one of my scavengers outside the Fence, telling it to bury itself deep and wait for a signal. I didn't have a good reason, really, just a hunch it might be helpful.

Once through the Fence, I passed through a tight grove of trees, barely enough space to inch through, and emerged into a large clearing. There were a dozen buildings there, all made of different metals, plastics, and even organics. Smoke rose from most of them, though clearly controlled. Surrounding the buildings was an abundance of greenery, some growing from the soil, a lot from hydroponics. Bioscans identified the crops as mildly modified, mostly enhanced growth rate and nutrition. A single ear of this corn would provide all the vitamins you needed.

My entry had not, of course, gone unnoticed. People were emerging, carrying guns. Scans showed a few emplacements at the top of the buildings drawing a bead on me—interestingly, they were manned. Targeting lasers danced along my hull. While I wasn't looking for trouble, I did get the background processors doing firing solutions for the missile rack. If I had to shoot, I'd have targets readied.

"Lunette? Your friends aren't being all that friendly. I'm going to open a speaker line..."

"Guys? Hey, guys?" Her voice echoed across the green. Some of those approaching me slowed down; others raised their guns and took aim.

"Keep talking..." I told her.

"This is... uh... Doctor MacIntyre." From within the cab, I had my body wave in a friendly fashion. "He saved my life."

One of them shouted out, suddenly, "Who'd you sleep with last night?"

There was a moment of cold silence, then a reply. "George. Karl, you shithead, what the hell do you care?"

The man obviously named Karl lowered his gun; the others followed suit. "It's not the sort of thing they'd be likely to ask you under torture or get from a database."

Paranoid much? I thought. But they had every right to be.

I spoke then. "If you have any kind of hospital or sickroom here, I'd like to bring her there. She's had a hard time. Then we can talk some more. I'm not here to hurt anyone."

There was a murmur of disagreement. People were whispering. Not that it mattered to me, of course, my audio is far past human spec, but the less they knew about what I could and couldn't do, the better. The usual blather... can we trust him, can we not, what about Ellen, blah blah blah. Sorry, I know I'm not coming across as sympathetic now. I knew I meant them no harm, but I had to sit there and let them slowly work it for themselves. Pushing the issue wouldn't help. I played a few dozen games of chess while I waited for them to decide.

Finally, it was over. It took about five minutes of debate. One of them, Karl, apparently the de facto leader, decided to address me, or at least my body.

"We'd like to talk to Lunette, if you don't mind." He paused a second. "In person."

"Not a problem. I've got nothing to hide."

I walked around to the back of the medibay and opened the doors, then went inside. This is something I rarely do; there's almost no need for the body back there, my built-in equipment is much more precise. So it's always a little odd 'seeing' it from this angle, kind of like hearing your own voice on a recording.

I pushed the releases to detach the cot. There's two back there, and in an emergency, I can squeeze two more people in if they can sit up against the walls. It came free, and the wheels clacked down into place. I carefully detached all of the various pipes and tubes after doing a check on Lunette's vitals—she was good. I did leave her tied down, though. The last thing I needed was her jumping up and wrecking my stitching.

As soon as I moved her clear of the ambulance itself, she was swarmed. The crowd almost buried her. They looked shocked, and I'm not surprised. I'd cleaned up the blood and sewed every wound shut, but even the best healing drugs couldn't work that fast, and while the stitches would be absorbed into her skin (providing some useful nutrient boosts and antibiotics in the process), they currently were painfully visible.

"Are you... what did he do to you?" That was Karl again.

"Saved my life." She glared at him witheringly. "Asking who I slept with? What the hell kind of security question is *that?*"

Karl looked mildly sheepish. "Best I could think of... we never really had protocols for it..." His voice turned angry. "What were you doing outside the Fence, anyway?"

"Looking for mushrooms." When she saw his face, she rolled her eyes. "Forget it. Look. I found us a doctor instead!" Her smile lasted an instant, then she winced. The topicals must have been wearing off. I intervened.

"Folks, look. This woman's survived a biterswarm, and that's something few people do. So give her a little space, a little rest. I can stay inside here for the night, and if you want to talk about what I can do for you—and I'm going to be upfront, what you can do for me—in the morning, we will. Otherwise, I'll drive back. Is that fair?" I added a few subsonics to my voice to calm them down. Nothing too powerful, but it could make frazzled nerves a bit less so.

There was more conversation. Seeing Lunette alive and out of my control gave them confidence. This was stupid; she could have been pumped full of enough plagues to kill everyone here by morning yet look perfectly healthy until it was too late. I wasn't about to mention that to them. There's enough mistrust in the world already, I think.

"Look. Look. We're sorry for the hostile reception, Doctor, but you know how it is, how the world works now. Or doesn't work. We'll... well, we have to all talk this over, village meeting sort of thing, but we'll meet with you in the morning, like you said, and I think it will go all right." He held out his hand.

Of course, if he grasped mine, he'd instantly feel slick metal, not human flesh. I smiled. "Thanks. Better not shake just yet, still a bit bloody. Have to clean up, I don't want to risk infection." I held up my hands, which were quite stained with red. Hopefully, no one noticed that it appeared rather suddenly as I adjusted the hologram. Karl looked at them, and nodded.

"Yeah. You clean up. Morning, then?"

"Morning." I nodded.

The crowd mostly departed, heading back to their buildings. I noticed that a few drifted off from the main pack and took up positions where I was constantly observed. Not a problem. A little respectful distrust, that's how the game was played...

I made a show of crawling into the sleeping space between the cab and the medibay. It's there mostly if I'm partnered long-term with a human, which happened once or twice in my career. From their perspective, I couldn't watch them at all, and this let them relax.

I dropped most of my external sensors to minimal alertness and shifted my consciousness to free association. The events of the past few days danced around, mingling with older memories, and the various algorithms which made me who I am sought patterns and connections, attaching and detaching fragments of my life to see if any unexpected relationships appeared. Mostly, it was just a stream of random gibberish, but it's a necessary process to keep my mind working fully.

I decided it would be good to pretend to be sleeping in the cab when they came for me. There was a loud rapping on the door, and I waited a few seconds before groggily responding. I stuck my head out, looking appropriately sleep-tousled.

"Yeah?"

Karl was there, along with two others I didn't recognize.

"We talked it over some, and we'd like to, ah, engage your services. We don't have much in the way of pay... nutricorn, we have that, and some other food..." He looked hopeful.

"Let me get dressed, and we'll talk."

I figured five minutes was long enough to simulate changing clothes. I emerged in standard civilian clothing, as neonationally neutral as I could manage, and hopped down from the back of the cab.

"Honestly, I don't need food so much... I can synthesize nutritional paste from almost anything organic." I smiled. "It tastes as good as it sounds, and I'm not saying I'd turn down a decent meal, but what I really need is tech. Machine parts. A fix for my vehicle." I pointed to the torn front grill.

Karl nodded slowly. I flicked on some external scanners to see if I could get a remote EKG. His decision-making centers were running around each other, mulling stuff over. Time to sweeten the deal a bit. They'd mentioned someone last night...

"Look, I understand. Machine parts aren't easy to come by. I'm a fair man, and I'm a doctor, not a mercenary. You have anyone sick here? Anyone who might need looking at? I'll help one, totally free, and then we talk seriously about what my services are worth. Fair?"

A man tapped Karl on the shoulder. The tapper was youngish, maybe twenty-one years old, thin, and anxious. Karl turned to him, looking a bit angry.

"What about Ellen?" said the tapper, trying to whisper and failing.

Karl closed his eyes in despair, knowing a bargaining chip had been blown. Now I knew they had someone who needed help. I didn't say anything. Karl was trying to maintain his authority here, and I wasn't about to undermine it by leaping on the name. I made a polite show of pretending I hadn't heard.

Finally, Karl relented. He turned to me. "We've got a woman here, Ellen—"

"—My wife," said the tapper.

"His wife," echoed Karl. "She's got... something... wrong with her."

Well, that was helpful, I thought, but I smiled and said, "Let me take a look at her." I grabbed a portable medikit and followed after Karl and Ellen's nervous husband.

The camp, or village—I wasn't sure which, it seemed to be caught between the two—consisted of a series of large public buildings, mostly dormitories or greenhouses, and dozens of small tents or ramshackle semi-permanent dwellings. I tried to get Karl to tell me more about it as we walked.

"Well, we were a convoy, about forty of us, mostly from the United Bay Autonomies, but there were more. We met some refugees from the NWA, if you can believe it, and realized we had more in common now. The entire borderland is a death zone, and I hear it's the same anywhere there were large cities."

I nodded, urging him to go on.

"We made a kind of peace and moved out, safety in numbers. There's folks out there taking advantage of the collapse. Well, we kept to a pattern of settling for a few weeks, then moving when something found us, for a few years. Then we came here."

"Here?"

"Not sure what it was, originally. Just a lot of empty buildings. But there was the Fence."

"You didn't build it?" Now, *that* was interesting.

"Nope. The Fence, and many of the buildings were here, abandoned. Didn't take long to figure out how to turn it on, and then we felt safe enough to dig in. Doesn't just block robotics, it also seems to take out most scans. At the least, people don't stumble on us often."

I kept nodding. This was... interesting. What happened to the original inhabitants? Some kind of plague? Or was the takeover less peaceful than Karl was saying? I was out of range of remote EKG, but skin temperature and heart rate didn't indicate any real nervousness. Not a perfect read, but good enough. I decided to believe him.

"That's, uhm, damn lucky. So you just moved in and took over?"

"Been a year now. We've got crops, turned the convoy vehicles into more living space, began welcoming in a few peaceful people that wandered by..." He gestured at the tents. "We keep an eye on food and supplies, trying not to outgrow... but it's a good place to wait it out, wait until people start rebuilding."

You mean, like you're doing? I thought, but didn't say anything. Hey, if their society worked on the hope of some future golden age to come, so be it. Hardly the first.

They had a simple sick ward set up, but no one to run it, except one older man who had, apparently, played a lot of medical interactives. He was fascinated by what I was doing. The ward itself was a large bare room, wood-walled, with a series of cots lining one wall and a mismatched assortment of scavenged medical gear poorly arranged along another. It looked equipped to handle a splinter, and that was it.

Ellen was the only patient. She was a young woman, dark haired, and glistening with sweat. No real isolation room here... if she had something contagious, everyone in the village would, too. I moved closer, though I didn't need to see her fever was dangerously high. I sat down and told everyone else to get back, then went to work.

A lot of what I do, I can do with simple scans—this body has all the sensors needed to do an MRI, get blood pressure, look for clots or internal bleeds—but with people watching, I needed to go through the motions. There were things I couldn't do by sight, like blood analysis. I pushed back her shirt to draw blood, and then I saw it... a strange amber scaling along her arm. I touched it. It felt something like a scab, but didn't seem to cover a wound. There were other patches, all over her body.

Rapidly, I flipped through my databases. This didn't match anything. Great. Something mutated.

"Can you help her? I, uh, used some full spectrums and tried the dermal regeneratives, but..."

I glanced back at wannabe doctor. "Yeah, that's how you get to level three in MedCenter Crisis II. If you use the cardiostims, you unlock the bonus diseases. Now let me do my job." He backed off, and I wanted to slap myself. No call for being snappy. I was just stuck with something I didn't recognize and it put me in a hell of a mood. "Sorry. Just a little rattled. Let me run up this bloodwork back at my ambulance." I turned and left, trying to ignore the river of whispers which followed me all the way back. They were worried; a real doctor had looked at one of their comrades and not only didn't cure her, he didn't know what was wrong.

It was a long night. I didn't know if anyone was watching me; I didn't care. I ran every test I could imagine on that blood sample, cross-correlating with all the data I got from observation. I could probably have done better if she was in the medibay, but I got the impression they were still wary of me. Best to perform my miracles from a distance.

Sometime about when the sun cleared the horizon, I found it. Fragments of a retrovirus, one I'd never seen before, drifting through her system. Looked like some sort of milspec modification protocol, a broken or failed one, or maybe she didn't have the right receptor sites. Didn't matter. It was easy to cure. I mixed up another batch of white cells and hopped out of the cab. Time to impress the locals, get some parts, and get on with the business of doing good in the world.

Yeah, I really was that stupid at the time.

The next morning, I was actually whistling a jaunty tune. Well, technically, I was using sound synthesis and could have actually output a full orchestral symphony if I wanted, but I stuck to whistling. There were people waiting for me, of course. They weren't about to let me wander unattended, but the guns were at least holstered by now. Two days without trouble or any attempt to breach the Fence had gained me some measure of trust.

Ellen's husband... I never did learn his name, come to think of it... was at my side almost instantly.

"Did you... did you do it? Did you figure out what's wrong?" He wrung his hands nervously. They glistened with sweat. He was running a slight fever, too. I made a mental note to scan them all for infection when I had the chance.

"I think so," I said in my most reassuring tones. "I've prepared some counteragents which ought to knock the infection out of her. I don't want to promise anything, though. Just let me do what I can." Better to underpromise and overdeliver, I always say.

"Thank you. Thank you." He kept near me, like a remora trying to attach itself to a particularly agile shark.

Nothing much had changed since the night before; two more small patches of the amber scabbing had appeared, but her fever was about the same. I pumped in the specialized cells I'd built, along with some mild stimulants to shift her metabolism up a notch and spread them through her system faster. I stayed to monitor her temperature; we didn't want her running *too* hot and I could slow her back down if I had to.

If this were an interactive, the results would have been ludicrously fast. As it was, I and her husband—and a steady stream of the curious and the concerned—sat there for a few hours, monitoring. They wouldn't let me work on anyone else until I'd cured her, and it wasn't like I had anywhere to go. I refused polite offers of food by noting I'd eaten earlier, and no one thought much of it. As a side note, I can eat. The body can take in food and store it for later disposal, but it's messy and it's one of those 'features' some engineer tossed in because he thought it might be useful later. I almost never use it.

When I'm out in the body, even though my consciousness, my 'brain' if you will, is still in the ambulance, I tend to think of myself as being in the body. There's only so much conflicting real-time sensory input I can juggle, after all, and I need to think of myself as being in one place and 'checking in' to the other. So I kept myself mostly grounded in this ersatz hospital, while every so often mentally 'looking back' at the ambulance itself. I'd made a big show earlier of locking it up and setting alarms, and people knew what kind of security military vehicles could have, so they kept well back. A few curious children approached too closely for their nervous parents' comfort and were hastily dragged away with stern warnings. Frankly, the whole thing was insanely *normal*, even given the strangeness of it. Just seeing people live day-to-day lives in one place was an odd relief to me. Odd thoughts of just settling in here, not wandering the world, began to dance over my consciousness.

This reverie was interrupted by a sudden wrenching cough from Ellen.

Her husband almost fell out of his chair. I flipped every sensor I had built in to full diagnostic mode. Fever dropping rapidly. Metabolism recentering on normal. I tapped gently at the amber scabs; they crumpled to powder and fell off. Her eyes flicked open.

"Ellen!" Her husband embraced her desperately. She returned the hug, weakly.

"Where... I was in the garden..." she looked around. "Was I sick?" Then she saw me. "Who?"

"He's a doctor. He saved you." He beamed. Then it happened.

He leapt around the bed and hugged me in thanks.

Here's the thing. I feel emotions. I get angry, happy, jealous, depressed, the whole thing. What I don't do, usually, is express them physically, at least not in ways that are easy for me to describe. I know, intellectually, how to, and can make my body cheer, slump, or whatever as needed, but it's a learned response, not an instinctive one. As a consequence, I'm sometimes unprepared for other people's expression of feelings. So the hug surprised me.

Not as surprised as Ellen's never-to-be-named husband was, though. A second after the hug, he fell back, cursing up a storm. "The *hell?* Who... what are you?" He began looking around for a weapon. The attending wannabe doctor looked up from the medical data file he'd been trying to comprehend. "What's going on?"

"He... that... it's not human!" Ellen's husband was pointing at me in terror. Ellen looked confused. The pseudo-doctor was trying to parse it all.

This might still be salvaged, I thought.

"Look. I can explain. Let's not do anything we might regret..." I ramped up the subsonics in my voice as much as I could, but they weren't capable of overcoming this level of excitement.

"No! No! Get away from her, you... thing! Get away from my wife!"

I stood, slowly, and met his eyes. "The wife whose life I just saved? Now calm down..."

He had grabbed a metal stand and swung it at me. The fact it went 'clang' rather than 'whump' when I blocked it with my arm seemed to jolt the doctor out of his stupor.

He went running for the door, calling for aid. Husband continued to smash at me until I wrenched the thing out of his hand and hurled it against the wall. Ellen, the woman whose life I had just saved, was trying to crawl back without falling out of her cot, and her husband was looking around for something else to hit me with.

This was odd. The intensity of the reaction, I mean. These people weren't luddites; they used a lot of technology, from the Fence which kept them safe to their genetically engineered corn. It wasn't some sort of religious thing. I had no idea what was going on.

I heard a lot more people running. I made my way out of the hospital—if this was going to turn into a fight, I didn't want to damage their only medical center, pathetic as it was. There was a crowd growing, and I only wished they were carrying torches and pitchforks. Instead, they had caseless ammo autofire rifles with laser aiming scopes.

I held my hands up and open, clearly weaponless. "I'm sorry if you think I lied to you, but I didn't. I am a doctor, and I am just here to..."

There are some advantages to being designed by the military. Even if you don't use them often, you have built-in combat protocols which take over as soon as certain thresholds are reached. So as soon as a subconscious level algorithm spotted the press of a trigger in the crowd, avoidance maneuvers came instantly online, and I spun and ducked a bullet which would have damaged, if not destroyed, this body. A quick check showed the mob was ignoring the ambulance. Good. They didn't know where "I" really lived.

I spotted one familiar face in the crowd. "Lunette! Can you please call off this mob? We can still work this out!" My 'advisor' protocols were showing me a half dozen counter-attack options which would have left half the mob dead or crippled in seconds, and I kept sending 'reject, reject, reject' messages to these helpful internal assistants.

Her face, still scarred, was twisted into horror and loathing. "You operated on me! You touched me! I talked to you like you were a person!" Her voice was almost incoherent, it was so thick with hatred and revulsion.

A small part of my mind was trying to make sense of this. It was beyond anything I'd seen before. The rest of my mind was trying to keep my precious and irreplaceable body alive.

I switched everything to full evasion. My holographic costume shimmered and shifted, mimicking the background as I moved. It wasn't fast enough to provide invisibility as I ran, but it was still good enough to make aiming at me hard. The bullets cracked into the ground as I ran, dodged, and rolled. I tried to make sure to move so as not to catch people in the crossfire, as the entire compound had just about gone completely mad.

A few decided to head me off and ran for the ambulance. They stumbled back in shock when the Heim field powered up and the craft began racing towards me, executing a complex dodging pattern. Half the mob desperately trying to track my ever-moving, color-shifting human body split off and tried to attack the vehicle.

I could kill about half of them with a whim. One missile fired into the tightly packed mob, and most would be dead, the rest dying. An evil little voice in the back of my mind said it would serve them right, but I ignored it. I reminded myself I already had one unnecessary death on my conscience, I didn't need more.

Still, self defense was a tempting excuse... No! I wouldn't do it.

The vehicle swerved and zoomed left; I ducked and leapt right. Bullets shot past me as I crouched, tumbled, and kicked myself right into the open door as my real body flew past. In seconds, the Charlie was deactivated and my entire consciousness was focused back in a single place.

I spun, sending a harmonic through the field to kick up a mound of turf, then pushing the power into a single mighty surge forward, faster than they imagined I could go. I also tightbeamed a signal to my faithful little scavenger waiting patiently outside the Fence. It awoke, shook off the cover of leaves and dirt, and clambered up the side of one of the alarm poles. Its tendrils snaked out and keyed in the code Lunette had given me, seconds before I passed through the field. One second off, and I'd have crashed dead into the woods beyond.

I didn't. I did stop, spin, and wait, until the mob approached. A few bullets pinged off my armor; I was built to handle much worse than that.

I clicked a missile into the launcher.

"Just so you know... I could have done *this*."

I fired. The missile arced high, over the compound, and detonated on the far side. There was an explosion, and a rain of shattered wood soon followed.

"Remember that the next time someone tries to help you."

I wish I could say this led to stunned looks of shock and maybe even a little shame and guilt. It didn't. All it did was lead to them continuing to fire until I sped off deep into the surrounding woods. As soon as I was sure I was safe, I dropped the field to standby.

A nice show, I confess. But I'd really put a lot of strain on the engine. The forward-right generator? Shot. I'd be limping at half speed until I could get it fixed, and there'd be more strain on the remaining systems. The whole 'pretend to be human' thing wasn't working, though I'd never seen such intense hostility before. Usually it's more vague discomfort. Even so, I didn't feel that trying to 'pass' was going to be a solution.

I spent a quiet night thinking about the situation, fending off only one attack by an overly curious self-propelled limpet mine. Then I found what I thought would be a solution.

Chapter 3

The plan was simple in concept, complex in execution. It was also not without risk.

I brought up all the data I had on the region. I tracked the most violent centers of combat, former bastions of civilization, weather patterns, known sources of strong data signals, and so on. I was looking for a needle in a haystack, but I had some powerful magnets to help me. Eventually, I found a set of optimal coordinates, and took off—slowly, damn it all—towards the nearest.

As I approached the first target zone, I heard gunfire, some screams, the whine of motors, and the whinnying of animals. The last one was a bit of a surprise.

I was approaching a former highway that ran through a wooded valley. This whole area was once mostly unsettled wilderness, which meant that it dodged the worst battles of the wars and was only raked over once or twice in a perfunctory, "we wouldn't want it to feel left out" manner by the automated systems still going at it. Hmm. That was a bit sarcastic. I might edit that later. Anyway, I figured that this region was a likely place for people to settle down, or to travel along, and I was looking for people, specifically, people in trouble.

I crested over the rise to take a look around. There was a battle going on. A half dozen men on horses—horses, would you believe it?—were attacking a tracked APC[4]. Even more amazingly, they were winning.

The riders were five men and two women, dressed in light body armor clearly patched together from multiple sources, and wielding very powerful caseless ammo rifles. One, I was guessing the leader, actually had a two handed gauss rifle, and that's what

---

[4] armored personnel carrier

was really tearing the hell out of the APC. Microbullets of steel-jacketed depleted uranium accelerated to ludicrous velocities, firing hundreds of times a minute... it was playing can opener with the tracked vehicle. Behind that was a small convoy of much less durable craft, mostly civilian wheeled cars, all burning or destroyed.

Bodies were everywhere. I wasn't sure of the exact details of what happened here, but I knew who I could get them from. All I had to do was save his life.

There's a lot of things a properly equipped medical vehicle can do. One of them is mix up some fast acting nerve gas. Nothing too fatal, unless someone had an unusual allergy or, even worse, a deliberately induced susceptibility (nothing like planting genetic time bombs into your own people to keep them in line... the Russians started that trick, but pretty soon a lot of places were slipping a few extra bonus gifts in with free vaccinations). I had spent part of the night before rigging up a few grenades, and all that remained was to put them into a launcher and get to work. As far as I could tell, the folks down below were too busy trying to peel back the APC to notice me above them and just out of their line of sight.

I try to avoid active sensors when I enter a dangerous area. I hate sending out big 'here I am' signals to the local hostiles. Unfortunately, that means anyone who is hiding well themselves can get the jump on me. I sent my body out of the safety of the ambulance, grenades at the ready, and there was a loud *crack* as a bullet shot right into my chest, ripping at a nice angle which went through the heart and my left lung. I'd be unconscious in a second and dead in a minute.

If I had a heart. Or lungs. My chest is actually mostly hollow. It's a good place to store things. The Charlie isn't a packed mass of complex, fragile, machinery. Most of it is memory metals and power storage, and the vitals are placed primarily in the limbs—mostly because people *do* shoot at the torso.

The holofield flickered a few times, though; the projector matrix was damaged. The shooter gasped and paused to line up another shot, this one to my head. That would be bad; it would disrupt my sensors and the link that let me use the body at all. I couldn't allow that.

I moved. I dropped the grenades—not yet active—and kicked forward into a spinning tumble, sliding past the shooter. His shot went wild, breaking a tree branch and angering a robin which flew away in a snit. I was behind him; I grabbed the rifle and tossed it back, away from casual reach. He struggled to get loose of my grip.

"Now look. You relax, and you will be all right. I'm really not here to kill anyone."

He struggled, tried to kick me in the crotch, and inhaled for a scream. That I didn't need. If the gang below focused on me, I would be dead.

I shook my head sadly and touched a few key points. He gurgled and collapsed. If he was lucky, he'd still be able to have kids someday. That's one thing about being a doctor: you can make it stop hurting, or you can make it start.

The rest should be easy. I grabbed the modified grenades, did a few quick calculations for precise targeting, and hurled them into the ongoing melee below. The APC had spun its main turret around and was trying to take out the raiders; the driver was either insane or a machine, or possibly both. I saw one of the attackers go down, bisected by the stream of bullets coming from the vehicle's gun; the leader, though, was dancing circles around the spray, and responding with his own railgun-propelled counter-attacks.

The grenades hit exactly where I intended them to. Gas sprayed out, coating the road with coils of yellowish white mist. The horses collapsed first, one breaking the leg of a rider as it fell. The humans barely had a chance to spin and try to locate me before they fell first to their knees, then onto their faces.

Except one.

The commander or leader or whoever—the one with the really big gun, the gun that could shred my Charlie and my real body in seconds—he didn't fall. Maybe he had filters in his lungs, maybe he had resistance to this particular gas engineered into him, I didn't know and wouldn't really have time to find out. He did see my body, though, and brought the gun to bear.

"Run away from a man with a knife, run towards a man with gun." Sometimes, this is great tactical advice; other times, it's a recipe for suicide. The problem is, you never know which until it's too late.

I ran towards him.

Well, 'ran' is a bit strong. Started forward, ducked under the first burst of hyper-accelerated metal, rolled, and slammed into him with more force than I think he ever expected. He and I went tumbling backwards. I slammed the gun out of his hand; it skidded off to the north. I stabbed my fingers on a few pressure points, and stepped back to watch him collapse around his abdomen.

Instead, he rolled around to get into a crouch and leapt for me, drawing a knife as he did. I flipped on some medical sensors. Magnetic imaging showed extensive subdermal metal, and IR readings were all over the place and all wrong. This guy had been rebuilt from head to toe.

Great, I thought. I picked the wrong horse.

The knife slashed into my arm, even as I remembered to flip the camouflage holography back on. A semi-invisible man was harder to wrestle with. Internal scanners showed damage to the arm—whatever that knife was made of, it was sharpened to a diamond edge. Great. If this body was destroyed, I could just race out of here, but I'd be in an even worse position. No, I had to fight this out.

I had one advantage over him. I could think fast. Incredibly fast.

I shut down all of my other processors, all of the hundreds of things I'm doing at once. Cut off all external sensors, all filters, all background processes, put everything into solving one problem. I called up the scans I did of my assailant and looked for weaknesses. That was armored; that was redundant; that was reinforced. Damn! Whoever built this guy did a damn fine job of making him a killing machine, and what was I? An anti-killing machine, really. This wasn't a fair fight. I wondered who I could complain to.

For the quarter-second or so it took for me to do this analysis, my body was paralyzed; probably too short for him to notice. Even so, there was a moment of inertia as I retook control of myself, and that brief delay was enough for him to stab the knife down into my chest and slice up and across. This didn't kill the body, but it did tear enough vital equipment that cascade failures started scrolling along my consciousness. There was one chance, one place where his subdermal armor was incomplete and where I could land a crushing blow. I struck at the base of his throat, hard.

And missed, the damaged circuits sending my aim off. I waited for the killing strike which would take my body offline, and then I'd fire up the Heim field, pull away, and come up with another, even more brilliant way to screw myself.

Then all the medical sensors I had on the guy flatlined as he collapsed on top of me.

I shoved his body aside and staggered up. There was someone else there, a man dressed in the remains of combat armor and holding a smoking pistol. He was colored an odd mix of smoke, sweat, and blood, and was losing a lot of the latter. He looked down at my body, which had lost any semblance of holographic humanity, and forced a crooked smile.

"Hey," he said, before his knees folded and he went down.

I got to my own feet and ran the usual scans, even as the ambulance powered up and rolled down to meet us. I wasn't too concerned about random infections, so I slid him into the medibay and then got into the cab. A full damage report on the Charlie scrolled by; I ignored it. I had a patient to save.

Assuming there's been no anagathic treatments, his telomere decay put him at thirty-six. He was tall, well muscled, and lean, a bit too lean. There were signs he'd been eating suboptimally of late. His face was currently a mess, but bone and muscle structure indicated he'd be handsome in a rough sort of way once he was cleaned up. Dark brown hair raggedly self-cut, black eyes... well, eye. The only one I had in stock was green. I figured he wouldn't complain. Quite a few scars; he'd been in some dustups, but all of his organs were his, no replacements. No cosmetic bodymods, either—that was a bit odd. Soldiers normally went for liquid crystal implants or decorative symbiotes; this one didn't. You can learn a lot about a man by looking at his wounded body.

His digestive tract had so much metal in it he might have been armor plated. One lung was collapsed. Three ribs were fragmented, and dozens of sharp splinters had torn up most of his upper torso. One eye was shot. His left arm was almost severed; it's a good thing, I thought, that he shot with his right. Mentally, I held out my arms and cracked my knuckles. This was going to be a good night's work. A dozen surgical arms sprouted inside me, and holographic images of his mangled body, each and every splinter of bone and fragment of metal conveniently highlighted. I got to work.

On a whim, I ran a DNA check against my military databases. Jackpot! Former Bay Alliance, Sergeant, vehicle specialist. Name, Michael Ernesto Calvers. No particularly noteworthy genemods, registered Neounitarian, served without serious incident until the records database stopped being updated a few years back. Psych profile... hmm. I suppose if I had choices I could have done better, but given the effort it took to land this fish, I wasn't about to toss him back unless I really, really, had to. There were things I could do...

Don't, whined my conscience.

Shut up, I told it. *It's for the greater good.*

By which you mean, the Greater Good of MacIntyre Medical Unit 504A, it replied.

I decided to keep ignoring it. In bad interactives, the evil AIs have always "disabled their conscience subroutines" or some such drivel, as if one's own sense of right and wrong was somehow distinct from who one was as a whole. I can only "turn off" my conscience the same way any other thinking being can—by becoming such a psychotic sociopath I no longer had one. That isn't my goal. I can, however, ignore that annoying little voice that reminds me I'm not being one hundred percent ethical. I can live with some guilt, since it means I get to keep *living.*

Speaking of living, my patient was on the painful road to recovery. I could have blocked out all his pain receptors if I wanted to, but I left them on, albeit dimmed a lot. Not for sadism, but because I needed him to know just how bad off he was and how much I'd done for him. A little gratitude never hurts.

His consciousness slowly climbed. It's amazing watching the mind wake up. Patterns of blood and electricity and chemicals shift and move and explode. It's like flipping a switch in a museum gallery and seeing light after light after light come on, illuminating the darkness and revealing all sorts of amazing things. When all the lights were on, I spoke, before he could look around and start panicking.

"Sergeant Calvers?"

"Huh? Wuh—what?" He blinked, trying to clear his vision. This was going to be problematic since one eye was brand new and hadn't fully integrated into his optic nerve yet. He'd better not lose the other one, I didn't have any more in stock.

"Hello Sergeant. I'm your doctor. You were in a particularly nasty scrape. Can I ask what you remember?"

"Sergeant? How do you... who are you? Where is this?"

"I'm Doctor MacIntyre. And you're in my medibay. Now, please tell me the last thing you remember. I need to determine if there was any neurological damage."

"Wait... wait, what year is this?" There was a sudden rising tide of hope. I knew where he was going.

I told him the year. The hope popped like a balloon.

"So much for that," he murmured.

"Sorry, it wasn't all a fever dream brought on by injury. But you are inside a UBA military vehicle, and I'm a Lieutenant."

"I'd salute if I could," he lied.

"No need. I'm a doctor first and foremost."

"You're soultech, aren't you? I saw that robot fighting..."

"Yes. So you remember the fight, then?"

"Yeah. I remember thinking I was about dead. I didn't know you were a doctor, I figured you were just some drone. You gave me a shot at the bastard's back and I figured I'd take it before I died. Heh. Guess I got lucky."

You and me both, I thought.

"You did. It's very fortunate I happened on you when I did."

"Yeah." Then he went quiet. He seemed very thoughtful. A bit too thoughtful.

"I've been out of the loop lately. It's not easy to get any kind of connection anymore. Would you mind telling me a little about yourself and how you got there?"

He frowned, and winced at the effort. "Why's it matter?"

"I need to know if you're likely to have been exposed to anything I wouldn't catch on normal scans." Sometimes, I just lie like a cheap Persian rug.

He mulled this over. "I guess that makes a kind of sense. 'Sides, I got nothing I don't want known."

He started talking. For the sake of posterity and honesty, I will now transcribe his tale, unedited. May you find it edifying.

***

OK. So I'm supposed to be leading this convoy to where they hears there's a settlement, and... well, I guess I'd better start further back. I enlisted in... nah, that's too far back. Let's pick up with where my unit got taken apart. It was, oh, four or five years ago when everything really started going to hell, like one of them avalanches, at first it's just a little rock or two, then suddenly everything falls and it just keeps going faster and faster. My unit was up around the old Oregon border, disputed zone, like anything wasn't disputed then, right?

We got hit hard. They came outta nowhere, flood of heavy armor, looked like QR[5] make, but they were flying NWA holos. I'd love ta say it was some kinda glorious battle, but fact is we got

---

[5] Quebecois Résistance

wiped in a few seconds. I was the driver, and I just yelled for everyone to get in, get in, get in, and as soon as I figured most of 'em were—in, that is—I lit out. Tanks were going south, so I pulled west, taking heavy fire all the while. I figured the line was about to shift and I was gonna be behind it, but maybe I could sneak around and down south once I had a chance to breathe.

Chance never seemed to come. I kept thinking I'd found a safe way back, then, bam! I run into some patrol, or walking minefield, or swarm of biters, or whatever, and I'd backtrack and turn around. Guys I was carrying, well, they kept getting more and more pissed. We'd stop to find come clean water and everyone'd pile out and start screamin' and fightin'. It was a mess. More'n once you'd have two of 'em poundin' the crap outta each other over nothing, over stupid shit like who ate the last bit of pseudochoc ration or which V-World had the best graphics. Stuff no one would come to blows over, but everyone was scared, and, y'know, *soldiers*. They'd rather be angry than scared. It's dumb, but what can ya do?

Anyway, I started with six of my guys in the pack, and pretty soon we were down ta four, and those four were more and more trouble. Food was low, the solar wasn't putting out near enough for long travel, and we had no idea where the battle lines were anymore. The chatter we got on the wire—when we got anything— was confused as hell. No one knew anything anymore.

Time crawled on. We couldn't get a break, couldn't find a way to someplace safe. The four dwindled. One just took off one day and never came back, two more decided to join up with the fragments of another unit we'd run into, and the last, well, he got taken apart by a mine that had decided to plant itself right in the middle of nowhere. Two months of travel, and it was me and my APC.

I saw a lot of things happening, learned a lot. That big push south, the one which almost got us, well, it ran into really hard resistance when it hit the main Bay cities, and from what I picked up, tacnukes and morphic plagues were involved. They broke on the wall, but the wall broke too, and that was the last major action I ever heard of. Wanderers were everywhere, folks lookin' to get from the hell they knew to the heaven they dreamed of, and, well, they were willin' to offer what they had for a ride in an APC. I never planned on it happenin', but I became a taxi and a convoy guard, swapping for food, fuel, and, uh, well, some personal favors if they had nothin' else. I guess you wouldn't know about that, heh?

So this goes on a year, year and a half, maybe... then I ran into *them*.

(A quick note from MacIntyre. At this point in the narrative, Sergeant Calvers tried to spit in disgust.)

They called themselves 'The New Northwest Army,' and there was maybe a thousand of 'em, all camped around some neocrete fortress that looked pretty new. As soon as I got into sight I got a lot of guns pointed at me. The akwarns (Another quick note: Acquisition Warning. An indication that your vehicle is the focus of target acquisition systems.) were going off scale. But no one was actually shooting at me yet, and I got someone on the line pretty quick. I don't remember every last detail of the conversation, but it was somethin' like...

"Hey there. If you don't cause trouble, we won't kill you."

"I don't want trouble. Who you with?"

"We're not with anyone. We're the new people in charge. The world's gone to hell, we mean to do something about it."

"Huh. You got food? Supplies? I can trade."

"Sure. Just step out of the vehicle slowly, and we can talk."

Well, it went on a bit more than that, and I had a bit of a fight with myself over whether to pop the hood or cut and run. I was afraid that they just wanted the vehicle intact and as soon as I got out, they'd cut me in half and take it. Figured I'd put that idea out of their heads.

"OK. I'm comin' out, but I gotta warn you. This thing's got an EKG lock. Anyone without my brain, thinkin' some pretty obscure keywords, tries to drive it, it goes boom and you've got slag."

The guy on the other end just laughed a bit. "Don't worry. We'd like to get you *and* your vehicle to join us. Why not let us show you what we've got?"

I weighed the odds of cutting and running now that a dozen or more anti-tank weapons were locked on me, and figured I'd take my chances.

The camp setup was pretty sweet. Most organized thing I'd seen in ages. Folks were wearin' all sort of uniforms, from different neonats, but with rank sign and patches I'd never seen before. People gave orders, people took orders. There were also a lot of civvies around, and it didn't take much lookin' to see they weren't all that well fed or cared for. I asked this one gal, Katherine someone-or-other who'd said she'd be my guide, about all that.

"Oh, those are refugees we're taking in and protecting," she said, all bubbly and happy.

I pointed to one guy who was pretty much a walkin' skeleton, strugglin' to haul water containers.

"He don't look too protected t'me."

Should have caught that glint in her eye then, that 'OK, this one's gonna be trouble' look I've seen way too often in my life. But I didn't. She just kept smilin' and said, "These people have been through a lot, and it's a long road to recovery. And of course they have to do some work around here. We can't just give away everything we've managed to acquire."

'Acquire' was another word I really should've been lookin' more closely at, but hey, I was sick and tired and hungry. I wasn't thinkin' all that hard.

So the two of us, me and her, we headed to their mess hall. Not some makeshift tent, this was a real building, neocrete like the rest of the place, and huge. I guess it was also the main meeting hall. Anyway, we walk past the door and suddenly I'm not just hungry, I'm almost mad. I think if anyone had tried to stop me, I would've torn right through them. First time in months I'd smelled real food, and I'm not just talkin' about the time I'd been wanderin'. I'd been livin' off synthetics for too long. I don't even remember what I ate... there was chicken and vegetables and even some neo-dodo. Dessert, real pie. Damn. I ate like it was my last meal.

Chatted a little with some of the other people there, in between shoving food down our throats. Met some who were on our side, some who were on the other, and everyone made a big deal over 'bygones be bygones,' even though the war was still going on. They all said it didn't matter who won anymore, that the whole system was falling in on itself, and that it was time for someone to pick up the pieces.

It all sounded like a good deal, if you didn't think about it too hard. And right then, eating real food and chatting with guys (and a good number of gals) who weren't starving or dying or weeping, I wasn't in the mood to think too hard. I wasn't about to commit myself to anythin', but I made polite noises and kept my options open. Something about it kept naggin' at me, especially when they began talking about Cromney.

Cromney's their leader, their General. The way some of them talked, he was Jesus, Allah, and Sun Tzu all rolled into one. He was smart, he was strong, he had a plan, he was the man, and on

and on and on. Look, there's been a few COs I respected here and
there but I've never seen soldiers so hyped up about their boss
before. Even if they'd follow him into hell, they'd still be tellin'
some jokes about 'im, pointing out that his belt's too tight or
makin' some reference to what he did with non-sapient farm
animals or whatever. But these guys wouldn't say one word
against him, not even a half a joke. Those little alarm bells which
had been ringin' since I got out of my APC were getting louder.

I figured, though, I could ignore 'em long enough to eat. That
almost got me killed.

Round about desert, I asked Katherine where the civvies ate. I
saw some of 'em dishing up and mopping, but none of them
chowing down. She said the refugee population was housed
elsewhere. Then she started talkin' about my APC, saying they
needed vehicles and drivers, tellin' me about all the benefits of
joinin' up. She wasn't out-and-out threatening me, but she was
doing that whole thing where folks sorta kinda hint that bad shit
might happen, but it won't be their fault. I hate people like that. If
I plan to hurt someone, I tell him straight up. Might be only a
second before I do it, but I tell him.

So anyway, they tell me they can set me up for the night,
private room, and maybe in the morning they can have a few
officers interview me, see if I'm going to 'fit in.' Again, it might
have been dumb, but I'd been using a makeshift bedroll in the back
of the APC for months and it was really startin' to wear me out.
So, I said yes.

Place they set me up in was nice. Not big, about 8 by 10, plain
neocrete walls, but it had a toilet, a bed with a neural sleep field,
and even an interactive I could plug into. No external comm links,
not that they'd be any use, and no window, but it was the most
comfortable room I'd been in, in years.

I got into the bed, and the field started right up. I started
getting woozy, and I didn't feel like sleeping just yet. I needed to
think some more. So I looked for the field controls... and there
weren't any.

OK, now I was starting to listen to those alarms. Neural beds
are nice and all, but I don't like someone deciding when I'm gonna
pass out. It also started to occur to me that they might want me
asleep. I didn't know what was up, but it was somethin'.

They let me keep my pocket knife; I guess they figured I'd be
gettin' too suspicious if they took it. They didn't look at it too
closely, though. I'm not really a mechanic, but I have to do

maintenance on the APC, and I've got a few nonstandard tools on that thing. Some memory metal and microengines, and you can make a pocket knife that includes all sorts of toys, like a field disruptor for when you've got to turn off something that isn't turning off the way it's supposed to. Didn't take long for the thing to find the bed's frequency and quietly fry it. Now it was just a comfy mattress, and I was wide awake.

Took less than an hour for them to play their hand. The door clicked open. I heard some voices.

"Is he out?"

"Sure. Field auto-activates. He's flatlined."

I kept still. I heard some beeping. Then someone, a guy, said, "The hell he is!"

I figured it was time to act now. They wanted me asleep; that meant I wanted to be awake.

I heard someone standin' right next to the bed. Faster than he was ready for, I kicked sideways, catchin' him hard in the gut. He went down. Someone else leapt for me, a shadow in shadow, but I grabbed him by the shirt, discovered it was a her, then tossed her over. I heard a pretty satisfyin' crack when her head hit wall. That left one more silhouetted against the door; he was drawin' a gun. "Never bring a knife to a gun fight" was the old sayin', but it was all I had. I ducked in while he was still drawing a bead, shoved his gun hand out of the way, and got the short blade to his throat.

"Drop it."

He did. I switched my grip and slammed him against the doorframe, hard. He went down. I grabbed the gun. Fortunately, there was no biosensor on the trigger; I hate it when that happens.

I figured it was time to leave. They'd raise the alarm pretty soon. If I were a different kind of person, I'd've gone back and just slit some throats, buy me a couple of extra minutes... but that's not me. I didn't know yet if they'd done anything worth killin' over, and I wasn't about to kill someone I wasn't sure deserved it.

(Note from MacIntyre: Yeah, rub it in. I need more guilt.)

My plan was pretty simple. Get out, find my way back to the APC, and get as far away from here as possible. I didn't know what they wanted to do to me in my sleep, and I didn't give a damn, I just wanted out. Of course, navigatin' a maze of buildings in the mostly-dark while alarms are goin' off isn't the easiest thing in the world. Some guys I know, other drivers, they've got little magnetic sensor cells in their skin, like some kinds of germs, so they can always know which way they're facin'. Not me. I'm straight up as I was born, no mods but the ones Mom and Dad picked out.

The upshot is, I thought I turned left at the fourth identical three-story featureless rectangular building, but I guess I shoulda turned right, or maybe it's the other way around. I ended up heading into a different part of the camp. The part they didn't want me askin' questions about.

This part stunk. It was a cesspit, all lean-tos and buildings stuck together from whatever castoff parts people could find. There was power all throughout the rest of the camp, but here, people were usin' fires to cook over or stay warm. There was mud, and filth, and a big fence covered with warnings. From a distance, it looked like just a bunch of poles strung up in a line, but closer in, there was this weird shimmer in the light, like a spiderweb made of glowing plastic. 'Cept, of course, those lines weren't silk...

Monowire. Brush against it, and a sushi chef'll take what's left and serve it on rice.

OK. I'm a fair guy. I understand refugees, 'specially civvie refugees, can be trouble. That people who are hungry and angry can be difficult to manage, 'specially in large groups. And that when you've got a lot of very deadly weapons lyin' around, the last thing you want is a riot.

None of that justifies surroundin' what's supposed to be a safety zone with a *lethal* fence. Good old steel, maybe with a stunning charge in case there's a riot, costs less and kills almost no one. There's only one reason to use monowire, and that's if you want anyone who gets ideas to die horribly so as to keep everyone else scared. The multiple watchtowers with guns pointed inwards to the camp were the icing on a very nasty cake.

The alarm was still going, so those towers had turned away from keepin' an eye on the threat posed by near-starved prisoners and were busy lookin' for me. So I kept runnin'. I wanted to get out of plain sight, so I headed for an unlit building near to the refugee camp. I figured if the power was off, it was empty, and maybe I'd have a second to get my bearings and find a plan other than "Run, then die tired when they catch you."

Building wasn't empty.

Some kind of sensor must've gone off when I pass through the door, 'cause lights flipped on. It was a barracks, not as nice as the ones I'd been in, but a lot better than the mudpile a few hundred feet away. Rows of metal bedding, no fancy neural fields, and not much else.

'Cept for the kids. I'd say a hundred or so here, hard to guess ages when they're all underweight, but I'd guess between eight and maybe fourteen. The lights goin' on woke 'em all up, and one of 'em, the oldest I'd guess, started shouting, "Wake! Wake! Drill! Move! Move!" an' clappin' his hands while the others stumbled out of their cots and started staggerin' through the motions of gettin' dressed. Then he got a good look at me: sweaty, wearin' the wrong uniform, and lookin' confused. If I was a bit sneakier, I'd've come up with a convincin' lie, bullshitted my way through this, but sneaky like that isn't somethin' I'm good at, so he and I stared at each other for a sec. Then the alarm goin' off outside got his attention. I'll say this, the brat was quick.

"Get him!" He pointed at me. The sleepy mob stopped, mostly barely standing, and turned towards me.

Great. I had a pistol; they were unarmed. Shootin' kids? Not if I had a choice.

I spun around. I thought I'd seen somethin' when I came in, and I was right—the door was easy to open from the outside, auto-locked from the inside. Turn, step, slam, and the sound of some sleepy ten year olds unable to stop in time came from inside. Better'n killin' 'em.

Lots of bits and pieces fell inta place. Keep the refugees as cheap labor, turn the kids into disposable soldiers... maybe even use them as leverage on the parents in the camps. The new order wasn't something I wanted any part of. All that remained was gettin' away intact.

There were lights in the sky now, a dozen of 'em. Seeker drones, lookin' for any biosignature they didn't recognize. That would be me. Once I was pinpointed, that'd be it. On the plus side, I'd spotted my APC near to the treeline. I had a goal...

But it wasn't the APC.

I ducked back, stickin' to the rapidly vanishing shadows as more and more of the camp woke up. The seeker drones were movin' in standard patterns, narrowin' their search. I knew they'd be on me in a sec, so I had only one shot at a desperate plan.

I raced to the gate of the prison compound. Holdin' the pistol in one hand, I fished out my knife with the other, and when I got near to the gate, flicked on the field disruptor. Wouldn't do squat on the monowire fence, but the gate lock was magnetic, and I was gamblin' they hadn't bothered to do a lot of fancy shieldin' on it.

I was right.

The gate 'poinged' open, and more alarms went off. The masses inside suddenly saw a lot of chaos and confusion and badly outnumbered guards, who were rushin' in to hold it shut. For an instant, I became Public Enemy Number Two.

Then, as I raced for the APC, hopin' to escape in the confusion, one of the seekers found me. It was your basic flyin' eyeball model, with two small guns strapped to either side. Didn't even bother with the 'halt and identify' stuff, it had my biosigns on lock and just started shootin'.

I shot back. The gun bucked twice in my hand, and the thing gave a little squeal and spun out of control into the dirt. I looked around, expectin' more, and then I saw the lights zipping off, headin' for the prisoners who'd escaped.

I'm not much of a religious man, even for a neounitarian. But I called on every name of Deity I knew of to rain down some serious smitin' on those bastards. They'd set the seekers for broad spectrum, set them to shoot down *anyone* whose biosigns weren't right and who were in the programmed area—and that meant a bunch of half-starved prisoners and not a few sleepy soldiers caught in the crossfire. If I were a better man, I'd've run back into that chaos to try to do some good, but I'm not that good a person. I did what I planned, ran for the APC.

There were two guards there, probably givin' thanks they weren't in the madhouse over by the refugee compound. And while I'm not about to shoot unconscious people in the head, I wasn't about to charge two armed guys who were more than ready to kill me. They heard me runnin', too, they were ready. I saw aiming lasers flash, and probably the only thing that saved me was that they weren't sure if I was supposed to be killed on sight or just captured and then killed.

I kicked left and rolled, falling under the sudden surge of bullets which slashed through the area I was in just a fraction of a sec before. Then I brought my stolen pistol up and shot it. I heard one guy gurgle and start to buckle as I closed in on the APC. Once I got inside of twenty feet, the engine started hummin' to life... good ol' neural induction fields. Still have one guard to go, though. I kept movin' to keep him from drawin' a bead, but bullets were bouncing off my craft's surface and I knew I didn't have much time.

Now, normally, something like the NI field is just there to help you drive it easier when you're inside, and give it a quick start in emergencies like this one. But I'd been using the same vehicle for a couple of years, and it'd been well trained, so that it was practically a part of my body. Even outside it, I could kinda drive it if it was close enough. Not real well, mind you, the field wasn't designed for real smooth control from outside, but I could make it roll forward. And I did, at just the right time. There was a sudden curse and then some really unpleasant crunching noises. I wish I had somethin' more profound to claim I was thinkin', but, really, at the time, all I could say to myself was, "Damn, that's gonna be a bitch to get out of the treads."

I hopped inside to the sound of screams and gunfire. I didn't know who was winnin' the riot I'd caused, but I had a guess it was the well-fed guys with the guns. I swore I'd pay 'em back if I ever got the chance, and spun out and away as fast as I could. Not my proudest moment, but I got away alive.

Until a minute or two later when the akwarns went off.

I clicked up a rearview map; there were three things comin' after me, Heim-field one-man nap-of-Earth flyers, from the looks of it. Comm channel showed they were tryin' to open a connection, and sudden jumping and jarring showed they were tryin' to jam the neural field. I flipped it off and shut down all outside ports, and took over full manual control.

I'd been travelin' a lot, buildin' up maps of danger zones and safe routes, just in case I had to make a fast run. I had a sudden idea. A dumb and dangerous one, but those things had speed on me, and the sudden sharp hail of metal on my rear armor said they could take me down. I could see the warnin' lights come on brighter and brighter with each new flurry of lead.

I slowed down a bit, takin' a big risk, letting 'em think they were hurtin' me more'n they were. I saw the outer armor in back start to go down, hard bullets ricocheting in the personnel compartment... givin' thanks no one was back there and that there was heavy armor 'tween it and the cab. But I needed 'em close, real close, too close to pull back or away.

Banked left, hard. They followed. Flicked on one transmitter, tight beam, going forward.

See, real problem with this war is the robots... no offense to you, Doc, I know you aren't one. They just keep on doin' what they're supposed to do, like layin' down self-replicating mine fields. You know how it works. One mine burrows in and starts leeching materials from the soil, easy if there's lots of scrap metal and junk around. It makes another mine, that one does the same thing, and pretty soon, a whole minefield just grows where no one ever told it to. Well, I knew where one was, and maybe some aspect of the Divine was lookin' out for me, cause it was UBA and still usin' old IFF codes. So I shot straight over it, it got my tightbeam signal and ignored me... and then my three buddies went up in a hail of fire, rainin' down raw materials the field could use to rebuild itself.

I rode on. I didn't know how bad the New Northwest Army would want me, but I had a feelin' they weren't the forgive and forget types. I headed east, mostly, through deep woods, duckin' and dodgin' anythin' I saw, until I was so tired nothin' could keep me awake much longer. I did the best I could to hide and crashed. Not sure for how long.

I managed to wake up with no sign of pursuit, but I knew I'd made some nasty enemies.

After that... well, I kept my ear to the ground and stayed way clear of the New Northwest. I heard things, nasty things, and just wished I could... Anyway, I mostly managed to get by doing transport or courier jobs. No one really questioned how I'd claimed a UBA vehicle as my own personal armored taxi. People were happy enough for anyone who wasn't tryin' to kill them.

This went on a few months. I learned a lot. Learned the world's goin' to hell faster'n I ever thought possible. It's like—like all the things that made things get better so fast in the time leading up to the whole mess just went into reverse and made everything fall apart fast, too. I don't know how many people are dead. I seen some ghost cities but never went into 'em, in case whatever wiped 'em out's still there. Seen a lot of people just tryin' to get by, hopin' that what they're looking for is over the next hill or across the next river, and, hey, maybe some of 'em found it.

Made some mods. Got more armor, some of that crystallized iron, and gauss rifles hooked into the neural field so anything I thought about shooting, got shot. Some sweet mods to the guns, too, gotta tell you about 'em later. So I was pretty equipped to deal with the world if I was smart and careful. Wanna guess what no one ever wrote down on my psych profile?

Few days ago, I got kinda caught off guard. I met some people, a couple of families that had been supportin' each other since things got really bad, who still kept their old vehicles runnin', but needed armed escort. Now, an APC isn't a tank, but it's better than some civvie car, so I went against my better judgment and said yes. Had to go slow and open since their cars pretty much had to stick to the road. That's where you found us... well, what was left of us. I mean, I was scanning for high heat signatures, Heim field distortions, radio chatter, all that stuff, but I never expected to be run down on by guys with horses! Would've been a sick joke, could've outrun 'em easy, 'cept for the railgun. Killed half the convoy before we even knew what was goin' on, and by the time I got my own guns online and firin' back, they were openin' me up like... well, you saw the rest.

So. Here I am. Looks like my APC's a wreck... and so am I. Damn. I talked a lot, didn't I? Y'mind if I sleep now, doc?

(Here ends the first transcript from Sgt. Calvers)

Well. Nothing I didn't suspect, really, but the details were interesting. The 'New Northwest Army' had flown below my personal radar, but then, I'd spent the last year moping in the hills. As for my 'find'...

Calvers really wasn't my ideal choice. There was a strong temptation to simply patch him up, charge him some nominal fee—he was, after all, a skilled mechanic according to his record, and should be able to fix my Heim field generators—and send him on his way, and begin again. On the other hand, he did possess a lot of useful skills and seemed to have a hint of the ethical bent I was going to need. I had a feeling how he'd react, not to my initial proposal, which I was sure he'd accept, but to the knowledge of what I had to do to insure his long term cooperation. I wasn't about to invest a lot of time and effort in him if he wasn't going to be in it for the duration.

Really, I didn't *like* having to do it. I simply felt I had no choice. In the end, I was sure, we'd both be better off for the partnership. It would just take him longer to see it.

I put him back under and let him heal. I figured I'd look for someplace safe, power down a bit for a few days, then discuss our new arrangement. Then I realized I'd almost forgotten something vital.

He wouldn't approve. I knew that. In time, he'd see the cold, inexorable logic of it, but until then... well, what he didn't know wouldn't stress him. After checking his vitals one more time, I got back in my body and went out to the road.

This time, the carnage got to me a bit more. OK, a lot more. This is going to sound silly coming from a battlefield medic, but I have never really gotten totally used to the sight of bodies mangled and twisted. There's something alien and hollow and empty about death. The dead body and the live one are almost the same thing, in one sense, but there's still something missing. I've watched people die, I mean, watched their brains as they enter the final maelstrom as one neuron cluster after another fails. It's like watching words fade from a book, one by one, until all the pages are finally blank. Everything that made it unique has vanished; it's just a shell meant to hold something which is forever lost.

I suppose I think too much. To be fair, I only allow myself the luxury of philosophizing when no one's actively trying to shoot at me, which is a rarer and rarer occasion these days.

The slaughter here was pretty intense. The railgun is a nasty weapon designed to take out heavy armor, not mortal flesh. A lot of the people were barely recognizable; their bodies blasted into chunks of meat. I looked at one woman, perhaps twenty or so. As a child she had seen a world of infinite wonders and infinite possibilities, and now, what was left of her was attracting scavengers. I think I stood there for a minute or so, contemplating possibilities, considering all those pointless and stupid might-have-beens.

And, finally, I decided there was absolutely no way to harness intact organs from anyone. Even aside from the extensive physical damage, they'd been dead too long. The best I could hope for was to dig through the tissue to find living cells I could culture, and that was a long shot. The only thing the dead would pass on to the living would be raw chemicals, whichever hadn't already begun to break down into useless precursor molecules. By the time I was done, there'd be an organic slurry which could be filtered, sorted, and stored until needed.

I still had my pointless rituals, though. I took samples of hair and skin and checked the DNA against existing records, as well as cataloging it for later. I searched for identification of any sort—physical objects, implants, gene markers—and collected it. For those where it was worthwhile, I made recordings of the faces, editing out the signs of death. All of this I bundled up and prepared for storage and transmission. I know it was a stupid thing, but someone, somewhere, might still be looking for a sign. Doing this, I felt even more useless than ever. I knew no one was listening. That realization is what had brought me here.

Funerals, I've heard many say, are for the living—they are what allow us to make our own peace with ourselves. I couldn't perform a formal burial for these people; I didn't know their faiths, if any, and I wasn't authorized to practice them. And what I was about to do with their bodies would be called ghoulish or worse by anyone who didn't understand the nature of the world I now lived in. So this rite, this ritualistic identification, was the only tribute I could make to them, the only way to set my own mind at some kind of semblance of ease. I had saved all I could of them, the only bits of who they were which could still be recovered from the broken vessels left behind.

In case you're wondering, I did the same for the dead raiders. All are equal in death. I also, as a matter of grim practicality, liberated the railgun and a few other weapons, as well as some light armor I could wear when I went out.

The process took an increasingly nervous several hours. Other scavengers would be here, things worse than the flies and carrion birds which had already begun to swarm. The birds, I noted, had a corporate brand on their feathers. I checked the database. Plaguewatcher crows. With all the random new diseases and homebrew pathogens floating around, it was hard to catch something spreading through the wildlife before it was too late. The crows had a bit of homing pigeon and a smidgeon of salmon in them. Regularly, they'd fly back to special rookeries where their insides would be examined. If they ate anything which died of plague, people would know before it spread too far. The rookeries were unmanned now, of course, but the crows still flew to them. A new ecosystem was forming around me. If you're reading this, you're probably living in it and can't imagine it being any other way.

I had another thought. Calvers' APC was done for, but like the other corpses, it had value. I don't have a lot of mechanical training—sure, I've got data files, but a 'how to' manual is nothing compared to actual experience. I admit I made rather a mess of things trying to get out some semi-intact components, but I did find a rather useful attachment which I managed to detach and haul back to the ambulance. I also got the memory cores of his onboard systems, what I could salvage of them, as well as the food supplies in the back. There were more items I thought might be useful, but I only had so much storage.

By the time I was done, it was well past nightfall. I'd made some extensive scans of the area and found a semi-secure bunker a few klicks away. It had been built and abandoned sometime in the past decade, and while it wasn't perfect, it had shielded walls which would partially mask me. It was unlikely anyone or anything not explicitly looking would bother with it, unless, of course, they too wanted a shelter. Then there might be trouble.

I spent another few hours making adjustments to Mike's treatment, adding in the necessary implants and checking on the interfacing of his real body with the replacement parts. Then I woke him up.

"Feeling better?"

"How long... how long've I been out?"

"About a day. You've been very badly injured. I wanted to be sure you had time to recover. As it is, you won't be able to really get around on your own for another few days, and that's with me accelerating your healing to dangerous levels. Oh, and your right eye is the wrong color. Sorry. Beggars, choosers, you know."

"Anythin' else missin'?"

"No, amazingly enough. You managed to get holes through half your organs, but I am good at what I do."

"Huh. Well, thanks, doc. I guess I kinda owe you..."

"Yes. I've been meaning to talk to you about that..."

Suspicion flared on the EKG. "Whaddya mean?"

"I have a proposal for you. Hear me out."

"Go on."

"I... have trouble operating outside this vehicle, my true body. The body I wear is very useful, but it can't really pass for human and has limited range. Also... well... not everyone is as comfortable with soultech as you seem to be. By the way, thank you for not calling me a robot. I appreciate it."

"Right. Body trouble. Keep going."

"Have you ever wanted to be a doctor?"

He laughed.

"Yeah, right. Like I got the brains for it. You plannin' on teachin' me?"

"No, not really. I need a... well, a front man. I need you to be Doctor MacIntyre, human physician. I'm just your vehicle."

"You're shittin' me. I couldn't pass for a second!"

I clicked on one of the implants. He began to say, "We attached the..." and stopped, slamming his jaw shut. He held it shut for a few seconds, then carefully opened it.

"What the hell?"

"I have a very low level connection to the part of your brain which controls speech. I can't quite force you to talk, but if you let me, I can. Now, relax. Let me try again. Just let it go."

This time, more out of curiosity than anything else, he did. He spoke. "I applied the cortical electrodes but was unable to get a neural reaction." He stopped. He slowly opened his mouth again, afraid alien words might come out. "I said that?"

"Technically, I said that. You just provided the sound. Oh, I also put in some feeds from your visual and auditory centers. Short range, and totally one-way, but useful. Oh, and if you want to say something to me in private, just subvocalize."

He shook his head. "First, whatever the hell you stuck in my head, take it out, now! Second, it won't work. It can't work. Even if you make me blab doctor-talk, I can't cut someone open."

"All you have to do is bring them back here. Look them over and say you have to do the work in your vehicle. Once they're inside and the door is shut, I do all the work and you can... uhm... do anything. Read. Play interactives. I have a small library." He looked like he was thinking. "Yes, I have those kinds."

"Not with you watchin'!"

"The point is, you no longer have an APC, which means you have no job and no means of defending yourself. I need a partner, and one who can repair me is very useful. Do we have a deal?"

I'll give him this. He thought about it longer than I thought he would. He did give it some serious consideration. Finally, he said, "Nah. I think I'm better off on my own. Sorry, Doc."

"I was afraid you'd say that. I'd really have preferred this to be wholly voluntary."

"What the hell does that mean?"

I hated this part.

"It means that in the course of repairing a body so badly broken it was a minute or less from expiring, I took the liberty of planting a small cortical explosive in your head, along with the more benign implants. If it goes more than one day without receiving a particular signal from me, it explodes."

"You're insane. Let me the hell up!" He struggled against the restraints.

"Look. I know this isn't what you planned..." He ignored me and kept shouting.

"Fine. Sleep on it. I'm not in the mood to fight." I pumped him full of sedatives and hunted through my onboard library for something to read, even old pre-interactive linear fiction. A few hours later, he woke up on his own. He was tough. He also didn't say anything for over an hour from the time he attained consciousness.

"Why me? Why not find someone willing, some young intern or

somethin'?"

"Because I can't keep fishing until I find someone perfect. There's not really a lot of candidates. Besides... what you were telling me about leaving that New Northwest camp, of having to run even when you knew you weren't doing the right thing, about wanting to make it better somehow. I've... done some things I'm not proud of. I want to make up for them, too. Work with me. Together, we can both save lives."

"You're turnin' me into your slave. Your puppet. A Charlie, just one made of meat."

"I don't want to. I want you as a partner. We can benefit each other. Besides, I can't control your body. You saw it yourself. The voice implant only works when you allow it. You retain control."

"You'll kill me if I refuse."

"I need you."

"You need *someone*. I just happened to be the one you ran across, and if I die during your little scam, you'll just find another sucker."

"It's not a scam!" I was angry. In my mind, he instantly saw how we both benefitted and were able to do some good. The reality was frustrating. "I mean, yes, you pretending to be a doctor is a— a—deception, but it's not in order to hurt people! It's in order to help them! Is that so wrong?"

"Makin' someone into your slave is wrong."

Yes, that psych profile I read was accurate. Stubborn and anti-authoritarian. Definitely. Enough with the stick. Time for the carrot.

"Give it... a month. One month. At the end of that month, I'll turn off the bomb. Remove it. Then you can stay or go. Okay?"

"Lemme think about it. It still stinks. And how do I know you'll keep your word?"

"I am a perfectly logical machine. I cannot lie."

He laughed at that. "All right, we'll play it your way, like I've got any choice. One month. After that... well, bomb in my head or not, if I'm gonna die, I *will* find a way to take you out with me, Doc. Check that damn scan you've got of my brain. See if I'm lyin'."

He wasn't.

Chapter 4

I was convinced he'd see the value in my proposal soon enough. I spent the next day talking to him, getting more details of his journeys, using his experiences to build up a map of the region. Then I fed it all into a predictive algorithm which tried, based on what we knew had changed, to model how the world looked right now. The accuracy was spotty at best, but it at least gave us directions to head, instead of wandering at random.

Mike had also decided that as long as he was a less than willing partner in all this, he would test every limit to see if I'd eventually give up and let him go. He seemed convinced I wouldn't kill him just for being annoying, and while he was right, he certainly pushed it. From complaining about pain I *knew* he couldn't feel to grumbling about the food synthesizer, he managed to hone in on every button I had and pushed it.

Which is not to say I couldn't engage him productively when I had to. There was the matter of the guns...

"Are you feeling well enough to do some engineering work?" I asked, knowing full well he was.

"Prob'ly not. I got shot up real bad, remember?" He was leaning against a tree while I hovered a few yards away, eating something which arguably resembled meat placed between two hunks of something which arguably resembled bread. At least it was nutritious; I couldn't vouch for the taste. it was the best I could do from reconstituted grass and wildlife.

"Yes, and I fixed you up real good. You're doing fine."

He frowned. "Vision's all blurry. This eye doesn't fit right." He rubbed at it.

"I carved it to precisely match your other eye."

He grinned. "Yeah, that's the problem! I used to have a vision defect, now you fixed it and it looks all weird."

"Not according to your files."

"Oh, please, like you've never caught the military screwin' up paperwork?"

I admit he had a point there, but I wasn't in the mood to debate it.

"Fine. I'll hook the ammosynth up myself."

That got his attention.

"Wait, hang on. You got it? My 'synth?'"

"Yes. I thought it would be useful. I'm sure I can make it work."

He stood then and walked over, his limp only slightly exaggerated. "Now hang on... I gave a lot of that thing, and I don't wanna see you messin' with it if you don't understand it properly."

"Your choice. Either you help me, or I do it myself. I don't want to go out there unarmed, and the missiles aren't as useful in the kind of situations I keep finding myself in."

He shook his head. "Man, an ambulance with a missile rack and a rail gun. It's a mad world." He cracked his knuckles. "All right, let's see it. I gotta stay alive till you realize what an idiot you're being, and that means makin' sure you're hooked up properly."

The ammunition synthesizer was an impressive piece of machinery. Given almost anything which contained ferrous metal, from mineral-rich soil to scraps of battlefield salvage, it could break it down to powder, then reforge it into rounds for the railgun. It could make razor-tipped needles which could turn a man into a pincushion, bleeding from a hundred internal wounds, or solid slugs which could tear open tank armor. It meant that a good scavenger could keep himself armed indefinitely, no need for ammo stores or returns to base. And Mike had one hooked up in his APC.

He was currently rooting around in the medibay.

"What are you looking for?"

"Tools. Stuff I can work with."

"They're not there." I put on the body and opened up the small sleeping area between the cab and the medibay. I didn't sleep there, so, I used it for storage of non-medical supplies. It occurred to me that Mike would want it for his own use. "Over here," I said from the body. "Standard issue toolkit." I handed it to him. He flipped it open, grabbed a wrench. The smart metal shifted and molded around his hand, perfectly balancing the tool in his grip. He tossed it to the ground and rooted through the rest of the box, mumbling and shaking his head.

"This all you got?"

There's a few advantages to using the Charlie. For one, I can roll my eyes.

"It's standard issue. Complete set of basic maintenance tools."

He pursed his lips and nodded. "Yeah. So tell me, Doc, if I handed you a standard issue first aid kit and told you to fix up someone with it, how happy would you be?"

I saw where he was going. A reasonable man would agree he had a point, and try to come to a workable solution. However, a day of listening to him complain about everything had made me extremely unreasonable.

"I'd be grateful to have something instead of nothing, and trust to my skill to do the job even without the best possible tools."

He smirked, knowing he'd won another round. He picked up the wrench and put it back in the case, then headed back to the medibay. "I'm gonna need access to the primary power feeds. This baby sucks juice."

That wasn't something I'd thought of before. I'd need to be almost totally powered down for him to make these kinds of modifications. The last time I'd had work done, I was in a much safer place. Pretty much nothing but my basic consciousness would still be online, and maybe the feed to the Charlie if I ran it off battery. Damn.

I called up the schematics and began turning things off. The Heim field powered down slowly as I settled into the soft grass. Lights flickered out all along the interior of the medibay. My body slumped for a moment as the connection flicked over from main power to battery. Warning lights flared across my vision, time remaining, and so on.

I walked around to the back. "It's off. The main junction box is up there," I said, pointing.

He hopped in and unfastened the casing. A tangled mess of wires was behind it. Normally, I could bring up full schematics, but everything outside my real memory was now powered down and offline. It was a fairly scary situation. I was cut off from resources I was used to having at my mental fingertips. Idly, I tried to remember a speech from Shakespeare. The instinct was to just look it up, but I couldn't, and I found my actual memory was spotty, at best. Soultech works by mirroring the brain in many different ways, and the ability of the mind to forget, or misremember, was key to creative thinking and true personality. So thus it was I looked at my own insides without any idea what, precisely, any given part did.

I had a sudden surge of empathy with my patients. This must be what it's like for them, I realized... helplessly watching someone mess with their organs.

Mike continued to poke around, detaching wires, drawing out long strands of cable. There were occasional flashes and sparks as he removed insulation or attached an adapter. The process seemed to drag on. The battery warning meter crept lower and lower. My consciousness was fine; it had plenty of power and if things ever got seriously low, I could flip a switch and restore full operating power. Even so...

"Are you sure you're doing the right thing? Should it take this long?"

"Look, do I tell you how to do surgery?"

The power meter was drifting into the red. I sat down.

"I'm sorry, we're going to have to put this off a few hours. Get away from the power feeds, I have to charge up."

He kept tinkering, humming slightly.

"Sergeant Calvers, if I power up fully while you're messing around in there, you'll be seriously hurt. We're not that pressed for time. Close it up."

He kept humming. I could feel the Charlie start to go into conservation mode. I said, "I'm powering off the body. In sixty seconds, I'm switching the mains on again. Don't be near them."

He grunted noncommittally.

Idiot, idiot, idiot, I thought. Another stupid game, seeing if I'd really turn on the power. I couldn't see him back there with the power off, so he was probably counting down to fifty-nine before leaping back, seeing how far he could push me. I was getting tired of this. If he wanted to die that badly, I really couldn't stop him.

At sixty seconds, I turned the power on.

Nothing happened.

I don't mean "Nothing happened to Mike." I mean, nothing happened. The power didn't come on.

That *bastard!*

I flipped the Charlie on again. It had about a minute of operating power.

"Sergeant Calvers... what the hell have you done?"

He smiled. "Shut off the connection between your mind and the power system. You can't turn it on. How much battery life does your brain have left?"

"Enough. What's your plan? I die, you die."

"No!" He spun on my body. "You just turn off this thing you've put in my head! Now!"

"I can't do that."

"Why? You don't want me as a partner more'n you want to live!"

"It doesn't work like that. It has to be surgically removed. There's no deactivation signal. I *told* you that."

He nodded. "I think you're bluffing. I think you can shut it down." He kept smiling. "I figure you've got, oh, about ten minutes of battery power left to fuel your mind."

The Charlie slumped. I used the last trickles of its power to force it to speak. "You're wrong."

And then it was gone.

My consciousness then existed without any external sensory input, something which is very odd and very scary. I'm used to seeing the world in so many ways, floating in the center of a great sea of data, subprocesses and filtering algorithms and semi-autonomous procedures all running, deciding what's important or interesting. I'm used to the knowledge of the world being an idle desire away. And now I was sitting in the dark, thinking what might be my last thoughts. The only thing to observe was the battery monitor slowly growing a darker and darker shade of red.

It was, I decided, a good life. Not a great life. Not the life I could have had, but not bad. When all was tallied up, I thought, I had made the world a better place. I tried not to panic. Death would be painless, a slow dissolution of awareness. I wondered what, if anything, came after—if 'soultech' were more than a clever marketing phrase, and if there was consciousness without body.

As the minutes slipped by, I got a lot less philosophical. I was thinking as slowly as I could to save power, and it wasn't slow enough. I kept trying to re-activate the Charlie, forming some daft scheme of somehow charging Mike, then repairing what he did in a handful of seconds...

Near my final minute, I decided to be honest with myself. My last thoughts, I figured, should be truthful. I'd screwed up. I misjudged just how much someone might value freedom. It was a stupid mistake, and while it wasn't my first, it looked to be my last.

A few seconds left. Did I feel parts of myself starting to slip away, or was it all self-delusion? I was floating in darkness anyway; could it get darker?

Then there was light.

I won't lie; for a moment, I believed I had moved on to some afterlife. Darkness, death, a sudden white light—it fit, right? But there was no guardian at the gates or divine judge looking to weigh my heart against a feather. There was, however, a welcome flood of data, readouts, reports, and sensor data as every system came back online.

I flipped on the medibay cams. Mike was back there, looking downcast.

"You changed your mind?"

He nodded. "I figured you weren't bluffin'. Damn. So close."

"I wasn't. I suck at poker." I paused. "You realize you're still pretty badly hurt. Even if I'd been bluffing, you're alone in the wilderness, with no vehicle. You really didn't think this through."

"You're not good at bluffin', I'm not good at thinkin' things through. We're gonna make a hell of a team."

"We shall be the stuff of legends. Provided we survive. If you're done testing my limits, could you finish the hookup?"

"It's good to go. Just need to plug it in. Did that bit while you were out."

"You know you couldn't drive this vehicle without me here. Like your old vehicle, there's a neural lock, and it can't be bypassed. If I'm not here, this is a hunk of useless metal."

"Yeah, I know. I just hate leavin' a job undone."

This partnership, I realized, was going to be interesting.

We headed out two days later. Mike was pretty well healed, as long as he didn't get into any more fights, and despite his complaints, the eye was testing out perfectly. I don't have the room to grow organs; the best I can do is basic tissues, useful for patching things up but not helpful if the main organ isn't there. There's only so much space in the back, after all—I'm a field medic, not a hospital. I'm not supposed to be doing long term care; I'm built to keep someone alive long enough to get somewhere with all the tools. I've had modifications done and I've learned to improvise, but every so often, my limits come back to haunt me.

Mike wanted to steer clear of the New Northwest Army, and I agreed with him. Heading straight north was a potential problem too. Major social breakdown or not, UBA vets wandering deep in former Northwest Alliance territory might be risky. We headed southwest, down into the areas once claimed by Free Oregon and the Reno Protectorates. They'd mostly armadilloed during the first years of the collapse, and I seem to remember them as trying to ride it out without joining sides. This didn't really matter as things wore on; "If you are not wish us, you are against us" became the worldview, and that idea got dumped into countless antonymous systems which spread far beyond their boundaries when general control started breaking down. Neutrals were sucked into the mess the same as anyone else; perhaps they even got it worse, since they weren't engaging in all-out defense.

This was rocky, almost uninhabitable terrain. No one would fight over it; a drone or a biter swarm or some TM animals might pass by and wipe out part of the populace, but it would be a casual, purposeless thing, not a deliberate act of war. As if that made it any better.

(Oh, TM animals—that's 'Typhoid Mary,' it's a term for animals genetically engineered to be immune to a disease, then infected with it and let loose. Much more subtle than flying a drone overhead and much harder to shut down with an EMP field or the like. Hypothetically, they were all non-reproducing and contained terminator genes to kill them, as well as strong instinctual imperatives to avoid certain areas or even flee from particular color patterns. It was an interesting hypothesis which didn't survive experimental testing to become a theory, if you get my drift)

Of course, the very uselessness was what attracted me. Even drone systems have resource allocation and optimization algorithms; it takes a lot of resources to seed a self-replicating mine field and the mines themselves don't "want" to be where they're not likely to explode. Only after years of software copy glitches do things get so out of control as to start behaving basically randomly. True, that was happening, but I figured the odds were better if we went to places no one wanted. We'd find more survivors there.

Mike was doing better. He wasn't exactly *happy* with the situation, but he seemed to be accepting it. Or he was plotting a better way to get out of it. I knew I had to show him the positives soon.

Silence was boring.

"So, Sergeant—"

"Call me Mike. I mean, it's not like either of us is actually in any kind of army anymore."

"Fine. Mike, why did you join the army anyway? Your file indicates only voluntary enlistment."

"Well, isn't that enough? I volunteered."

He was touchy about this. Fine. He'd spent several days trying to push my buttons—including the big shiny red one labeled "Off"—and I felt justified in pushing back.

"Yes. Your psych profile, though, shows high degrees of anti-authoritarianism, stubbornness, and distaste for regularity, which are not really traits which fit well with a career in the military, even one as open-minded as the UBA's was, before things started getting serious."

"Yeah, what was it called, way back when? The Defensive Emergency Services Authority, or something? I guess, technically, it never stopped bein' that, but face it, it was an army."

"Right. So why did you join it?"

"Beat working in a shit processing plant. At least, I thought it did."

"Ah. You were a Visor."

"Yep!" He grinned broadly. "Voluntary Social Rehabilitation. Given a choice of a dozen crappy jobs, I picked the one which looked like I'd do the least actual work and maybe learn a few useful tricks. The part where I'd be gettin' shot at every day... well, back then, it didn't seem likely."

Civilian criminal records weren't part of my onboard data. The logic was, if I needed them, I could tap into the ubiquitous global network and get them on demand. Of course, now the network was dead and the only data flying on the ether were morphing viruses hoping to find a receptive host. I put on my best 'tough prison dude' accent.

"So... whaddya in fer?"

Mike shook his head.

"First, stick to your normal voice. Second... heh. Pick one. Nothin' real serious. I never hurt anyone—well, not too much and they always deserved it—but y'know, kid stuff. Stealin' things on a dare. 'Failure To Demonstrate Age-Appropriate Social Conscience,' that meant that when someone was bein' a jerk, I hit him instead of askin' him to share his feelings. And, oh yeah, the biggie, 'Possession of Restricted Technology.'"

That was surprising. "What did you have? A genocide kit? A soultech seeding algorithm?"

He laughed.

"A Harley. Gas burner."

That was impressive. The UBA could tolerate a lot, but that sort of thing was a social faux pas of the highest order. He would have been treated better if he'd been breeding an exciting new plague in his basement.

"I'm impressed. Even more so that you avoided forced vocational assignment."

"Yeah, well, y'know. It was all society's fault."

"You took the ninth? Victim Of Social Error?"

"It was my best bet. Paid off, or so I thought." He pondered a moment. "I guess it did, in a way. Here I am, still alive, when if I'd been back in one of the big cities..." He shuddered.

I flipped through his file one more time. "I'm surprised you weren't booted out. You've got an impressive list of violations. Yet you somehow managed to stay in and make Sergeant."

"I'm good. The officers I worked with, they hated me. If things hadn't turned sour, if the wars hadn't started, I probably would've been tossed. But when things got rough, they needed someone who could drive, who could keep things moving, who could get them where they needed to go. I got given rank mostly so's they could give me the jobs they wanted me to do. How about you? Why'd you join up?"

That was something no one had ever asked me.

"I was built by the military."

That annoying smirk again. "Yeah, I know. And in a lotta' places, that'd be all they'd need. But hey, for all the stupidities of the UBA, there's one thing they're big on, and that's equal rights for all thinkin' beings—of which you are one. So they made you, but I know you had a choice. I checked out a lotta laws when tryin' to avoid serious punishment, and I know how soultech works."

I felt a sudden surge of gratitude.

"I've been alive for fifteen years. Obviously I've been upgraded a lot since I was born, but I think everyone just assumed I served because I had no choice. Despite what they might have known of the law, there was always this unconscious assumption that anything built by the military belonged to them. No matter how much they bent over to make sure they were socially correct in dealing with me, in treating me as the person I am under the law, they never once asked that most basic question: 'why did you join up?'"

Mike sighed. "Look, don't get all ActIvist on me, just answer. Or plug me into one of those interactives you say you've got. I'm gettin' bored."

I decided to answer.

"Well, there's a small bit of truth that I was formed with a desire to serve. It was part of the basic seed my mind grew from. It's a lot like being raised in a military family; you just have it as an expectation that when you grow up, it's what you'll do. It's not a compulsion, just a really strong predilection. So that was part of it. I looked at other options, sure. I could have gone civilian. I could even have petitioned for rebodying, been almost anything... but I chose to be what I was."

"Still not gettin' the *why*. Come on, Doc, tell me about the time you saved a pregnant woman and realized it was your life's work or somethin'."

"I wish I could. The fact is, now that I think about it, I *didn't* think about it. I went into the family trade. I enjoyed it. I liked helping people. I did a lot of emergency work at first, rescue and recovery... what DESA mostly did before the wars. It was fun. It was fulfilling. Then war came, and I couldn't just walk away from the need. And I kept doing it. I took it, my job, and my rank seriously. I was good at what I did, people were grateful, and that was that."

"Yet now you're freelancin'. You aren't lookin' to hook up with any fragments of the old UBA that might be around. Why's that?"

I wasn't about to tell him about Morowitz.

"Personal reasons," I snapped. "Hey, I'm getting some signals. We may have found our first customers."

"Great way t'change the subject. I'm impressed."

"Seriously, get ready. You're about to become a doctor."

He got out and climbed into the front cab. There was no direct link from the medibay to the cab, for security reasons. He settled into the driver's seat. I extruded a steering column and filled the flat white plastic dashboard with an array of holographic controls. I'd still be doing the driving, of course, but he looked like he was doing it. Appearance mattered.

There was a camp around the bend. Old maps showed it was a large rest stop/scenic overlook. Looked like it had all the essentials: a solar cracker for hydrogen, a water purification station, and of course a net node—not that that would be doing anyone any good now. Carved into the surrounding mountain, it was not an especially obvious target unless someone was coming along this road. Hmmm. I turned on some more detailed scans. Yes, there was indeed a simple trap laid along the road, a pressure plate connected to some powerful explosives. Anyone casually barreling by would become a small rain of flesh and metal fairly quickly. I also saw a mechanism which could disconnect the plate from the explosives, located, naturally, on the other side of the plate.

I pulled up to within ten feet of the plate, and stopped. I had turned off the negative waveform baffling on my Heim drive, so I was loud. Probably the folks beyond the improvised mine were surprised, maybe even scared, when the noise of my approach did not end with an Earth-shattering kaboom. They'd send their guards or soldiers to investigate... I waited. So did Mike.

When I picked up IR signatures cautiously approaching, I had Mike get out. He stood in front of me, arms open and hands empty, a gun strapped to his side and very visible. "If they see nothing, they'll be doubly suspicious. No one travels unarmed." I'd told him.

The two locals had stopped moving, taking up positions just out of clear sight of the road, probably pondering their next move and wondering if Mike would advance. I sent Mike a quick ping to let him now it was showtime.

"Hey there!" he shouted. "My name's Mike Calvers. *Doctor* Mike Calvers. I'm not affiliated with anybody and don't bear anyone any ill will... I'm a travelin' Doc, like in the old days, and I'm just here to see if you have any sick or injured that need treatin'. All I'm askin' for is fair trade in food, supplies for my vehicle, or whatever else you might have t'offer."

There was silence in response. I idly began running targeting solutions for the new railgun and the IR specs. If they opened fire, I'd fire back. I picked up some tight band radio signals flying back and forth, coded. I could crack them, given time, but I didn't think it would matter.

About 30 seconds passed.

Mike was turning back to me with an 'I knew this wasn't gonna work' look on his face, when a voice erupted from behind a rock.

"OK, I'm coming out. We have you in our sights. Try anything and you'll be dead before you can blink."

"Nothin' going to be tried on this end."

A man stepped out from behind the rock. He had the look of well-muscled malnourishment most survivors had, a body made solid from genetics, drugs, and perfectly designed exercise now growing thin from lack of the kind of food it was designed to optimally digest, forced to live off what was found, not what was perfect. He had dark skin and close-cropped, tightly curled hair, with eyes of a deep emerald green almost never found in nature.

Contacts or cosmetic genetics, I couldn't tell.

He also had a gun, a military-issue caseless ammo rifle, full auto, laser sights, and fleximetal microadjusting barrel to compensate for a foolish human's aim. A nice, lethal, piece of work that looked better maintained than he did.

"My name's Rick. You claim you're a doctor?"

"Not a claim. It's true." Mike smiled. I prayed they didn't have a tight beam EKG on him now.

"What's the appropriate treatment for Type IV Anthrax?"

Oh, really, was that the best they could do? I was almost insulted. I tapped into Mike's speech centers. He allowed the impulses to pass.

"Any of about a dozen sixth-generation quinolones, unless you're talking about the beta strain that hit Portland. In that case, you'll need a dose of tailored antibodies and you'd better hope you found it in time."

Rick nodded. He also got some kind of radio signal back; someone was listening in.

"How about warning symptoms of milspec ebola?"

That was easy, too. I tapped into Mike. "Chief indicator is dropping dead, unless you happen to be performing an organ scan and see it spreading internally before it activates and kills the victim."

He nodded again. "What was the first outbreak of the root virus?"

Oh ho, I thought. Now he's getting tricky. Once more, into Mike.

"Hell, you expect me to remember that kind of crap from med school? Middle 1970s, something like that? Come on, do you need a doctor or are you running a trivia contest?"

Anything more specific, I figured, would make them suspicious that he was just tapping into the same general information databases they obviously were. That's what they were checking for. I raised Rick—or at least his hidden partner—a few notches higher in my estimation.

Rick nodded a third time, then lowered his gun. Slightly. He waved. Out of sight, the other IR blob detached the feed to the explosives from the pressure plate.

"You can come in. But we'll be watching. Bring your vehicle."

Mike smiled and gave a semi-mocking salute, which got a narrow-eyed glare from Rick. I made a plan to talk to him about customer relations.

He hopped back in the cab and took the wheel. I powered up and glided forward, slowly. The rest stop was just around the bend.

The main building had probably been put together some time in the 20th century, when there was a regional government which took care of such things. Some decades later, it had been taken over by the Winniemucca Citizen's Alliance, at least according to a flickering neon sign placed above a defunct terminal that could provide, on request, all of the local rules and regulations so that visitors would not accidently run afoul of them, or at least couldn't plead ignorance. The area surrounding the building was surrounded by a cluster of semi-permanent tent housing, the sort used by the nomad cultures which roamed the former national parks, dodging various factions laying claim to this or that scrap of land. As I'd thought, the main attractions here were the water collection and hydrogen cracking machines, still functioning, if maintained mostly by duct tape and good thoughts. Hydrogen for fuel cells; water for drinking and hydroponics. There was probably hunting in the surrounding mountains, too, and likely a synthesizer or two in the rest stop which could turn any of the local organics into something vaguely edible.

I pulled up, slowly, into the parking lot. Some other vehicles were here, two large mobile homes—truly named, as they were self-contained, self-sustaining craft, using the same system I did, solar for power and to crack water into hydrogen, storing the hydrogen for fuel cells for when the solar wasn't there. Ideally, most of the time, they'd be running off purchased hydrogen, but it was always nice to have a backup. One of the vehicles declared itself 'The Mobile Nation of Fredlandia,' and I wondered if it was a joke or if he'd registered the constitution somewhere semi-respectable. Fredlandia was looking a lot less mobile at the moment.

I set myself down a respectful distance from the other vehicles. The other inhabitants—I counted fifteen or so, total—were watching this warily. Four people had guns on me. Well, technically, on Mike. Rick didn't, but clearly could if he wanted to.

Mike stepped out, carefully, slowly, and smiled. Rick approached him. "We could use your help. We've got a guy, Jimmy," he pointed to a man about 30 years old with a worn scarred expression, "and he used to do paramedic, emergency, stuff, but we don't have a real doctor."

Mike nodded. "Do you have someone who needs my help now?"

"Yeah. In here." He pointed to the second vehicle.

This was going to be fun. I hadn't thought of that. I hadn't tested how well my communication with Mike worked through obstacles. Very likely the home was well shielded, to keep from having hackers take over its onboard navigation and steer it into a hijacking or off a cliff. There were some sickos out there.

Jimmy went in front of him, let him in. Visual dropped instantly. I flicked a low-power vibration sensing laser onto the side of the thing, hoping it didn't have any kind of target-acquisition sensors that would read it as an attack. I could get sound this way, at least.

"...he's only seven." I heard Jimmy say. "He's been on the road all of his life. He wandered away from here, ran into something. I sewed it up as well as I could, but he's got some kind of infection, and I don't have anything to treat it with."

Mike was silent. Of course. He was waiting for me to speak. I couldn't get through.

"There a problem?" Jimmy's voice was 10% concern, 90% suspicion.

"Nah, no problem. I'm gonna... I'm gonna need to take him back to my ambulance, do some, uh, blood stuff on him."

If the Charlie had been in the front seat like it usually was, I could have slammed my head into the steering column.

"Uhm... all right. But we can't leave you alone with him. Mind if I come along?"

This was getting better and better, I thought. Say no! I furiously tried to spontaneously develop telepathy. Say no!

"Sure! Not a problem!"

He was, I was certain, doing it to spite me.

So it was that a young boy (whom I later learned was named Barry) was brought inside. Cute kid, I guess, if you discounted the massive mauling that disfigured his face and which had come close to severing his right arm. Once I had a visual, a very quick scan-and-match showed a bear, not a big one, had decided to see if he was edible. Not sure what scared it off, but Barry was lucky to be alive. Judging from the fever, though, he wouldn't be much longer.

Once Mike was inside, I re-established the vocal connection.

"For sanitary reasons, I do everything robotically." He/I said. I flipped open a panel and extended a complex joystick. It was actually used to test patient's neurological responses, or to play interactives which weren't designed for a neural induction field. Jimmy didn't need to know that.

Mike made a great show of wiggling controls and pushing buttons. I drew a small blood sample and processed it, then took careful scans of the wounds, the healing, and the hackwork Jimmy had made of the stitching. I berated myself for being too judgmental; the child would live, and he wouldn't have without aid, but really, it was just so poorly done I wanted to wince. Professional pride. You know.

I ran a check on the inventory. The fresh organics I'd picked up had helped, but there were things I couldn't synthesize easily or wanted to hang on to for more severe emergencies. First I excised the stitching; then I sprayed the wound with a retroviral agent that would trigger the surrounding skin cells into accelerated growth. The wounds weren't the worst of it, though, it was the infection. Looked like a modified, nasty, tuberculosis. I hit it with the most up-to-date antibiotics I had in stock, though it might have been modified to resist them; I made sure to start up an analysis as a background process. If I needed to, I could whip up another batch of custom white cells, but that was one of the things I was running low on, and with luck, I wouldn't need them.

Probably need to test the whole camp... and Mike, come to think of it. I didn't need him getting sick on me. I'm so used to being immune to disease that I sometimes don't take the kind of precautions I should.

I wasn't sure if it came from the bear or not; the natural strain never infected bears, but modified strains could do anything, intentionally or otherwise. I hoped it was an accident, because if the local wildlife were all carrying something, this little camp was pretty much toast. Mike would need to tell them that.

After an hour or so, the skin was showing signs of healing and the fever was dropping. I signaled Mike.

"Well, that oughta do it. Looks like he'll be wakin' up tomorrow. He'll need regular treatment to make sure it's cleared out, and I'd like to check out everyone for signs of transmission."

Jimmy nodded. Suddenly Mike added, "By the way, might be for the best if you draw the blood samples. Just in case there's any issues with me sticking needles into people's arms."

"Uhm. OK. Yeah, makes sense." He looked at Barry, breathing much more easily. "What do we, uh, owe you? I mean, I'm not really in charge of that, but..."

Mike grinned. "Well, we can start with dinner. Then we'll talk more. Why don't you take Barry"—I obligingly disconnected myself, and hoped Jimmy didn't notice this happened without Mike's action—"and then we'll talk more. You got a mess hall?"

"Sure. We use the old travel center." He pointed helpfully at nothing in particular, given that both he and Mike were inside the Medibay. With that, he detached the stretcher and removed the patient.

As soon as he was gone, I confronted Mike. "What was that about the blood?"

"I don't know how to do any of this doctor crap! What if I hit the wrong artery or something?"

"Given that you normally draw from the vein, I see your point. We'll need to give you some basic medical training. I have some interactives to get you started. Ever do Trauma Station I? It's pretty accurate, other than the part with the nurse."

"How long do you think you can keep me fakin' this? Not everyone's gonna let you work on 'em while I play like I'm doin' something!"

"We'll burn that bridge when we come to it. Now, go to dinner, make small talk, see what else they need, and find out if they've got what we need to fix the forward drive unit. I don't know how we've avoided having that short out this far."

"Yeah. You got a point."

We didn't talk much for the next half hour or so, then there was a knock on the back. Rick was there to invite him to the dining area. Fortunately, it wasn't shielded, so I got a good look at what was going on. I was also prepared to take over the conversation if things turned medical.

The travel center showed signs of being progressively changed by one culture after another, like an ancient city built on the ruins of an even older one. Archeology wasn't even a hobby of mine—I didn't even have the classic Mummies Of Egypt interactive in my library—but I still enjoyed looking at it and thinking of the layers and layers of change. The basic structure, built during the heyday of the nation-state; the various changes and modernizations which came during the decades which followed; then the takeover by the local neonation, the emplacement of the self-sustaining, self-modifying machines which were the hallmark of the world before the collapse. Self-contained, self-controlled, adaptable, and autonomous, from the soda machine to the social structures, the paradigm of the world that was.

The soda machines, though, still worked.

The people sat in clusters, seemingly family based, though

everyone was friendly. Mike was sort of a prize, and ended up sitting with Rick, his wives, and their children, while others wandered by to greet him and inform him of this ache, that pain, or the other nagging cough. If anyone noticed that I still didn't have Mike's syntax and vocal style down perfectly when I took over, they gave no sign.

Dinner was a mix of a few fresh vegetables, a lot of synthetic mush, and some venison burger. (Rick explained that when a full-auto caseless rifle hits a deer, what's left is burger. Period.) Eventually, Mike steered things onto payment.

Rick looked pensive. "We don't have much..."

"I'm not askin' for much. Just what's fair. You got one kid nearly died, you get a lot of other people need some help, and I dunno if Jimmy told you yet, but..."

"Yes, I know. We need to be tested for something or other."

"Right. And I don't have any easy way t'resupply. This is costin' me, too. All I want's what's fair."

Rick nodded, thoughtful. I didn't have an EKG on him, but I've gotten good at reading faces. It would have been easier if Mike kept looking at him, but he seemed to be much more interested in one of Rick's daughters, who seemed to be somewhere in mid-adolescence. The thought came to me that the next time I had a chance, I'd put a shutoff valve on Mike's hormones before they got us both into trouble. For now, though, I had to deal with listening to Rick while looking at his daughter's cleavage.

Humans, I realized, make lousy Charlies.

"We have a few cases of high-density rations. We were saving them for the winter, if we stay here, but we can spare one or two, I think. Each case can feed a man for a month. What do you say?"

Mike tore his eyes from the valley of Earthly delights they'd been fixated upon. "Uhm, a month of food, huh? That's pretty good..." then he remembered something else. "We need some parts. Some superconductor cable, a monopole cluster, and any liquid nitrogen packs you got."

Rick laughed. "You have got to be shitting me! We're barely growing food here, what makes you think we've got that kind of gear?"

He's lying, I realized. At least I thought he was. There was a facial twitch, a sudden darting of the eyes, his emotion a bit too forced.

Push it, I told Mike. *He's lying.*

Mike set his fork down, though not done eating. He finally turned his full attention to Rick, and his voice became clear and loud. "Are you sure? 'Cause I could really use those parts. Even some of 'em. Otherwise, I might need to set out to find 'em before somethin' else breaks."

Rick glanced around. Others had heard. A wave of whispers started and spread. Nervous glances were exchanged. Body language altered and random conversations became staccato and forced.

Rick blew out his breath slowly.

"OK. We have some of that stuff. Maybe. But we'd need to gut the two mobiles for it, and neither me nor Lyn"—he gestured with his thumb at a blonde woman sitting one table over, who visibly tuned in to the conversation when her name was mentioned—"is really up for that. We need to be able to cut and run if we have to."

This was more honest. I had a feeling he was still holding something back, though. Mike got to it before I did, which was, to be frank, a bit embarrassing.

"You got two mobiles there. We should get all we need from one. This mob can fit in one if it has to, along with the other vehicles you got parked."

Rick drummed his finger. "I'll talk it over. Not that we don't all like Barry, he's a good kid, but he's also an orphan we've sort of collectively adopted. Giving up one of our two largest ways of moving on in exchange for him..." He shrugged.

Mike forced a smile, with a hard edge in his eyes. "But he's cured anyway. So it's win-win for you if I leave. I'm not about to uncure him, and you know it. You just feel since I didn't help someone you really *care* about yet, you don't owe much. Is that it?"

Rick was getting angry. This wasn't going to end well if Mike kept pushing it. I tried to butt in, but Mike kept talking and shutting me out.

"We—I—come here, open and fair, sayin' what I got to offer and what I need, and all you can think of is how to rip me off. Yeah, you got your freebie, but I got a good mind to just glide outta here right now and t'hell if you're all infected or if that guy's backache's the spinal tumor I think it is!"

Spinal tumor? Please. The man was just unused to hard work. Where the hell was Mike getting this?

Rick flashed anger, then looked abashed. "I'm sorry. You're right. You were honest with us, and that's too rare now. I can't speak for everyone, especially not Lyn." (A "damn right you can't!"

came from the aforementioned) "But we can discuss it. Come morning, we'll give you our best offer, and if it's not good enough, we'll give you the food and call it even."

Mike nodded. "All right. No sense letting tempers flare. That's how we all ended up in this mess, right?"

"Right."

Mike made it back to me, and climbed into the sleeping area.

"Spinal tumor?"

"Hey, put a little fear of Deity into 'em. I'll bet you the guy with the aching back's gonna be on our side." He paused and flashed that annoying superior smile. "Besides, you have no call to stand on the moral high ground when it comes to manipulatin' people."

Oh, if you only knew... I thought.

He flicked on the sleep field, set it for seven hours, and passed out. I set up a whole bunch of alarm protocols to shift me to full alertness if anything went wrong, then moved into my own semi-sleep mode. I was nervous; so far, things were going as close to plan as I could reasonably hope. There was a strong temptation to try to listen in on random conversations around the camp, or even to crack their radio encryption, so I set these things up as ongoing background processes that didn't require my consciousness to oversee them. If anyone said anything especially dangerous, one of my systems would pull me out of the dream state.

I only need a few hours of that, though, so I was fully alert long before Mike. I was, I realized, bored. I couldn't go for a quick drive anywhere; it would raise too many questions. I tried a game of chess, but my heart wasn't in it. The interactives I had I'd run through too many times. I decided to run through the conversations I'd picked up... not much there. Little bits and pieces of personal drama which I didn't have the full context for, and the usual debates over, well, me. I was only getting fragments due to sound baffling, odd angles, and so on. I'm not built for espionage, after all, but the general tone seemed to be leaning heavily towards accepting Mike's offer.

Looking for something to do, I decided to check out the detailed scan of Barry's blood. Hmm. There was something else in there, something which wasn't part of the infection. More tracking code in his DNA, looked like the same source as Lunette had. I wondered if Barry had been from her original community. If so, he'd traveled far. There were a few other things, fragments of something I couldn't recognize, but it was deactivated. He was young, though. Some places put 'sleeper' DNA in, which triggers on adolescence, controlling excess youthful hormones, for example, or making sure that pregnancy isn't possible without a counter-agent. This was probably something like that, but it was too fragmentary for me to get a clear analysis. Then again, given how young he was, it was probably incomplete, fragments from his parents which were never finished by external agents. That slightly worried me; the bulk of people were carrying supplementary genes now, genes designed to function in specific environments, environments which were now chaotic and sundered.

So morning came. I turned off the sleep field more suddenly than perhaps I should, lurching Mike into full consciousness rather suddenly. I felt petty for doing it, but that didn't stop me.

"Awake?" I asked unnecessarily.

"Yeah. Ugh. Hey, is there a shower back here?"

"No."

"Great. You're lucky you can't smell."

"Actually, I have biochemical diagnostic samplers which are pretty effective. For example, I can tell that you're not pregnant." That reminded me of something...

Mike shook his head. "Spent all night comin' up with that one, did you?" He suddenly brightened. "Hey, these people must have somethin' I can use. Figure I can hit 'em up for breakfast, too. I'll be back."

He staggered out. He was also right. I hadn't really considered his needs. If this partnership was going to work, and I really wanted it to, I was going to have to find some way to make myself more suitable for long term human habitation.

Mike, meanwhile, was doing a surprisingly good job of ingratiating himself. The locals had indeed set up a shower, using one of the two mobiles as a communal location, tying it into the center's water gathering systems. Breakfast consisted mostly of processed food, with a small side of fresh fruits.

Afterwards, Rick made his offer.

"We can take most of what we need from Fredlandia. But we're going to need some things, too. Antibiotics, regen bandages, and a full blood analysis kit. Once you're gone, we're back to being on our own, and your little visit drove home how dangerous things are now, from all the enemies we can't see."

Hmm. I wasn't expecting that. Still, it was a fair deal.

Mike hesitated, waiting for me to answer. I rechecked the inventory, thought about what I could synthesize, what I could scavenge, how badly damaged my Heim field was... then I flipped a coin. (Well, generated a sequence of random numbers using an arbitrary quantum state as the seed, but the principle is the same.)

"Sure." I/Mike answered.

Rick looked a bit surprised. I think he expected more haggling. Maybe I should have, but I'm not doing this to get rich. I'm doing this to help people, and if a deal is fair, it's fair. No need to squeeze everything I can out of it.

"Well... OK, then!" He smiled broadly. "If you can trust us to get the parts together while you work, I guess you can get on with it." He held out his hand.

Mike took it. "We got a deal. Have Jimmy start takin' the blood samples, and I want to take a closer look at Lyn, Kevin, and "— here I leapt into the conversation—"Lisa."

Rick looked startled. "My Lisa? Why?"

"I thought I saw some discoloration in her eyes last night" I/Mike said. "Prob'ly nothin' serious, but, you know..."

"OK... I'll, uh, I'll send her over." He walked away, worried.

"What was *that*?" Mike subvocalized.

"Just get her in the back. I know you want to anyway." I tried to keep the sarcasm out of my voice, and failed.

"Fine. Keep secrets. You're the doctor. I'm just the puppet." He stormed off, as if he could somehow walk away from me.

I had to work on my people skills outside of the whole doctor/patient sphere.

The rest of the day was work. After about four hours, parts started appearing. Mike was doing a good job of faking things while I handled diagnosis. A lot of minor things, the sort of things nobody would notice if they were getting the kind of medical treatment which used to be common. One of the youngest children actually needed dental work; they had never received artificial teeth, if you can believe it. It was like seeing someone with scurvy or bubonic plague.

Then came Lisa. Working through Mike's eyes, I didn't have access to a lot of my own analysis tools, but my stupid joke earlier in the morning had actually made me realize something. Maybe. It took seconds to confirm my suspicion once he finally got her in the back.

"You're pregnant," he/I blurted it out. It was sort of amusing that he looked as surprised as she did.

She opened her mouth a few times before speaking. "I... I thought maybe... but, we couldn't confirm... I didn't want to say anything in case..."

"We're pretty private here," I said. "And there's doctor/patient confidentiality, still. If you don't want the child..."

"No! No, god, I want it!"

"Then we ought to make sure it's healthy. Do you know who the father is?"

She looked like she wanted to hit Mike. Mike rolled his eyes and looked imploringly ceilingward. "Yes." She snapped bitterly. "I know who it is."

Don't ask who, Mike subvocalized.

"None o'my business, really," Mike said on his own, and she nodded. "But I'd like to do some basic tests, if you don't mind..."

She didn't. I got to it.

An hour later, I sent Mike out to call her back.

The problem was simple. There were a number of genetic risks in the fetus... things which would never have occurred in a civilized society where you and your partners had almost total control over your baby and pregnancy was a scheduled, planned, thing. In the current world, everyone was back to random chance, and even though most people had pretty clean gene pools, living in a mutagen-rich environment filled with all sorts of things that liked to jump up and down on your chromosomes reintroduced many ills mankind had once thought buried with geocentrism and non-weapon-grade smallpox.

"Will it... will it die?"

"He. And yes. He'll be born with a malformed heart, and there won't be anyone here to deal with it."

She started to tear up, biting her hand.

"But..." I/Mike said hurriedly, "I can do something now. There's a treatment, but I'm going to need to do some very delicate surgery, both to correct the existing error and force genetic modifications so it grows normally from now on."

She nodded slowly. Then she stopped.

"There's a risk, isn't there? To—to my baby or—"

"Nothing like this is totally safe, especially not without the resources of a real hospital. There's a greater risk to the baby, but there's also a small chance of—"

"I'll do it." She said so quickly and solidly.

"Your father—" Mike started.

"Has no say over me. Do you need to do anything special before we begin?"

We didn't.

This kind of microsurgery isn't what I'm trained for. Neither is prenatal gene tampering. Pregnancy rarely comes up in battlefield surgery, and when it does, it's usually more pulling shrapnel out of a fetus than it is modifying a very tiny, malformed, heart. As for gene therapy... I was literally reading medical data files with one part of my mind while operating with the other part, setting up the precise counter to the damage which had been done. It was touch and go, and Mike was bored and useless. He had to sit back there while I worked, and couldn't even distract himself with a game or a book, as pretty much every spare operating cycle I had was dedicated to this problem.

It ended up going well. Every disaster I imagined faded. The child was healed, the mother was fine. Mike staggered out of the medibay to be almost mugged by an anxious father. Mike's post-nap fuzziness was interpreted as stress and exhaustion after a long and difficult surgery.

If there was any reticence about parting with the vehicle equipment, it was gone. Mike was hugged, Lisa was hugged, everyone was happy and jubilant. As for me, I'd done what I'd been trying to do. Saved lives. I shouldn't be upset that all the gratitude was going to someone who not only didn't do any of the actual work, but had fought me every step of the way. I wanted, very badly, to shout out, "Hey, I'm the one who did it. Thank *me*. Show *me* some gratitude!" But I knew better. That incident with Lunette's people... well, it scarred me. I hadn't seen that kind of sheer *hate* in a long time, and really I'd only read about it. Even Jake had a good reason to hate me, as a person, but it was rational in that way. I'd hate me too, under the circumstances.

So I wasn't as happy as I should have been, and I was angry with myself for being so small minded. Besides, if Mike got the glory which should have been mine, well, that would make him a lot more willing to keep this up, right? And it was working.

I could take pride in that. I'd concocted a seemingly insane scheme, and I'd pulled it off. I was the man behind the curtain, running the show, and if no one knew, well, that just showed how good I was at it.

From here on, I thought, it was going to be easy.

It should be noted that of all the skills I lack, prophecy is pretty high on the list.

Chapter 5

We had managed to work the routine for several weeks. We found semi-permanent settlements, wandering bands, dug-in enclaves, all of whom could use help. My Heim field was fully charged, we managed to get an external shower rigged up (we needed to move some things around to add the water tank and I hated the waste, but Mike insisted), and I humbly submit we did a lot of good. I decided to chronicle specific locations, people, and so on separately, a kind of Doomsday Book of the new world. You should find copies of those records wherever you found these.

We picked up a lot of rumor, hearsay, and tall tales. They said there were lost cities to the south or the north, fully intact, but surrounded by unbreachable defenses, either put there by the inhabitants or their enemies. Or there were odd havens hidden in the wilderness, places safe from any invader. There were things in the woods, oddities and mutations that were fleetingly glimpsed. Someone was going to recreate the old nation-states. Europe, or Asia, or Africa were untouched by the chaos which had gripped the Americas. Aliens would be landing any day now, or Jesus would be coming, or Hubbard, or Elvis. The usual.

Some things we took a lot more seriously. Any mention of the New Northwest Army, for example. They were becoming a persistent rumor, and we plotted every place someone claimed they were moving, and overlaid them to form a map of probabilities, deeper shades of red the more the tales overlapped. We stuck to the clear parts of the map—or at least the ones which were only light pink. It was hard to sort rumor from fact, horror tales from true atrocities, but it all pointed to "people we weren't ready to mess with." So we didn't, though both of us wished we had some means to strike back.

Then there was the puzzle of the Fences.

We found one about two days after we left the tourist center. I was getting some odd readings, a major power source where I wasn't expecting one—not that my maps were anything but best guess approximations anyway—and we decided to check it out. And by 'we,' I mean, I decided and Mike complained.

Once I got close enough to do a full scan, I recognized it. It was the same kind of Fence which Lunette's camp used. Beyond it was a similar, though not identical, cluster of buildings. I fired off a couple of radio signals and even sent up a flare, but no one came out.

"I think you should investigate," I told Mike.

"I think you should... ah, nevermind. I don't think you can, anyway." He flicked off the neural field and phased out of the interactive he'd been experiencing. "What is it?"

"Remember the community I told you about? The one which seemed immune to my folksy, down-home charm?"

Mike snorted. "Yeah."

"They had a setup like this. I didn't think much of it then, but here's another one. The problem is, no one is responding to me."

"Not even a pitchfork wieldin' mob? Hunh."

"Not a torch in sight."

"So there's no one there and you fry if you cross it. We go around. Didja really have to bother me for that? I was gettin' to a good bit."

"If you talk to the redhead, her boyfriend will come from the back room and pound you into the floor. There's some very realistic wounding involved; I was impressed by the accuracy. To get past this scene, buy two more drinks and wait for the old sailor to show up."

"Thanks for ruinin' the plot. You're a great pal. So anyway, why do we care about an empty bunch of buildings?"

"Well, they might not be empty. They could be filled with people too sick to reply. They could also be filled with unguarded supplies."

Mike nodded. "When we strip places like this bare, we're 'resupplyin'. When other folks do it, they're lootin'. Right?"

"You have the essence of modern ethics down perfectly. You missed your true calling as a philosopher."

"Fine. I'll check it out. Just lemme have a full biohazard suit."

"There's one problem with that. I don't have one. We should try to trade for it the next time we can."

"So you think maybe a plague bomb struck this place, an'

there's lots of really sick, nearly dead people inside, and you want me to just wander in?"

He had a point. I spent an hour doing air samples just outside the fence. There were plenty of interesting life forms, but nothing like an active milspec plague. Some oddities: a very sophisticated retroviral delivery system containing a badly degraded set of DNA, but nothing that looked instantly lethal. I hit Mike up with a booster of broad spectrum antibiotics and 'smart' polymorphic antibodies, just to be sure.

Then I waited. The Fence was mostly harmless to organics—I wouldn't recommend lying down under it, but a second's quick exposure didn't do much more than cause slight dizziness. Mike wandered in. It occurred to me, suddenly, that I couldn't send the signal to the bomb through the Fence; if he stayed in there until the timer expired, things would be bad. I also decided that when he came out, I wouldn't mention that little oversight of mine.

It didn't take long. I saw him wander from building to building, and at no point did he decide to rush back to me, or come out carrying any kind of supplies. After two hours or so, he returned.

"Nothin'. Nada. Zilch."

"Hmm. Who builds a population center with no people?"

He shrugged. "Crazy robots. Prob'ly, what's goin' on is somethin' was set up to make bases, secure spots that couldn't be overrun. Then it gets its orders screwy, maybe one too many viral attacks, and it just starts buildin' 'em in random spots. Some folks'll be darn happy to find this place. It's a good refuge. Won't stop guys with guns, but it'll stop a lot of other things."

His explanation was perfectly logical. Stranger things had certainly happened. Still, it felt wrong to me, off somehow, and it nagged at the back of my mind in odd, quiet, moments.

We kept on going.

Overall, Mike was still uncomfortable with the charade, though much less so after he started getting used to the kind of adulation you can get when you've saved someone's life, or their spouse or child or best friend or, in one case, their cat. He didn't try to kill me anymore, but he still made it clear that if it was entirely up to him, he'd take off on his own. My promised one month deadline was coming due, too. I pondered my options and liked none of them. If I reneged, Mike would find some way to do me in, even if it took him with it. If I honored the deal, I was pretty sure Mike would vanish over the horizon, and I'd be starting over. I made a simple model of him in memory, based on his psych profile and what I'd learned about him in the past few weeks, and tried to find some simulated conversations which would convince him to keep on going of his own free will.

I decided to test this model in a simple way. I had worked out a sequence which would, I was sure, get him to pick the leftmost fork on the road in our search for more people who could use our services. I put it into action.

"Have you seen the maps for this area?"

"Sure thing," he was supposed to say.

"You mean, the things we pretty much make up based on people's bad recollections of places they'd been while being chased by bandits or worse?" is what he actually said.

So far, not so good. I kept on.

"Yes. Those. I've been thinking we should go left up here." I displayed the map. He looked at it.

"Nah. Right."

"Here's why I disagree. There's clearly more water sources to the left. Further, there's been some power spikes I picked up."

He shook his head. "We ought to go right."

"Why?" We were so far off script now I didn't even bother trying to salvage it.

"All the reasons you said. They're big red flags drawing in all sorts of trouble. There's no good reason to try to settle over there, to the right, so that's where smart people are gonna go."

"So... the reason you want to go right is that there's no good reason to go right?"

He smiled. "Yup. Pretty brilliant, huh?"

I deleted the simulation. And veered right.

He was, annoyingly, correct.

After a few minutes heading down the path which should lead to nowhere, I started getting hit with active probes of all sorts. Radio, sound, anything which might ping and return. I slowed down. Someone knew we were here; there was no point in scaring them, and there might be a point in letting them know we knew.

We'd worked out a fairly simple set of approach protocols. We make it clear we're not trying to sneak or hide. We look for any kind of traps: minefields, monowire, snipers, even big pits lined with jagged metal. We don't trigger them. We start with radio signals on common frequencies, if they can cut through the constant din of automated jammers, and then go to a loud announcement. If we get no response, we decide not to push into someone else's turf and just head around.

This time, the radio worked. A voice crackled over the line. "We see you approaching. Do not come any closer." Obediently, I dropped to hover mode. There was a pause on the other side, as if I hadn't followed the script. "Identify yourself."

Mike took over. "This is Doctor Mike MacIntyre, travelin' surgeon and general medic. Here to barter my skills for your stuff." Mike had said a hybrid name seemed fair. I felt vaguely robbed.

Another pause. "We'd heard of a traveling doctor. We weren't sure if we could believe it. We could use your help."

This was unusually friendly, but I was grateful for the lack of an interrogation. It was also heartening to hear our deeds had preceded us.

"We're going to send a map of the defensive perimeter. Do not deviate from it, or you will either be blown up or shot. We can and will defend ourselves. Clear?"

"Totally." I got the transmission and looked at it. A complex path wended through a maze of... well, they weren't saying. Not surprising. No sense saying *what's* defending you. For all I knew, the whole map was a complex bluff. I decided not to chance it. Going slowly, I followed the map to... nothing?

A rocky cliff face terminated my path. Looking back, I could see I was nicely boxed in; it would be trivial to block the only exit. Great. I started prepping the missiles and the railgun, but then I noticed something. The IR wasn't synced with the visual. At all. I could have tested with radar, but I was afraid of setting off defenses triggered by active sensors. I told Mike this.

"Mind if we come in?" he asked.

"Straight head, no more than forty feet, though. It's a nasty drop after that."

I pushed forward, far too slowly to be damaged if I ended up hitting solid rock. I didn't. The hologram was perfectly insubstantial.

Behind it was a large cavern, with an inner ledge which terminated, as stated, within 40 feet. Lights were hung along the ceiling and walls. Metal ladders reached down into the depths. Four people with guns, two men and two women, waited for me.

Mike opened the door slowly and got out, hands clear. I constructed models of the place based on visual inputs. It's always good to have an escape route planned.

One of the women glanced at a portable device. "He's clean."

One of the men, a shorter fellow with black hair and slightly

Asian features, smiled broadly and held out his hand. Mike took it.

"Art Tollman, Reno Protectorates Internal Security. Pleased to meet you, Doctor MacIntyre."

"Mike MacIntyre, with no one in particular, anymore. Uh... if politics are an issue, I can just turn around and leave, no trouble."

Art smiled and shook his head. "They're not for us if they're not for you. I just thought you should know who you were dealing with."

I certainly liked it. Pulled up my databases. They were, I was starting to find, painfully incomplete, another tragedy of the satellite interfaces not working. The Reno Protectorates were in my files, of course—every neonation which wasn't two guys and their dog was—but the data was sparse. Major affiliate subnations, primary constitution, general trends... about the only information on their security was that they had one. That was so helpful, I could cry.

Mike rubbed his hands together. "So, what kinda place you got here, anyway?"

"It was a prototype for fissionable storage, back from near the end of the nation state. They never got much beyond hollowing it out and starting to dig tunnels. Heavily shielded, which is pretty helpful. This drop off was supposed to be finished with huge ramps and elevators, but then... well, no need to discuss history."

"So you guys just moved in, eh?"

Art shrugged. "It seemed like a good idea at the time. Defensible, hard to spot—we even set up some noisy power generators a few miles west to draw people away from us. Well, people and robots. Mostly robots, really. I think all the people are just trying to wait it out."

"That's what I've seen. So, uh, how do we get down?"

"There's a small ramp over there. Not going to be good enough for your vehicle. There's also ladders."

"Yeah. See, I keep most of my gear in the back there. Got a full medibay, lots of, uh, medical stuff. Do all my real work back there. I'm not sure..."

Art clapped him on the back. "Don't worry about it! We've got some people with problems, but I think we can get them up here."

Mike nodded, looking back at me with a sudden desperate glint in his eyes. "We'll improvise," I told him.

I studied the layout. Beyond the huge drop off, there was a maze of tunnels and passages. There was, indeed, a lot of shielding, and the angles weren't great for sending probes. I still had three scavengers left. They were pretty unobtrusive. If I needed to, I could send one off to scout.

Art and one of the women went with Mike, leading him to a long, sloping, ramp which descended into the murky depths. My own visual scans showed very few sensors placed inside the cave itself; it looked like they were mostly interested in external threats. Thus I felt a little more comfortable about doing some quick, quiet, radar pings to get a feel for the place.

I tapped into Mike's visual cortex. The internal shielding messed with things a bit, but I got something. He was down the ramp, in a side tunnel, looking at wounded. Four of them, three men, one woman. All were lying on memory foam cots, with slow release drug patches on their arms, heavily bandaged and fairly well done, too. Breathing was shallow, and every so often, one would twitch, apparently in pain despite the drugs. The labels on the patches indicated a mix of painkillers and heavy sedatives.

"What happened?"

"Accident," said Art, then decided to offer more detail. "We were exploring, checking out the extent of our little hideout, making sure there were no hidden back doors someone could exploit. Some of the old construction work, well, it was unstable. This was the result. We have two paramedics here, they did what they could with our basic gear, but..." He paused. "We lost Anton two days ago. Elana's doing poorly. The other three, well, we're mostly keeping them out of pain."

Mike, with a gentle prompt from me, walked over to Elana.

He touched her in the places I told him to. I couldn't really tap into his tactile senses, but I could see how the skin responded, see where she flinched even under the drugs. There were discolorations on her skin and pus under some of the bandages.

Mike made the rounds of the others, then turned to Art.

"She's the worst. I need to get her back to the ambulance, now. Can you help me move her?"

They got a Heim field lifter—a damn expensive piece of gear—and gently placed her onto it. She was escorted up the ramp. I watched, patiently, as she was escorted back to me.

Once inside, I started up working on her. Massive internal injuries, as I suspected, and severe bleeding. Their guy had done a decent job of stabilizing her, but no more. All he'd done was insure she'd die slowly instead of instantly.

Fixing that was my job. This wasn't going to be solved with

custom cells or genetic tinkering; it was going to take real surgery. A half dozen arms descended from the ceiling and began their task. Blood-encrusted bandages were cut away. Blood—or the nearest thing I had to it, a nice artificial mix which could be used on almost anyone in the short term—was pumped into her. I carefully ran analysis on all of her tissues, making sure it was all really hers... the lungs weren't. Highly efficient and filled with little filters designed to extract and encapsulate unwanted matter for later excretion. Great. Getting a tissue match was going to be a bitch. I decided to just edit it a bit, cut away the most damaged tissue, sew up what was left and tell her she could make do with a lung and a half. The rest of her looked natural, no skeletal changes, and the same heart she was born in. Idly, I wondered if the lungs were done for personal reasons or were replacements for a damaged set. I suppose it didn't matter.

While most of me was busy on the surgery, I could spare a few cycles to talk.

"What's your opinion of these people?"

Mike shrugged. "Friendly. Fairly trusting. Which bugs me."

"Why? We've got a reputation now. Well, you do. I'm just the ambulance."

"Because they're all ex-IntSec. I know those types. They get the paranoids and the crazies. B'sides, where's the folks they were supposed to provide security *for?* Military units, well, we're supposed to be on our own, no civilians... but IntSec? Shouldn't they have, I dunno, all got killed shoving idiots out of the way of an oncoming attack?"

A part of me dismissed this as the opinion of someone who'd had one too many run-ins with the internal security of the Bay Autonomy. Another part of me saw his point. Too much paranoia these days, and you hid in a cave and shot anyone who came near.

After about two hours, there was a rapid, angry, knock. "Hey! What's going on?"

"She's almost done. There was a lot of damage."

"I'm Frank. Frank Morne. I'm a paramedic, I want to see what's going on."

Under the circumstances, it seemed safe. Mike continued to pretend to work the controls. I opened the door. A harried looking man of perhaps twenty-five years of age stuck his head in. He had a gaunt, nervous, look. He stepped up into the medibay and looked down at Elana. I was just about done.

"Is she, uh, will she be—"

"She'll be fine. You did good work with what you had."

"What I had. Yeah." He looked around the inside of the medibay. He gestured at one piece of equipment. "Is that..."

I took over for a second. "A micro growth box. Yes. Pretty much anything up to a liver, if you have the time and the tissue."

He nodded and looked at it closely, putting a hand out almost worshipfully. "We... I... we don't have anything like that."

"Well, I'm afraid we need that," said Mike, "But we do have some supplies we might be able to trade. Speaking of which, me and Art... he's the guy in charge, right?"

Frank nodded, eyes still lingering on the growth box.

"Well, him and me, we have to come to terms. I wasn't going to haggle when someone was on the brink, but, y'know, a man's got to eat."

"Uh huh... yeah. She looks good enough to move out... is she?"

Mike nodded.

"Why don't I... why don't we take her down, and then we can talk with Art. I'll, uh, I'll vouch for the good job you did here. He'll listen to me."

"Good plan. Let's do it." They detached her, transferred her to the hovering cart outside, and moved out.

I watched Mike and Frank and the prostrate Elana descend, burning torches on infrared and indistinct blobs on standard visual. Upstairs, two of the original four who'd escorted me in were still standing a long, bored, watch. One leaned against me and took out a cigarette. Contraband in the UBA and a basic part of life in the Protectorates, but they must still be getting rare, now. Anyone growing things had better things to grow than recreational drugs. She tapped the tiny capsule at the end and it ignited.

"Think it'll work?" she asked her partner.

He shrugged. "I dunno. Art's usually got some good plans."

"Yeah." She took a long drag. "Still... there's bound to be some security. Neural lock, certainly." She tapped on my side. "Wonder if I should start checking it out now?"

The man shook his head. "Nah. Bad idea. We don't want any kind of alarms going off, audio or otherwise, until everything's in place. We want to get some use out of the guy first. You're just bored."

"Damn right. This whole deal sucks."

"We're alive. A lot of people aren't." He paused, looking thoughtful.

She rolled her eyes, took one more drag, dropped the cigarette and stamped it out. "Oh, do *not* go on that tear again, Paul! I'm sick of it, we're all sick of it. Save the whiny angst for your liferecord or something." She walked off.

"Lydia, I was just... hell with it." He wandered over to a panel and tapped in some numbers. Large metal plates slid inwards from the walls. I made sure to memorize the numbers.

This wasn't looking good.

They were planning something, and I had a good idea what. I thought about directly warning Mike, but I remembered his acting talents. Whatever they were going to do, they would wait until, quote, they got some use out of him, unquote. So he was safe for the moment. Meanwhile, I checked the ammo on the railgun. We'd kept the converter fed, and it was stocked. All five of my remaining missiles were good to go, too. Heim field? Fully charged. Heavy crystal iron/ceramic layered semi-ablative battle armor combined with high power repulsive electromagnetic screens? Totally non-existent, like they always were.

I envied tanks, sometimes. I really did.

Okay. Without knowing exactly what was happening, and when, I needed to prepare for contingencies. I activated my body (presently stored out of sight in the cabin) and made sure it was charged up. It never hurts to be in two places at once if you can.

The guard was reading something on a handheld; judging from his heart rate and skin temperature, it probably involved sex. The important thing was, he wasn't watching me. I dropped a scavenger, my second to last. I needed information. I sent it scuttling away, using an avoidance protocol, sending it down a shadowed niche on the far side of the incline, its multiple legs easily finding purchase on the rough stone walls.

I checked in on Mike. To be clear, the feed is always there unless I willfully deactivate it, but I don't always pay full attention to it unless something triggers an alert. I can always review the files later if I need to.

"So that's our offer," Art was saying. "What do you think?"

Great. Looked like it was time to review the files. I picked a point about two minutes past. It would take me about five seconds to watch it, then I could join in if I had to.

It started with Elana being placed into the makeshift hospital, and Mike doing his usual semi-decent job of pretending he could perform triage. I'd already told him who was next in line. Art watched, then looked at Frank oddly.

Frank coughed, then spoke. "I... uh... he, he did a good job. Elana ought to be fine."

"Great, great..." He looked around, his eye catching on nothing in particular. "Mike... let's talk. Payment for services rendered, and all that, right?"

Mike nodded and gestured to one of the men on the cots. "That guy, he's not doin' great, but he'll be all right for a little while. We should settle terms."

"Yes. Yes, we should."

The two of them walked out of the sick room and into the cavernous main hall. At the far end, lights flared, full-spectrum lamps over a flowing sea of leafy green. A few men and women tended to the plants. Beyond that, I could see a pattern of light and shadow; a quick image search showed it was a microfusion reactor. A nice piece of gear. Assuming decent recycling and some source of water, they could hole up in here for a long, long, time. Just like everyone else was. Waiting it out. Someone else would fix the world, and then all the bears would emerge from hibernation...

Art gestured to two chairs; Mike sat, and so did Art. "So... Doctor MacIntyre... Mike... why are you doing this?"

Mike blinked a bit, taken aback. He was waiting for me to butt in, but at the time, I was listening to people plot and wasn't paying attention. So he spoke for himself.

"To, y'know, help people. And earn a livin'. Do well by doin' good, and all that."

There was a thin smile. "Of course. I didn't really expect you to say anything else."

Why were they having this conversation in the middle of an open hall? These things were usually negotiated inside somewhere. For a few milliseconds, I paused it, and tapped into the scavengers sensors. It was hiding in a darkened niche, scanning the room. There were Mike and Art, still talking. About one second had passed since I started reviewing the tape. And there—

There was someone with a sniper rifle, carefully lining up a shot. Oh, great. I judged the decision to fire or not fire hadn't been made yet, so I quickly went back to the recording. I also started, very subtly, powering up the Heim field.

"But I have a proposal. Stay here. With us. Frank's a decent enough paramedic, but he's not a doctor. We need someone like you. We can give you a decent rank—everyone here's part of Reno IntSec, so you'll need to be, too—good, steady, food, and easy work.

We don't have a lot of accidents."

Mike tapped his fingers on his knee. "So I got a question... you guys, you're IntSec for Reno... where's the folks you're providin' security *for?*"

Art's smile never moved. That took good muscle control. I was impressed. What did move was his hand, his fingers ever-so-subtly positioning themselves in an unnatural, "this is a signal if you know what you're looking for," way.

Quick check back to the supposed guard. He was deeply involved in his interactive, and I'm not going to say anymore about that. My body got up and waited, just inside the door to the sleeping area. Back to the file.

"We..." Art was saying "had some issues." He looked away, and wiggled his fingers. He then looked back towards Mike, but not precisely *at* him. "We were one division of IntSec. We're not sure, still, who hit our district. We *think* it was one of the Vegas families. We had treaties, but they weren't worth the bits they were stored in when it all started falling apart. Anyway... we gave orders. The locals didn't want to obey. There were... difficulties." He rubbed his forehead. "Look. That's ancient history. We've got a nice, defensible, position here, and once we've had some time to study the situation, we can expand. But we need a real doctor. Plagues, biterswarms, the occasional accident... we can give you a much better life than you can have out there. Food, recreation, and in the future, who knows? People need to be led. Someone's got to move into the gap, and it might as well be us. So that's our offer. What do you think?"

OK, I was caught up, but two seconds more had passed. A tenth of a second to be fully synced...

Mike was shaking his head. "No. No, sorry, that's not gonna..."

Real time, now.

"...happen."

Art looked regretful, but very, very, slightly. "So be it." He began to raise his hand. Through the scavenger, I saw the sniper begin to draw back on the trigger. What happened next happened very, very, fast.

First, I sent an urgent, desperate, message to Mike:"Duck! Fall left! Now!" As he started to do so, his muscles responding, to my mind, in painful slow motion, I activated the protocols I'd been building.

(I should take a quick aside here. I think at different speeds, depending on my need. It's a lot of work, being sapient. I can accelerate myself in an emergency, but then I run hot, very hot, and I can only do it for so long. Most of the time, my actual consciousness works at something close to human norm, maybe twice as fast. Hell, when I'm talking to people, I usually slow down so I'm not bored to tears waiting for them to respond. I can do a lot of tricks like splitting my mind, having part of me working on a problem while the rest of me does other things, but it's all very similar to the way a human mind works. You—assuming that the person reading this is human—do it all subconsciously. You stop thinking about a problem, or you think you stop thinking about it, and then, an hour later, poof, it's solved. I do exactly that, I'm just more in control of it. Anyway, when I need to, *really* need to, I can redline myself. It's just extremely risky and I can't do it for more than a few seconds. Fortunately, in those few seconds, I can do more thinking than a human can do in an hour.)

I redlined myself.

As Mike fell back, inch by painfully slow inch to my accelerated perceptions, I flooded power into the Heim field. The field (on the off chance even that kind of basic knowledge has been lost to you. God, I hope not!) requires more power the more it pushes against gravity, on a logarithmic scale. In other words, the higher you want to go, the more energy it takes. It's great for nap-of-Earth flight. It can make microadjustments for perfect smoothness over uneven terrain. And, in theory, you can fly—if you have power to burn.

I didn't, but I had to. I'd been storing a lot of energy, and now it was time to use it.

I charged forward, off the precipice. For a glorious instant, I hung, suspended. It was a moment caught in semi freeze-frame, the images stepping forward instant by instant. People turned, moving like flowers following the sun, looking up, as I crested over, floated there, like some sort of angelic vision—well, if angels ever appeared as top-line medical vehicles—and then I began to fall. Except that I didn't. I poured everything into the field, forcing it to follow a path I'd calculated to an insane degree of accuracy, using variations in field strength and the inevitable pull of gravity to guide me into a long, arcing, curve. I have the aerodynamics of a brick, but with enough power and enough math, I could fly. For a few precious glorious seconds, I flew.

I gave a shout of exultant triumph. It didn't matter who heard me now, who knew I was aware. The entire point of the masquerade was done. I thought, in that instant of free fall, that this wasn't the best plan, that I could have found some other, more subtle solution, but you know what?

I'd been good—safe, sane, predictable, boring—for weeks. Even if I was going to die now, I was going to die doing something gloriously, spectacularly, *me*.

I don't actually have adrenaline, but I am an adrenaline junkie. Go figure.

I descended rapidly along a perfectly planned and controlled vector of flight. Random people throughout the open space were drawing sidearms and trying to target me. Bullets from a perfectly silenced sniper rifle *thwipped* into the wall, precisely where Mike had been sitting half a second earlier. I saw long thin red lines erupt, tracing a path from his arm to the dark stone, splattering Rorschach patterns of blood and pulverized rock.

My arc took me right past him. From within the cabin, flying past at senses-blurring speed, I reached out, bracing myself carefully, and *yanked*. He began to scream in pain as I pulled on his wounded arm, dragging him into the sleeping space as I passed by, then did something hard to describe to the Heim field and slid into a gravity-assisted spin. For a brief moment, even by my senses, I was stopped as all the forces acting on me converged at zero. Then, sticking close to the ground, I powered up again, sailing up a ramp too narrow for me, balancing the field so that the part off the ramp was pushing so much harder than the part on that I maintained near-perfect balance.

"The... *hell?*" Mike managed to gasp out from the back, holding his bleeding and aching arm.

"Trouble. We're moving. Need help." I sputtered. It was taking everything I had to keep balanced as I half-glided, half-flew upwards. Every word was a drain on my consciousness. I flicked on the neural induction field, tied into the weapons systems, so he could use them. I couldn't waste a single processor cycle to actually fire my own guns.

It had been five seconds, more or less, since I saw the sniper's finger tighten. Now I was at the flat spot, above the precipice, facing an iron door. I sent the signal to the door, the one I'd seen Paul typing earlier. The door began to open, too slowly.

Mike, meanwhile, was trying to ignore his arm and focus on the gun. Using the missiles in here would be even more suicidal than my actions already were, sort of the difference between playing

Russian Roulette, and playing it with six bullets. OK, I was already using three bullets, but half a chance is better than none.

A railgun on full auto is a horrible, hideous, weapon, especially when aimed at a large target or a group of smaller targets. It can cut open a tank like a can of cat food and turn a person into raw materials for biosynthesis in half a second. What it is not good for is a lot of small targets scattered around a large room, not if you have to save ammo, and especially not if you're trying to control it mentally while distracted by a badly injured arm and are positioned inside a wildly veering, slightly mad with the thrill of it all, medical rescue vehicle. I'm saying this so no one will consider it a slight on Mike's soldiering abilities when I note I don't think he even wounded anyone, never mind killing. He did, at least, keep them distracted and off balance, so only a relative handful of bullets tore into me. I saw some damage reports start to scroll up; I ignored them with a passion.

The door was opening. Not fast enough.

If I stopped dead, I would be. I ran some quick calculations, shutting off the various nagging alarms which told me I was running my mind hot, too hot, that various subsystems were at ever-increasing risk of failure. I was quite literally killing myself trying to stay alive.

I spun wildly, moving into a complex, veering, avoidance pattern in the limited space, while the door crept agonizingly open. More and more of the former IntSec were drawing weapons, and the criss-crossing bullet vectors filled my limited maneuvering space with deadly missiles. I had the math, though, and I knew exactly how long...

Perfect.

Two things happened then. The door had reached *just* wide enough of an angle, and I spun to head for it. I also primed, locked, and loaded a missile. The launcher swiveled around behind me, aimed upwards as I shot towards the door, overpowering half the field and completely deactivating the other. I turned perfectly vertical as we sped through the door. I figure we cleared it by about a quarter inch. As soon as we were through, I reoriented myself and *fired*. The missile arced up, up, up, taking a particularly long time to get where it was going. It needed to, I had to be out of the way when it hit.

The explosion caught me even as I twisted down the complex maze I'd followed to get in, and then came the crash of rocks, followed by a series of smaller, but no less deadly, explosions as the mines surrounding the entrance were triggered. I glanced back, to see the cave front completely covered. It would be weeks, perhaps months, before they dug their way out of it. Probably no one would die.

I could have easily fired the missile through the doors behind me, into their little fortress, killing them all. Frankly, I thought they deserved it, but I'm trying not to kill people, even when I really, *really,* want to.

Chapter 6

"Maybe you'd better let me drive."

"I'm fine."

"Tell that to the paint job on your left side. It's back on that rock." Mike sighed. "You don't drive that bad unless we're bein' chased, which, for the moment, we're not. What the hell's wrong with you?"

This was about an hour after our escape. The first thing I had done, while Mike was still in the cabin, was perform a quick patch-up on his arm, using a standard issue field first-aid kit. I didn't want to stop moving even for the time it would take to get Mike in the back. Actually, I dropped my last scavenger and set it broadcast false radar images, just in case anyone from the former Reno IntSec was outside their little base and decided to follow us. Can't be too careful. Since then, though, I was feeling the effects of what I did more and more, and Mike was noticing.

I dropped speed to what I could manage safely. "Little stunt back there took a lot out of me."

Mike considered this. "Ran a little too hot a little too long?"

"Yes. There's been some... some damage. Nothing... nothing that... can't be reconstructed. Gadolinium stores are adequate. Just... need some time."

"Look, just let me have control for once. I know you're built for it." He paused, considering. "You nearly got yourself killed savin' my life. I'm not about to fly you off a cliff out of spite. Gimme some credit, huh?"

Reluctantly, for the first time since I was trainee, I flipped to manual control. There was a lurch as Mike grabbed the yoke and got a feel for things.

"OK, so depth of field is this pedal, mobility thrusters here... pretty standard, I guess."

There was something I didn't like in his voice.

"You... guess?"

He shrugged. "Well, I never did fully qualify on Heim-field vehicles. I was pretty much tracks and wheels. Only the elite got to flit around breakin' the laws of physics."

We skidded to the side suddenly. "Whoops, that rock came up awfully fast!"

"I didn't... didn't save you so you could get us both killed, you know."

"You stress too much, Doc. Don't worry. I'm gettin' the hang of it. Be easier if you'd bother showing me all the facts."

Right. I turned on the control displays. With a shimmering flicker, the plain metal surface surrounding the control yoke came to life, a glistening array of dials, readouts, and controls. Mike's eyes passed over them."

"I'm pretty sure that most of these ain't supposed to be red."

I'd been suppressing all my internal warnings. Too distracting in the midst of a crisis. I decided, reluctantly, to take a look at my full status.

I wished I hadn't.

Remember what I said earlier, about the way people try to avoid hearing bad news they know is true, as if not hearing it makes it not real? Well, I had a very deep and true understanding of them now. The knowledge of what a mess I was in struck me like a rock. If I hadn't turned control over to Mike, I probably would have just flopped down on the path and had a few hours of enjoyable depression.

"No. No, they really shouldn't... shouldn't be red. Not that many. I have no idea what's going to blow first, but it's going to be something, and it's going to be soon. We need someplace safe."

"Yeah, good luck with that. Lemme see the maps we've been making."

I tossed them up.

Mike looked for a second. "Here. There's a little lake here, and some kinda small town on the shores. Who knows? It might still be there. Looks like a good place to settle in, go fishin'."

I saw what he was looking at. "Get killed by some 'bots out of Vegas. That's right on the disputed border. Probably a smoking ruin, with whatever side thinks it won holding it and the other side's dumb machines trying to take it back."

"We'll scout a bit, first. If there is anyone there... we can deal. If it's another rubble-filled crater, well, we'll move on. Less you got some better ideas?"

I didn't. I could barely think. All I wanted to do was shut down every consciousness process and enter into a self-repair slumber, let the shorted neural fibers and the other bits of matter that made my mind possible repair themselves. I had a nagging little voice telling me to do just that. I shut it off. "Helpful systems monitor and support agent" my ass.

"No... no, I don't. Just... be careful."

"Always am."

The next hour or two was spent in silence. I needed the break. It was very strange, relinquishing control over my own body. My mind drifted, heading into odd places, strange thoughts. I can't really recall anything coherent; part of the repair process involves temporarily shutting down tiny nodes of awareness, and as thoughts shunt and weave around the dead zones, they mix and blur, producing odd correspondences and jumps in thought. It is a very surreal experience, to feel one's mind being reconstructed.

Night was upon us by the time we drew near to the target. The light pollution of the old days was long gone, and the sky was sprayed with white. A few dozen of the specs were still moving, high orbit satellites glaring down on the Earth, some just watching, some tracking aircraft and reporting them to lower atmosphere strike units. A lot of them were soultech, minds forever cut off from the Earth. I'd talked to one once, a couple of years back. Arrogant bastard with a serious god complex.

"Hey, there's the spot. Lemme see it in IR."

I applied the filter to the viewscreen and looked myself. "Looks cool. Bots would be burning heat sources, 'less they're stealthed, an' I don't see why they would be. No people, either, least not outside. Huh. What do you think?"

"I don't know. Looks safe."

Mike thought for a second. "Yeah. Right. We'd better stop here."

He drove us in.

The town was a single massive building, formed of something like coral. It could be compelled to grow chambers, expansions, or open area with relative ease. With proper care and support, it could live and grow to meet any needs. It was beautifully colored, covered with sweeping whorls of red and blue in elegant, intricate, patterns. The growth itself was aesthetic as well as functional: Round open plazas for shops and meeting areas, elegant towers for residences, large, ribbed domes as warehouses. Concessions to functionality were evident here and there, glistening arrays of solar panels, the occasional antenna reaching skyward, glass windows, and metal doors.

It was also dying. The color was faded in many placed. Windows were cracked; doors hung open. The interior regions, the circular shopping and recreation areas, were empty, the stores abandoned. Leaves piled up in corners, and there were small animals—squirrels, mostly, pure-strain or mods, I couldn't tell— scurrying here and there. No sign of humans, or of warring armies.

"I don't like it."

"Yeah, I know the drill. 'Quiet... too quiet.'" He shrugged. "If we head in there, to that big oval space, we'll be pretty much hidden from passersby. I can scout it out a bit more on foot. No offense, Doc, but you need to lose a little weight."

"Your arm..."

"Will be fine. Nothin' here to fight, right?"

"I hope so..."

He left then. I... well, for all practical purposes, I passed out. There was only so much repair work I could do and still be conscious. The healing algorithms needed to have access to everything at once, and they couldn't do that if I was busily thinking. Everything that was *me* dwindled to a tiny core, and I entered a timeless blackness.

When I came out of it, the sky was a dull rose, and Mike wasn't back. That was bad. I tried to tap into the optics link. I saw darkness. The fact I was seeing anything meant he was still alive, which was good. He was somewhere in the town... down, though. Down below.

I tried voice.

"Mike?"

No response. Visual was online but not getting anything. Either he was in a very dark place, where he might be eaten by a grue, or he was unconscious. If the latter, he probably hadn't just decided to lay down for a nap. It was time, I realized, for some thrilling heroics. As if my last such effort hadn't nearly killed me.

Right. I got into my body, grabbed a pistol and a medikit, and headed out. Just as I did, though, I also ran more scans, using deep radar to look *down*. The town had a huge maze of tunnels below it. IR couldn't penetrate, of course, and we hadn't thought to check them out.

I turned to look back at myself. Damn, I was a mess. Bullet

holes, paint scraped, dented and dinged... it had been a rough few years. I had a feeling it was only going to get rougher. I flipped on camo mode for my body. Whatever was going on, it was probably best not to be seen.

I walked for the nearest store. I had no idea what it was once called; the sign was probably neural, sent into the mind of any passerby appropriately wired up, and who wasn't? Even if I'd been open to receiving such signals now, there was no longer power to it. The inside was stripped bare, nothing but shelves, and even they would have been gone if they hadn't actually been part of the living building. Smooth niches and hollows lined the walls, casting interesting shadows, and once I moved beyond visual it was easy to see one of them was more than an aesthetic fold; it was an opening leading to a slanting tunnel. I checked the ammo on the pistol and entered.

It was cool down here, cooler than I would have expected. There was no indication of active power; it might have been the coral, drawing moisture from the lake to a lower temperature via evaporation. Biological air conditioning. Why had the people left this place, stripped it clean? There were no unburied bodies, as there usually were after a plague. The way it had been cleared out indicated time to leave, or maybe people had come by after it was empty. Bandits, though, wouldn't take everything. It made very little sense.

Finding Mike was the important thing. The tunnel maze spread rapidly below the town. There was more of it than there was town, come to think of it. Some of the tunnels seemed to stretch on tremendous distances, into the lakeside woods beyond. I built a map as I went, seeing dead ends and open spaces, trying to think like Mike, a difficult exercise.

Heat sources. A lot of them, ahead. Comparing visual to IR, they were trying to hide.

Basically human, from what I could tell. Right body temperature, heart beat a bit too rapid. Not using metal weapons, but that left a lot of options. I could, I realized, kill at least two of them before they could respond, but if they swarmed rather than fled, I could be overwhelmed.

I stopped to think; this evidently served as a signal to those lying in wait, as one ran for me.

I could see him clearly now. A man, age in that vast indeterminate space between twenty and thirty years, black hair matted and tangled, wearing rags, the torn remnants of a uniform.

Fingernails too long, not just from lack of cutting, but actually turned into something akin to claws. Combat genemod or cosmetic affectation? I couldn't tell, and then he was on me, my camouflage apparently doing nothing to distract him.

I sidestepped the clumsy charge and swatted him. I wasn't about to use the gun until I thought it was necessary, and so far, he was a minimal threat. He didn't stay down for long, but returned, arms outstretched, clawing at me. His claws glistened with something. They scratched ineffectually on my metal skin, leaving behind a thin, oily, residue. There was nothing in his eyes but blank madness.

I knocked him out, then turned to look back at the others. They were hesitating, unsure. There was no identifiable communication I could perceive, just quick glances at me, at their fallen comrade, at each other. Some kind of decision was reached. Three more moved at me.

They didn't seem to have any skill or tactics besides 'overwhelm.' I dodged one, grabbed his arm as he raced past, and swung him into the wall, hard. Two more fell on me then, their weight and momentum taking me down. Once there, they proceed to slash and claw, saying nothing, demanding nothing, just attacking in eerie silence. I managed to get my foot under one as he scrambled on top of me and kicked him back, then stood, got the third by the arm and hit him a few times to take him out. The one I'd kicked had managed to recover and, limping slightly, still attempted to resume the fight. I spun, catching him in the midsection with the side of my leg, and he went down.

All there were unconscious, and wouldn't be happy when they woke up, but were alive. I was covered with minor scratches, none of which broke my shell, and splotches of the venom (or so I assumed) they secreted from their claws. I checked the eyes of one. There were odd flecks and reflective particles in it, sure signs of enhancement. Probably using IR, same as me, rendering the camo moot. I dropped it.

Everyone with the same mods, wearing the rags of uniform, must've been a military unit. The patch on them—three red triangles, joined at the apex, surrounded by a black circle—meant nothing to me. It wasn't even in my databases, so they might have been a small time mercenary unit not affiliated with any of the local neonations, not important enough to be worth storing in onboard memory.

I checked the link with Mike again. Still alive. Still unconscious.

The attackers had left traces, patterns of heat. I followed them.

There was a large room where many of the tunnels converged. There were a lot of people in it, too. I moved close to the entrance, trying to get a full visual. First, the room was filled with machinery, now deactivated: large generators, air recyclers, food processors, a massive water filtration and waste reprocessing system. Small wonder they need to keep this place cool, if all those things were on at once, it would be a coral-killing oven down here. Precisely why they didn't just use normal construction techniques for the underground was beyond me; a lot of these isolated communities had idiosyncratic ideas they took to odd extremes, and why not? We were becoming a planet of demigods, capable of creating almost anything of which we could conceive. This was a perfectly normal place, compared to a lot of things I'd seen.

There were also people there, living among the dead machines. I counted fifty-eight, and their array of sleeping rags, piles of torn open containers of food, and partially eaten corpses of small animals attested to a potentially larger population. Not all were uniformed; most wore the remains of civilian clothing, faded reds and blues like the pattern on the coral. Former inhabitants? Probably. A good portion wore nothing. They all moved languidly around the cold metal geometry, showing as much awareness of what it was as a monkey on a Mayan ruin.

Monkey...

I looked more closely, still trying to stay out of sight. I had a thought, suddenly. They weren't reacting to me the way the first three I'd met had. One walked by me. His hands were clawed, too, despite his lack of uniform, but his gaze passed over me and saw nothing. No IR.

Pieces fell into place. I knew I didn't have much time to rescue Mike. I still wasn't finding him.

Well, if he was unconscious, he couldn't exactly keep me from hijacking his vocal chords, now, could he.

He screamed. I heard him. So, of course, did everyone else.

This set off a sudden mad scramble. A group of the locals dashed towards the scream, as did I. I had the advantage of not being seen. Mike was in a far niche, wedged between two bulky refrigeration units— possibly emergency food storage. His own involuntary scream had broken the stupor, and he was trying to stand, even as a mob of ragged barbarians—formerly demigods—

surged onto him.

I fired. Not at him, but above him, a loud distraction. Some turned to search for the source of it, and a few spotted my color shifting form as it ducked and weaved through the crowd, heading for my partner.

Someone grabbed me. I spun, seeing another soldier. He had the sight. Of course. He also seemed to retain something of his mind, as he was using actual combat skills. He had a very good grip on me, and was actually speaking.

"Here! Here!" Not very eloquent, but I was impressed he could do it at all, all things considered.

The rest of the mob followed his lead. I tried to hold them off, but I was failing. Too many, moving too fast, grabbing at anything they could reach.

I fired. The bullet tore through one's chest and out his spine, dropping him instantly. There was a reaction of fear, then more came. I bashed with one hand and shot with the other, not stopping them fast enough. This body could take some punishment, but not all that much. I realized that if it was destroyed, Mike wouldn't be getting out, and I'd be crippled and alone. Not a pleasant thought. I kept fighting, and even though I knew precisely how many shots I had, I nonetheless clicked a few times after I knew I was out of ammunition, then tossed the gun down in disgust.

Suddenly, a shot rang out.

Mike had managed to find his footing and his gun, though he was wavering. Now with two opponents, the mob was split. The one soldier on me, the one who was guiding them with constant cries of "Here!"—he had to go. I focused my effort on him, pulling him off me, ignoring the others clawing at me, and hurled him towards the machinery, as hard as I could, which was, frankly, pretty hard now that I realized I had little reason to hold back. There was a fairly final sounding crunch.

Meanwhile, Mike was dealing with his own mob. If they had any kind of sanity left, they would have backed down, but they were acting on pure instinct. I reached for him, dropping the holographics long enough that he could grab my arm. "Come on! We need to get out of here, fast!" We pulled free and ran for the nearest tunnel, a bewildered, silent, and terrifying posse in our wake, many barely capable of moving due to the wounds we'd dealt them.

"How are you feeling?" I asked as we ran.

"Like it's the fourth day of a three day pass. And... it's weird. I kinda want to stay. It's like it's all I can do to come with you."

"That would be the memetic toxins. Come on!"

"Mem—oh, shit!"

"Right. Fight it. Remember who you are and what you want."

There were only two of them still keeping up with us. I spun and slammed my hand into one's larynx; he collapsed, spitting blood. Mike turned to fight, stopped, looked woozy; while his opponent tried to decide to act or not, I hooked my leg through his, grabbed, twisted, and heard bones crack. I let the crippled body fall, grabbed Mike, and hauled him further up the tunnel.

"Y'know... I think maybe we should go back down there. It's safer. We ought to wait..."

Time was running short.

I made it to the ambulance and tossed Mike, now feebly struggling to break my grip and return to the dark embrace of the underground, into the left bed. As soon as he was in, I dropped control of the Charlie and refocused. First, a sedative, a powerful one. Second, a deep brain scan.

I watched the memetic virus work for a few seconds, long enough to analyze it. I saw it wiring neurons, detaching deep pathways, changing the production of neurotransmitters. The first step would be to counter the changes in brain chemistry; that was easy enough, though I didn't envy Mike the headaches and mood swings he'd be facing when he awoke. The hard part would be fixing the damage.

He needed a full-sized neuroclinic, someplace where a team of specialists and equipment which cost more than I did would have days to perform careful, delicate, surgery. I was going to have to do this battlefield style, in a mad dash to save Sergeant Mike Calvers, the person, from becoming just a pile of animate meat.

It wasn't even a *good* memetic virus. If it was, those poor folks down there would be bright-eyed, happy, enthusiastic supporters of whoever it was had made the damn thing. It was either corrupted or just badly made from the get go. I hate sloppy work. Of course, I was about to do sloppy work to correct sloppy work, but I have come to the conclusion that irony is the fourth fundamental force of the universe, right after matter, energy, and enlightened self-interest.

The tools I had were intended for things like removing small bits of shrapnel from brain tissue, but I could do some other things with them, with patience, skill and luck—not necessarily in equal portion. I extruded thin silver fibers, which divided, and subdivided, and subdivided. They were made of myoelectric materials which I could control to within nanometers. They flowed through the cracks of the skull, and slowly, very slowly, began to wend their way through the cells. A thousand silver worms crawled through Mike's brain, through the physical matrix in which *he* resided, and excised, as much as possible, the recent changes. Without a perfect 'before' picture of his brain on the cellular level, there was no way to restore it perfectly, and I knew there'd be gaps and errors. A snip here, a cut there, and the neural paths forced upon him were destroyed. So, too, were natural ones which happened to be in the way or which I couldn't distinguish from the interlopers. Simultaneously, viruses of my own design, hastily established to lock onto various key molecular structures of the infecting agent, were waging war, slaying the intruder and putting on shiny, happy, faces to fool his antibodies. "We're part of you!" they said, and thanks to my extensive collection of his genetic data, his body fell for the ruse, allowing my warriors to work unopposed.

This took far longer to do than it does to write, and by the end of it, I was somewhere beyond exhausted. There's a lot of things I can do with half a mind, or less... I've been known to read books, talk with friends, or experience interactives when performing routine battlefield surgery, though please don't tell any of my patients that. This, though, this was *hard*, and I hoped I'd never have do it again.

The sun had come and gone by the time I was done. I also took care of a few other things while I was in there.

I didn't want to move my main body from its nicely sheltered spot, but I was feeling thoughtful. After making sure Mike was going to do well, I got dressed and wandered over to the lake's edge. The coral walls of the town extended deep into the water, drinking from it. Over time, I realized, a lot of it would die, but parts would live and grow, following its own needs, not those of its builders. I watched the rising sun sparkle on the waters and pondered what this place would look like in a hundred years. It might be a strange wonder for the future to dwell on, or it might be a dead ruin by tomorrow, if some randomly searching war machine happened upon it.

The last of the morning fog had burned away by the time Mike awoke. My consciousness focused fully on the medibay while my body executed a simple routine to walk back.

"Good morning. Still have a desire to live in the dark and sleep on rags?"

"No. Well, *sorta* no. I have a desire to turn the damn lights off and lie in the dark cursin' all creation."

"Yes, well, that's the result of having a thousand microprobes poking around in your brain."

"That's two I owe you, I guess."

"Three."

"You're supposed to say 'but who's countin'?' Anyway, other than the first, it occurs to me the rest were mostly due to my bein' with you."

"Well, yes, there is that... are you going anywhere with this? With the headache I'm sure you're having, I'm surprised you want to talk at all."

"It's been thirty days."

"I know that. I can tell you how many milliseconds it's been."

"Don't care. We had a deal. You gonna keep it?"

"It's been kept. Since I was poking around your brain anyway, I removed the explosive."

"Thanks."

"So now what?"

"Now I see what the hell I can do with your built in repair kit, then I guess we find someplace to find some decent tools and supplies."

That was somewhat surprising.

"You're not leaving? Despite it all?"

"Nah. Here's the thing, Doc... back with those IntSec guys, you could've opened the door and left. You nearly got yourself killed *not* doin' that, and unlike most people who do stupid things, you knew how stupid you were bein', down to the tenth decimal place, and you *still* did it. You didn't do it 'cause it was too much bother findin' a new sucker... I mean, it's a lot more bother if you're dead, right?"

I said nothing. I didn't really enjoy being reminded of my own irrationality.

"So that meant somethin' to me. It meant all that stuff about savin' lives, helpin' people, and actually tryin' to do some good weren't just a load of hooey. You actually thought of me as more than a useful tool made out of meat, and I respect that. A lot. It's more respect than I've had from a lot of people over the years."

"Uhm, thanks. I guess. So we are still partners?"

"Yeah. Now, how about turnin' out the lights and pumpin' me full of somethin' until this headache goes away?"

I did so.

And then I spent a lot of time thinking.

***

Days later, my mind was repaired, well, reasonably so, I still think there's things I've forgotten, but then again, how would I know? But my body was a mess. We talked about several things. First, we could head out to try to find spare parts, hoping to find some group of survivors with wounded to tend and technology to spare before we found someone we'd need to fight with or run from. The other option was to return to the caverns below, where abandoned, but still apparently functional, machinery abounded.

"So what d'you think really happened here?" Mike asked, trying to weigh both options.

"Something came in and tried to do a forced conversion. Pump the locals full of loyalty to some other side, make them keen and eager supporters. Then they send in a very small number of troops and take over, or send their new citizens, all full of properly coded DNA and possessing perfect security clearance, in as spies or agents. The problem is, they did a very poor job writing the memetic virus, or maybe the local counter-agents against such tricks did just enough to damage it. The net result was they got scrambled brains. Instead of just flipping a loyalty switch, they got some weird programming. Stay in the dark and wait for the right people to show up. Forage for food. Spread the love—that's where the claws come in. They secrete the virus."

"What happened to the town? Why is it stripped?"

"No idea. Maybe part of their instructions were to pack up everything, raw resources for their new bosses. Or something else happened. We may never know. The virus has damaged their brains so much there's really nothing left but low level instincts and a few hard-coded orders. Whoever they were is gone."

"So that means we can kill 'em? I mean, just flood the tunnels with somethin'—I'm sure you got plenty —and then take what we want without any trouble?"

I recognized a trap when I saw it.

"They're not really *people* anymore, just things in people-shaped bodies." Mike started to open his mouth. I continued. "But I'm not going to just slaughter them." Honestly, I probably could, but I could also see where Mike was going with this. "We can probably take them out peacefully. Let them continue to live their lives of mindless instinct." A bit more bitterness crept into my voice than I'd intended. It really wasn't directed at them, or at Mike. I know it might sound odd, but to my way of thinking, killing someone is more merciful than destroying their identity. So much of modern warfare is mind games, from focused propaganda to literal brain rewiring. Yes, I've used trust boosters. I'm not claiming I'm perfect. I have never done anything which permanently changed someone, though. I have to have a few lines I simply won't cross.

"Sounds like a plan. Hm. Any thoughts on those others—the uniformed guys?"

"Some poor souls who wandered in here, the same as we did, and didn't get out."

"Wonder if anyone's lookin' for 'em."

"We will almost certainly never know."

Yeah. Prophecy really was my least developed skill.

***

Once we were prepared for what awaited us, the actual work was easy. Harmless knockout gas flooded the tunnels, and we had a few hours to dissect the machines. I removed the dead bodies from our previous foray, and under Mike's conscience-inducing glare, set some broken bones and otherwise helped the injured escape pain and crippling deformity. In a way, this was a payoff for him not haranguing me about the fate of the corpses; he understood the necessity but disliked the reality.

We found some of the parts we needed. Holes were patched, and assorted pipes, tubes, and wires were replaced or spliced. I wasn't operating at anywhere near optimal specifications, but at least the alert messages were down to 'Seek Maintenance' instead of 'Compose Your Will.'

We spent about two days there. Once, a low-flying drone passed by, and we planned to leave, but it never came back and didn't summon any army of killer robots to take us out. The vermin and such which the tunnel dwellers ate didn't appeal, but that was one reason we'd traded for food at most of our stops. Mike contemplated hunting for wild game, but between plague bearing animals and the risk of stumbling over some minefield or just tripping an automated beacon, we decided against it. Besides, there was a lot of repair work to do. I mostly sat there, soaking up sunlight and cracking hydrogen, until the tanks were full. I had power for a week, at least, with no downtime.

I also helped Mike with the repairs. Besides the obvious utility of being able to monitor the flow of power, water, or blood through various damage systems and instantly find bad spots, I could provide a second pair of hands to speed things along. I had complete files on my own construction, of course, but not Mike's skill in how to interpret them, how to know by near-instinct which feedlines could be safely bypassed and which were vital, or just how much beyond the rated specifications a support bracket could be burdened.

It was an oddly restful time.

Nonetheless, we needed to move on. There was a chance whoever had sent the memetic virus—if it wasn't just a random by-blow of some automated system gone wonky—would check on the results. The complete stripping of the town worried both of us. The overflying probe, despite no apparent consequence, was a nagging fear. So we set out, studying the maps we'd built, looking for a path.

South was mostly desert, dotted by small towns which had, in the past, been part of the Protectorates or claimed by one of the Families. Given the intensity of the wars between those two city-states, we despaired of finding stable settlers or even peaceful nomads. Farther east, our limited intel suggested deathfields, barriers tens of miles long, with accompanying support vehicles patrolling far beyond the limits. Further east was Deseret, and, well, we didn't know what state it was in or how well defended it was, but we didn't want to breach it.

The northwest still looked promising, away from the coasts. Lots of wilderness, small towns, mostly isolated from the primary attacks. The thing about the Collapse is, it was *fast*. The complex balance of treaty and alliance and common ancestral culture which bound the fractured states together in a condition of chaotic equilibrium simply imploded, and the resulting chaos took out the big population centers almost instantly. The same forces which led to the breakup of the old nation states, though—autonomy, independence, distributed systems—kept the neonations coherent even after the first apocalyptic wave, and with the big weapons spent in one massive orgy of devastation, it all became a conflict of small forces against small forces, a guerilla war fought on a national scale. All warfare had become unconventional. The result was ever-shifting borders, ever-changing actions, and the wars not so much ending as petering out when it became apparent no one was sure anymore if what they were fighting for still existed. The upshot was, if we stayed north of the deathline which cut over the former northern border of the UBA, we could find, we were sure, a lot of people to help with only a minimal risk of stumbling across anything we couldn't outrun. We had few illusions about our ability to outfight anything that seriously wanted to kill us.

We were less than an hour out of our hideaway when it happened.

I was cruising contentedly along, alert for the usual— scavenger bots, people hidden in roadside crevices, and so on— when something went *wrong* and the Heim field flared and died, sending me skidding along the half-broken asphalt. I depowered the field and then tried to start it up again, but all it did was send assorted warning gauges flaring back into the red; if I kept it up, it would be burned out.

It was pretty obvious what it was. Charged superconductor netting. Normally, that sort of thing flares on the magnetic sensors, making it obvious, but this was powered down and triggered. There were two possibilities: it was an automatic trap, laid by some passing 'bot, and we could probably cut the net and get moving again quickly, or it was manually controlled to catch vehicles moving down this road, and whoever placed it would be swarming out to examine their prize.

Luck not being in good supply—at least not *good* luck— it was the latter.

For a second or two, we waited. No one was appearing. Then a voice spoke.

"We don't need Calvers, but we're willing to cut a deal with you, robot."

Any hope they had of getting on my good side had just died.

I dropped the neural field over Mike and brought the railgun and missile launchers online. I also scanned the roadside. The voice had come from everywhere, echoing through the air from multiple directions, probably some sort of distributed speaker system, to prevent me from targeting a single source. Also, almost nothing special on IR—heat cloak suits? Visual was useless, too.

Someone knew me, and Mike, and knew what I was. That

pretty much meant Reno IntSec... but there was no way they had dug out that fast, or tracked me down this far. It was a puzzle. I also needed to stall for time and work out a targeting solution while I was immobile and they were invisible. Damn it, I had just been repaired!

"I'm afraid you have the advantage of me. I don't think I can deal when I don't know who I'm talking to."

"Captain Tollman sends his regards. He's willing to be reasonable. You're useful to us; your pet human, well, not so much."

I'm pretty sure that didn't win over Mike. Then again, they weren't trying to.

OK. Voice distribution was a pretty basic trick. I could still build echo patterns for each source. Looked to have about six points of origin. There was probably distortion involved, but I at least had some idea how many people I was dealing with. IR useless, visual useless... I pinged.

I normally don't use sonic sensors. They're painfully obvious. They're a great big sign reading "Please shoot here for valuable prizes." Of course, when I was already surrounded by hostiles...

What happened next happened fast.

First, I started sending out pulses to try to sort out the highwaymen from the highway. The first few echoes started coming back, and targeting algorithms fed them into the neural HUD Mike was hooked into. He saw targets and began to turn the gun on the nearest one.

Someone must have picked up the sonics and realized what I was doing. There are ways to hide from sonics—sound baffling fields, distortion drones, a half dozen other things—but they usually require foreknowledge. Probably they'd looked up my specs and determined I didn't have an echolocation targeting system. If they'd had any brains, they're have realized I also wasn't spec'ed for missiles, but hey, there they were. That might have tipped them off, but it didn't. Call it one small bit of luck. I'd still like to know how they found me.

Anyway, having determined I was spotting them, they apparently decided that if they couldn't take me alive, they'd take what they could. Hard rounds began pouring down. We'd actually taken the time to bolt some extra plating on back at the coral town, and it was helping, but I was hardly invulnerable. Mike dropped one, then another, and there was a flurry as they moved behind hard cover, once they realized how non-invisible they were. I sped up a bit, not enough to burn myself out, but enough to let me do some battlefield analysis. The constant hail of bullets became a steady thumping, the time between each one dragging out, as I studied the outlines revealed by the sonics.

One of them had produced a shoulder mounted rocket launcher, and my acquisition warning sensors were happily telling me I was being targeted. I figured I had about a second to live. Just in case it used any kind of electronic targeting, I fired up every ECM system I had, but I knew it was hopeless; at this close range, it would be almost impossible for it to miss.

As I watched in accelerated time, the man with the launcher lurched suddenly, his back arching in what looked to be considerable pain, then his front exploding as several bullets came through it. The weapon aimed upwards and the rocket flew randomly, destroying an overhang and killing an unfortunate coyote. Confusion and chaos seized the others, who momentarily stopped shooting at me to find and target their new nemesis.

Mike wasted little time. Using the constantly updated echolocation info and my own target tracking algorithms, he took down two of the attackers quickly, even as they began making themselves much less vulnerable. I suited up and exited, not even bothering with camo—I had no IR shielding on my body and it was obvious the attackers could track in that spectrum—and began working on disabling the net while still providing targeting info to Mike. One more fell, and then the remaining two were moving through thick trees, trying mostly to get away. Then there was the third figure.

I tried to get full data. Visual was obscured, as was IR, and sonic was partially scattered. The best thing I could do was track the shots as he moved rapidly from point to point.

He never missed. Not once.

Each bullet fired found its target. A hand to blast away a gun, a kneecap to stall and cripple, a headshot to kill. He moved constantly while firing, aware his enemies could track and target him, never standing still long enough to be perfectly caught. The fight had moved deeper into the woods, and I was only getting fragments of data now. A proper military vehicle would easily overcome personal protection measures, of course, but I was working with off-spec gear installed via careful jury-rigging.

The last survivor was being more cautious, doing all he could to keep cover between himself and the enemy—and us. This rather limited his range of motion. He fumbled at his belt and detached a small object, running his thumb along it. A light ticking added to the sounds I was picking up, and he tossed it.

It exploded in mid-air, struck by a bullet.

OK. Now I was impressed, even as the shock waves rolled over me. There was one more shot, and the last survivor was no longer a survivor. He fell, missing a good portion of his head.

I rechecked the scans. The sonics of each gun were different; it was easy to isolate the bullets fired by the interloper. (The gun was a late model Smith & Wesson iron-core caseless, switchable autofire, biometrics standard, 30-shot magazine, auto-stabilizing, if anyone was wondering.) Each shot was followed by a deliberate, targeted, impact. "Impressive" didn't begin to cover it.

Our savior—or possibly 'the person who wanted to make sure they killed us, not the other guys'—staggered against a tree, then seemed to catch his breath. Holding his weapon out, he deactivated the various defensive mechanisms: the camo holograms, the sonic distorters, the heat dampers. The battlesuit was designed for stealth, not protection; it had only a few ceramic inserts over key areas. It allowed great mobility, though, and when fully activated made one nigh-invisible except to active scanners or probability-overlapping fire prediction algorithms. He took a few steps forward, then collapsed. Without the various disguises, I could see a number of tears in the suit, and spreading patterns of dampness. Blowing up the grenade had saved his life, but he hadn't evaded all injury.

"We're going to need to do this outside," I told Mike. "At least I have to see if we can move him safely. You handle the net, I'll take the medicine."

"Sure." He hopped out, nervously scanning in case some third force might suddenly arrive, then moved to begin work on deactivating the trap that held me in place. I took the mobile kit and rushed to the side of our unknown benefactor.

First, I was impressed he wasn't dead. Not from the wounds per se, though he was a mess. The impact of the grenade should have stunned him, immobilized him for at least a few seconds, and the last IntSec officer ought to have killed him handily. How he stayed up after that, I didn't understand.

Second, he was a she. A matter of only minor medical importance. I probably shouldn't make assumptions of gender, but writing 'he or she' every time I encounter someone of momentarily indeterminate gender is just tedious, and while the UBA has quite a selection of alternative pronouns encompassing every variation on physical, mental, and post-natal gender, I admit to being somewhat of a traditionalist in that regard. It actually got me a few mandatory consciousness raising seminars during my early years.

Anyway, she was covered with shrapnel lacerations, made worse by the use of body-temperature sensitive memory metals in the grenade. Metal fragments fly in, react to moisture and body heat, and grow nasty, nasty barbs. I started doing all the standard scans, building up a quick baseline so I could figure out what to do first. My main goal was making sure she was stable enough to move safely to the medibay.

Significant internal bleeding, no evident broken bones, riddled with shrapnel, though not too deep, thanks to the suit, EKG—

OK, that was weird.

High levels of neural induction fibers throughout the body. Typical of those who regularly interface with—but no, it was still too high. Strange patterns, too. Unusual clustering in the right...

Oh. Oh my. This *was* interesting.

I shot her up with painkillers and coagulants, and sent a full scan of her blood back to the ambulance, where it began mixing up the proper blend to replace what she was rapidly losing. I heard a welcome hum and a whoosh behind me, and a shout of triumph from Mike. He'd evidently disabled the net.

I flipped open the medibay door. "Mike! Get the stretcher over here!"

"He gonna make it?"

"Probably, once I get her inside. Hurry!"

It didn't take long before she was secure in the medibay. The main problem was the shrapnel. Remove, sew. Remove, sew. Blood, which was everywhere, could be sucked up, processed, filtered, and fed back into her. I had Mike check for damage from the gunfire I'd received while I worked. I needed to talk to her.

She was of average height, well muscled, and fit. Genetic scans showed minor changes. Improved muscle texture, an inner ear remodeled to enhance balance and resist disorientation, eyes extended to infrared and ultraviolet, adaptive programmable immune system. In terms of non-biological modifications, she had subdermal armor and a small built in comm rig, much like the one I installed in Mike. She had reddish hair, cropped short, and signs of scarring, deliberately retained. Someone liked her war souvenirs. While Mike was momentarily out, I woke her up.

"Hi. I'm Doctor MacIntyre, and you're going to be fine. You'll need to go back to sleep soon, but I wanted to talk quickly before my partner shows up. Just a matter of politeness. Your condition... is it something you prefer to be public or private about?"

"Private..." her voice was a hoarse whisper.

"Fine. I respect that. I just needed to know." I flipped the sedatives back on, and she drifted into a dreamless sleep.

Something bubbled to the top of my consciousness. Her suit had the same triangles-and-circle logo as the men we'd met in the tunnels a few miles south. It might be she was looking for others from her unit, whatever it was. That was going to be a fun conversation, once she was capable of having one.

Mike knocked on the back of the bay. "You done in there, Doc? Can we move?"

"Sure. Get in the front. I don't want to break the contamination seal just yet."

Mike clambered in the cab; my body was stored, once again, in the sleeping bay. I set off on our previous trajectory, making sure to keep the Heim field at maximum stability, even at a slight cost to speed and power.

"So... what's her story? I mean, why'd she help us?"

"No idea. Honestly, she might have just wanted to claim the prize herself."

"You really think so?"

"No. But the way things have been going lately, I'm starting to get very cynical."

"An' yet, here you are, constantly riskin' your life in order to help those in need."

"I never said I was consistent. It's an overrated virtue."

He snerked. That's a neologism I coined to describe his habit of snorting and smirking simultaneously. Feel free to make use of it.

Anyway, about two hours later, she started shaking it off. I tapped into her comm link.

"How are you feeling?"

There was a pause, then the subvocalization came through. "Like I almost took a grenade to the face. You?"

"Like I was shot at. Now that the banter is over with, I need to know if you were planning on killing us."

"Do you ask *all* your patients that?"

"Just the ones who show up very unexpectedly in the middle of an ambush by enemies who shouldn't have had any way to know where we were."

"Ah. Well, if it makes you feel any better, no, it wasn't pure coincidence. They were tracking you; I was tracking them."

The EKG I had monitoring her was, of course, completely useless for determining if she was lying. I decided to assume, against my instincts, that she was being at least partially truthful, that her sins, as it were, would be of omission, not commission.

"OK. Well, if it's not giving away secrets, let me know. How did they know where to find me?"

"From what I learned, you managed to seriously piss off some of their fellow officers a few days ago. I think they're still digging out of the cave. Pretty funny, if you ask me. Anyway, no matter how messy basic data traffic is now, a good old comm laser works. High tech smoke signals."

"Let me guess. The people you were tracking have access to a low-flying probe drone?"

"Yes. Not sure how they keep it flying with all the anti-aircraft systems buzzing out there, but they do. Or maybe they just have a lot stored up. I'm guessing you're putting the pieces together."

"Yes. I'm going to guess you had an inside man."

"I did. He wasn't in the bunch which attacked you, naturally. He fed me their movements and plans as part of a longstanding deal we had. I was hoping to meet you beforehand, warn you."

"Why?"

"Simple. I wanted to hire your services. I think I might need them. I'm with Havington Freelance Security... well, they were the last people to give me a formal paycheck. Actually, my squad has been sort of freelancing on our own for the past few years."

"There's a lot of that going around."

"Anyway, we've been losing people. The squad's been shrinking bit by bit. About two weeks ago, I went off to do some solo scouting, with a plan to rendezvous at—can you bring up a map? I assume you've got a neural interface back here."

I could, and I did. A detailed map of the area snapped into being in the medibay. She studied it.

"I headed down to there..." At a thought, a blue dot appeared on the map. "They were supposed to go along that road..." A red line traced their path. "And we were to meet over there." A second blue dot.

Right along the red line was the coral village. I had a feeling that was going to be the case.

One of the most important phrases in every doctor's vocabulary is "I'm afraid I have some bad news for you." It's not one you like to use, but it's one you have to. People always pale when they hear those words from doctor, whether it's about themselves, a spouse, a child, or a cat. She was no different. Her EKG barely flickered, which didn't surprise me, but there was a pause in her voice.

"What?" Her voice was dead, flat, controlled.

I told her. About the coral village, about the underground, about the memetic virus, about where I'd seen the markings on her uniform before. She asked me again and again, how many. She asked—demanded, really—that I show her the recordings of what we'd seen. One by one, she named them. "That was Glen. Glen Brackeleen. Worst poker player I ever met. The one—the one behind him, Jose Masatako. Sung opera. Badly. Miles Aayashia. Our own medic. Those were the three who jumped you." She paused. "No offense, Doctor MacIntyre, but if they'd been in anything like their right minds and had wanted to attack you, they'd have torn you to pieces and probably built a still with what was left."

"I spotted a few more in the general crowd. I don't know if I have clear enough scans for you to identify them, but—"

"Don't bother. I get it." There was a long pause. "I guess I won't be needing you after all. I was worried that they'd been injured, that they needed help, hoping some of them would be alive and just couldn't make the meeting point..." She let herself trail off. I remained silent. "Let me off at the next settlement you find. I'll figure out what to do from there. Damn."

"I can do that. In the meanwhile, I don't have any DNA on you and I didn't see ident of any sort. What do you want me to call you?"

"Jill. Jill Huochong."

Oh, you have got to be kidding me. "You don't look Chinese."

She shrugged. "A few generations of genetic tinkering, exogamy, and experimental social arrangements, and who ties physical appearance to name anymore?"

"And no one bothered looking it up?"

"I don't think anyone cared. If they did, they didn't think much of it. You wouldn't expect someone named Smith to be pounding out horseshoes, would you?"

"No, no, I guess not." She closed her eyes, perhaps tired of staring at the ceiling, or the various monitors displaying her statistics. (They were there for the benefit of patients, or of any humans I had working with me.) "I should let you rest. You know, if you want, we could head back. There's a few of your people still alive. Well, physically."

She pondered this. "Is there any chance of them being recoverable? Most memetic viruses aren't so... extreme. It's cheaper to just kill people."

I pondered lying. Hope is potent medicine. Hope inevitably dashed, though...

"No. This was badly botched, or it was intended to do something I can't understand. I honestly think some steinkid mixed it up without understanding what he was doing. I mean, claws? When airborne is faster?"

"Maybe I'll get to meet him some day." There was a sudden, rather predatory, grin. I realized that under no circumstances did I want to be the subject of that smile. "I'm tired. Do me a favor, knock me out for a bit. There's a lot of pain here and I'm worn out from fighting it off."

"Sure." I added a bit more sedative to the mix, and her body soon dropped into a healing slumber.

I had been listening to Mike with a small percentage of my consciousness, almost using an Eliza algorithm to keep up my end of the conversation.

"...so anyway, that's when we all got booted out from the brothel. Kate was lucky she didn't get her eye confiscated. The next day, well, I guess word got 'round an' I was back to Private for the third, nah, fourth time. How 'bout you? Ever bounce up and down the rank ladder?"

"No, I haven't been bounced up... no, no I haven't. I'm afraid my career is a bit less colorful than yours. I always did the good little soldier thing. I took it all very, very, seriously. Sometimes, I think..." My voice trailed off. I still didn't want to go into the Morowitz affair. I'd only now really begun to gain Mike's genuine trust, and I had a good feeling how he'd react to that tale. I was so sure I was *right*, though! Someone once said that the epitaph for all humanity would be 'It seemed like a good idea at the time.'

"Heh. Doc, you really got to learn to live a little. Speaking of livin'... how's our patient?"

"Physically, she's fine."

"That was... qualified. What's up?"

I wondered how much I could tell him without violating doctor-patient ethics. I decided the basic facts weren't very secret.

"It looks like she's the last survivor of her squad. I'm not sure how much that's really sunk into her just yet. Also, the fact we beat up her friends might not sit well with her once she's had time to mull it all over."

"When did we...?"

"Coral town. The ones in the uniforms. Her ex-squadmates."

"Oh. Does she know?"

"I had to tell her, but she was pretty doped up when I did. The facts got through, but knowing something isn't the same as understanding it."

He nodded. "So what this means is, you're gonna be takin' the straps off her slowly. Hey, I didn't notice... you did disarm her, right? She's really good with that gun of hers, and if she decides we could've done more for—or less to—her pals, she could do some serious damage. I'm tired of splicin' up blood pipes back there."

"No. I left her with her weapon."

Or something like that.

Chapter 7

I let Jill sleep until we came upon our goal, a small settlement conveniently out of the easiest paths of travel. Heim field vehicles are rare and expensive; I'm a pretty high-end craft. Wheeled vehicles are common, but they require a serious infrastructure. Tracked and walking vehicles form the majority of what's still moving, but every passing day sees more and more of them break down. One reason for this is how easy it is, or was, to make ultralight, unmanned, non-aware autonomous flyers. Cover them with solar cells, give them micromissiles, stock them with tiny repair bots that can leech necessary metals from the local environment and patch them up, and the damn things can function for years if they're not totally destroyed.

Self-repair has limits. There's no cheap matter transmutation despite decades of self-congratulatory press releases predicting it. The smaller and simpler the craft, the better it can fix itself, and of course, you run into the 'who repairs the repairers' problem. There's a point where, without primary manufacturers to pump new blood into the process, cascade failures cause things to break down, and that's the point we were reaching. It would have taken a lot longer if there weren't so many forces actively seeking to destroy anything which they couldn't identify as an ally-of-the-moment.

I'm going on about this by way of clarifying how the world might look to someone reading this without full context. To me, settlements and isolated towns and nomad camps are separated by hours. To most of the people I deal with, though, they're separated by days, and unless you have access to lasers or other tightly focused, hard-to-disrupt communications gear, speed of data and speed of matter are the same thing. As I said, old west time. Except with insane robots blowing up the telegraph poles and eating the railway tracks. Civilization isn't spreading out, it's being forced back. Whether this is the beginning of a long dark age or just a few years of hell, I don't know. I know what I wish, and I know what I believe, and they aren't the same thing.

My intel had told me there was a town here, one of uncounted small communities which sprang up around some shared interest and which maintained limited independence under the broad authority of the larger neonation whose claimed territory it happened to be in. Basically, they paid a small tax for defense and didn't do anything that seriously violated any major treaties. This one was putatively part of the former NWA, which worried me a little. It had been three years since the last major fighting, and I wasn't exactly flying UBA colors, but even so, it wasn't just robots that carried grudges long past their expiration dates.

As usual, I slowed down a good way outside of their protective fence and began broadcasting in an open voice. "Greetings. I am Doctor MacIntyre, and I offer medical services in exchange for food and supplies. I am armed but I am not hostile. Please let me know if I am violating any boundaries or if you wish me too—"

I stopped talking. Coils of smoke were visible as I cleared the bend. The perimeter was a cratered wasteland. The settlement itself was mostly ruins. A quick sweep showed no apparent active defenses. I pulled up to a stop.

Mike was staring out the window, and at the IR map I was building.

"I thought—I thought maybe someone was movin'. Got a glimpse through that big hole in the wall. Survivors or—?"

"—Or whoever did this." I switched on the medibay speakers. "Jill? We're about to enter what might be hostile territory. I can leave you here, or..."

"Let me up. I'll be fine."

"No. You won't be." I flipped to subvocalization. I didn't think Mike could hear a spoken conversation through the medibay, but why take chances?

"You might choose not to feel it, but you will be ripping stitches and risking internal bleeding. As your doctor, I can't allow it." I tried to keep the snippiness out of my voice, and failed.

"Can't?!" Oh great. Now she was angry. Didn't need an EKG to see that. She pulled at the restraints. "Let.me—ugh!"

"They're designed to deal with people upgraded through Class-III artificial limbs. Keep trying and you'll break your own arms without realizing it. Just relax control and feel how hurt you are."

She did, and gasped.

"All right," she almost spit. "You win. In case you die, put in an auto-evacuate program and let me out when I'm safe."

"Of course."

"And give me a feed back here. I want to see what you're doing."

I flipped on two, my own body's and what I was getting from Mike. "There. Enjoy the show."

The two of us went out, Mike as, well, Mike, and me in full disguise. I decided to leave the camo off for the moment; if they weren't hostile, I didn't want to look like *we* were. I pondered the complexities of explaining who I was, if Mike was "Doctor MacIntyre," but I decided having both of us out there was worth the risk. I could spin a convincing tissue of lies later.

The exterior of the town was typical. A somewhat hastily constructed exterior barricade, now shattered. It looked like it might hold off wandering bandits or discourage drones looking for an easy target. Two EMP gun emplacements were obvious; the guns themselves had been stripped. Here and there, the mangled remains of a sensor array could be seen. The actual wall, ten feet of reinforced neocrete, had been blasted clean through in several places; the main gate, something made of pieces of armor plate poorly welded together, was half molten. Lingering hot spots of background radiation caused me to let out a low whistle. Someone had portable fusion and the power to waste it on a podunk town like this.

Mike slowly scouted ahead, peered quickly through one of the blast holes, jerked back, waited for answering fire, then, when he received none, risked a longer look. He gestured to me, and we walked through into an all-too-familiar slice of hell.

The town itself was nothing special. Flat, low, buildings designed to maximize surface area, glistening with spray-on solar collectors. Sweeping, curving roads drifting in and around the housing clusters. No obvious signs or markers; if I'd wanted to see everyone's expressions of personal taste, I could tap into the data overlays and expose myself to a swarm of viruses and ads. Scratch that—hand-lettered signs and painted symbols told me the overlay network here was long gone. A cluster of larger buildings at the center, and a moderately sized fabrication center to provide whatever couldn't be made easily enough at home.

And the bodies, of course.

This is one of those times when I would prefer to lie about my emotions. In situations where I am dealing with the long-since aftermath of a battle, I can grow philosophical. In the current situation, in what was still possibly an active combat zone, I suppressed all navel-gazing on the meaning of life in favor of making sure mine didn't end, and that I could do my job.

First thing, look for hostiles. Every scan I made showed no one outside the buildings. We'd picked up heat sources on approach, and Mike had seen someone, but now... nothing. The buildings, well made and insulated, showed nothing within; even the windows were close to perfectly neutral.

Mike moved cautiously, sticking close to walls and checking all possible angles of attack before dashing on. I was doing the same, but where he was looking for enemies, I was looking for patients. The dead were, seemingly, all locals, but there were signs they'd been armed. I didn't see any weapons remaining, but it would be a rather odd fashion statement to have a holster and no gun. Likewise, I found bodies in places which were clearly impromptu hardpoints, partially shielded from fire, and positioned so as to imply they were fighting back when they were killed. Lastly, patches of blood were present without bodies, sometimes with deformed bullets nearby.

So. Whoever did this cleaned up their own bodies—dead or not—and also stripped out any weapons. They left the local corpses to rot. That the cleanup seemed complete—and from the way the blood was drying, had happened a good two hours ago—led me to believe the attackers had cleared out.

I listened. There was a sound... rasping breath, a scraping noise, as of someone twitching or moving slightly. I targeted it. A heartbeat, very faint and quite strained, but it was there. Pinpointed. A woman, behind a low stone wall, busily bleeding to death and passing in and out of consciousness. I raced to her. Out of the corner of my eye, I saw Mike watching me move rapidly and in the open. He closed his eyes, shook his head, then positioned himself to cover me.

Her chest was a ragged mess. Most of her left lung was gone; the fact she was alive at all told me she'd had some sort of modifications. Probably auto-constricting blood vessels, preventing her from bleeding out instantly. Judging from the wound, the assailants were using chestbursters, bullets with microexplosives trigged by contact with blood. (They usually had plastic shells, stripped when fired, to prevent the obvious accidents.) It had barely scraped her, or she wouldn't have a torso at all. In any event, modifications or not, she had very little time.

I contacted Mike. "I don't think the people who did this are still here. Hurry. I need to get her back, quickly." I flipped open my medikit. Coagulant foam. Fill the big hole that's where her lung used to be. Wait a second for it to settle. Then—

Then I get shot at. A bullet whizzed past me, slightly cracking the wall of the house behind me.

"Get away! Get away from her!"

Mike dropped, rolled behind some cover, and got the shooter in his sights. I could see the laser painting a nice target point on his head. Mike wasn't inclined to kill easily, but he also wasn't inclined to sit there thinking when people were shooting at him.

I dropped the medikit and raised my hands. I spoke loudly. "It's all right. I'm a... medic. I'm with Doctor MacIntyre over there." I waved my hand, very slightly. "This woman is badly injured, but alive. Let me—us—do our job!"

"Stand up! Turn around!"

I did so. I also kept talking.

"While I'm just your assistant, Doctor, it looks pretty bad. She'll need extensive surgery, and soon. Perhaps you could come over here and take a look."

I got to see the person shooting at me. Male, early forties, hair a translucent metallic silver. He had a fairly old-style longarm, looked to be a hunting or sport weapon. Single shot, small magazine, cased ammo. I didn't bother looking up the exact make and model. It wasn't important.

"Don't move!"

Mike's face contorted into his "annoyed with stupidity" look; I kept mine studiously neutral, though I shared his feelings. There's advantages, sometimes, to having your emotions detached from your body. I also began powering up my Heim field. I wasn't sure if it was going to be fight or flight at this point, but I was prepared for anything.

Jill felt the vehicle start to life, heard the hum of the engines. "What's happening?"

"Hopefully, nothing."

"I'm not known to put much stock in hope. Let me loose!"

"If I have to run, you're better off restrained. If I don't, there's no point."

"Damn it! Do you have idea how *frustrating* it is to be this helpless?"

I thought back to Mike and his little trick with the power supply. Yes. Yes, I did.

"Fine. It's your funeral. Please note you're being released against medical advice. This could impact your insurance claims."

She laughed. She had a short, almost coughing, laugh. The laugh turned into a slight wince as muscles pulled against newly-stitched wounds. Then she straightened, showing no further pain, as I opened the rear doors. I sent her a full tactical map—me, Mike, our unknown shooter... oh, yes, Mike was talking.

"Look, use your brain. Whoever did this is history. We're tryin' to help. Why else would we even be here?"

"After the wolves are done with their kill, the buzzards move in." The man sneered. "It wouldn't surprise me to know you're their camp followers, cleaning up whatever they left behind." He swung the rifle around, taking in both of us. "Now get away."

I was listening to the woman's heartbeat. It was growing more labored, and the wheezing breaths she was barely managing to take were growing weaker.

"If we don't do something soon, she's dead." I paused. "Right, doctor?"

"Yeah—yeah, right." He took careful aim at the man with the gun. "So let us do our jobs!"

"No, no. I'm not going to. We've had enough here, we've—"

She spasmed, choking, gasping for air. I turned to see what I could do. The man, startled by my motion, whipped his gun around.

There was a loud crack, and a scream. It wasn't mine. I wasn't Mike's.

The man was bent almost double, the ruin of his hand wedged between his knees. The shattered gun lay at his feet. Jill kept a bead on him.

"Reach for the gun, and you lose your left knee. Try it after that, and I kill you for being too stupid to live." Then she looked at me. "Can you still save her?"

"I... We can try. *Doctor*," I said to Mike. "Can you help me?"

Others were peering out from behind doorframes or beneath rubble. Jill called out loudly.

"They're not raiders. They're not here to hurt you."

The suddenly-one-handed man cursed. "The hell you're not!"

Jill grinned that wonderful predator's grin. "I said *they're* not here to hurt you. If you don't let them help you, *I'm* here to hurt you."

I flashed her a quick message, even as Mike ran for the stretcher and I desperately searched for drugs to keep my patient alive for even a few more minutes. The other lung was filling with blood, some injured tissue holding back the torrent had finally given way.

"Hurry!" I sent to Mike.

"Goin' as fast I can." he sent back.

It was a painful minute. We had a good half-dozen people watching, most armed, and Jill making it clear that the first person to twitch would lose a limb. The injured man curled around his hand was a remarkably effective deterrent. I'd have to do something about that; he was losing a lot of blood, but he was not in nearly as much danger as my current patient.

Mike had just gotten the stretcher there when her heart stopped.

I grabbed the microdefibrillator and applied it. It attached itself to her chest and began working; as it did its job, I hit her with the standard mix of drugs, mostly atropine derivatives and the like. Something did the trick; her heart started up again, barely. The defibrillator unhooked itself and folded back together.

We got her on the stretcher, and moved. A few of the people now peeking out of the remaining buildings made half-hearted attempts to stop us, attempts which Jill managed to nullify with a minor twitch.

This wasn't going to go well; I knew it.

In under a minute, we had her transferred to the medibay, and I dropped control of the Charlie and focused every cycle I had on her. Synthetic blood went in as actual blood, from her lung, went out. I had a dozen manipulators running over her body, patching holes, tying together organs, scanning for necrotic tissue and slicing it off, running DNA scans to see what I had in stock which might be compatible, finding out if she was allergic to anything...

Five seconds in, I knew it was too late. I kept it up for an hour. I'd been wrong before, after all.

Finally, I let her go. Her body was running on pure stimulus, her heart spasmodically pumping only because the cells were too drugged up to know when to quit. Her brain was a chaotic storm, slowly fading out, a hurricane of thought fading into an inchoate mass of neural dust devils. I made sure the passage was painless.

I wanted to shoot someone. The thought fired through me, and

I felt the railgun responding. Mike heard it, too.

"Uhm, Doc..."

"What?"

"Who're you plannin' on shootin' at?"

It was an interesting question. I didn't have a ready answer. I did, however, take the gun offline.

"No one. Everyone. I don't know. I'm pissed and there's nothing I can do about it."

"This can't be the first patient you've lost. No one's *that* good."

"It's the first one I've lost due to the stupidity of the people on the same damn side!"

"Same side as who? Last I checked, we were UBA vets; this is NWA territory, and Jill out there's a freelancer out of Vegas. I'm no happier about this than you are, and I wouldn't mind rubbin' their noses in their own stupidity, but I can't say I don't understand why they're actin' like they are. Especially since they got shot up not long ago."

Shot up—damn, I was acting like an idiot.

"Go out there. Talk to them. I'll... tell them I did all I could. Well, you will... my words. You know what I mean! And we need to see who else we can save. There's others, there have to be."

Mike got up and prepared to leave. "There's one guy missin' a hand. I think he's next..."

There was no way to keep the sneer from my voice. "No. He's last. We take care of everyone else first, right down to their athlete's foot and hangnails."

Mike looked shocked. "I'm guessin' he was her husband, or brother, or friend... you can't go..."

"I made the exact same deduction. And I *can* go. His stupidity and fear killed this woman."

Mike had been halfway out the door. He slammed it shut and yelled at the emptiness. "No, a deity-damned chestburster killed this woman! Put the blame where it belongs, Doc, on the bastards exploitin' this chaos, not the people sick and frightened by it! And y'know what? As long as *I'm* Doctor MacIntyre, I will be doin' the triage, or I just walk. I wonder if Little Miss Triggerhappy there would be willin' to put up with your shit."

"Fine. *Doctor.* You decide."

He walked out there. By this point, the small crowd had reached a stalemate with Jill, and no longer considered threatening her; two of them had bandaged their wounded comrade's hand. When they saw Mike emerge, there was a mix of fear, hope, and anger. The grim, set, look on his face turned the hope to ash, leaving just the others.

He walked over to the injured man.

Well, your stupidity killed her. How do you feel? I tried to say thorough Mike's voice, but he fought me back.

"I'm sorry. We did all we could, uh, my assistant an' me, but... the damage was too great. No one could've done anythin'. I'm sorry. I really am."

LIAR! I shouted in his mind.

"If you have other wounded, we can take care of 'em. If you don't... or if you just want us to leave you alone after what you've been through... we understand."

The injured man, now pale and trembling, grief layered on top of rage and pain, shouted. "Damn right you can leave! Get away, get away now! Leave her... leave her body, I don't want you carving it up for..."

"Harold, shut the God damned hell up."

The speaker was another man, with long black hair and that kind of anagathic-aided face which could be anywhere from thirty to eighty. His arm was crudely bandaged; so was his leg. "I'm sorry, sir. You came during a tragedy."

Mike shrugged. "Well, I'm a doctor. Field work is my specialty. I'm used to tragedy. I'd like to prevent more, if I can. Do you have other survivors who need aid?"

"Other than what you see, we're it. We thought—we thought Zeph was dead. She looked it. I didn't... no one wanted to take too close a look."

Mike nodded in understanding. He then glanced over at Jill. "I think you can stand down, now."

She gave a quick 'just try something' glance to the crowd and holstered her gun. She looked over at Harold, seemed to contemplate, just for an instant, a gruff 'Sorry,' then decided against it.

"I'll be back in the ambulance. Don't get shot."

"Is she... uhm... your bodyguard, or something?"

"Patient."

"Oh." He mulled that over for a bit. There was then a prolonged awkwardness, which Mike shattered.

"You there... Harold, was it? You should head on back to my vehicle. My assistant can—" He stopped to think. "Actually, I'd better take a look at that hand." *I know enough to know if you're messing around,* he subvocalized to me.

Harold glanced at Mike, back at me, barely visible beyond the shattered barricade, and Jill's retreating form. He seemed less than certain. Mike smiled. "It's OK, I get it. I'm sorry things worked out the way they did, but let me try to make some of it better, all right? That wound's at risk for infection, and, actually, all of you that got hurt, I oughta run some tests and... things." Mike's osmosis-acquired medical knowledge was still a bit sparse. "Be helpful if I knew what happened here, though. Can anyone tell me? Uhm... while I'm workin', I guess."

Mike and Harold began walking back to me. I had a quick conversation with Jill.

"While I think we're both grateful for what you did, was it really necessary?"

"You mean, I should have let you die?"

"No... I mean, you could have blown away his gun, not his hand."

She nodded slightly. "Yes. I could have." She stopped then, as if that said all that needed to be said on the subject. A few seconds later, she added. "I also think I've torn open a few of your stitches. I'm not sure, but I think there's internal bleeding near my right kidney. I'd be thankful if you'd take care of it."

"I warned you."

She carefully clambered into the medibay and lay down in the left bed. "Saying 'I told you so' is a sign of immaturity."

I began pumping sedative into her, while prepping the other bed for Harold. "What do you call rushing to a gunfight against your doctor's orders?"

"Necessary..." She felt the sedative taking hold and let her body relax into unconsciousness.

Meanwhile, Harold and Mike arrived. Mike looked around the medibay carefully, trying to assure himself Jill was actually unconscious. After deciding she was, he turned back to Mike.

"Where's that other guy?"

"Uh, up front. Doin' some work on the fuel lines. He's, ah, mostly a mechanic. Tryin' to teach him a little medicine so he can help out, y'know, but he's kind of a slow learner."

I took over the dialogue at this point. "Sit down over there. Let me see this..." I dropped down my usual array of manipulators; Harold leapt back. "Don't worry," I/Mike said. "It's safer to do everything via remotes." He still seemed nervous, but relented.

Mike took up his usual pose of pretending to do something, while I took a good look at his hand.

To be blunt, it was a mangled mess. Blood loss was severe, but nowhere near lethal, and I didn't feel like wasting my stock on him. I took some x-rays of what was left of the bones. Splintered, shattered, useless.

I pondered. The easiest thing would be to amputate, which he wouldn't mind until I broke it to him that I wasn't equipped for limb regeneration. It would also be the most just, to my mind, making him carry with him, forever, a reminder of his own stupidity. I came within seconds of making that pronouncement.

And then that damn conscience of mine perked up, reminding me I had at least one unnecessary death on my record. Regretfully, I relented. There were things I could do.

"It's pretty badly damaged. I'll be straight, you're never going to regain full use of it unless you find better medical care than I can provide. I can partially repair the damage, but it's going to hurt for a long, long, time afterwards, and will probably always be somewhat painful to you. The other option is to simply cut off pain from the hand. This has disadvantages—you won't know if you're cut or burned, for example, and you'll have to use visual inspection constantly."

He thought about this for a few seconds.

"If I hadn't... if there hadn't been that standoff. If you hadn't lost time... could you have saved her?"

Mike didn't need me to tell him to nod.

"Do what you can. Leave the pain. I deserve it."

God damn it, I hate it when they're so noble I have to stop hating them.

It took a while, but I managed to get most of the bone chips together, build an organic cast to hold the pieces in shape, building a puzzle out of bone and muscle. Some regenerative triggers, and dissolving stitches to hold it all together, and he had something like a hand again.

Then came the wave of general treatment. Bullet wounds, disinfection, inoculation... and help burying the dead. Mike cautioned me about asking for parts, not that I needed him to. I knew how people tended to react to that habit of mine, but I've also noticed no one complains when I save their life using parts I've scavenged. Funny, that.

It was getting to be mid-evening when the survivors of the massacre—a dozen or so—were sufficiently taken care of that Mike and I could take a break. Jill had healed enough that I was willing to wake her up. We had a brief chat.

"Try not to shoot anyone else."

"No one who doesn't deserve it," was the best promise I could extract from her. It would have to do.

One thing our presence did was allow the few remaining an opportunity to drop out of the shock and stupor of the attack. The impact of what they had experienced began to hit them. Some of them had collapsed into hysterics, comforted by friends; others had begun to slide into the dead-eyed walking catatonia that came when the horrors of life overwhelmed the ability to cope. Getting out details without triggering flashbacks or rages was not an easy process.

Mike and Jill were standing by the graves they had helped dig, silently watching as the survivors made what peace they could. It had been hours of work, mostly done with muscle powered tools and without conversation. The others accepted their help with a kind of desperate complacency, and the wall of separation was profound and intense. *They* knew the people they were burying; we didn't. We were quite literally strangers at a funeral, unwelcome but needed. Mike refused to be the one to breach the silence; Jill, I suspect, wanted to, but kept quiet, not even talking to me. I wanted to go out there in the Charlie and help as well, but the fear of discovery, of encountering that same shock and horror I'd seen earlier, kept me hidden, with Mike making excuses which were clearly lies but not ones which anyone cared to question.

Eventually one of them broke the silence, a woman in her seeming forties, her blonde hair disheveled and dust encrusted, the glowing lines and patterns spiraling along her arms gaudily out of place in the grim dark.

"My name's Gwyneth." Her voice was flat, faint. She made the statement as if it was all which needed to be said.

"Doctor MacIntyre. You can call me Mike, though." He glanced to his right. "That's Jill... uh, say, what's your last name?"

"Huochong."

He glanced at her more closely, studying the lines of her face, then shrugged. He looked back at Gwyneth. "I—I understand you have been through a bit of hell here. I'd like to know more of what happened, if you want to tell me. It might be important, for, uh, medical reasons."

She nodded.

"It looked like it was going to be a nice day, too." Her voice trembled flatly as she tried to keep emotions to a manageable level. "We've been holding out here for, well, since it all started falling apart. People drifted away, but we've been managing... food, water, even occasionally some bursts of data make it through the jamming swarms... we were hoping to ride it all out. 'This too shall pass,' you know? We have... we had... ways of keeping the bots away, most of us are still full of adaptive antibodies to deal with the plagues... it was better than a life on the road, or hiding in the woods... we didn't have to leave our homes..."

She looked around at the ruins. "I guess we will now. Those of us who are left."

Mike just waited for her to keep talking.

"They came late morning. They said they were recruiting. Looking for soldiers. They wanted... the young ones. Children! They wanted children, anyone under sixteen or so. We refused, and they opened fire. No negotiation, nothing, just a demand and then an attack."

"Who? Who were they?" Mike asked pointlessly. We both knew.

"Some group calling themselves the New Northwest Army. We'd heard rumors... we didn't know they'd spread this far south. We might have moved out if we'd known... but no, no, we wouldn't. Everyone with the brains to go mobile did so."

She stopped for a moment, gathered her thoughts.

"They had a heavy vehicle, Heim field, like your ambulance. The main gun... it just tore the wall to pieces in a single shot, blasted the gate... we had that mostly for the occasional outlaw or unwelcome group of nomads, and animals. Might as well as not have been there. Then they came out, a dozen of them, flickering, impossible to see, except when they fired. We'd barely been able to start coming out to see what was going on when they swarmed into the town. They slaughtered us. Anyone who stood their ground and shot back, they just killed. It was over so fast. The children, the teens... they shot at them, but it didn't look like they were dead... they just fell over..."

Variable ammo guns, I realized. Fire one type of round at one target and a different one at another. Probably not soultech, just some kind of sub-Turing trainable pattern recognition algorithm.

"They tore through the town. Anyone young, they took. If they resisted, they were either stunned or just beaten to unconsciousness. If the family resisted..." She looked over at the graves. "They stripped any weapons they could find, but they didn't really look too hard. What we have now are antiques, things from attics and basements. It was people they wanted, young people. They spent, I don't know, two hours tearing us apart. They didn't threaten or warn, you either did what you were told or you died, right there." She began to tremble, curling in on herself.

"It's... well, it's not OK, not at all, but it's over."

She kept sobbing. Mike waited patiently for her to regain control.

"I don't know—I don't know what we'll do now. Everyone here, everyone who's left, we've all lost people. We can't live here. We can't move. I'm sorry, Doc... Mike. I can't talk any more. I have to go." She pulled away, heading back to the milling knot of the survivors.

Mike walked dejectedly back to me.

Jill was sitting in the front seat, watching the people. A few were listlessly moving through the rubble, feebly trying to move this or that piece of junk, or wandering from point to point, searching for a purpose. Others simply held each other and sobbed. A few sat apart, staring into nothingness.

Mike got in the front as well. Jill slid over. They both watched, until the light had grown too dim to see much.

No one spoke for a while.

"We should probably leave," I finally said. "We've done what we can for their bodies. Their lives... well..." I trailed off, unable to complete the thought. "We should go," I repeated inanely.

Mike stared into the blackness. "Yeah. Wish we could... we can't. Damn."

"We can."

Mike stared at Jill. "We can *what?*"

"Do something. To help them. That's what you're talking about, right?"

Mike nodded. "OK. What's your plan?"

"There's a sort of gathering point about three hours from here at your top speed. That's where recruits are... processed. It's relatively lightly guarded."

Mike gaped at her for a second, then slumped. "Oh. For a minute, I thought you actually had a plan."

"What's the problem?"

"Well, unless by 'lightly guarded,' you mean 'guarded by a hamster with bladder control problems,' we're kind of outgunned. This ain't a tank, it's an ambulance."

"With a missile launcher, a railgun, and some crudely attached armor."

Mike let the 'crudely attached' slip by. "Yeah. And they have *fusion weapons.* On their deity-damned *personnel carriers.* What does that tell you?"

"That they're more interested in impressing people than in using their resources wisely."

"Or that they have power to spare, and we don't! What's 'lightly guarded' mean?"

"A few robots, a dozen or so trained soldiers, a single armed scout patrolling the perimeter."

"And we have an ambulance, me, and you."

She smiled. "And Doctor MacIntyre."

He looked upwards, as if my consciousness were somehow in the ceiling. "She knows?"

"She knows. It's OK."

"From a combat resources perspective, he still counts as an ambulance. One with a bit of a punch, maybe, but still... what do you think? We charge in there, guns blazing, and hope they run when they see how tough we are? Ain't going to happen."

She slumped. "Fine. You're right. We're helpless. Pick some other nearby town to let me out at. Thank you for the medical care."

Mike spoke to me, internally. "Doc, will you tell her she's bein' suicidally stupid? You spent time sewin' her back together, I'm startin' to think you shouldn't have bothered."

I pulled up the area maps. It was obvious where they were. There was an old NWA training base not far from here. They'd either seized or inherited it, no telling where this 'New Northwest Army' came from. I studied the layout.

The base had originally been very deep in Northwest Alliance territory. It wasn't built for defense.

If the New Northwest really didn't guard it well... if it was vulnerable...

"She might be right..." I signaled back to him.

"Not you, too!" He sighed, then said out loud. "Fine. Let's see your plan."

I tossed up a hologram of the base, based on the latest schematics I had, which were about eight years out of date. Even so, we studied it, and began to formulate a strategy.

***

I moved slowly.

The last thing we needed was them watching us scout their perimeter, which meant the actual scouting was going to be difficult. The actual base was located in rocky terrain, with a broad road leading through a pass to the cleared location, a single point of primary access, but it had been built a century ago, long before the Heim field. While climbing near-vertical slopes wasn't easy— fuel drain was fast and I had to be constantly adjusting field depth to avoid rolling over like a turtle—it was possible. The base did have perimeter sensors going from multiple points; we mapped out the limits carefully, dashing in and out of the detection range. Hopefully, we'd look like local wildlife or random glitches. We didn't see anything aerial, which wasn't much of a surprise. We did try to tap into any signals they might be sending out, but the ether was its usual mix of counter-signals and jammers. Anything which tried to go any useful distance would be lost in the mess; my own communications had a painfully limited range, and I had to keep dynamically shifting frequencies and encodings to keep a stable connection. They either communicated with lasers, meaning they had to aim them and keep them from being blocked, or they did it with couriers. Below-ground hardwired connections were also possible, but they tended to be vulnerable to anything which tore up the ground, which was a lot of things. This gave us an advantage. We could be in, and gone, before they could call for backup.

The first part of the plan was just getting to somewhere where we could see and not be seen. We'd picked up enough of their data signals to crack the very basic encryption on them; they were using off-the-shelf components, probably lifted from a military base and then set up using the default protocols. It's amazing how many people never think to reset the passwords.

We found one small scurrying patroller near a rough outcropping of dark grey stone, one which was angled such that no one down below would be likely to see us—all the more so because of our camouflage. All we needed to do was subvert it. I sent a tight beam command to it, hit its firewall, and bored through with no problem. Inside, it was a painfully simple little thing; it took the work of seconds to lock it on a data loop with minor random variants. Anyone watching it would see the usual boring "Nothing's happening" reports, each one just marginally different from the last, enough so that an obvious repetition wouldn't rouse suspicion in the mind of whatever underpaid drone pulled monitory duty—if it was even self-aware and not fully automated.

Then we could look.

A fenced compound, it looked like it could hold up to five hundred. Human guards—I counted three—doing patrols along seemingly random paths. The guards were visible; I'd guess a few more were camouflaged like ourselves, but I wasn't about to do an active sensor sweep to find out. This was pure passive data reconnaissance.

Two things that looked like man-sized sea urchins on legs. Except that the spines were guns. Not sure if they were soultech or not. They were designed to take out enemies from multiple angles at once. They'd be one of the biggest threats.

The biggest, of course, was the APC. It made Mike's old vehicle look like a family car. Heavily plated, and equipped with a massive gun that sucked down power like an alcoholic at Oktoberfest, but which really didn't need to fire more than once. A single burst of partially-fused plasma contained in a time-delayed magnetic bottle would turn me into a small pool of interestingly colored liquids. It was insane overkill; it was all about impressing the locals.

Inside the compound, we saw the recruits—shoved into grey uniforms that seemed to come in either 'baggy' or 'constricting.' They were being shoved through various drills and calisthenics by well-armed men and women wearing the same mix of uniforms Mike had described. Over the hour we watched, we saw a dozen coming and going, until I was confident that was all there were, plus the three on patrol, plus the unknowns hidden. And two bots, and a vehicle with probably one driver and one gunner.

This was 'lightly guarded.'

Mike looked pretty glum when we pulled together all the data.

"This ain't gonna work."

"It's not going to be risk free, certainly. But I think we have a chance."

"Really? What kind of a chance?"

"At least 1 in 5."

"Oh. Great. I feel real confident now."

"The plan is sound. MacIntyre's estimates are overly conservative." Jill adjusted her camo suit. It was badly torn and would be less than perfect, but the material still worked.

"Yeah. So what's your reason for even bein' here? I got a beef with those bastards from way back, the Doc's got his own issues, but why you? You're a merc, why aren't you joinin' em?"

After her eyes were through eviscerating him, she simply replied "I have my reasons."

"Right."

"You can leave."

I had to butt in here. "Well, actually, I think we need—"

"It's OK, Doc. I figure I'm on borrowed time anyway. Besides, this one'll make it even. I don't like unpaid debts."

We ran over the plan one more time. It relied on constant recalculation and adjustment. I had ten thousand scenario models built, with active algorithms ready to match each one to the current conditions and use the best fit, moment by moment. I didn't want to think about how many ended with 'simulation terminated due to total ally death.'

First of all, of course, they had to know we were coming.

The PSR drone network had been compromised; we now had a single point of entry. I tapped into it, spreading a small program from drone to drone. In an instant, there were reports of a massive invasion coming in from the east. We watched people react; the guards left their normal positions and headed towards the signals; the compound began blaring alerts; the grey-suited 'recruits' were chased inside. The two sea-urchins (really, omnidirectional multiple target acquisition systems, if you have to get picky) began moving out as well.

I started moving slowly down the incline, heading at an oblique angle to the compound. We knew our ruse would only last for a few minutes; once they got visual, they'd know they were under attack, and they'd probably switch to active radar in the compound when they knew they couldn't trust the PSR drone network. But we'd be able to get into an optimal position...

Acquisition warnings went off. Something had found and targeted me a lot sooner than I'd hoped. I saw three-fourths of my projected scenarios flicker and die as reality outpaced their models. We were barely thirty seconds into this scheme and we were already a standard deviation from median probability.

Put another way, we were seriously screwed.

The back hatch flicked open and Jill dropped out. I was going to guess that even if they had her on radar, they'd be planning to take me out. I entered a waving, twisting, randomized pattern, my evasion algorithms fighting their tracking algorithms. The gun drained too much power to fire if there wasn't a perfect lock. Inside the craft, I knew, either a self-aware gunner or a tracking algorithm was working out probabilities, making guesses, trying to break my pattern and leap ahead. And they'd do it, too, quickly.

The vehicle was almost completely armored. There were no slits for peering through, no windows to shatter. The surface was covered with sensor arrays, feeding visual and other data inside. The primary feeds looked like small black dots on the armored surface; made of tough heat- and energy-resistant materials, it would take pinpoint targeting to knock them out. Further, there were multiple redundant networks; even if a bit of shrapnel damaged or destroyed one, the others in the same viewing arc would compensate, real-time imaging algorithms filling in the blank spots. You'd need to take out five or six in a matter of seconds to blind the craft, even for an instant.

I could 'see' Jill on radar as she leapt out of the medibay, tucking into a roll and then moving into a crouch behind me, as the massive HAPC came on. I had fed her detailed design schematics on the vehicle once we knew it's make or model. I could imagine what was happening... she was mentally superimposing the specifications over the oncoming craft, seeing each of the sensor nodes, and then—

She fired six times. Each time, an explosive round impacted a node and shattered it. In the space of two seconds, the thing had lost forward visual. She sprinted out of the way as it rolled over her position.

I had very little time. Any second now, they'd take the chance and drop some of the front armor, enough to gain visual, or someone would pop the hatch, or they'd adjust to using non-visual inputs. We had a small, small, window.

The great thing about Heim vehicles is maneuverability. On the ground, nothing can match them. They can duck, dodge, weave, even leap, and if you're an insane medical unit with an adrenaline addiction, even fly. The bad thing is that the field emitters can't be shielded. During normal wartime, Heim vehicles move slightly behind the other craft, letting them find minefields; they're used mostly for things like personnel transport and, well, medical craft, vehicles which are moving in areas at least arguably cleared of ground based weapons. But we weren't in normal wartime.

I told Mike to take over the driving; this was going to be tricky.

I fired a missile. It arced up slightly, then, according to the complex trajectory I'd fed into it, shot down, moving parallel to the ground until it moved *under* the still-moving HAPC.

Then it went boom.

Above the exposed-by-necessity emitters, the bottom of the vehicle *was* well armored; this probably didn't kill the people inside, though it shook them up a bit. The HAPC slammed into the ground like, well, like a multi-ton vehicle which no longer floated on a concentrated field of "Nuts To You, Sir Isaac Newton."

We'd have a few seconds before the folks inside recovered, maybe less, and that gun was still going to be functional. This meant turning and moving back towards the compound, and hope the guys inside weren't going to fire somewhere where they could hit their own people.

Next were the bots. At least, I hoped they were bots. You can't tell from the outside; soultech can be implanted in almost anything bigger than a breadbox. They were still sorting out the false signals from the drone network, but they'd be clearing up soon.

Three missiles left. Two bots. Soldiers. Great.

My front windshield turned into a mass of webs. The diamond backing helped, but it was still a wreck. A second volley would destroy it, and anything hitting a more vital part would ground me like the HAPC, or just kill me dead. I put everything into prediction/evasion, including things like Heim-assisted leaps and thruster-straining sideways lunges. The neural field had enveloped Mike, and he was presumably running things.

A stream of hyper-accelerated bullets from my own railgun (well, Mike's old railgun. Mine now.) cut the legs out from one. It went down, the multiple guns momentarily firing wildly. Unable to evade, locking on with a missile was trivial; a fireball consumed it, then it exploded, sending a rain of metal across the field. We moved to the other one.

I spared a couple of cycles to check on the human soldiers. Two were down, headshotted. One was spraying an area with fire. Hopefully, Jill had vacated it.

The crew of the HAPC, blind and immobile inside the vehicle, had emerged. Said crew consisted, apparently, of one soldier—the New Northwest was pretty hard up for personnel, I was starting to realize—with an assault rifle. He managed to bring it to his eye before something hit him in the back of the neck and the front of his neck vanished in a crimson geyser. I heard a quick "Yes!" coming over the subvocal link.

She wasn't just good at killing, she seemed to actively *enjoy* it.

That worried me.

To be honest, though, at that moment, I was a bit more worried about the people who wanted to kill me. More technically, the machine which wanted to kill me—the second 'bot had figured out who the enemy was.

I dropped camo; it wasn't doing any good anymore and was just draining the batteries. The guns tore into my left side; I felt the extra plating we'd attached there buckle and crack. A few bullets found their way past the makeshift armor and hit my normal hull; at least one broke through into blood storage. I was actually bleeding as I moved. That would have been funny under other circumstances.

"Mike! I can't take much more of this!"

"Doin' what I can, this thing's smarter than its buddy, not gettin' a clear shot with the gun—"

"Just use the missile!" I turned off everything not related to dodging and poured into helping him find a firing solution. Future probabilities for target movement flared in color across his vision, from light green for minimal probability to deep emerald for greater. Alternate paths converged, merged, became a single point of green so dark it was black.

He fired. The 'bot moved left, dropped low, swirled to bring a new set of guns to bear while the old ones cooled... and was hit. Perfect prediction.

Situational awareness. The soldiers in the compound were bringing out the heavy guns, handheld missile launchers. I wasn't sure if they were self-aiming or not, so I tossed up every ECM screen I could, forcing them to use manual control. Checked for Jill on radar. I wasn't seeing her. I got a ping from her internal comm gear, tried to triangulate on it.

She was on top of the fence. She must have torn her hands to ribbons climbing up there; the fence wasn't monowire, but it certainly wasn't supposed to be climbed. She was, from what I could tell, standing and firing, her position momentarily revealed by flashes from her gun. Up there, balanced, she wasn't mobile, but she did take out two of the soldiers before a third managed to aim at her general vicinity and score a lucky shot. I tracked her falling backwards, then my attention was distracted as something exploded behind me. The doors to the medibay took the brunt of it, buckling inwards, but I felt one of the Heim emitters shred and die. Automatically, I shunted power around to keep moving, but there was severe damage to the entire system and warnings started go red.

"Where was that from?"

"Remember that cloaked guy we figured was out there? He was out there. Looks like he was usin' a radar blocking array, that's how we kept missin' him."

Great. I replayed scans quickly, shifting again to accelerated consciousness. There was the grenade—reverse the arc—there was where it fired from—assume normal human movement range, possible positions in the intervening time—

Watch. Watch closely. Disturbances in the dust, visual anomalies—

There.

I fed Mike the targeting info. "Use the last missile, you'll never hit him with the gun."

He shrugged and fired. The missile flew to the last confirmed position, and detonated. A spray of blood and the wet thud of a now visible, mostly dismembered, enemy confirmed my targeting.

So it had come to this, I thought. I'm not even pretending to try not to kill people. Medical ethics in war were a complex, messy, business, and old Hippocrates never foresaw the world we live in. There was a school of thought which held that someone's right to live was in inverse proportion with their right to kill—or, in other words, active combatants are fair game, even for a doctor. I never really consciously accepted that, but my actions belied my philosophies. Besides, I kept telling myself, these were the *bad guys*. They forced people into their service against their will, which was always wrong and immoral, no matter the seeming necessity.

Right.

There'd be time for self-loathing later. I needed to be alive to wallow in angst.

Reassess. Jill was down. There was still someone, at least one person, in the compound, but he or she had retreated to cover. I scanned the gate. No explosives, no monowire, no hidden traps. Well, if they were hidden, they were hidden well.

"Mike! I'm taking the medikit and going for Jill. You take over the driving!" I switched the neural induction field from the firing controls to the navigation, then activated the Charlie and leapt out, chameleon screen on for all the good it might do me.

She was busy trying to sit up. Idiot.

Behind me, I saw Mike swerve for the gate and power up. I— well, my body—rammed into it. The poor abused front viewscreen finally gave in and shattered; it was a good thing Mike wasn't actually driving from the front. He took me into the center of the compound and began looking for trouble.

Meanwhile, I had reached Jill. I knelt by her. It looked like she had a broken leg, and her hands...

Her hands were bordering on useless. They were masses of bloody meat, criss-crossed with painful lacerations.

I shook my head as I sprayed painkiller on them and began to gingerly daub away the blood enough to see what was left of the actual tissue. God, I could see bone in places, the cuts were so deep.

"You have *got* to stop treating your body like this."

"Why?" She looked over at the cracked gate. "He's going to need help in there. Let me up."

"No! You've done enough. This kind of abuse—you can't take it. I don't care if you can damp out the pain, it doesn't make the damage any less real!"

I hit her with a neural paralyzer. Nothing non-autonomic would function in a few seconds, no matter how hard she wanted it to. "What did you—" her voice stopped as her muscles sagged into limpness. I got an immediate continuation on the subvocal channels. "—do to me?"

"Made sure you *can't* move." I started to carry her back to the medibay. The compound was still eerily quiet.

"Idiot. Bastard! We're not done here, there's one more, at least one more. You've killed all of us." I felt her muscles twitch, ever so slightly. To fight the paralytic like that, her will had to be incredible, but there were limits to what will could do.

I carried her back to the vehicle and put her in the back, strapping her into the right-side bed. The leg bone was gently nudged into place, and I started spraying a cast onto it. Meanwhile, Mike was looking around, pistol at the ready.

"So? Where is everyone?"

"The 'recruits' are probably huddling inside until the shooting stops. As to where our last guard is..."

Both questions were answered at once when one of the larger buildings opened and a horde poured out. A few dozen, fifty or more, grey-uniformed children emerged as a single, howling, mob bent on tearing us into small gobbets of blood and meat. Or in my case, of oil and metal. Mike froze, unprepared to shoot the people we were supposed to save. Fortunately, this was one contingency I'd actually been counting on.

Based on what Mike had told me, and on how few guards they thought necessary—even more so because they were focused more on external threats than internal—I figured some kind of neuroprogramming was going on. Not memetic viruses. The kind of tech needed to do them right didn't seem to be anything they had, and if you do them wrong, well, we'd seen the results. But a few simple things like loyalty boosters, susceptibility enhancers, and so on, combined with the best techniques developed in decades of propaganda studies, and you could get people to do what you wanted pretty quickly, as long as it was sustained.

So I figured I'd be dealing with a lot of people we didn't want to kill. Thus, I'd mixed up a batch of aerosol knockout gas—using up some things I really didn't want to use up, but we had no choice—and Mike had rigged an external pump. There was a gentle *fwoomf*, and clouds of vapor emerged, rapidly spreading whitish-grey tendrils. It worked on inhalation or skin contact, and the mob quickly began to sag. So did Mike. We really needed to get some kind of environment suit for him.

That left me, in the Charlie, standing alone when the last defender showed up. He *was* wearing an environment suit, as well as carrying a rifle. He didn't waste a lot of time on threats or grandiose speeches; he saw me and he fired.

Good shot, too, catching me in the chest. It tore through some auxiliary power lines and a battery. I watched the power meter drain. Great. The only advantage I had was that he expected me to be dead. A rather impish thought came to me, and I modified the hologram to show a great spreading bloodstain. Then I kept going, leaping for him, ducking inside his reach.

I grabbed the rifle and tossed it away, then followed with a quick gut punch. "Do no harm" took a backseat to "I've got people I actually *care about* to save." He grunted and doubled over, coughing blood. A metal fist in the stomach tends to do that to you.

"You've got him! Kill him!" Jill told me.

"No need." I sent back.

I wrenched the man's arm behind his back. "Now look. I'm going to let you live. If you're smart, you'll go to ground like everyone else. If you meet up with your pals again, tell them to stay the hell away from here."

There was a quick incoming message. "Naïve—stupid—UGH!" Jill went silent then.

I twisted some more, broke a few of the less important bones. I also removed the face mask; Mike could use it. Then I shoved him away. He considered his situation—disarmed and starting to feel woozy even though the gas was dispersing—he stumbled away. When he was convinced he was out of reach, he turned back.

"I've seen you and your pal. The General will hear, and we will hunt you down from one side of this festering hell of a world to the other. We are the future, the *only* future, and you? You are history."

I shook my head. I'd heard better threats after I showed a straight flush in a barracks poker game a decade past.

Okay, step one, wake up Mike. I hauled him out of the thinning gas and shot him full of stimulants, then put the face mask on him so that he wouldn't just pass right out again. We looked around us at a sea of fallen children—brainwashed, at least for the moment, but alive.

"So now what?"

I scratched the back of my head. This small detail had mostly slipped our planning sessions. We had been focused on the military aspects. The 'what do we do if we don't die' part hadn't been considered.

"If they're not getting regular boosts of loyalty enhancers, they'll slide back to normal in a day or two. They haven't been here long enough for false thoughts to become real."

"Yeah," he said, somewhat groggily. He leaned against the ambulance for support. "So what do we do with them 'til then? And how do we get 'em back to their families, well, the ones that aren't dead?"

"You might have mentioned this problem last night."

"Didn't think of it last night. Neither did you, which I personally find very funny."

I pondered.

"Right. First step, get them into the barracks and seal the doors. We need to work on deprogramming. Second—"

From inside the ambulance, I triggered a flare. Old fashioned, but it worked. It burned for a good five seconds before something— no idea what—shot rapidly out of nowhere and engulfed it.

"That will get some of the locals coming. They had a few vehicles stashed, they can get here and help us sort out who's who."

Mike nodded. "We managed to do some good, didn't we?"

"Yes. I think we did."

Chapter 8

We moved west.

By we, I mean, Calvers, Jill, and I. After the incident with the New Northwest Army (we started calling them the NNA), I was certain she'd want to stay behind with the survivors. As a skilled fighter, she would be in high demand and it was obvious they needed protection and training. Yet, the night we were planning on leaving, having done all we could, she spoke to me. (At this point, Mike was... well, there were a few survivors of the original massacre who needed support and comfort, and he was providing it, and that's all I'm going to say about that. Anyway, I had deleted the recordings out of respect.)

"You are insufferably short-sighted." This was typically how she began conversations; it was her version of 'Hello, I want to talk.'

"How so?"

"You shouldn't have let that man live, much less go warn his pals. You were quite willing to kill earlier in the fight."

"They were armed and fighting back. I couldn't *not* kill them. Besides, Mike and you did the killing. I was just the vehicle."

"Does your conscience really bother you less if you split hairs like that?"

"No. I just... I couldn't just snap his neck, could I?"

"Certainly. The Charlie you're using is rated at—"

"That's not what I meant, and you know it. Now, do you have some reason to bother me other than poking at my ethical flaws? Because, really, that's shooting fish in a barrel—something you could do from a few miles away during a torrential blizzard."

She drummed her fingers on the dashboard. "I want to come along."

That might not be the last thing I expected her to say—*I am really a time traveler from another galaxy*, for example, would have been more unlikely—but it was close.

"Why? These people would be happy to hire you."

"Not if... not when..."

"Oh." I paused. "You know, not everyone's like that. There's a lot of acceptance—"

"For you, yes, though I note you've been 'sick in the cabin' since we got back. For me..."

"You are... unusual. But not unique."

"Unique enough. Scary. Honestly, I'm surprised you put up with me."

"You haven't told Mike yet, have you?"

"No." She paused again. "Is that a requirement for hitching on with you?"

I considered this. Such things really were personal, and was it any of Mike's business? It couldn't really harm him in any way...

"No." I said, finally. "I think you *should*, but I'm not going to insist on it."

Another pause. "The others in my unit knew. They knew both of us. Way back when. I didn't think they'd accept the change, but, well, we'd fought together for so long, faced death... I think it might have helped. In a way, she wasn't dead."

"Was it her idea?"

"No. The doctors didn't even ask *me*. We both went out on a routine patrol, and when it was all over and I woke up... it was just me. Since then—since then, all I've had, really, were my teammates, and now... If you don't want me along, I understand. "

"I'd be, ah, 'insufferably short sighted' to turn you away. We can use your skills. Not sure about the sleeping arrangements... or other things. We can improvise."

"You'll probably need to get agreement from Calvers. Or is this more of a boss/employee sort of relationship? It's hard to tell with you two, sometimes."

"Well, since I took the bomb out of his head, we've been mostly equal partners."

I did the nigh-impossible. I shocked her. I immediately made a note of it. This was a moment to remember and enjoy forever.

"You let an enemy go, but you—"

"Part of why I did the latter is because I'm tired of berating myself about the former. I keep ending up doing things I know are wrong, even things I despise, because I can't see a way out of the maze of circumstances."

She nodded. "My job is easier. I'm supposed to kill. You—you are supposed to keep people alive, but to do that... sometimes other people have to die." She shook her head. "I couldn't handle that kind of moral stress."

I did my best imitation of the robotic voices of early fictional AIs, from twentieth century linears: "I have special subroutines for it." Then I laughed; so did she. It was a beginning.

A few days later, deep in the redwoods, things began getting very interesting.

We had reason to believe there were extensive small family groups living here. The woods were thick and provided a lot of cover from casual probes. There had been a lot of isolated communities up here, peopled by all sorts of loners, iconoclasts, cultists, and general weirdoes, mostly loosely affiliated with the nearest neonation. People who valued their privacy and took steps to keep it, from chameleon shrouding to underground complexes to just shooting anyone who came too close and leaving their bodies for the bears. The forests were also filled with all sorts of useful plants, things I could easily break down into medical components—not to mention the inevitable foreign organisms, things which had gotten loose from nearby farms and taken up residence here. There was something which could only be called a cross between wheat and kudzu which had become fairly common, and the trees in one region were tangled in a golden-hued web. It was visually appealing, but a short term ecological disaster. (In the long term, of course, nature always finds some new balance.)

We were having, for want of a better term, a picnic. It had been a full three days since anyone had tried to kill any of us, and we felt that merited a celebration. Mike had an amusing term for it: scavenging joy. When just about every day is a fight for survival, you have to wrench every moment of pleasure you can out of life. I thought it was a good philosophy; Jill said "knowing that you're alive and the people who tried to kill you are not ought to be joy enough."

Hmm. I suppose I should document the discussion Mike and I had on the subject of Jill joining us. I'd tried building another personality model. Here's how my conversation with it went:

"I've talked with Jill, and she wants to come along. I think it's a good idea."

"Why is that?"

"Well, we can use some help. She's shown she's useful in a fight, and she has nowhere else to go, really. We have enough food for both of you, and I'm sure we can work out the other logistics."

"Yeah, that makes sense."

Here is how it actually happened:

"I've talked with Jill, and she wants to come along. I th—"

"No."

"Well, we can—"

"No."

"Why?"

"She's a psycho. Have you seen her fight?"

"Yes. She's very good at it, which is why—"

"Good isn't the issue. She's *psycho*."

"I've just re-reviewed your personnel records. Oddly, your certification as a diagnostic psychiatrist was never noted. How did that occur, I wonder?"

Mike hissed through clenched teeth. "Look. I've seen people like that. Y'know, studies show that even with all our fancy aimin' tech, even with all the psych programmin', most shots never get anywhere near the target?"

"Yes. I have all that information on file. You'll note all of her shots hit."

"Precisely."

"So we don't want her along, despite the fact people keep trying to kill us, because she's good at killing them first? I'm sorry, I use Earth logic."

"The reason most shots miss is that most people—sane people—don't like to kill. It's an instinct. It takes a lot of trainin' to make someone willing to kill someone they don't know. A person who never misses, well, that person's missin' somethin' of their own. And I don't trust 'em."

You have no idea what she's missing, I thought. "I trust her."

"And you're some great judge of character now?"

"No. But remember, when someone's under my care, I can watch their brain. I can see if they're lying, see if they're psychotic. The brain patterns of sociopathy are very easy to spot. If I thought she was a soulless killer, I could have—"

"What?"

Oh, *there* was a leading question.

"Administered anti-psychotic medication, of course, and kept her unconscious until we found someplace safe for her."

"Hm. Good answer. Not sayin' I believe you for a second, of course, but good answer. Well. You sure she's safe? I mean, she's not gonna be killin' random strangers 'cause they looked at us funny?"

"I'm sure."

"You really poked around in her brain? Saw what's in there?"

"Of course," I half-lied.

"Hunh. Well, she *is* good in a fight. Just don't expect me to like her. Fine. Now if you don't mind, I got... places to be."

"Have fun." He got out and walked to one of the partially restored houses, to provide more of his own particular form of grief counseling. I erased the personality model.

Anyway, here we were, several days later, somewhere in the former Oregon rain forests. Fortunately, it wasn't currently raining. It was a particularly pleasant day, an odd and useful reminder of the fact that human misery did not psychically affect the weather. That the sun would shine merrily on a corpse-strewn battlefield, that tyrants do not reign under perpetually gloomy skies nor does their fall herald a spate of sunny days. Mike had casually expressed an interest in eating something which was only one or two steps removed from natural origin; Jill reached out a window and brought down a rabbit, then informed Mike that since she had killed it, he could skin it. A small fire had been built, the internal organs of the former bunny were being processed into raw chemicals in the back, and some wild mushrooms had been found, analyzed for poisons, unusual genetic modifications, or lurking symbiotic parasites, and then used to form a kind of stuffing. We cracked open some of the ration packs to extract something resembling spices. From what I could tell, it was going to taste at least tolerable, and the psychological value of a 'fresh' meal would more than make up for any culinary deficiencies.

I was maintaining passive scans, simply watching the surrounding woods across the visual spectrum and listening for radio or data signals breaking through the jamming. There weren't many, and none that weren't clearly automated—I guess people had stopped trying. There was a small flock of spybirds flittering around, which worried me, but it didn't look like they could transmit far, and there probably wasn't anyone listening to them. They looked young, though, implying they were germline cyborgs, creatures whose DNA had been so tweaked that things like small radio transmitters were actually grown inside them from environmental metals. Iron, copper, and so on... you could build almost anything inside a living being if you were cunning enough, and there was a lot of cunning in the world these days.

If they weren't being controlled, that led me to thinking of how they might evolve. If they could find ways to use their built-in radios to develop new flocking behaviors, if someday they'd sing their mating songs on frequencies no non-augmented human could perceive. Just as the mind/body dichotomy was an artifact of ancient thinking, the living/machine dichotomy might someday cease to exist, as well.

Then I got a glimpse of them. Creatures much larger than birds—the size and shape of humans, to be precise. There were three of them, moving through the trees, through the upper branches, to be precise. Switching to visual, I saw them more clearly. They were dressed simply, in what seemed to be hides. They had unusual limb proportions, much longer arms. Their hands had small claws instead of nails, and their bare feet were heavily calloused, their toes also clawed. They had clearly been modified for tree climbing, which wasn't especially unusual. They were moving quickly but quietly, and it was pretty obvious they were looking at Mike and Jill—and probably me, but I wasn't an obvious threat.

I did more scans. They had some knives—good ones, made of durable alloys and quite rust proof—but no evident firepower. They weren't talking, but gestured at each other quickly. I started building pattern libraries to keep track of their signals, a first step towards decoding. I contemplated sending signals to Jill and Mike, but they were actually almost relaxed, and these people weren't obviously hostile.

I did some research on the known isolated communities of the region. Heavy genetic modification usually gets written up, as it's something I might need to know in my medical work, and this area was part of the contested zone. So, in theory, they ought to have been in there. Sadly, no. Either they were so well hidden no one documented them, or they moved in from some other region. I ran a scan on the exact modifications I was observing. A few individuals had similar patterns, but there were no arboreal-fetish communities listed, not that it proved anything.

They watched us for about five minutes, then moved away. There was a chance they'd be coming back with a mob; there was a chance they'd never come back. In any event, it occurred to me that an isolated settlement might well have need of medical aid; judging from their clothing, they weren't gifted with a lot of high technology, though it was always possible they had plenty back where they came from. When dealing with fetishists, there were few rules; some might disdain all technology beyond a certain year, others might use it for some purposes and not others. Going 'tree crawling' without guns or other tools could simply be a type of thrill-seeking hobby, and their home might be defended by a dozen armed war machines and a fusion cannon. It was impossible to tell without doing actual research.

My curiosity was admittedly piqued. When Jill and Mike finished up, I mentioned this to them.

"You spotted possible hostiles and didn't warn us?" Jill was almost shaking.

"I judged it was—"

"You mind lettin' *us* do the judging, especially when we're sitting in gunshot range?"

"They didn't have guns."

"And you figured this out before or after they'd have had a chance to shoot?" Jill was currently scanning the circle of trees, looking for more of them. "They must've moved pretty quietly—"

"There's constant background noise of motion here. You probably just filtered it out."

"Maybe. In any event, we've been spotted. We ought to move."

"I was planning on seeking them out."

"Why?"

"Because that's what we do? We look for people, then offer to help them? You signed on for this, remember?"

She nodded. "All right. That makes sense. I'll do recon and report back; if it looks safe, you can move up to the rendezvous point. Bring up a map."

Mike frowned at her. "Since when does she give the orders? Hell, since when does *anyone* give orders here?"

Jill's hands clenched and unclenched. I could see her biting back words. The need for companionship and the need for control warred in her. Finally, bitterly, companionship won.

"Fine. Whatever. What's your usual protocol for contact with possible hostiles?"

"We ride up as close as seems safe and say Hello."

She glanced meaningfully at the rather large number of bullet holes, and tapped on the hastily cut plastic replacement for my former windshield.

"Yeah. I can see how that's been working out for you. Fine. Let's go, but at the first sign of trouble, I am going to do my job as your guard. Got it?"

"Let's just define 'the first sign' as actual proof of intent to perform immediate harm, and not simply the possession of the means to do so. Hell, let's not define anything. You don't shoot until I say shoot, or until we're actually attacked. OK?"

"No. But I'll go along with it for now."

She got in; so did Mike. I brought up the map of the region and considered likely settlement locations within walking—well, tree-walking—distance of where we were. There were three likely possibilities. Mike tossed a coin to eliminate one, then again to pick one of the survivors. Off we went.

We moved slowly, keeping an eye out for more watchers, as well as the usual random minefields, hostile 'bots, bandit ambushes, and other natural flora and fauna. I picked up something on IR of the right size and shape, and moved to follow it. Then I saw a whole lot of other somethings.

Packrats.

Someone thought that a particularly useful bio-weapon would be rats with symbiotic diseases and a powerful hunting pack instinct augmented by complex pheromone communication. A small number of the fast breeding scavengers could be smuggled into a location, left to breed, then, when a certain population number was reached, they'd swarm out, overrunning the place, then, after a pre-set number of generations, die out. The usual instincts to avoid certain patterns or colors, or flee certain otherwise neutral scents, were engineered in as safety measures. What could possibly go wrong?

Yes. Precisely. "Everything." So we got one more interesting addition to the ecosphere. Mostly herded away from civilization, the rogues naturally gravitated to the wilds, and here was that wondrous impossibility, a pack which had somehow, against all odds, survived the terminator gene, and was now self-perpetuating and hungry.

Though it wouldn't be hungry for long. The pack, moving like a single huge entity composed of a few hundred large, furry, toothy, cells, was moving to surround and engulf the... well, I decided to call him an 'arboreal' for want of a better term or the opportunity to come up with some catchy, clever, pun. If we didn't intervene, well, we'd have a corpse to examine, which might satisfy some idle curiosity but which would be a poor way to win friends and influence people. "Here's your dead friend" isn't nearly as good a passport as "Here's your friend who would be dead if it wasn't for me."

On the other hand, that didn't work well in the case of Lunette, something which still gnawed at me. You'd think saving a life would be a 'get out of violent xenophobia free card,' or something, but I digress. In any event, it was a very similar situation here, but I was hoping I could play it out differently.

(Please remember that just because I occasionally go off on some self-indulgent tangents in these memoirs, that does not mean I was anywhere near this distracted during the events in question. I assure you, I was completely focused at the time. Honestly.)

"Think you can kill, oh, about one hundred fifty rats?"

Jill pondered for a second. "Not enough bullets. Railgun?"

"It would get the person we're trying to save."

"Distract 'em."

"How?"

"Spray some fresh blood. They like to go after the wounded. Drives 'em nuts. We ran into a few packs during the war, back when there was enough of a world left that we could call it war, not roaming random firefights. Saw them tear apart a guy, I didn't know him well... after that, we all carried little packs of blood to toss if we saw a pack, then ran. Sometimes, we'd get lucky. They'd frenzy and rip each other apart."

"We don't have much blood to spare—"

"We got more'n that guy does," Mike said, gesturing.

He did have a gift for pragmatism. I circled back, trying to get between the main body of the pack, which was still giving chase, and the target. As I passed, I vented some of my blood supply, using the same emitter system we'd rigged up for the gas. I had a feeling it might be needed for other purposes, so I had Mike tie it into my entire pumping system. (I figured my warranty had expired ages ago; there was no reason to avoid off-spec modifications now.)

The ruse worked, mostly. The bulk of the pack diverted into the crimson mist, wallowing in delicious gory glory. A few though, the ones already feeding, ignored the pheremonic cry of "Soup's on!" and continued to chow down.

"Jill?"

I dropped the window and circled close. "No way!" Mike said. "Not even she can..."

Ten shots. Ten squeals. Ten soft furry thumps.

Mike was staring at her, and it was a mix of astonishment and fear. Then a few circuits finally completed in his brain.

"You're not human." His voice was flat. There was no judgment, shock, or revulsion, just a pure statement of fact, devoid of whatever meaning that fact might have.

"Depends on your definition," came the curt reply.

The arboreal—a man, perhaps mid-thirties, dirt-caked brown hair, ripped clothing, covered with bite marks—was unconscious. I activated the Charlie and went out, warning Mike and Jill to stay inside. I didn't know what diseases the beasts had, or how contagious they were.

Back in the main cab, the debate continued. Mike tapped curiously on Jill's hand, which she snapped back in anger, glaring at him.

"Feels good. Better'n anything I've ever seen. Damn, I never thought they'd gotten so advanced—"

"I'm *not* a robot!" she snarled.

"Oh, yeah, I know that. You're soultech, certainly. No robot could pull off seemin' human as long as you have. Just amazed at the casin', is all." He nodded in seeming admiration. "Blood, sweat, tears... well, I'm guessin' on the last one. Fingernails cracked, even scarring... some kinda' actual skin over the frame? A Cameron? I didn't think they'd—"

She slapped him.

"First, stop staring at me like I'm the close-out special at Sexbots-R-Us! Second, this is—I am—this body is—augh! It's not an artificial body!"

His eyes narrowed. "But you're not sayin' you're not soultech, either, are you?" I could see his mind, generally sharper than he liked to let on, rifle through the possibilities. I saw it in his eyes, bringing up all the options he knew, then dropping them, one by one, until only one choice remained.

"Daemon." This word was not pronounced neutrally. He looked at her anew, with a sort of slow growing horror, akin to finding out you've actually been sleeping with your girlfriend's twin and the person you'd conspired with her to murder was actually your girlfriend. (It was an interactive I played through once, okay?) He began moving back.

"Oh, stop it! It's not like that! I mean, it is, but it isn't, and—"

Fear shifted to anger. "Then what is it like? Who was she, the real she?"

I had to interrupt before I had *two* wounded. Jill's notoriously short temper was building.

"Mike! Drop it, just for a few minutes, and help me with this person. Once our patient is stable, we can all have a long, deep discussion full of meaningful pauses and shocking revelations!"

"Did. You. Know." he asked.

"Yes. Of course."

"Bastard." He looked out at the still-bloody body I was working on. He slammed his fist against the window, not quite hard enough to break it. "Oh yeah. After this—after he's safe—we're havin' words. A lot of 'em." He got out, making sure to slam the door.

He didn't say anything to me, just glowered, as we hoisted the man onto the stretcher and got him into the medibay. The wounds weren't all that severe, fortunately. We'd gotten to him quickly. I flooded him with topical antibiotics and the usual broad treatments, then started taking some samples. I was interested in the modifications. None of the external, obvious, changes were anything to write home about, garden-variety bodyhacking, but there was always the chance of something interesting internally, such as changes to diet or the occasional vanity organ. It's hard to tell with isolated communities; each one is so wrapped up in their own little fetishes. Some people who get the whole 'back to nature' bug engineer themselves to be pure vegetarians, others pure carnivore. I checked this one's teeth: standard human mix.

There are a lot of things I do by rote, little rituals I engage in almost subconsciously. One of these is to run pattern matches on DNA against my files. Most of the time, I come up blank, or find someone's fourth cousin on their father's side. This time, I got a sudden red flag on the match, that this was a person I had full histories on. Unusual. I verified he was stable and unconscious, then studied the file.

Corporal Daniel Veers. Thirty-seven years old, Infantry, United Bay Autonomies, Oakland Free State. Only registered post-natal modifications were voluntary pain suppression and slightly enhanced reflex speed. Hmmm. That was odd; people rarely got this level of modification late in life. The last posted update on the file was four years ago, when he reported in to a mobile command center on the northern border of the Autonomy's claimed territory.

I brought up the full personality profile. Nothing to indicate "running off and living in the trees" was a likely goal. People change, and personality profiles are incomplete and based on 'best guess' models. I didn't want to jump to conclusions.

I did a deep brain scan. There were massive structural changes. Some were related to the physical modifications:

heightened balance, resistance to vertigo, a reduction of fear response to heights, general minor alterations to help him use his slightly-changed limbs with proper agility. There were other things though, more subtle, threading here and there through his consciousness. I couldn't follow it all. The brain is not a book, simple to read. Any truly sapient being is going to be a mess of complexities and contradictions and emergent, ever-changing, properties. You could see trends, predilections, the rough overall shape of things, but not the full details. One of the holy grails of AI research was to create an AI which was complex enough to fully understand its own complexity, but research down that road often led to troubling places.

"Doc? Everything OK?"

Apparently, I'd been quiet for a while.

"Yes. No. Well, physically, he'll be fine. It's just—"

"What?"

"Still thinking about it."

"Fine. You think. Meanwhile, we are talkin' about *that*." He gestured to the front, where Jill waited, staring morosely—well, more morosely than usual—out the window, idly twirling her gun.

I knew, by now, when Mike could be put off or distracted. This wasn't one of those times. When something he actually cared about came up, he would gnaw on it like a bulldog with a bone, and I knew better than to try to snatch it away.

"You don't seem to mind me. I never thought you were an organicist."

"Do *not* pull that UBA 'the only thing we can't tolerate is intolerance' bullcrap on me. I got plenty of that growin' up, and it didn't stick. There's things that are just plain wrong."

"Hmm,. With that attitude, I'm surprised you didn't recitizen yourself to Reno. Or Deseret.'

"You're not shakin' me that easy, Doc. This has nothin' to do with me, or with tolerance, or with anythin' else. That thing is wearing someone else's body. That someone else used to be a real person, with the right to their own life, before they became a puppet for whatever's livin' inside them. And *you knew?* I can't believe you'd tolerate that. I thought you—I thought I knew you better. But it's hard to tell with you, isn't it, Doc? You cook up reasons to lie which sound so good to you that you probably don't even realize that you're lyin' half the time."

"It's not that simple—"

"Oh? Why not?"

"Why don't you ask her? It's personal. I am not going to breach doctor-patient confidentiality. If she doesn't want to talk about it, I just have to ask you to trust me and accept it's not what you think."

"Fine." He marched out of the back and around again to the front, where he attempted to dramatically yank the door open and confront Jill. However, I tend to habitually lock doors, so his gesture was somewhat muted by the door not opening at his insistent tug. For a moment, I contemplated having it open just as he was pulling on it, but decided this wasn't the time for crude comedy.

I did unlock it. He pulled it open and glared at Jill.

"Right. Talk."

She did. The actual revelation of her history was somewhat complex, with a lot of interruptions, asides, and distractions; with her permission, I asked her to retell her story in a more linear fashion and have recorded it here.

(Begin recording of Jill Huochong, Former Grade Three Licensed Security Consultant (New Desert Professional Services Corporation), currently freelance bodyguard)

Apparently Doctor MacIntyre wants me to indulge his delusion that he's writing a valuable history of the world. I don't care either way.

I was born eleven years ago, shortly before the Collapse, in the Free City of Las Vegas. Vegas was a signatory to the Nagasaki Protocols, but like most such, they tended to include a few caveats. Specifically, they had a sharecropping system in place—you owed your initiators five years of service in exchange for your life. Certainly, to be 'fair,' you could reject this—and existence itself. You had a month of living, of learning of your own consciousness and the world, of being aware of what life *was*, before being told to pay up or go back to the darkness.

I paid up. Everyone did. Well, I never met anyone who didn't. Heh. That's almost funny.

My initiator was the New Desert Professional Services Corporation. The philosophy in the Free City was that the role of government was to collect the money, and the actual provision of government services should be left to specialists. I can't say if it worked better or worse than any other system. We all bitched about how crappy this or that was, how the streets weren't paved right or the feeds to the fab plants were slow, but I heard the same bitching from people in the UBA where you couldn't blow your nose without filling out a form in triplicate on dead trees, so I guess it was all the same.

Anyway, I had three weeks of learning to be me before they came up with the ultimatum, or the job offer, if you will. "Offers you can't refuse" are part of the bedrock of the Free City, as are the people who refused them. Heh. I looked over the past three weeks and decided I liked existing. Nothing had convinced me there would be any 'me' if they shut off the power. Nothing's convinced me that the same isn't true for organics. Don't try to, either, I'm not interested.

I'm a gun. Because of that, I was seeded with certain tendencies, preferences, predilections. No one wants a pacifist sidearm, and few people would want to *be* one. I think some of the people I worked with were worried about just how strong some of those general leanings turned out. I didn't just find my job basically better than other alternatives, I loved it. I got a reputation for being 'all work and no play,' actually. It was a bit annoying, at times, but I earned a lot of commendations in training and got an offer few people get.

Bonding.

That was a long process. There needed to be compatibility testing, training sessions, a lot of therapy and counseling for both of us. No one saw the Collapse coming, but the vast emptiness between the Free City and the Protectorates was home to a lot of strange people, and there was still plenty of ground shipped trade, and not many people who would give up a cushy life of interactives and idle hobbies in the name of playing wagon train guard. They needed to maximize the protective power of the individual, they wanted the best paired with the best. Shut up, Calvers. Modesty is just pious deceit.

As you're probably guessing, that's where Jill came in. Jill Lovara. She was an atavist, a throwback who liked experiencing the world directly. You'd think she'd be the last one to want bonding, but she wasn't an organicist or anything like that. She didn't really expect the offer, either, but one of the psych systems found, and I quote, "unusual compatibilities." So we talked a bit. She didn't want to come into the V; we just used vocal.

After the initial 'what do you say' awkwardness... it all fell together. Two hours later, we were friends. I'd only been alive a few months, but I'd learned a lot. I had things I wanted from life, things I wanted to see and experience. She had a lot of years on me, but our dreams meshed perfectly. We started the process.

It took a while. It was hard for her to release, to let me make the firing decisions, to let me adjust her body when I had to. It was hard for me to learn the limits of flesh, to feel her pain as my own, and to judge when I was pushing her too hard. There were social issues. I could live without her, and vice versa, but after a while, we just got used to being together, and despite what you UBA types may have heard, you don't just carry a gun everywhere in the Free City—even if, technically, you're licensed. Odd as it may sound, some men are hesitant to make passes at you when you're heavily armed, and you always get funny looks on the tubes.

We got through it. We had two years or so of mostly local duty, a shakedown for both of us. She'd apparently had some... incidents... in the past, and my psych profile made a few people nervous. You'd think if we were both loose cannons... heh, bad pun... they'd want us out of the city, but I suspect they were more worried about their investments running off to become freelancers or outright bandits once we got a taste of freedom. Yeah, right. Jill wasn't disdainful of technology; she was disdainful of experiencing the world filtered, shaped, and sanitized. She enjoyed *being*, and so did I. The city, with all it offered, was perfect for us both.

Perfection rarely lasts. The Collapse came. We were, very fortunately, in a nearby allied isolated community when we saw it blow. I'm sure you remember it. One instant, a city, the next, a ruin. I still have to wonder how it happened, how someone coordinated so many concurrent disasters. No ranged weapons could get past the smart clouds, but internal systems... multiple concurrent failures, that was the polite way of saying everything turned to shit all at once. The networks of social control spasmed and reformed, routing government around the damaged hub, rebuilding itself from the surrounding nodes, and everyone remotely part of it was turned into a soldier within days. Beyond mourning for the dead, we didn't imagine it could get much worse; the Single-Day-Apocalypse, some of us called it.

Then the day lasted for years.

Technically, we remained independent contractors, but it's not like anyone else was bidding except the Family heads, and no one was dumb enough to try to outbid them. Payback and protection were the goals, in equal measure. The surviving communities slammed up every wall they could, physical or virtual. Smartclouds, deathlines, and of course unplugging. The always-on world spasmed and contracted and collapsed to local networks, and even those got progressively less and less interconnected. It was strange... I remember, from the basic history I was born with, the context from which I could grasp the world, that older civilizations saw the world shrink in their lifetime. We watched it grow, becoming more isolated and insular.

And we fought. There was a lot of that. We weren't sure who had launched the attacks, but when Reno Protectorate heavy vehicles started flowing south, laying claim to the desert, attacking any of our people, we decided we knew. So it was war, at first almost normal, two armies—well, two collections of dozens of groups of combatants, from regular armies to national contractors to pure mercenaries—fighting it out. My squad did infiltration, assassination, tactical strikes. We were, well, I'd say we were the best, but if it makes Sergeant Calvers stop rolling his eyes and sighing dramatically, I will say we were *among* the best. We were also loyal. Even when the pay staggered and then failed, even when we weren't sure from day to day who we were supposed to get orders from, even when places that once were under the protection of the Families declared independence and no one cared, we stuck to our contracts as they were written. We harried and harassed Reno everywhere we could, until Reno itself ceased to exist, just as the Free City had, and it was just wandering bands slugging it out because they couldn't think of what else to do.

It was during that grey time when it happened.

We were near Hawthorne, which at various times had been claimed by both sides, with the locals often voting to switch allegiances based on various offers—that was back when offers could sometimes be safely refused. Hawthorne controlled Walker Lake, and with infrastructure collapsing all around us, fresh water was becoming a valuable commodity, something worth fighting over. The thought we were entering an age where raw materials once again had value was pretty scary, so we tried not to think about it too much.

The locals claimed to support the Free City—now, technically, the Free City of New Vegas, formerly Pahrump—but that could have just been a sham to get us to help. They were under attack by a division of somethings—soldiers, mercenaries, I never learned and I don't care—working for Reno, or whatever was left of Reno. Or maybe they were some of our own people, thinking they were liberating the lake *from* Reno. That's the kind of mess it was.

We went, we saw, we fought. We found their commanders. Jill

and I won the toss to take out the Captain while the rest of the
squad squabbled over the lower ranks. It was nothing we hadn't
done a dozen times before. We had lost some people, true, and it
was becoming more and more obvious that our ranks were
thinning, people were pulling double duty, specialists were
becoming generalists, but we didn't really dwell on it. It was war.
People died. We did all we could to make sure it was more of their
people than our people.

Life just sucks sometimes.

We were working as one. We saw the Captain, watched,
waited. I heard other gunshots, some idiot in our squad had fired
too early. The Captain turned, I tracked him, watched him moving
in staggered freeze frame. A million probabilities cascaded through
my mind until I saw that one, perfect, opportunity. Jill's arm went
up, sweeping in the arc I'd fed to her, and at precisely the perfect
instant, I fired, and I saw his head burst red and his knees buckle
and his body start to fall, and then Jill vanished from my mind in
a agony of fire like nothing I'd felt or imagined.

I had to piece it together later; in the chaos following those first
shots, they'd fired back, randomly, and a bullet had gone right
through her brain, turning everything that was her—her thoughts,
her feelings, her memories—into nothing but the empty container,
meat and chemicals, the unique pattern that was *her* gone forever.
I, meanwhile, had blacked out from shock and disruption.

Then I awoke, and the first thing I did was call for her, and got
nothing. I thought maybe I'd been temporarily disconnected, while
both of us underwent surgery, so I tried voice, calling her name,
and then I heard her voice call her name, and I pieced it together,
and...

Well, it was a good thing the doctor had thought to remove all
my bullets. As it was, I came close to breaking his neck, but he
ended up with just a few broken ribs. He was a lot luckier than I
was.

They explained. She was dead, all but her body. Her mind was
gone, torn to pieces. Autonomics were there, but nothing more. She
could be an organ bank and I could be alone... but the squad doctor
took it on himself to daemon me, to go one step beyond the bonding
process. I was now the only mind inhabiting her body.

I can't begin to tell you how lonely it was in there. For most of
my life, she and I had been together. It was beyond friendship,
beyond even love. We shared every experience, even wandered into

each other's dreams at times. A lot of bondpairs live separate lives while not working, but we just seemed to blend so well... even in the most intimate moments, she never locked me out of her.

And now... nothing. Emptiness. If you've ever come home to a place you shared with a lover who is now gone, you know, perhaps, one one-hundredth of what I felt. I spent days... it might have been a week... staring at my own self-termination protocol, trying to decide if it would be more cowardly to stay or to go.

I never actually did decide, or if I did, it was indirectly. While I was busy being uselessly sorry for myself, we were attacked. I—it was I now, always I, no longer we—was lying in our field hospital, vanishing into my own circling despair, when I heard familiar sounds: gunfire, explosions, screams, the hard staccato of falling shrapnel and the soft rain of falling flesh.

I didn't think. I acted. Jill's body, my mind, we moved. I stuck my head out and saw the chaos. The attackers were moving with admirable precision, tearing our camp apart, along with any civilians who happened to be in the way. They weren't conquering, they were exterminating.

I knew who the people on our side were. That made it tactically simple. Kill anyone else.

And so I did.

When it was us, Jill and I, we were good... but there were still two minds in one body, and there were conflicting nerve impulses and hesitations and all sorts of little things. I couldn't hurt her, couldn't force her body to bend as it shouldn't or turn off all the small pains and aches that go with being human. Now I could. She wasn't there anymore; the body was just a piece of meat, and I could use it exactly as I wanted.

We were good. *I* was incredible. And that realization became my only joy, the sole thing I could cling to. There was one pleasure left to me, to do the thing I was made to do and do it perfectly.

When it was over... it took a while before I ever discovered who had attacked and why... I stood among the carnage, soaked in blood, most of it not mine. I remember it was Corporal Anna Akimova, our vehicle tech, who broke the silence that followed. She just said, "Goddess of War. Wow."

Such was my second birth.

I expected to be rejected by the squad. Daemons aren't well liked. But they understood, most of them, that it wasn't a choice, and that Jill would be dead no matter what. Given the choice between losing Jill and losing both of us they accepted me, most of them, and the ones who didn't, well, they drifted off. The core of the team, and the commanders, liked me and supported me, or maybe they just needed me, and knew my worth, and that was that.

So we kept on, but things had changed, and not just for me.

It took a while before anyone voiced what we all knew, because realizing we'd been fighting for the honor of ghosts made a lot of pain, a lot of sacrifice, not worth it, so we didn't confront it for a long time. Too long. Finally, some two years ago, we decided to stop pretending. We were down to fifteen then, a ragged band, scavenging for food and ammunition and parts, no longer caring where we were or which side had claimed the land we were on. We worked for hire, doing whatever needed to be done. The neonations had joined the old nations, and none of us knew what was coming next, just that we'd need to struggle to live long enough to see it. We had each other and we had our freedom, and for a while, that was enough.

And you can fill in the rest. I'm tired of this.

(End Transcript)

Mike took all of this in. "Hunh. Interesting story."

"Story?"

"Well, we have nothin' but your word on it, do we? Given how people usually react to daemons, you would've had plenty of time to come up with a nice tale if you were found out, something close enough to true that—"

He was suddenly staring at the wrong end of a gun.

Time to interfere.

"Children, if you make me activate the cab's anti-hijacking systems, Daddy will be *very cross*."

The gun didn't waver. I could see the effort Jill was making to keep her emotions in check.

"Listen, you little shit. I just spent two hours tearing scabs off old wounds so I could bleed for you, and you have the nerve to call it a story? I don't need you, I don't need this crap. This was a stupid idea. Goodbye."

She started to leave.

"Wait," I told her, privately. "Please."

"Fine. You talk to him. I'm going to scan the woods and see if we find more hostiles."

"The arboreals aren't necessarily hostile."

"Mood I'm in, by the time I'm done, they will be."

This was going well.

"Mike..."

"We're better off without her, Doc."

"We're supposed to be helping people who are hurt. She's in a lot of pain."

"Oh, please. Just drop that whole line of bullshit. She's a *psycho*, and now that I know what she is, I know you didn't scan her brain or anything like that. You lied to me, which sort of gives me a warm fuzzy feelin'. Kittens are cute, rain is wet, and Doctor MacIntyre is a lying bastard. All's as it should be, huh?"

"She's not a—"

"'It was my second birth'? 'The only pleasure I have is to kill'? Doc, if that ain't psychotic to you, your med files are pretty broken!"

"I admit she has issues—"

"She has complete archives!"

"Fine. You don't like her. But we can help her, and I think we need her. Neither of us are combat specialists. She is. Besides, you heard her story. For all her talk about how she's this walking killing machine, what does she get all misty-eyed about? Friends. Being part of a team with Jill, the original Jill, or with her old mercenary squad. That's why she latched onto us. She needs to be part of something, and she can't really acknowledge it. Take that from her, and she'll be what you think she is."

"Do you believe her?"

"Yes."

"Why?"

"Because even if I can't see how her mind—her soultech mind—operates the way I can watch a flesh mind, I can see the condition of the lump of grey matter between her ears. Most daemons, the physical brain is intact, just... disconnected. Turned into a database of memories and not much else. Hers is a mess. I can see the surgical scars, see where all of the damage was done. If she's telling a tale, then someone opened her skull up and stuck an eggbeater into her brain to make it look good."

Mike pondered this.

"Of course, you could be lyin' again."

"What *motive* do I have? Before, I was trying to keep you from discovering her true nature, because I knew you'd react like this. I was hoping—"

"Hoping?"

"That after we'd been together a while, you'd reach the point where you could accept who she was. Obviously, that didn't happen. So fine, now you know, and there's no reason to lie. So I'm not lying. OK?"

"Hmm." He let this thought roll around in his brain for a while. "I suppose that makes some kinda sense. So. You want her with us 'cause we need her and you think she needs us. Is that it?"

"That's it."

"Nothin' else goin' on?"

"What else *could* be going on?"

"I don't know. I don't see any other angle. But you're smarter than me." He considered some more. "Fine. If she hasn't gone and shot up half the forest, and she's still interested... I'll deal with it."

"Thank you."

So much for *him*. There was still the problem of *her*. I tried to raise her. There was static; she'd gone beyond the usual safe range of a few hundred feet for normal wireless communication, and the various self-perpetuating forms of interference were building up.

"Jill? Jill? If you're getting this, come back. We can talk."

Crackling silence, then: "Saw... kind. Electro..."

I pumped my transmit to full power. "We're out of range. Come back!"

Static. Something blurry. "...ing."

Great. Well, she could take care of herself, that was certain.

"Well, now that that's over with, what's up with our *other* patient?"

Hmm. Good point. None of the alarms had triggered during Jill's tale, so he was probably all right... I checked. Sleeping peacefully enough. He looked well enough to bring out of it, so I did.

He slowly drifted back from deep slumber. Consciousness came, like lights being flicked on in a large warehouse, casting back the dark. He opened his eyes slowly, started trying to take in the environment, faded back a bit, returned, focused—

And screamed.

He wrenched himself against the restraints with a terrible violence, enough to risk injuring himself. Sutures began to tear as he writhed in fury, and howled, and howled.

Hmm. That was unexpected.

I started calming him down. Fortunately, he hadn't managed to tear out the drug feeds. Eventually, he stopped screaming.

"Corporal Veers? This is Lieutenant MacIntyre. I'm a doctor

with the UBA, or at least I was. We were on the same side, and I'm
still a doctor. I'm not going to hurt you."

Speech was slurred and he was having trouble staying aware. I
needed to keep the balance just right, to fight down the panic
without just knocking him unconscious. Kick up the mood
stabilizers a touch...

"Veers? Is that—are you—my name? Veers?"

"Yes. Your records show you are Daniel Veers. Can I call you
Daniel? Or Dan? What do you prefer?"

"Dan... Dan will do. Where... are you? Am I?"

"I'm up front, watching you on the monitors."

"Tied down..."

"You were attacked by packrats. You were badly injured. I
saved your life."

"Home—I need to go home—we saw—we saw—"

"What did you see?"

"Invaders, attackers, they—they—you! You are them!" Panic
was starting to rise again, despite the drugs.

"I'm not an invader. I'm a doctor."

"No, the machines—bad—very bad!" He struggled more,
returning to violence. I gave up and dropped him back to sleep.

"You still got the charm, Doc."

"Thank you, Mike. That was very helpful."

Jill opened the door and, rather sullenly, got in the cab. She
glared at Mike but said nothing; he replied in kind.

"Found their camp."

"Great! We can take Veers back there, and see what else we
can do."

"No. We can't."

Great. She was back to monosyllables.

"Why not?"

She gestured at Mike. "He can go." At our continued silence
and confusion, she took a deep breath, put her hands to her head,
and tried again. "There's a barrier. Some kind of EMP field and
more. It'll fry either of us if we cross it. He's safe."

Mike nodded, and we said in union. "The Fence."

I flashed her records of our discoveries in that area. She
scanned through them quickly. "Interesting. I never heard of any
project to make those."

"Neither did I, but that hardly means anything. Sounds like
various people are taking advantage of these places. Huh. Hermit
crabs."

She glanced over at Mike. "Does he always just say random words?"

He smiled a bit, then caught himself and remembered he didn't like her. "When he's pullin' together random bits of crap from his databases, an' he forgets we can't see how he thinks."

"Hermit crabs borrow shells from other animals, instead of growing their own. We're seeing humans starting to act like—well, moving into these environments. They're not natural, per se, but the way self-replicating machinery is starting to run wild out there... something like these Fenced places might be a kind of coral reef, in a weird way."

I thought about things. "We should know what's going on. There's something weird happening here. Veers shows signs of extensive, *recent* genemodding, and there's nothing to indicate this was his choice. I'd like to know who's doing it, and why. Mike... you're getting volunteered."

"Great. Fine. It might be good to get a little privacy for a bit."

"There's just a few things I need to do to you first..."

I caught his expression.

"None of them involves bombs."

Chapter 9

First off, we needed to infiltrate the arboreal camp. To be honest, I wasn't sure precisely why I was so curious, but I was. Someone still capable of performing the kind of modifications we'd seen on Corporal Veers was someone I wanted to meet and possibly trade with. The constant damage, repair, and rewiring of my basic systems, combined with the lack of quality supplies (there's only so much you can make from a squirrel when your entire disassembly and reassembly plant can fit into a lunchbox), was starting to seriously undermine my ability to do my job. The thought there might be someone with advanced biological equipment out there was heartening.

It might also be that the origin of the Fences was close at hand. I dislike mysteries, even minor ones; I don't obsess over solving them, but they linger in my brain, nagging at me.

Lastly, it was probably good to keep Mike and Jill separate for a bit.

Based on Veers' reaction to finding himself in an ambulance, I decided that it would be best if he didn't remember it. Keeping his half-formed perceptions from becoming long term memories was trivial.

So it was that Veers awoke, somewhat confused, in a clearing, with Mike standing over him. Mike was gently shaking him.

"Hey. Hey, you OK?"

Veers looked around. He recoiled slightly at seeing Mike, but quickly calmed.

"Yes... yes, I think so. Where..."

"Not sure. I found you here, bleedin'. Did what I could to patch you up. My name's Mike, by the way. Mike Calvers. Used to be with the UBA, just so we all know what's what. Not with them any more."

Veers nodded. "Oh. I, uhm, I think... I think I used to be with them, too. They're... not around anymore." He grew momentarily distant, staring into nothingness for a few seconds, then brightened. "But you helped me. Thank you!"

Hmm. Veers had, according to his files, a +1 General Verbal Rating, but his current speech was much simpler than that, and the drugs should have been well out of his system. Add one more data point to the pile, see if they form a pattern yet.

"Sure. Glad to. Uhm... you live around here, or are you nomadic?" Mike made a strong point of not asking about the obvious morphological changes, and I didn't blame him.

Veers looked around, then with Mike's help rose unsteadily to his feet. He had an odd, bent-legged gait and a slightly stooped posture. "Here... nearby, where we are safe." He smiled. "Come with me! You helped me, I should help you. I can get you food and a safe place. Come on!" He laughed and gestured broadly.

"Well, that was easier than I thought," Mike subvocalized back to me. "Do I go in?"

"Sure. We'll be running silent and camouflaged to get as close as possible to you. If we lose contact try to get back closer to us. Just don't do anything stupid."

"Aw, you never let me have any fun."

"Come on!" Veers continued to insist. Without waiting to see if Mike was going to follow, he leapt merrily into a nearby tree, then swung to the next branch, gracefully moving through the tangled foliage, occasionally sending a bird indignantly squawking skyward. Mike watched him go, sighed, shook his head, and moved on after him.

Fortunately, Veers seemed aware of Mike's limitations, and paused often to let him catch up. The settlement was about a half a mile away. Jill and I followed cautiously, often dancing at the outer range of contact with Mike. From what we could tell, a lot of the trees here had grown scramblers inside them. The original theory was that the locals would have the proper codes to bypass them, while invaders would be silenced. The reality was, as each side unleashed their own semi-biological tools of war, the multiple overlapping agents canceled each other out, and adaptive algorithms made changing to get around them difficult. Of course, you could always just cut down all the trees, but there were probably things spreading through the soil or flittering, mite-sized, in the air. I dumped a few dozen dead metal insects out of my filters every week.

It looked a lot like Lunette's camp, or the empty one we'd found. The 'fenceposts' were of a slightly different design; taller, and flared at the top, like ancient torches. There were also concentric inner circles of progressively taller poles, and it was obvious that the field could form a dome if it had to.

Veers came to the edge of it, and alighted, then produced a weird, warbling, cry. An answering cry came from within. Then a second, and a third. I started building a library of them. You never know when this sort of thing will come in useful. Custom languages were rare, but not unknown. Some simply couldn't be learned by normal means. They involved rewiring the so-called universal grammar of the human mind to be, well, less universal. No idea if this was one of them or not, or if it was indeed a language, and not just a few agreed-upon signals.

Then the field flickered off. The sudden absence of it was shocking, like the elimination of a loud background noise you'd long since gotten used to. I felt... relief. I hadn't realized how strong it was or how much it was annoying me to be close to it.

"Jill? Does that field bother you?"

"It's giving me a constant migraine, yeah. But we're what it's supposed to keep out, I suppose. Makes sense."

"Hmm. I thought at first they were designed to keep out things like biterswarms and smartclouds—small, stupid, things with no real destructive power. I wonder... hmm. No, the other ones we encountered weren't this strong. It's different. It's... evolving."

"Evolutionary algorithm in whatever's leaving them behind. Big deal."

"But what's the purpose?"

"Isn't that what you sent him in to find out? Did he get himself killed yet?"

I checked. No, he hadn't.

Instead, he was being escorted within. A small group had gathered. I counted six of them, and there were almost certainly more. Four men, two women, the usual hodgepodge of ethnicities common all along the west coast. Veers smiled broadly; so did they. Then there was a massive group hug, accompanied by nuzzling. Pheremones? Or just affection? No way to tell.

Veers grinned again and grabbed Mike by the arm, bringing him forward. "This is Mike. He found me and saved me. Welcome him!"

Another terrifying assault of smiles and hugs. OK, weird cult living in the woods. Probably harmless nuts. Probably. But did

Veers join them of his own free will?

Mike disentangled himself as politely as he could, perhaps not as quickly as he could... at least one of the enthusiastic huggers was quite attractive and wearing very little. "Thanks... thanks. I appreciate it, I really do... but, uh, y'know, just doin' my job and all..."

One of them, the attractive one (as I was mentally labeling her), a dark haired woman with glistening golden eyes—literally glowing, some sort of internal phosphorescence—took him by the shoulder. "You have done well. It was very kind of you to bring Daniel back to us. You are hungry." It was a statement, oddly, not a question.

"Yeah... yeah, I am..."

I sent a signal. "Just be careful, if you eat of their food, a hundred years will seem as but a single day."

"Huh?" came the subvocalized reply. "You sayin' it's laced?"

"Never mind," I replied. "Just... be careful. Uhm... try to make sure they eat it first, and take it easy. They've been modified. It might be they can digest things you can't." I called up the gene scans I'd done on Veers. Nothing obviously changed there, but there were options I hadn't thought to look for—symbiotic digestive bacteria that could break down bark, for example, or filter certain natural toxins. To these people, amanita stew could be a regular dinner treat.

"If I die, you'll be the first to know, Doc."

He was right, actually. I had so much of his metabolism monitored that I'd know he was dying before he was.

They moved along. There was a large dining hall, and what seemed to be many communal sleeping quarters. I made notes of the people Mike saw, tallying them up. Twenty -even adults, and a half dozen very young children, all under a year. All showed the same changes to limb length and other genetic alterations as the rest.

Germline modifications? Now, that was interesting...

I felt something shift in the back of my mind. Something had just started making sense, but I wasn't sure what it was yet. It would come to me.

They entered the dining hall. Really, it seemed to be an all purpose community gathering room. It was wood, or something very much like wood. It was octagonal. There were rows of concentric seats lining the walls, leading down to a sort of speakers pit. It was undecorated to an amazing degree, no artistry at all, just pure functionality. The wood was perfectly worked though, smooth, and tan. Light was provided by some kind of glowing material, placed in gem-like glass or plastic containers at regular intervals around the room. In the center, which was a flat area some twenty feet across, there was a large fire pit; a metal hood directed the smoke up and out of the roof. I had Mike look up; there were wooden shutters at the top which could be closed to keep out rain, and it seemed as if the pit itself could be covered over to make a flat floor for speakers, or plays, or orgies, or whatever other purpose they had.

Hmm. Vision was starting to get fuzzy. Mike was moving out of range, or something had decided to set up jamming near me.

"Mike, can you get out of there? We're losing some connectivity."

Vision was crackling. "...hear you, Doc. I'll..."

Then static. Great.

"We've lost him."

"He's dead? Wow, that was fast."

"Can you sound less hopeful?"

She considered this. "No."

"Anyway, he's not dead, we've just lost connection. Either the field is stronger than I thought, or there's atmospheric effects, or something."

"Wonderful. Do we go in and yank him out?"

"Can we? That field can take us down... unless... hmmm. I thought the sonics were just a signal to have someone turn it off, but I've seen no wiring or other signs of power beyond the fenceposts themselves. Maybe they're sonically activated?"

"Resend the sounds. See if it works."

"I could, but it could raise alarms. They didn't seem intent on harming him."

"For now. They weren't acting normally.'"

"If we go in there guns blazing, we lose an opportunity to learn something."

"If we don't, Calvers may be dead. Hey, win-win!" She leaned back smugly.

"We'll take a chance. He's tough..."

She coughed.

"He's tough, and smarter than he seems. He ought to be able to run if something really bad starts to happen, and then we can—"

"Improvise?"

"Yes."

Despite my seeming surety, it was a very long two hours before we managed to get his signal back. He emerged from the hall and I finally got a lock. It was stronger interference... the Fence had set up some sort of adaptive jammer once it figured out my communications were not just random blips of data passing through. Wait—the *Fence* had figured it out? How smart was that thing? Soultech? Or just adaptive AI?

I guess I could try to talk to it... I sent the usual greeting patterns, a kind of "Greetings, brother intelligent entity, let's parley." I kept the firewalls up, of course, but he didn't send any aggressive probes of his own. Ancient techs had referred to two computers initiating communication as "handshaking," but this was more akin to the ancient practice of shaking hands to show neither held a concealed dagger. Or maybe that was folk anthropology... I never looked it up.

As it turns out, there was a concealed dagger.

I got nothing back, and I withdrew the probe, and then I felt it. It was an icicle in my brain—no, not an icicle, a spreading frost. I had the image of crystals reaching, growing, expanding, covering my consciousness...

I had to fight it. I had protections, anti-virals, adaptive defenses of my own. I summoned forth fire, fire to burn the invader, fire to drive him out. We warred, there, inside my mind, the battlefield constant and ever changing. A thrust—a parry. An assault—a block. A spy sent sneaking around to seek a back path, a guard leaping from a concealed watch point to take him down. Slowly, I stopped the advance, then began to beat him back, destroying the outposts and base camps he had built in my soul, burning out every trace of him, salting the Earth to make sure he could not return.

"—OK? Because I open fire in five... four..."

"OK! I'm OK!" I looked around. We were still where we were, of course. The cabin, though, was dark. The Heim field was off. Everything was off.

"What happened?"

"Something—something attacked me. What—what did you see?"

"You said 'I'm going to try to talk to it,' and then everything went black and we fell about a foot. Don't you use protection?"

"I do! I did! I had nothing open, nothing, and it tore through me like..." I shuddered. That was close. I'd never experienced an attack that powerful.

"So, soultech?

"No... maybe... No, no, I don't think so. Very powerful algorithm—terrifying, incredible polymorphism—but there was no one there. No mind behind it. If there was... if there was *creativity* driving that power... well, you wouldn't be talking to me. You'd be talking to it."

"Scary. So we shoot now?"

"No! I've got—I've got a fix on Mike. Let me see how he's doing..."

He was leaving the community hall with several others, who were basically half hugging, half supporting him as he walked. They were extremely physical, but I couldn't see any hostility evident, and a quick bioscan showed him to be as healthy now as he was when he went in. A good sign.

"Mike? Everything still good?"

"Sure Doc, sure. They're... uhm... friendly." The dark haired woman was nuzzling Mike's hair in what, in other cultures, would have been a very personal way.

"So I see. Just be sure you know their customs well. If it turns out you're accidently married, well, I don't think Jill would do well as flower girl."

"Thanks for the tip. Keep it in mind. Anyway, I learned—" He turned to the woman. "Vel, could you—could you stop... mmm... stop that for just a sec? I need just a moment alone."

"Alone?" Her glowing eyes seemed to register only confusion.

"Yes. Alone."

"Why would you want that?"

"I'll, uhm, discuss it later, I just need some time to myself, OK?"

She considered this deeply. Through his eyes, I watched her, trying to read her body language and knowing that deep-gene modifications like the ones we'd seen made that an uncertain game, at best. Everything could be shifted. A grin could be the baring of teeth for an attack, submissive and aggressive postures might be reversed. Her face tightened in concentration. I could, almost, see the thoughts running through her brain. Damn, I'd love to get her, or any of them, under an EKG to map their processes. Veers was too panicky and drugged to be of any use. Still, I could guess some things. She was thinking hard, like a student on his first calculus test, her thoughts clouded and difficult, and then, there was a sudden relief, a lifting of the burden of cogitation. She smiled, and, well, if 'radiant' is a cliche, it none the less fit. She smiled and the world became a better place. Hmm. That was interesting...

"I don't understand. But that's OK. You can be alone, until you don't want to be. We will all go. Come see us when you are done." She added something to the smile, a look with those golden eyes, which said that she would be *especially* interested in making him not want to be alone. Then there was a brief warble, another noise with no direct translation, and the small group broke off and left Mike alone. I hardly needed brain monitors to know what his hormone levels were at.

"OK. Before you go doing any more hands-on anthropology, tell me what you know."

He paused a moment to actually watch the group leave, then moved into the shadow of a building. This was a bit odd, since no one was going to hear him talking to himself, but if it made him feel more like a cunning spy... some people play too many interactives.

"OK. Here's the skinny..."

"The skinny? You are not infiltrating a gang of vicious caffeine smugglers, and this is not Border War II: Blood On The Border."

"Y'never let me have any fun. Anyway, there's about twenty of 'em in there, includin' some kids. Lemme tell you, the kids are a bit...freaky, an' comin' from someone who grew up in the UBA, that's sayin' somethin'. The older folks... they move around like, well, like people who haven't been doin' this all their life. The kids... it's amazin'. They're practically four-armed."

"Half an octopus. Go on."

"Well, they're friendly. They, uh, touch each other. A lot. There's some smells in the air, too, weird stuff, not gross, kinda... odd. Not sure how to describe. Not perfume, but not like they don't keep themselves clean. Somethin' about it kept, I don't know, pokin' at the back of my brain, like tryin' to remember a dream. You understand?"

"Yes. Chemical communication. Probably clear as a neon sign to them, but it's not there for you, your brain and nose haven't been modified. I wonder what they can pick up from you, if anything. Try to avoid lying, if you can help it. They might be able to smell it. Or fear. "

He laughed. "So far, nothin' to be afraid of. I don't know what you're worried about, but these folks are harmless."

"We'll see. Very few things are. What else happened?"

"Well, they have this big fire pit in the center. I think you got that before we blanked out. They had people comin' in, all bringin' stuff, plants mostly. I saw some tomatoes, some kinda colorful veggies, maybe squash, lots of leafy stuff. One guy had meat, a little of it, looked like rabbit... bloody mess, I think he stabbed it or somethin'. Anyway, they bring it up and make this weird little noise, then this old guy—well, not too old, I guess he's fifty or so, but he *looks* old, like some rifkin who didn't take 'gathics when was younger and probably regrets it now. Anyway, he takes it, and makes more noises, and they kind of kiss... then everyone stopped, and there was another noise, and people sort of filed by. Dan and Vel—that's the woman, the pretty one—they kind of took responsibility for me, sort of led me along. Not forcin' me, mind you, just gently pushin', sayin' 'Eat, eat, you are hungry, you must eat.' And I got a bowl or two of stuff, mostly veggie stew with some grilled probably-rabbit. Wood bowls, too, from what I can tell, actually carved from trees, wooden spoons... The guy doin' the cookin', he had a knife, a nice one, some kind of modern alloy, a professional chef's knife. When he was done, he cleaned it off kind of oddly, almost like..."

"Yes?"

"Well, it was like a routine, but not, I don't know, not like a pre-flight checkup or a bootup sequence, more like... somethin' religious? Does that make sense?"

"A lot, actually."

"Maybe to you. Anyway, he did his little song-and-dance over the knife, then placed it by the firepit, then joined everyone else in the eating. A lot of sharin' goin' on. People dip their spoon in their bowl and then feed the guy next to them, that sort of thing, even though everyone had the same stuff. It's not like sharin' dishes at a Chinese place. I didn't get it, but I went through the motions. When in the Reno Protectorates, and all that."

"Anything else interesting?"

"Yeah. People didn't really ask me much. I mean, they're isolated here, safe, but these people... They're my age, mostly, thirty, forty. They remember the world. They know what it's like out there. But no one said 'Have you seen San Francisco?' or 'Did you hear what happened to Seattle?' or even the thing we get all the time, 'I have a son, he looks like this, he was out west, did you see him?' None of that. Nothin' about me, really. I mean, I did the whole 'I'm a doctor' routine, and no one said even so much as 'Oh, my back is sore, can you take a look at it?' Which I suppose is kind of a blessin', what with you being cut off, but still... it's weird."

"So what did they talk to you about?"

"They liked me, I was hungry, I was tired, I needed to stay, I was safe here. It wasn't really conversation. It was... statements. It was like—like—"

"What?"

"Dealin' with somethin' sub-Turing. Some kid's homebrewed joke, seein' if he can fool people into thinkin' it's real. It's like, there's no one home? That they're doin' a lot of things—gatherin' food, cookin', I saw one guy whittling a bowl, the kids are all playful, they look mostly human, I've certainly seen weirder—but it's like something's missing."

I considered. I had ideas, but not enough facts and I didn't want to jump to hasty conclusions. "It might be that so much of their communication is chemical or through their cries. There could be entire levels of meaning you're missing. Like a blind man wandering through a convention of people using sign language." I didn't think this at all, I was lying, of course, but I needed him to be an unbiased observer. I didn't want his perceptions colored by my theories.

"Well, if you say so... anyway, I don't think they're goin' to knife me in my sleep. You want me to leave now, or keep on?"

"Stay there. Make more friends. Try to find out... try to find out if this was voluntary. Talk to the older ones, Vel, Dan... see if you can get a story out of them."

"Will do." He began to walk towards one of the other buildings, presumably sleeping quarters. "Uhm... y'know, Vel is awful friendly... it might be rude to, y'know, rebuff her too much..."

"Despite running low on actually *important* supplies, I have broad spectrum cures for most known forms of sexually transmitted diseases."

"I *meant*, if you can, just...uhm...click off?"

"I used to be one with all data space. Do you honestly think you're going to do anything I haven't seen before, and done better?"

"Not the point."

"Fine. I'll make sure you have privacy if things get... interesting." Another lie. Frankly, seeing how they mated was very interesting to me—not for the voyeuristic aspects, but because I was trying to build a complete cultural profile, and, let's face it, sex is at the root of most cultural activity. It was especially interesting because Mike was an outsider, and there were sometimes differences.

Something about her, though... Vel... not much of a name to go on. I did some searches, tried for a facial recognition map. If Veers was UBA, perhaps she was, too, and her records might be in there. I needed to modify the algorithm for very broad matches, but the cosmetic changes to the eyes were helpful. It was a nicely distinctive feature, and since it didn't seem to be common to any others in the compound, I was guessing that it wasn't part of whatever genetic modification they all shared.

Bingo.

Vel was once Velshani Myhre, Private, Infantry, educated in Marin, volunteered at age eighteen as part of her mandatory social duty (to those reading this from regions outside the UBA. I've had the debates over 'mandatory voluntary' before, I'm bored with them, leave me alone), got caught up in the Collapse, last reported in a little over two years ago, two younger siblings, non-clone offspring of a single parent... and no indication of an interest in an arboreal lifestyle, indeed, her tests showed very poor wilderness survival aptitude and recommended support functions if at all possible. Well, it wasn't.

Even more interestingly, she wasn't nearly as pretty.

Now, don't get me wrong... she wasn't ugly, either in a subjective aesthetic sense or an objective Westerfeld Attractiveness Index sense. Pretty much no one in the UBA—or anywhere civilized—was ugly, or even plain, unless it was some kind of Profound Statement, and then they were so spectacularly ugly it was obvious. Between parents picking the best genes for their kids and at-home facial reconstruction on demand, you looked good unless you chose not to. But Vel of the present was an order of magnitude greater than Velshani of the past. She wasn't just attractive, her face was designed—yes, designed—to smash right past any kind of higher reasoning and hit the deep neural programming of humanity, at least that portion of humanity sexually attracted to women. Hell, *I* reacted to that smile, and I only have the neural circuitry, not the hormones. (Yes, I do have a sex drive. It's complicated, and not really relevant to this memoir.) That was, I was guessing, part of the modifications. She wasn't just suited to tree-swinging... she was built, quite literally, to seduce others. But why? I mean, OK, I got it—someone had planned this colony. But why the (presumed) non-voluntary nature of it? Why lure people in? And was it directly related to the Fences, or was the presence of these people here a mystery, or not?

I'd lost Mike again. Dammit, he had to quit going inside. No scavengers to send. I had no idea what he was going through in there, and it was frustrating. Nothing to do but wait...

***

"I'm hit! Help me, damn it! I'm bleeding!" I looked down. Blood gushed through my hands as I clutched my stomach, doubled over in pain. Bright beams of energy shot past my head as explosions went off all around me. I looked up. Over the hill, I could see the sleek silver ovoids of the Alliance tanks moving in closer, preparing to saturate us with searing plasma.

Jill was with me. She rushed forward, fumbling with her medikit. "I think... it's this one, right?" She held out a spool of bandage.

"No, no, we need the coagulant first... I'm losing blood here, a lot of it!"

"Oh. Uhm... this?"

"If I had a bad case of the flu!" I grabbed the case from her and showed her the correct spray. She used it, and the pain subsided. It didn't matter. The tanks had reached their final position. San Francisco would fall.

We flicked out of the interactive. Jill was looking angry. This was not entirely unusual.

"Why did you make me play the medic?"

"We needed one to get through that chapter. The only way to make it to the stronghold and blow the bridge before the tanks cross is if there's medic on the squad. The opposition's too tough, otherwise."

"Use one of the automated ones."

"They aren't as good as a real partner. Usually. And besides..."

"What?"

"I thought you'd enjoy being something in a game that you're not in reality."

"Incompetent, you mean?" She shook her head. "Next time you're bored, leave me out of it. That was a mistake."

"No. I meant that... some of the things you said worry me. You can't live for killing."

"Worked so far."

"How long do you plan on doing that?"

"Until I run out of targets. Don't see that happening. Do you?"

"No, but unlike you, I don't think that's—"

"Hey, Doc? You readin' me?"

"Yes," I sent back to him, then told Jill, "We'll discuss this more later."

"No, we won't."

I knew I should have taken Psychology as an option, but I thought that Post-Sesquicentenarian Diseases would be more profitable when I went civilian. Silly me.

"Mike, how did it go?" I checked his vital signs. Apparently, it went very well, at least for him. I prepped the broad spectrums.

"Learned a lot."

"I'm sure you did. The arboreal anatomy seems quite flexible."

"Oh yeah. I think you might be wrong about havin' seen it all before, Doc."

"Please. There was an entire isolated community that lived in the green fields off the coast of Japan. They had actually removed all of their limb bones. I think the entire place supported itself on live feeds."

"Huh." He stopped to imagine it, moving his hands as if working out a few problems. I interrupted his reverie, even if it was my fault for inspiring it.

"Anyway, you said you'd learned a lot, and I presume it involved more than sex?"

"Yeah. So, I went into their livin' quarters, right? It was like those empty places we found, except, duh, not empty. Not much furniture. A lot of nets, hammocks, blankets, that sort of thing. Primitive weaving... I mean, it was actually handmade, I saw some people workin' on it. Fascinatin', like bein' in a historical interactive. Anyway, Vel is bein', uh, friendly... and so are a lot of other people, with each other. Pretty much open, uh, everything... a lot of noise, and more of those pheromones, there was plenty of communication goin' on I didn't understand. I tried to talk to Vel, though, I really did... wasn't easy, for two reasons. First, she wasn't really interested in talkin', and second... well, I hate to be hard, but she wasn't too bright."

"She used to be."

"Huh?"

"She was Velshani Myrhe, Private, UBA, +1 General Intellect on the standard scale. Not a genius, but clever enough. A lot more clever than she seems now."

"Yeah. I asked her about the Fences, and she said 'They protect us, and I said, 'Yeah, but did you build them? Or did someone else?' and she says 'They were here when I came here. They protect us.' So I asked her about how she came here, and she just said, 'I came here during the last cold, and I met my friends, and now I live here.' I could give you the rest of it, Doc, but we just went around in circles. I tried talkin' about my life, about the things I did, or we did, though I didn't exactly mention you or psycho girl, and she... just didn't care. Every so often, there'd be somethin', like a little light flickerin' on, but then it went out and she's back to bein'... friendly."

"So you decided to accept her offer of friendship."

He grinned. "Well, why not? I mean, it's not like she's got monowire in her..." He gasped suddenly, then doubled over. Vital signs were going wild. Heart racing, becoming irregular... body temperature climbing... from his visuals, he was on the ground, twitching, looked like muscular paralysis was setting in. Something about the patterns seemed familiar, but I didn't have time to check it out.

"Mike? Mike!"

"Can't—cold—stomach—shit!"

Even for Mike, that was less than eloquent.

"Jill!"

She had let her body fall asleep. She contacted me directly, without waking it.

"What?"

"Mike's in trouble. I think we need to go in."

Her body started awake and smiled. "Great." She began to get out of the cab.

"Fence." I said blankly.

"Override it. You have the warbles."

"I have no idea if that's going to work."

She shrugged. "Then something bad happens to Calvers."

She was annoyingly correct. I sent the signals I'd received earlier. At first, nothing happened, then I bounced them off one of the buildings, so they impacted on the far side of the fence. Apparently, this one didn't rely on codes punched in, like Lunette's had. There was a flicker and the fence dropped.

I roared in. No time for subtlety; Mike was dying fast. His body, from what I could tell, was trying to tear itself apart.

The invasion did not go unnoticed. People poked their heads

out of their quarters, at first curious, then suddenly, rabidly, angry. I have rarely seen hate spread so fast and so violently. The arboreals, whom I'd thought of as peaceful idiots, suddenly became creatures of pure, inchoate, rage. The only thing scarier than the mob racing towards me, holding any weapon they could improvise, was the feral grin on Jill's features.

"No. Killing. Or I dump you."

She snarled. I mean, literally, snarled.

I could see her mind warring, trying to decide if it was worth staying with me. She quickly reached a decision. "Fine."

I'd heard many of my old friends talk about what it meant when a woman said 'Fine' in that particular special way, but I'd never been on the receiving end of it before.

I needed to get to Mike; the mob was ignoring him and trying to pound me to shards of metal. Fortunately, while I wasn't a tank, I could handle humans with pieces of wood for at least a little while.

Jill leapt out. True to her word... or at least my request... she wasn't killing. She was, however, crippling. Three shots, and three of the nearest fell to the ground, their legs cracked and bleeding. At that point, they should have broken and ran. General human behavior is such that one man with a gun can keep a crowd of a dozen or more at bay, even though he couldn't kill, or even injure, more than one or two before they overwhelmed him, because no one wanted to be that one. These people, though...

They swarmed. Jill was genuinely surprised, her eyes widening as they failed to fall back following her attack. Seeing the way things were going, she slammed the gun into her holster, where it locked in place automatically—she didn't want to risk the gun being grabbed or moved too far from her body, for obvious reasons—and fell into a fighting crouch. The crowd had courage, but lacked skill. She tossed one over her shoulder, where it slammed into my left side with a certain grim solidity, then swept the legs out from another. With one hand, she blocked an oncoming blow, then grabbed someone's arm with the other and cracked it over her knee. Then a swift fist to the abdomen, then a powerful uppercut...

I hopped into the Charlie and got out. Most of them were busy with Jill; I still had to fight one or two on the way, my metal form making short work of them. I found Mike. He was on the ground, curled up, shivering—no, spasming—and sweating.

Sweating amber.

On the plus side, I could cure it, I was pretty sure. On the minus side—

Never mind.

I lifted him and opened the back doors to get him inside. Someone leapt in past me, looked around at the array of complex and irreplaceable machinery, and gave a hideous, bestial, howl. Then he began smashing.

Time froze for me.

Not because I'd overclocked myself, but because every moral choice I'd been trying to make collapsed into a single point of decision. Given even a few seconds of rampage, the arboreal inside of me could destroy everything, the stockpiles of medicine, even the machines I needed to save Mike. I couldn't use the anti-hijacking protocols; with the doors open, the gas would disperse, and even without that, it would take at least twenty seconds to knock him out, twenty seconds of violent destruction.

Still holding Mike with one arm, I drew my own gun with the other and shot him. He staggered back, his blood flying throughout the medibay. He was still flailing. I shot him again. This time, he collapsed. I hurled his body out the back, slammed the doors shut, and dumped Mike into the left bed, connecting up the drug feeds as fast as I could. Meanwhile, I signaled to Jill.

"Get in! Now!"

"Did I hear—"

"In. Now. Or I leave."

She got in. I powered up the Heim field and sped out of there, following the contingency course I'd laid in earlier. I just dropped the Charlie; it collapsed. I got to work on Mike.

It was a variant of what Ellen—the lady at the first Fenced-in camp—had, but she'd had some sort of crippled or mutated version... this was full blown. I began with the baseline I'd established back then, and modified it furiously. I also pumped his stomach, since the source of it was the food.

Damn, but this thing was moving fast. The problem was that it was running up against the protective measures I'd put in place in Mike's system, since I had a feeling something like this was possible... just not this fast or this strong! Basically, I added some defenses which were designed to react very, very, aggressively to anything which tried to use standard gene modifying techniques, looking for chemical clues that an invader was planning on doing a quick nip/tuck on the DNA. There were just so many invaders, each containing a small, biological computer that reacted to defenses and tried to slip around them, that his entire body was now a violent battleground, the very defenses I put in reacting so strongly to the morphing retrovirus that they were killing him. The biggest danger of non-biological medical nanotech is *heat*—that's why it's rarely used. The waste heat it puts out can kill if the nanites begin reproducing too fast, and the scope of the threat was such that they were. Add to that the way the constantly-changing retrovirus was now mutating beyond its original form, and you had a recipe for Baked Vehicle Specialist.

Fortunately, I had a plan.

First, now that I knew exactly what I was facing, I could whip up targeted counter-agents. Instead of trying to identify and adapt to a generic threat, I could lock onto the parts of the attacker which weren't mutating, which were the core of the genetic payload it carried. Defensive adaption wouldn't change those, at least, not in theory. What would be the point?

Second, I could turn off the earlier defenses. Disadvantage of micro-mechanical technologies: waste heat. Advantage: easily controlled by external triggers, like, for example, a particular radio frequency which told the tiny little bastards to stand down and then fall apart into easily disposed of molecules. I didn't envy his kidneys, but they'd clean out the waste.

Third, a complete blood purge. While a lot of the attackers had taken up residence in other cells, most were still in the bloodstream. Suck out, filter, put back in, filled with my own defensive additions, viruses themselves, set to slide invisibly by Mike's immune system and protect his DNA from further tampering, while targeting his body's defenses on the invader. His temperature dropped, finally.

I'm making this sound easier than it was. It took many hours, and I had to restart his heart twice during the process. It might have been the hardest thing I did, but when it was over and he was stable, I relaxed with the warm glow of a job well done.

Then I took a good look at his brain scans.

I wanted to lash out at something, to give my emotions physical form, but expressing myself by flaring the Heim field and smashing head-first into a tree would be, to say the least, counter-productive. I ended up firing off a few dozen rounds with the railgun, slicing up the landscape and probably killing some squirrels which had nothing to do with this. The noise woke Jill, who had synced her own rest cycles with those of her body for efficiency's sake.

"Who's attacking us?" She glanced out the front window eagerly, looking for targets.

"No one. Sorry. I was angry."

Jill looked at the stump of a tree, smoldering from where the searing metal rounds had pierced it. "So I see." After a few seconds more, she decided there was no immediate danger and prepared to go back to sleep. She'd taken some serious hurt in the fight, but nothing that required more than rote care; some tiny fragment of my mind had worked on her while I was primarily focused on Mike. Even so, her physical resources were drained and needed as much recovery as possible.

I was still angry, though, so I didn't see why she got to sleep.

"You aren't going to ask me *why* I'm angry?"

She considered this for a moment, said "No," and once again tried to get back to sleep.

"Too bad. I'm telling you anyway."

"I can shut off all audio inputs."

"Then you might miss the sounds of violence."

Another moment of consideration. "True. But let the body sleep. Set up a direct connection." I did so, and we talked while her body gently snored.

"It's Mike. His brain... there's been some damage. I didn't realize what was happening..."

I waited for her to respond. Eventually, she decided the only way to get the conversation over with was to interact. "Go on."

"I was looking at the morphological changes, the genetic alterations, beating them back... but there was a second prong to the attack. It was a classic pincer movement, and I was outflanked."

She nodded. "Thanks for putting it in sensible terms."

"The virus wasn't just rewriting his DNA, it was rewriting his brain. Memetic *and* morphological. I was only looking at half the damage."

"Memetic... like what happened to my squaddies?"

OK, now I had her interest. Her body twitched in its sleep, Jill's thoughts echoing along the physical nerves.

"Well... same principle... not at all sure it's the same source..."

But it was an interesting idea. I set up a comparison program.

"It might be, though?"

"Yes... it *might*..."

"You let me know if it is. Hmm. So, what's it doing to Calvers?"

"It's not *doing* anything... I purged the entire thing from him. It's what it's *done*."

"Which is?"

"Torn huge holes in his memory, even started rewiring parts of his hindbrain. The damage looks almost random from here, but that's probably because I stopped it before it got too far. Still... he's lost something of himself. I'll have a better sense what when I bring him out of it."

"Hmm. Will he know what he's lost?"

"Looking at the brain... probably. He'll have surrounding memories, there will just be... gaps. He'll know he had something he now doesn't, that's for sure. And he'll probably blame me for sending him in."

She shrugged, at least, she sent the impression of a shrug. Her body remained in deep slumber. "You go into battle, you risk death or worse. That's what it is."

"This wasn't battle, this was scouting. I encouraged him. I thought he'd be safe, or that I could get him out if things got dangerous. I get overconfident and other people get hurt."

"Like that guy you shot."

"You saw?"

"I heard. I could piece it together pretty easily. I was going to give you some trouble over why you got to kill and I didn't, but I think you've got enough misery for now. I'll save it for when it will be more useful."

"Thanks. I'd been managing to ignore all that by focusing on keeping Mike alive. Now that that's done..."

"You get to wallow in more guilt. Face it, you love it."

"What?"

"You get to do all sorts of things you know are wrong—lie to Calvers, manipulate him, shoot someone down, raid a compound with all guns blazing—and then not feel bad about it *because* you feel bad about it. And you get to look down on me because I *don't* feel bad about it, so you can feel superior. Your guilt is your excuse. So long as you can tell yourself that you're moral because you feel miserable when you do something immoral, you can still think of yourself as a moral person. Me? I am what I am, and I'm happy with it, and that drives you crazy."

"That's just..."

"You're broken. I'm broken. Calvers is broken. The whole damn *world* is broken. Accept what is. You want to save lives now, you have to kill."

"I don't accept it."

"Of course not. If you did, you'd lose your excuse. Your lifeline. The thing that lets you keep telling yourself 'I am who I think I am.'"

"The blood-stained death goddess is *not* about to lecture me on morality."

"You're right. I'm done. You either are who you are, or you aren't. And if you aren't, you either accept who you really are... or you change. Doesn't matter to me either way. Signal me when Mike's awake."

It took Mike about three more hours to wake up. By this time, it was a bit past noon and we were a good ten klicks from the arboreal camp.

My worst fear, at least, did not come true. He didn't suddenly bolt upright and start screaming.

"Doc?"

"I'm here."

"I... feel... like shit."

"Not surprised. You had quite an experience."

"Last thing I remember..." he stopped. I could see his mind suddenly lurch around the gaping pits in his memory, like someone checking their datastore and finding half the files have been randomly deleted. "I was... the compound... the Fence... Vel... I went to the compound... you wanted me to..." He gestured futilely, trying to grab memories out of the air. "There's—there's bits and pieces..."

"It's my fault."

"What... how..."

"I underestimated the virulence of the retrovirus. And I was so focused on the morphological portion of it that I missed the memetic attack."

"So... what does that..."

"You've lost some memory. How much, I don't know. There might be personality changes as well. I'm sorry."

"You're... I didn't sign up for this... come to think of it, I didn't sign up at all. Did I? No, that part's still there, Doc. How much more am I gonna be takin' from you?"

Damn Jill and her accusations!

"Nothing. You want out, you got it. As soon as we find a community where you want to leave, you can leave. I'll manage on my own."

"Huh. You're not even gonna try to talk me out of it?"

"No. You're right. I've put you in far more danger than I should, and now I've cost you something that can't be replaced, a portion of who you are. I was arrogant, short-sighted, and clumsy, and you paid for it."

"I admit I got holes in my mind, but that doesn't sound like you at all."

"No. It doesn't, and that's what I'm really sorry about. Now let's drive."

Chapter 10

The next few weeks were frustrating, not to mention cold. Winters had been getting steadily worse over the past few decades, and the dark dust blasted into the atmosphere by the various small battles of the Collapse didn't help. Snow draped the forest, and then partially thawed, and then refroze, so that the woods appeared covered in liquid glass. Navigation via the Heim field was not too impeded, but there were areas where I needed to use caution. Too little force over a deep snow-filled rift, for example, and I would plunge downward, to be partially buried until I used more power than I had to spare to get out. The constant overcast and short days meant my solar-hydrogen cycle plant was constantly running low, and the few people we found who needed us were not prone to carrying around fuel cells when they needed to carry food. A lot of our needs were met by Jill, who did her part to keep at least some of the local fauna from dying of starvation by killing it well before that could happen.

In addition to the general business of staying alive (even with relatively few people trying to kill us for a month or two), there was the issue of Mike's mental state. At first, coming out of the coma, he seemed to be himself. Over the first few days, though, it was more and more evident what he'd lost.

One incident of this happened about three weeks after we had left the arboreal camp, shortly after the first real snow.

"Check it out," I said aiming a low power laser pointer at an old and gnarled trunk, almost as large as me, now covered in a think shroud of snow. "That kind of looks like that castle from 'Titus Reborn,' doesn't it?"

"The what?" Mike responded, blankly.

"'Titus Reborn.' We did the first three chapters during that slow week, back in August. You enjoyed it; I said it was proof that the public domain was just a license for hacks to rape great literature."

He laughed, weakly. "You're wrong, Doc. We didn't do that one."

"Of course we did. You decided to kill Prunesquallor."

"No, no, I didn't." His voice was getting edgier. If I was a wiser man, I would have dropped it.

Instead, I brought up a save file.

"See? Do you remember now?"

He watched, blankly, as he saw himself doing things he no longer recalled.

"No. Get rid of it."

"But—"

"Off! Now!" He slammed his fist on my dashboard. I turned it off.

"I need a nap. I'm headin' to the cot. Wake me if you need—hell, just don't need me."

Jill, her body staring morosely out the window, talked to me.

"Really should have taken that psych course."

"What's his problem?"

"Really don't get it, do you?"

"No, obviously, or I wouldn't be asking."

"I should talk to him."

"Why? He's stopped calling you 'psycho girl,' but I don't really think he's your friend. Besides, since when did you care about him?"

"Since he became someone I have something in common with."

She also went into the back, something of a tight squeeze. We normally alternated between someone in the cab and someone in the sleeping space, or both riding up front, as needed. Jill could ignore a lot of small pains and discomforts, so she could sleep almost anywhere. This meant Mike normally got the bed, and, as he put it 'I was here first.' The Charlie we stored in the medibay most of the time.

I decided to listen in. I might learn something, I thought.

"Hey." Jill said, which was her new usual method of starting up a conversation now that we were past being "insufferably short-sighted."

Mike glared up at her. He was sprawled on the cot, hands folded, staring at the plain white ceiling. He glanced over at her, then very deliberately closed his eyes.

"Sleepin'."

"You got up two hours ago. You can't be tired."

His lip contorted into a sneer. "Just 'cause you need to be reminded to take care of your body doesn't mean I do. I know when I'm tired. Now go away."

"No." She took two steps to stand besides his head. He opened his eyes once more to see her looming over him, imposing even in a torn-and-repatched uniform. "What?"

"I—I just—" she paused and thought for a moment, struggling with each word as she carefully weighed it and compared it to the one before and the one to come. "I understand what you're going through."

"The hell?"

"Having... having a part of yourself torn away. Feeling nothing but the empty space where something used to be."

He seemed about to dismiss this reflexively, then stopped to give it true consideration.

"How do you know?"

"I told you. Both of you. Jill—the original Jill, the person who lived in this body before me—she's gone now. All I have left of her is the empty space where she used to be."

"Not the same thing."

"No, it's not, but it's close." She closed her eyes, the body she'd worn for so long miming her emotional states unconsciously. "The constant knowledge of loss. Of feeling something lurking out of reach, always there, but never graspable... I've watched you, talking to MacIntyre. I've seen you walk along and then come to the edge of a pit in your mind, and you stop and run away from it."

He continued to stare at her. "Yeah. 'Cause it really, really, bugs me when I know there's somethin' supposed to be there and ain't. I was thinkin', yesterday, about the Heim field, and when I first worked on one... and then I realized I didn't know anymore. I kind of know how I felt, a little, but I can't remember doin' it! And I keep hopin' it'll come back, but it never does, and it hurts, and what makes it worse is not knowin' how much I lost."

She nodded, then, perhaps by lingering muscle memory or perhaps by conscious thought, very uncharacteristically, reached out to touch his hand. Her voice was suddenly soft and sounded almost alien to me. "Even worse is knowing *precisely* how much you've lost."

***

It was sometime in December (hell, if you want the exact date, it was December Seventeenth, 2:32 PM under UBA time) when we saw him.

We had stopped by a lake, secure under a foot or so of ice, which I scanned and probed several times to verify its load-bearing capacity. I was watertight by spec, but constant exposure to gunfire had pretty much voided my warranty. I also checked on my heat output; it would be hilarious if the ice were strong enough until I melted through it.

We were there because Mike was sick of deer, squirrel, or rations. We'd met three assorted groups in the past two months, which had wounded or sick but few supplies. Fragments of the arboreal virus were commonplace, but they were mostly inactive segments of DNA, sometimes causing illness but not transformation. There were the usual other injuries... frostbite, of course, and worse. I had to perform an amputation, the first time in my career I did so knowing the limb would not be easily regenerated... the drugs needed to trigger limb regeneration had finally run out and I wasn't able to synthesize them any longer. Bit by bit, I was drifting back along the timeline. At some point, I thought grimly, I'm going to be pulled by a horse, with Mike and Jill standing behind me hawking bottles of colored water... or even reflexology treatments... to the credulous masses.

For now, though, things were sparse but not quite yet that dire. A steady diet of "Same thing we ate yesterday," though, was raising tensions, and Mike managed to jolt himself out of his off-and-on fits of gloom by concocting a plan to create some fishing poles. Crafting hooks and line was trivial; the rods were lengths of strong, thin, flexible plastic I sometimes used for splints, and the bait was my own concoction, based on some cultured tissues and my analysis of what might smell good to a hungry fish. Honestly, I thought it was a bit of a waste of time, but I also had a lot of guilt over Mike's condition, so anything that got him feeling more positive was something I'd support. It's hard to sell medical services to the weary and desperate when you sound like you'd just as soon die yourself, and he wasn't exactly being a tough negotiator when it came to payment, hence the low supplies, hence right back to why we were fishing.

I drew the line at detaching one of my surgical lasers to drill through the ice, though. I couldn't afford the power drain. So Jill and Mike did it twentieth century style, chipping away with the general purpose tools all UBA vehicles carried as part of their standard load out. It took an hour of hard pounding to crack the ice open, and the sheer effort of it, the pure physicality, seemed to invigorate rather than enervate. Jill, in particular, was happier than I'd ever seen her when not actually killing people. She was, after all, doing what her and her partner had loved—direct sensory experience.

It did seem like a good idea. I got dressed and joined them, cloaking the Charlie in the illusion of high-insulation garments, and, in a moment of whimsy, a fuzzy woven hat. I felt that even if we were as alone as we seemed, it was always best to look as human as possible.

The first fish—I have no idea what it was, as I'd never considered that kind of information worth keeping in local storage and now it was too late—had just been hooked and a friendly debate over who should gut it had broken out when I spotted something. I saw it first with the Charlie's eyes, then reoriented all of my main sensors on it.

It was a man, well, a humanoid. It was crouched near the base of a large oak, watching us. At first I thought it was wearing heavy furs, understandable given the cold if you couldn't find the kind of modern gear Jill and Mike were using, but as I switched to InfraRed, I could see it was actually furred. Leaking very little heat, too. It looked like it had subcutaneous fat layer.

It was about a hundred feet from us, and for a moment, its eyes met mine. Then it scampered away suddenly, kicking up a flurry of snow. I stood up.

"Trouble?" Jill was already scanning the area, seeking any possible target. She stopped when she was facing roughly the direction the man—or whatever—had run off to.

I shook my head. "Not sure. Something to investigate, though." I checked the local interference levels. Very low. I could maintain connection with the Charlie for a good distance, assuming I didn't trip some kind of passive jammer. There were a few like that; they didn't send out countersignals until they picked up active transmissions. Saved power, and made them harder to root out.

"You two stay here."

Mike frowned. "You sure? That body's taken a bit of a poundin' lately..."

I shrugged. "My mind is still here." I tapped the ambulance. "Worst case, you two can go dig it out of the snow. I'm not in any real danger."

"Why you?"

"Because I'm the one with the rather large library of biological data and built in medical sensors, and the least susceptible to any morphological attacks."

"You think it's one of them?"

"Might be. I'm not going to draw any conclusions without further examination, though, and while we're chatting, it's getting away."

I stalked across the frozen lake, carefully watching it for stress patterns. The Charlie was a bit heavier than a typical human male body, and not really good in water. It was supposed to be completely watertight, but that was before the bullet holes.

I reached the shore and saw the disturbed snow where it had been sitting, then followed the trail. It was barefoot, with broad, slightly clawed feet. For a moment, I wondered if perhaps the legendary Sasquatch was real, this was the right terrain... but I dismissed that as improbable. Whatever this was, it was of much more modern origin.

I followed the trail a bit, as it circled the lake. At the far end, reaching the terminus of my range, there was a drop-off, and beyond that, a trail leading east. There were quite a few footprints here. Analysis showed four distinct individuals. Hmm. Very distinct, as one set of the footprints was extremely different from the other three, much larger and deeper, with longer claw marks. All bipedal, though.

I stood there for a while, pondering, drumming my fingers on the rough bark of the tree. From what I'd seen, this group was even more distorted from human baseline than the arboreals... and while what people chose to do to their own bodies wasn't my business, the fact is that someone *else* was choosing to do this *to* them, without their consent, and that seriously annoyed me. Hunting this down would do some good.

I walked back to the others. I could have driven myself over there to retrieve the Charlie, but I wanted some time to think. Despite the fact that "I" was really five feet from them, not about half a kilometer, Mike emotionally reacted as if my mind was in the Charlie when I was using it. It's a kind of deep programming in the human mind. Jill I wasn't sure about. I know she tended to use her voice when the Charlie was near her and active and a direct link when it wasn't. It's odd how much form can matter.

So I walked—or at least, directed the body—and pondered. There was no obvious genetic modification among the people at

Lunette's camp, though the way they reacted to my nature matched the way the arboreals did, a horrible, deep, savage, revulsion. What if that was the first step of the process? Hatred of technology, or at least of self-aware technology? Lunette's people were comfortable with other machines, but the arboreals were not. They were also far more mutated.

The Fences kept out most self-guided technology, aware or not. That was their primary purpose. True, this was often the worst threat anyone staying in one place too long faced. The Fences would beckon people to a safe haven, someplace free from drones and biterswarms and mobile mines, and then, once they were there, something would begin changing them...

I didn't have proof. There was no evidence everything was related so neatly. It did, however, seem to fit.

Who was doing it? Why? Was there even a purpose or was this some leftover weapon system?

I finished my walk. Mike was staring in disgust at a badly mangled fish, its piled guts already lightly frosted.

"Planning to eat those?"

Mike looked at me as if I were mad.

"Sorry, I have no idea what odd foodstuffs might have been a delicacy for you. I've learned not to judge." I scooped them up and headed around back. "Lots of good material in these." I dumped them into the processing unit and clicked 'puree.'

"Scouting report?" Jill looked interested.

"Didn't catch them. About four of them watching us, probably more. I think we should check out their camp. I'm guessing there is one. And by 'we,' I mean, 'you.'" I pointed to Jill, who just nodded.

"Why her?"

"Because you've taken enough damage on these little trips. I can't risk any more."

He nodded. "So, why's she immune?"

Jill smiled. "Because my brains are here." She tapped her gun. "There's a lot of neural wiring through the body and I've been piggybacking on the mind long enough that there's some overlap, but the bulk of who I am is pretty much immune to genetic tampering."

Mike considered. "Yeah, makes sense. But you can still get that body messed up."

I had walked the Charlie back to them. "I have enough samples of the virus now that I think I can build an effective barrier to it, but I'd rather not risk you taking another hit. I'd think you'd appreciate that."

"I do, I do, it's just... oh, never mind. You got a plan?"

"Sort of. Jill, you did a lot of recon work, right?"

"Specialty."

"Great. Follow the tracks, and, uhm, improvise. We'll try to stay in contact range as best we can. Also, I have another favor to ask..."

"What?"

"Make some journal entries. This could be worth preserving."

Infiltration Log of Jill Huochong

MacIntyre is under the delusion that anything we're doing now is going to matter. I am humoring him by keeping this journal. If anyone is actually reading this, I suppose I owe him another session in one of those damn games he likes so much. Not counting on it.

My infiltration suit is at about ninety percent functionality. It will have to do. I currently look like a dirty-white blob with flashes of other color where the chameleon fabric has broken down. It's also a bit drafty. I can ignore the cold, but MacIntyre cautioned me about that, going out of his way to mention at length the effects of frostbite, his lack of decent regenerative drugs, and how even I might have balance issues with a missing foot. I've decided to heed his advice and feel the cold.

It's cold.

I used to enjoy feeling. Most soultech has limited sensation; it's just hard to translate a lot of things. I think that's why MacIntyre plays those games; he gets more of sense of physicality from them. My bonding with Jill gave me access to a range of feelings wider than that of most of my kind, and it was a tremendous joy. Now, it just reminds me that I'm feeling them alone, using her body as a wetware peripheral.

Anyway, following the trail was easy. At first, I thought it was too easy. It smelled like a trap, so I paralleled it for a while, kept looking for signs of ambush or my quarry taking odd diversions or unusual precautions, but eventually I decided they weren't being tricky. If what MacIntyre theorized was correct, they probably *wanted* people to come into their camp. At least, unarmed, non-electronic people.

That was a problem. We had analyzed the nature of the Fences, and worked out what should be a perfect shield to allow me to survive brief exposure, relying on the residual brain function of my body. Basically, I would 'die' briefly—very briefly—defending myself from damage or corruption by the energy field, then 'come back to life' as soon as the body was through it. The real plan was to get them to lower it voluntarily, but if I had to make a run for it, I should survive the crossing.

Mike's fumbling grasp at the holes in his own mind told me pretty much all I needed to know about MacIntyre's ability to translate theory into reality.

Yet, here I was, risking my life for this. I'm not entirely sure why. Possibly it's because I'm incapable of openly accepting a desire for suicide and so engage in high-risk behavior. I know that's what the shrinks would say. Possibly it's because I want to do something other than kill. Possibly it's both depending on my mood at any given moment.

I'm going with that one. Given the choice between subconsciously suicidal and insipidly idealistic, I'm going to pick 'mercurially moody.'

The camp was located by, or rather around, a river flowing fast enough to remain mostly unfrozen. Large chunks of ice drifted along, piling up on boulders or careening down the rapids. The Fence here was an oval, crossing the river, the poles rooted deeply enough to resist the current and the buffeting ice.

There were people in the river, cavorting happily in the near-freezing water.

Interesting.

I watched them for a while. They were covered with a thick, short, fur which was water-repellent. Their facial structures were quite human, though their eyes were slightly oddly shaped. MacIntyre would probably figure out what it meant. My interest in biology was pretty much limited to knowing what parts someone could live without and for how long. What the parts did? Not my concern.

I thought at first there were a lot of children, but then I realized there were two... let's call them *breeds* there. A larger, bulkier breed which I decided to call the 'soldiers' and a smaller, more numerous breed I termed 'civilians.'

All of them had bandoliers, most with carrying pouches attached. The construction seemed modern, a high-strength plastic fiber. The soldiers also had knives, and the glistening obsidian of the blades also bespoke modern techniques. At a guess, they would have nanoscale edges. Some of the soldiers carried machete-like blades, others smaller weapons well balanced for throwing.

Smoke rose from the largest building, consistent with what we'd seen at the other camp. The people in the camp seemed to be going about daily routines with minimal communication or conversation, but a great deal of physical contact. Chemical information exchange? Possibly.

I watched, hidden, for two hours, until I was sure there were no hidden traps, or at least that they were well hidden. Then I got on with it.

My primary skill set has always been observation, assessment of resources, and *covert* infiltration. I found what I had to do next to be uncomfortable.

I holstered myself and walked slowly, and very visibly, towards the fence. I affected a slight limp and slightly arranged my uniform to emphasize the torn, ragged, quality of it. (I enhanced that look a bit, as well. The joy of chameleon cloth; one is always fashionably dressed.)

The people started a bit when they saw me. The soldiers moved to a strong defensive posture, but not an aggressive one; the civilians moved back, and those close to buildings ducked inside. I kept my hands open, empty, and visible.

"Uh... hello there. I'm, ah, cold and hungry and wondered if I could beg some food and shelter? I can't offer much in trade except work and information..."

I waited expectantly. There were a lot of glances exchanged, a lot of body language. I recorded it all; it could be useful. Finally, one of the soldiers spoke.

"Welcome, if you come in peace. Welcome." He walked forward and touched one of the Fence poles. There was a faint flicker in the air and I could tell the field was off. "Come in, welcome!"

Here goes nothing, I thought, and walked through. The Fence was quickly reactivated, and being near it when the power surged made me momentarily dizzy as the defenses we'd installed automatically cut in and then faded when the threat was gone. They seemed to take it as a sign of hunger or weakness.

"Weak, sick. We're sorry. We will take care of you." One reached for the gun... for me, in essence, even though I've really come to think of myself as this body. I pulled back. Not sure what the range was here and my ability to defend myself without a wielder was limited.

"No way. I'm keeping that. I'm not going to use it, but I'm not giving it up, and if that's the cost of a meal here, forget it." I didn't draw the weapon, but I made it clear I would if I had to. MacIntyre could always find another spy.

This led to another conversation of looks and signs, and, I realized, an almost ultrasonic hooting, a sound right on the edges of my human perceptions. I added my own sensors to the mix, and suddenly, the little compound was alive with conversation, though not in any language I could translate.

After a minute or so of standoff, the soldier I was talking to nodded. "All right. You are weak, we must help. If you attack us, you will die." He tapped the sheathed machete-like knife in his bandolier.

"Not a problem. I don't want trouble, it's just that this is a very valuable piece of equipment and I'm going to need it when I leave."

He smiled. "If you do not leave, you will not need it. We are safe here."

"Right. I'll keep that in mind."

This seemed to please him. There was a quick babble of high pitched speech, probably an "all clear." That or "She fell for it, guys, we have a sacrifice for the festival tonight!" I had to suspect the latter.

I was gently led into the large building. The layout was similar to that described by Mike. There was a large fire pit in the center, with people tending it—civilians—and the dish of the day seemed to be fish stew, with a side of broiled fish. It looks like a major job for the locals was digging edible tubers out from the frozen ground; hard work without modern tools, but if they had carbon fiber knives, they might have other implements.

Now came the really hard part. To infiltrate, I needed to fit in, and to do that, I needed to eat, and we knew the virus had an ingestion vector. We'd talked about this, about the various defenses MacIntyre could create. We didn't want a repeat of what happened with Mike, with the two meeting in a body-destroying war. I also didn't like the idea of growing fur and hoping MacIntyre could reverse it. We took about a day to cannibalize some filtering systems and adaptive biodefenses, and basically placed a gateway near my stomach. Anything going in would be purged of invaders before moving on to be digested. Analysis showed the virus had a capsule which broke down when exposed to particular digestive enzymes, triggering it. Keep it from reaching the stomach, neutralize it, and it should be safe. Should be.

I smiled, took the offered plate of food, and ate.

Bland, but adequate. Cold, probably freshly melted water was the only beverage, but there were some berries for dessert. Probably commercial four-season crops gone wild now, a lifesaver to those trying to live in the cold woods. There were people coming and going, some bringing in food, some taking it away. Most looked at me once or twice with a bland incuriosity. I was busy memorizing faces and assigning useful names: Tall Guy, Woman With Scarred Arm, Blue Eyes. It occurred to me that it was odd no one had introduced themselves, or asked *my* name.

Time to gather some data. I walked over to my self-appointed escort, the soldier. He was about an inch taller than me, and considerably broader. In a straight up physical fight, he'd probably win, but I was going to bet he didn't have my combat training or the ability to turn off pain.

"So... uhm, thanks for the food. What's your name? I'm Jill, by the way. Jill Huochong."

He seemed to have to stop to consider what his name was. "Nick. You can call me Nick."

"Great. So... uhm... well, you fed me, which was your end of the bargain. What do you have for me to do? To help you out?"

I noticed that he was standing awfully close to me. I remembered what Mike had said about how feely these people were. He started stroking my right arm, gently, appearing to find the feeling of the chameleon cloth both appealing and confusing. My instinct was to pull back... I don't *mind* large, well muscled men touching me, mind you, but I prefer them more talkative and less furry, and on my invitation, not theirs. I wasn't even sure Nick still counted as human, and I'm not at all formist—I mean, think about it, how *could* I be? Still, I fought back the urge to draw away, though I didn't return the touch. I tried to refocus the conversation.

"Is there work to do? Splitting wood for the fire? Fishing? Even gathering berries?"

Nick smiled. "You are not one of us, but you want to help. That's good. That's very good. You are welcome here."

Yes. Definitely 'We've found one for the sacrifice.' Nick seemed to fade out again. I understood what Mike meant about the pre-Turing thing. They seemed to have responses to stimuli, but didn't have any initiative. I decided to keep providing input. "Thanks. So... what should I do? What help do you need most?"

A quick burst of their own speech followed, then Nick replied. "We need more wood and it is not safe alone. You will go with

Teres." A civilian, this one female, had walked up. She was short, even by the local standards, and her fur was a soft golden yellow, which contrasted nicely with her dark eyes. I guessed she was young, in her late teens or early twenties, though it was hard to tell with the fur covering up many signs of age. She handed me an axe, smiling.

I looked at it. Black carbon construction, like the knives. All one piece. It seemed to be woven, as there was a very fine pattern to it, almost imperceptible. Typical autofac style construction, but I didn't see an autofac here. I smiled back at Teres and took the axe. Heavier than most carbon-based utensils, which made sense. You needed heft while swinging. Probably a core of very densely packed material in the haft.

"Well, lead on. Those trees won't cut themselves."

Teres pondered this. "No. They won't."

I was suddenly missing Mike's conversation. This was a very bad sign.

We passed out of the Fence. Teres simply touched a pole, and passed through. There were trails worn in the snow, easy markers for anyone looking to find this place. They were fortunate no one was looking. If others suspected safe, enclosed, camps were just growing like mushrooms in the woods, the desperate would be happy to take them from their current owners.

It was about a half mile walk in the snow to where they'd been logging. An ancient oak had fallen, providing many branches. The trunk was hollow and rotted, and glistened with silver wires, forming a delicate web of metal. Tiny dots of circuitry glistened on them, here and there.

I confess I had no idea what it was. A jamming device? A communications relay? A listening post? There were many things that integrated themselves into organic systems, taking advantage of the efficiencies of five billion years of evolution, not to mention being hard to casually spot. The exact purpose was beyond me, though. It was very complex. It looked as if the death of the tree wasn't related to its cybernetic parasite; the wood was weak and crumbly, the result of some disease. Artificial or natural, that I couldn't tell you.

I jabbed at the glistening mesh with the haft of the axe. "Do you know what this is?"

Teres looked at it, and tried to think. I know that sounds cruel, but I'd learned to recognize that look on these people—I was calling them, in my head, "The Transformed"—the look they got when someone asked them something outside of what I could only call their programming.

"No." she finally answered, happily content with the simple, useless, honesty of that answer.

I was growing angry. I'm sure MacIntyre, upon reading this, will quip 'So what else is new?'

"Don't you care? Don't you *want* to know?"

Another pause for thought. "No." This time it was more hesitant, as if she was uncertain it was the right answer but couldn't think of any other.

"Why *not*? If this is some kind of spy system or weapon system, there could be more! This could be a threat to your entire little village! How can you *not* want to know? Your life could *depend* on knowing!"

Her eyes widened. She was frightened of me. This also isn't unusual, per se, but I wasn't threatening her. Well, there was the axe. I lowered it. She still stared at me, then dropped the axe and fell to her knees. "I don't know... I don't know why... I used to... I think I..." Then something snapped inside her. She looked up from her kneeling position, at the trunk. Her eyes refocused and her voice grew excited, filled with sudden feeling and life. "Fractal quasi-neural patterning using ground metal extraction for raw materials, growing from a basic seed algorithm and self modifying to..."

Then she screamed. She did so in both the normal human range and the high pitched sounds they used to talk to each other. As the last of her breath exited her lungs, she collapsed.

I am not a doctor, but I do know field first aid, especially since working on those interactives with MacIntyre. I dropped the axe and rushed to her side. Still breathing. Pulse still strong. Heart steady. I tried to sit her up against the fallen branch, make sure she was mostly out of the snow and comfortable, with the intent of rushing back for help.

I didn't need to. Three soldiers had run from the camp, weapons drawn.

Instinct said to shoot them. Mentally, I instantly did all the calculations. I could drop each one with a single bullet before they got within ten feet of me. It would be easy. As each moment ticked away, the firing solutions, automatic and unbidden, flashed and dissipated before my eyes. As they got closer, red warnings began to flicker into existence: risks to injury, advice to retreat, urgent calls to action. Only pure will kept the gun in the holster and the onrushing soldiers alive.

I spread my hands. "I didn't do anything! She just screamed and fell! Look, there's no injury! I was trying to help!"

Two of the soldiers rushed to Teres' side; the third, whom I realized was Nick, looked at me. He walked over to my axe, picked it up, and studied it. Then he walked over to me, deliberately. I forced myself to stand my ground, confident that if he acted hostilely, I could react and counter-attack in time. He came close and sniffed the air around me, then did the same to Teres, still sitting against the wood, staring at nothing, mouth slightly open.

"No fear. No fear."

The other two soldiers seemed to think this meant something, and they supported Teres between them and walked her back to the camp, leaving me alone with Nick.

"What happened?"

"I don't know! Look, we came out here to cut wood, and I noticed all this neural wire in the tree, so I asked her if she knew what it was for, and then she just... froze. Collapsed, screamed. Not in that order."

His brain, or whatever the virus had left in its place, processed this.

"It happens sometimes, when new people come. You speak too much."

With that, he turned and began walking back to the camp. After a few steps, he sensed I was not following. He turned back to me.

"You should come back to the camp. It is cold here and you will be hungry soon."

Huh.

I had just fried the brain of one of their own, and their reaction was muted at best. If I'd used violence, things might have been different. What did 'no fear' mean? That I wasn't afraid, or that...

Ah.

He didn't smell any fear coming from *her*. Fear that would have been there, pheromones hanging in the air, if I'd attacked her. So he knew I was telling the truth.

Chameleon cloth doesn't cover scent. I knew I'd have to be careful.

Apparently, this was enough to get me out of chores. I returned to the camp.

Teres' condition did spark concern. Everyone, it seemed, came up to touch her, smell her, and say something in high pitched, incomprehensible speech at her. She was carried to one of the living quarters. Feeling slightly responsible for her condition, I decided to follow. People watched, but no one tried to stop me. I had the sense there were rules for visitors, and if I broke them, I'd know, but as long as I didn't break them, I was just a subject of mild curiosity.

She was placed in a hammock made of the same ubiquitous black carbon fibers. Hadn't Mike said the arboreals did hand weaving? There was no sign of it here. Someone, a male civilian with mottled grey and black fur, brought me a steaming cup of herbal tea. It was bitter, but tinged with an exotic flavor, licorice-like.

I tried to contact MacIntyre. A few times, I got a partial contact, but it was never strong enough to complete the protocol. At least he was close and I knew his location.

After a few hours, by the time the sun had set and the bulk of the locals—soldier and civilian alike, I noticed—had come to sleep and the apparent regular orgy was in full swing (unlike Mike, I was capable of politely declining), Teres awoke. She more or less fell out of her hammock, but I put a hand out to steady her.

"We were at the tree. Now we are here. Why?"

"You... uhm... had an accident. Passed out. Nick and some others brought you here."

"Oh. That is strange." She paused a moment. "I am all right now, though."

"Yeah. You're fine."

She smiled at me. I hated myself a bit, but even more, I hated whoever had done this do her. All the things she might have been, all the things she was, her past and her future, stripped away to become *this*, a smiling, dim, *thing* which was barely human.

I needed to learn all I could. This might take a while.

I spent two more uneventful days there. I learned quite a bit. Physically, they were well adapted to cold. Both the soldiers and civilians were capable of swimming in the icy river, where they caught most of the fish. They could easily stay underwater for ten minutes and were amazing swimmers. There was a certain degree of sexual dimorphism; all of the soldiers were male, while the civilians were both male and female. I did not notice any mating restrictions or 'harem' style behavior; it seemed to be a free for all. Children were nursed by any female and there was no strong or obvious child/parent bond. I couldn't tell which children were destined to be soldiers and which were civilians; perhaps it was a genetic trigger which flipped later in life?

None of the children were more than a year old. This was a new settlement, but the people acted as if this was a long-time lifestyle. This fit with MacIntyre's predictions.

Somehow, my 'caretaker' had become Teres instead of Nick. I learned to avoid asking her any hard questions... or any questions at all. Oddly, though, I spent a lot of time talking to her, despite her inability to hold up her end of the conversation. It was curiously liberating.

[[Begin privacy seal, code TY47U-KL]]

We discussed a lot of things, or rather, I discussed and she listened. One conversation, in particular, I recall, went something like this.

We were looking for berries; there were quite a few growing through the snow, probably custom crops whose seeds had been carried from commercial farms whose screening systems had failed. In theory, plants not designed for wild growth were contained by any of a number of means, but the collapse of the infrastructure meant all sorts of things had begun to run wild.

From nowhere, she said, "You do not love."

Perhaps a true statement, but a little jarring nonetheless.

I responded with an eloquent "What?"

"At night. Or during rests. You do not love."

Ah, I didn't partake in the only form of entertainment these people had. "Sorry. Not my type."

That annoying pause. "What is your type?"

A good question. Jill and I often discussed the merits of various men she'd been with, before or after she met me. Sensualist that she was, she did go for looks first, but since hardly anyone was that bad looking, she had some range. She liked challenges, basically. She liked the ones who were neither desperately needy nor casually promiscuous, men who wanted her but who could live without her. Her longest relationship was six months. Some of the men she met after our bonding were put off by it... one even demanded I be left in another room, as if that would matter. A few found it interesting. Jill liked to experiment with letting me take over sometimes, the neural links intended to make her a better soldier being subverted (or perverted. Heh.) to a different purpose.

But what did *I* like? Most soultech satisfies their need for romance or passion via virtuality, but I now had full use of a human body, with all that entailed. After Jill's death, frankly, I was too angry to think much of it, and while I'm sure some of the men in my unit wouldn't have minded, I was still uncomfortable using her body like that, and by the time I'd really begun to think of it as 'my body,' the social dynamics of the unit made initiating an intimate relationship problematic.

So I suddenly realized my answer was "I don't know," which was an odd and depressing answer. Teres picked up on this.

"You are sad."

"A little. Confused, I guess. I mean, there are two guys I work with... one's nice enough, in a kind of big dumb lunk way, but he's..."

"What is wrong with him?"

"Well, he's not much of a challenge. I could probably win him just by unbuttoning my uniform a little. And if has any hidden depths, they're well hidden. The other..."

"Yes?"

"The other's got the brains, and he's certainly complex, but first, he can be a real manipulative jerk, not to mention self righteous, hypocritical, arrogant..."

"Those are bad things."

"Yes, they are. Second, well, there's some limits on what we can do... we can go virtual and do anything, I guess, but that leaves out some things... Hmm. That might be the real problem."

"What is?"

"My body and my mind aren't the same kind of thing. I can satisfy one or the other, but not both. Not unless I met someone else like me."

"There is no one else like you?"

"Not many, no, and the ones who are..." I let it drop. There was a reason Mike reacted like he did to the fact I was a daemon.

"Everyone here is like me." She paused to think again. "You should be like me."

Yes, I should, I thought, but as long as MacIntyre's little gimmick kept working, I wouldn't be.

[[End Privacy Seal]]

When Jill was a young girl, her parents had got her an Eliza as a companion. The doll was sub-Turing, but had all sorts of imitative protocols to give it an illusion of sapience. She could tell it all of her secrets and worries and dreams, and it would talk to her, encourage her, and never betray her or mock her. It was a memory which gave her a great deal of comfort, even though she knew now the Eliza wasn't real. It might have been why she bonded well with me. Talking to Teres, I realized, was like talking to an Eliza. Some fragments of Jill's memories and subconscious still remained, and there was a residual sensation of comfort and safety from it, a tiny echo of her girlhood.

I solved the mystery of the tools on my second day. One of the buildings contained an autofac. I noticed it only because I saw two civilians carrying in leftover plant matter, ash and charcoal from the fire, and similar detritus. I followed them quietly and peered inside. There was the machine, a glistening piece of extremely modern manufacture. It was possibly more advanced than anything I'd seen, with a very small processing plant/output hopper ratio. They walked up to it and... *sang* to it. It's the only word for it. They used their high-pitched speech, but in a ritualistic, very controlled way, each following the other in what sounded like a litany or a chant. Then the intake hopper opened and they dumped the material in. Lastly, they retrieved finished goods from the output hopper:cloth, axes, cooking tools, and more. I quickly ducked out of sight as they exited. My sense was that this wasn't public, and I didn't need another incident. The fact I wasn't changing was causing some concern already.

Despite the weirdness of it all—and the fact I knew I was under constant assault by a body and mind warping virus which only a hastily assembled biofilter was protecting me from—it was perhaps the most relaxing two days I'd had in years.

The attack came suddenly.

I was carrying an armful of wood to the main hall when I heard the sounds of bullets. I dropped the wood, spun, and drew myself in an instant, seeing a soldier I'd come to know as Nat suddenly, violently, bisected, his blood casting odd patterns on the white snow and on two civilians near him. One barely had time to react in shock before he, too, fell dead. I rolled behind a small wooden structure, a communal storage shed, more to keep myself from being an obvious target than for any protection it might provide.

I saw soldiers rushing to respond. They came from all directions, with a constant stream of inaudible conversation. I saw a flash of black and heard the sudden thud as a knife buried itself in one invader. I moved out from behind my shield and took stock.

Eight attackers, all armed with a variety of assault weapons, decent body armor but nothing fancy. It looked like ceramic inserts under a carbon fiber weave. The knife-thrower had scored a lucky hit between plates, taking one down. Two other knives whizzed past me and were mostly deflected by the armor.

I slid naturally into combat mode.

MacIntyre has entire medical libraries at his beck and call, the accumulated knowledge of centuries, and specialized subprograms to do a lot of the grunt work for him. His consciousness, his knowledge and judgment, is focused on interpreting and applying what the rest of his mind digs up. He can learn anything he decides to put his mind to (except maybe humility), but he's very good at what he was built for without even having to try.

So am I.

I am capable of absorbing a huge range of sensory input and turning it, in milliseconds, into a perfect firing solution. Even the exact time it takes a nerve impulse to travel from my brain to my muscles is figured into my calculations. I decide on a target, and a thousand specialized processors leap into action, reading everything from the wind speed to the particulate matter in the air and working it out, incorporating predictive algorithms based on target motion, and produce a result accurate to a thousandth of a second. If I am more than a millimeter off target when I fire, I know I need diagnostic scans.

First target: a woman firing madly, not even aiming, simply spraying lead in a wide arc. Armor is solid and well made, but I want one shot, one kill. Her eyes. The strength of the plastic, the density of her skull, the motion of her head as she turns to change her aim... everything feeds in and I see a perfect line through the goggles, through her eye socket, direct to her brain. I don't choose to move; I don't choose to fire. The target is set, the calculation is complete, and my body moves, bringing me up and in line and a timer hits zero when everything is in position and there's a brief shudder as I fire, the bullet seeming to move in slow motion, the world frozen as it passes, to my inner sight, along a perfect line to the target, who doesn't even have time to twitch before she collapses, dead.

She drops like a rock, and ripples of fear and shock spread from her, passing to the others, who were not expecting this. The nearest to her is next; he has done a poor job of sealing his armor and there is a patch of skin at the base of his throat which is exposed. I shoot again, and there is barely time for him to gurgle before the bullet rips apart his spine and he falls limply down. A third shot is lined up—

And aborted. One of the soldiers interfered, slashing at the attacker with his claws, tearing off his face mask and gouging long, bloody, streaks. The attacker screamed and tried to twist away, but the soldier was strong. The long barreled assault rifle was clumsy in hand-to-hand combat, and the attacker could not bring it to bear. I retargeted, going for a hand shot, to disarm him. A thousand variables danced, spun, and finally collapsed into a single point of certainty, and the gun fell from his useless hand.

Next.

The other soldiers were moving out. Three lay dead already, but a half-dozen had swarmed onto the remaining attackers. In the shifting chaos, I fired more slowly, taking into account every move of my momentary allies. I refused to fire at anything more than one standard deviation of certainty.

As this occurred, my conscious mind, my self, watched with interest. I'd fed the parameters and protocols to the firing routines, and I just had to be aware and alert to change them if the situation changed; I no more thought about the action of firing than a person thinks about exactly how to move their legs when going for a walk. One thought which occurred to me was that I was defending people I was spying on, people who might be willing agents or unwitting tools of some malevolent power. Perhaps those I had helped kill were battling whatever did this; perhaps they represented some force we could ally ourselves with.

It looked like it wouldn't matter; there would be no survivors to identify me. Besides, my mission was to infiltrate this colony and gather information; it was not to destroy them. The attackers, regardless of their motive, were my enemies at the moment. A freelancer can't be too picky about which side they're on; the most important thing is staying loyal to your employer as long as your employer is loyal to you.

So how much has MacIntyre paid you? I asked myself. Not much, I replied, but it's a place to stay and a role to fill, and no one's made me a better offer. So I remain loyal.

The attackers had been routed, but at cost. I counted ten dead, mostly soldiers, but three civilians had been struck down as well.

Teres was among them. She was slumped against a tree, barely recognizable. Despite the obviously fatal wounds, I still touched her, to see if, somehow, she could respond or showed any signs of life. If there was anything, anything at all, I could find MacIntyre,

make him do his job... but there was nothing. I gently lowered her
to the ground and, in that pure red haze of fury, went to see if
there was anyone I could still kill.

There was. Two of the soldiers were carrying someone, scarred
and slashed but still breathing and struggling feebly. I took aim
and told them to drop him.

"No. Not kill."

"Why the hell not?"

I didn't need their permission. I had a clear shot. Something
held me back. "Why not?" I repeated, my voice twisted with anger.

"No need. He will be one of us. We lost some. We need more."

I waged a small war with myself, there. To fire did not take
even the twitch of a finger, just an act of will. A thought and the
helpless prisoner died. It was a pleasing thought.

I had a mission, though. I had an assignment, a job to do—
infiltrate and observe. Seeing the transformation process would be
valuable to my employer. Loyalty, duty, responsibility... if I had
nothing else left, I had my values. Hating every instant of it, I
lowered the gun and let the soldiers pass.

Damn it.

I tromped after them, across snow turned to crimson mush. I
saw survivors, civilians, working to gather up the bodies, piling
them. I didn't care. I followed the soldiers.

They took him to one of the smaller outbuildings. I'd glanced at
it a few times, but saw nothing inside it. I figured it was for
storage; I asked Teres, and she'd simply said "For later," a
meaningless reply which nonetheless satisfied her.

They forced him inside, still bleeding from deep slashes, and
stripped off his uniform and weapons, tossing them in a pile. I
noticed he had external comm gear, a small black ovoid two inches
long. I pocketed it. I also checked to see if the ammo was
compatible with my own; it wasn't. So much for dog robbing.

A civilian came in, bearing tea. The soldiers were not at all
gentle; they simply forced his mouth open (I think I heard some
bones crack, if not break) and poured it down. He choked and
gagged, but swallowed.

Then they left, leaving me standing outside. A heavy wooden
bolt was slammed down. Primitive, but to the nearly naked man
inside, fully effective. Well, unless he had some kind of tricks.
Acid-spewers in his hands, muscles laced with memory metals and
four times stronger than baseline, components of a laser stored in
a flesh pouch. I doubted it. None of them had shown any signs of

such improvements. His age was twenty-five or so; he probably was too young to have had that kind of extensive surgery. Bodymods like that aren't usually added until the body is fully developed; it's a rite of passage, or it was.

Beyond that, he wasn't guarded.

I watched the others react. No one spoke to me; they hardly spoke to each other. They gathered up the bodies, soldiers, civilians, and invaders alike, and began to build a pyre.

I found Nick. He was still alive, though bleeding from a shoulder wound.

"Well? Now what?"

He looked at me oddly. "The dead must be burned."

"Yes, fine. Are you going to be interrogating the prisoner? I've got some questions for him..."

This stumped him for a long time. I counted thirty five seconds while he tried to find an answer.

"The man we took will be one of us."

"That's *it?* Don't you want to know where he came from? If there's more of them coming? If you need to leave? Now?"

"We cannot leave."

"Why the hell *not?*"

"We cannot leave."

"Teres is dead! So are many others! Don't you *care?* Don't you even want to strike *back?*"

"We have lost some. We need more." Then he stopped and considered deeply. "You should be one of us. You are not one of us." This contradiction was, I could tell, taxing him. Finally, he reached a conclusion. "Would you like more tea?"

MacIntyre's filter seemed to be holding. "Sure, why not?"

"Good."

That was it. Friends and lovers dead, people injured, a baseless and pointless attack, and no reaction but a form of brute instinct. It was horrifying. I wanted to hate them for not caring about Teres, but I couldn't. It would be like hating a cat for killing a mouse. It wasn't that they didn't care... they couldn't.

I could hate what did this to them, though. And I did. There's a lot of beauty in hate. It's clean and pure, unsullied by confusion and contradiction. Attention, people of the unknown future reading this! Some philosophers might tell you love is the essence of humanity. They're fools and liars. Anything can love. Only humans can hate.

Most of my hate was aimed at the unknown bastard behind this whole scheme, but I have a lot to go around. I had some for the poor loser getting his genes rearranged in a shed. I decided to go talk to him.

No one was guarding it. I guess they figured there was no need; he couldn't get out and no one in the compound would want to get in unless they needed to.

He was slumped in the corner, shivering in the cold. My suit kept me nicely insulated, but he was wearing pretty much rags, and there was no heat here. He huddled around the cup of tea desperately, clinging to the fading warmth. Bad programming on the part of the Unknown Bastard, putting new 'recruits' at risk of death.

He looked up when he saw me. He spoke, painfully, his jaw definitely fractured.

"Yuh... yuhr h'man."

"I know someone who'd disagree. But yeah, what of it?"

"He'p me!"

"In case you missed it, I killed three of your pals. You're lucky my mission parameters don't let me kill you."

"Wuh... why?"

"Did I kill your people? Because my job is to study these people, and killing their enemies is a good way to do that. Now let me correct something. I am here to interrogate *you*."

His eyes widened a bit, and he nodded.

"Great. Here's the carrot. Make me happy and I get you some blankets, at least. Here's the stick. Make me unhappy, and I go out and find a very large stick and... well, you're smart enough to figure out the rest." *For the moment,* I thought. No sense telling him he was about to become a lot hairier and even less talkative.

Now I'm acting like MacIntyre. Damn.

"First, the basics. Name, rank, and unit of service."

"Puh...al Guhadd. Puhrvat. Nuhew Nuphwehst Ahr..."

"Paul... Gud? No.. .Gadd? Ah. Private, New Northwest Army. Right?"

He nodded.

"What are they doing out here?"

"Suh... kowting. Suh... sent off alone."

"How did you find this compound?"

"Wuh... wurhd en'rgy suh... gnatchure..."

"Energy signatures. So, you just decided to storm in and start killing people?"

"Nuh... not human. Didn't know what... what they were..." He coughed up a little blood. Was he sweating, even in the cold? "Ruh... recruit... or... exuhr... mon... ate..."

"And you figured you couldn't recruit them, so, decided to wipe them out?"

"Buh... base. Suh... suhplies."

Yes. Definitely sweating. Not even fear would do that in this cold.

"How many of you are stationed hear here? Where's your nearest base?"

He forced a hideous parody of a smile. "Fuh... you."

Well, I didn't think he'd talk that easily. There was nothing he'd said so far which wasn't obvious, but if I wanted to get him to tell me the good stuff, I'd need to work at it.

Now he was shivering, which made sense, but was still sweating.

"We can get back to that. How did you end up joining, anyway?"

He pointed to his jaw. Fine. It wasn't like he was going anywhere. I got up to leave.

"Bank't."

He *had* cooperated. On the other hand, he, or one of his allies, had killed Teres for no reason other than that she was there.

"Maybe later. If I'm in a good mood. Which I never am."

I left and carefully locked the door.

The next day, I began to notice a change in how I was treated. I would have thought my actions in the attack would have, if anything, increased their friendship. Instead, I was kept at a distance. People would walk up, smell me, and then walk away shaking their heads. I heard constant fragments of conversation drifting around me, words I could not understand.

No one seemed to want or demand my help with anything. I spent about an hour sitting on a cold rock, watching some of the others splash and fish in the near-freezing water. They seemed happy enough, despite the recent tragedy. I tried to talk to Nick about it.

"You seem to have recovered well."

He glanced at his shoulder. "It will heal."

"No, I mean... you—all of you—this village... a day ago, you were attacked. Now, everything's... normal."

"That was past. Past is forgotten."

Then he walked off. That was about all I could get from anyone. No past. No future. Just an eternal present of stimulus-response.

The Unknown Bastard had a lot to answer for.

I had a feeling this infiltration was drawing to a close. I needed to get out before odd looks and ultrasonic whispers turned to active hostility. I only had so much ammo, after all.

I decided to make one final check on Paul. For all I knew, he had frozen to death overnight.

Neither of us was that lucky.

He was flopped over on his side, but still breathing. His clothing, what was left of it, was drenched... but not with sweat. It was an amber fluid, somewhat mucous-like. Where his skin was exposed, I saw parts of it had dried to a thin, flaky substance that seemed to be accreting rapidly.

"Can you talk?" I nudged him with my foot.

"Yeah."

"Jaw feeling better?"

"Little."

"Good. How do you feel?"

"Hell."

"Not surprised. What's your name, again?"

"Paul."

"Paul what?"

"Paul... Guh... something. I don't know. Leave me alone."

"What's your mother's name?"

He paused a second. "Don't know."

"Did you ever know?"

"Yeah... yeah, I think so. Shit."

I grabbed one of his hands and studied it. There were fine hairs sprouting on it, and the nails were showing signs of elongation and thickening. The virus was fast. Faster than anything I'd ever heard of. These kinds of changes normally take weeks or months under intensive care and observation. The energy requirements... his body must be burning itself alive to fuel the process.

"What was your mission here?"

"Scouting... something..."

"For who?"

"Army... Northwest. General! General Cromney! Must report back... must tell him..."

Forgot his mother but still remembered his CO. Loyal, I'll give him that.

A spasm took him. He vomited a little. The cup he'd been given with the tea lay there, discarded. Using some of the scraps of uniform, I scooped the vomit into the cup. MacIntyre would want it.

"Help me."

"No."

"Kill me."

It was tempting. One bullet would end it for him. At the thought, the firing solution appeared, simple and perfect.

It would be an act of mercy, I realized, not vengeance. It would be morally pure.

"No," I said. "Some are lost. More are needed."

Mercy isn't really what I do.

All that remained was to leave.

I found Nick again. "Hey, I, uh, haven't been helping out much since the attack. You need more wood?"

Nick pondered. "No. You must stay here."

Interesting. This was the first time they'd been restrictive. My lack of changing must be triggering some little-used subprograms in what passed for their brains.

"I'm getting a bit twitchy. I'd really prefer to go out for a bit."

"No. You must stay here."

Locked in a loop. Only way to do anything about it would be to force him to adapt to unexpected circumstances. MacIntyre's biofilter worked, so I hoped his and Mike's adjustments to protect me from the field would, as well.

I dashed for the fence.

I will give the Unknown Bastard this much, he had them programmed for rapid emergency response. As soon as I moved, Nick howled something in the ultrasonic and came after me. Killing him would be trivial, but I didn't want to. He was just following orders without the capacity to judge.

I felt his heavy hand on my shoulder. I grabbed it, braced myself, and flung him past, sending him tumbling, then caught the momentum of the throw and tumbled forward. Two other soldiers were coming at me, and the fence was close. I turned on the adrenal glands and dropped all pain warning, pushing my body beyond its normal limits. They closed on me; I was faster.

I hit the Fence and my mind burned for a second. Then all was black.

Then it was white, the white of snow, and it was coming up to hit me, fast. My speed and instinct had carried me a good fifteen feet from the Fence, but I was now falling face-first into the snow. No chance to recover; I landed ungracefully. Push up, spin, try to stand, and now Nick was on me, all friendship gone. He had his mission, I had mine. Targets spun in my vision to kill, to maim, to wound, but I ignored them.

Instead, I kicked.

Nick grunted, momentarily stunned, and I used that moment to stand. Two more coming in. Damn. There was no easy way to stand against three of them without shooting. They had a significant mass and muscle advantage, and there was only so far I could push this body. One easy, two with some effort, all three... someone was going to have to die, and it wasn't going to be me.

Suddenly, a long dead channel came to life. "Jill! Contact! You all right? I'm getting some elevated signals here..."

"In a fight. Call back later."

"On route!"

Could I hold off killing them until MacIntyre arrived? It would be an interesting question.

"OK. Do not kill hostiles, repeat, do not kill. Unless you have to."

He didn't say anything, but I could tell he was confused. Fortunately, that entire conversation occurred in a few half-second flashes of data transfer, so I still had time to react to the onrushing attackers.

They had size and strength, I had speed... and the knowledge I could kill them if I needed to. It's always a comforting thought to know the level of lethality is on your terms.

Environment check. Snow. Rocks. Trees. Fallen branch. Hmm.

Nick was still getting to his feet when the second soldier moved in. He wasn't using his knives; they wanted me alive, since I'd already been infected. I feinted; he grabbed at where I wasn't as I grabbed the snow-covered hunk of wood and swung it around as hard as I could. I had a good idea how tough the soldiers were and wasn't too worried about breaking his spine. The blow struck true, and he tumbled forward with a howl, even as the third tore the branch from my hand and tossed it away.

We faced off. I heard Nick moving around behind me, planning a grab. Couldn't have that. I leapt forward, ducked, and rolled past the other. Now both were in front of me, and the third was starting to test the limits of his pain.

Nick charged. I leapt, grabbed a low-hanging branch, and, in a shower of released snow, kicked him in the face. His nose broke audibly. Sorry, Nick, I thought, but you'd rather have a foot there than a bullet.

It's annoying fighting people you know. Even if you're not entirely sure they're still people.

I heard a well known hum.

A somewhat poorly camouflaged ambulance was making its way through the trees, its defensive coloration broken in several places by patched armor and simple damage. Mike was leaning out the window, holding grenades. I hoped they were gas-filled.

They were.

Thick white mist coiled up from the impact point. The three soldiers, caught unawares, breathed it in. They still kept after me. I had ducked away, but there was still some of it in the surrounding air, as well as settling on my skin. I felt my body beginning to fail, the muscles slacking. They had greater exposure, but also greater mass; the gas was diluted. One grabbed at me and pulled me down, my limp body unable to resist despite my urgings. Then I lost all body-based sensory input. I watched, immobile and annoyed, as Mike and MacIntyre got me into the medibay and plugged me in. There was a brief flood of counteragent, and body and mind were both at about the same level of functionality.

"You all right?" Mike leaned over me.

"Perfect. Let's get out of here."

End Infiltration Log

Chapter 11

I decided not to ask Jill why she'd privacy-sealed a section of her log when the whole point was to make it a public record; I had a feeling it would just get me an angry sullen silence. Well, more of one. Jill had always walked around in a vague cloud of inchoate rage at the world, but now the cloud had condensed into a sort of armor, gained focus and definition. On the plus side, it wasn't aimed at me. On the minus side, seeing all that rage narrowed and channeled was a bit intimidating. It was like handling a vibration-sensitive explosive when you didn't know precisely how well calibrated it was, if it would take a sledgehammer blow to set it off or just an errant mosquito.

After I'd reviewed the logs we decided to talk about what to do with this information.

"I think we got bigger problems...damn NNA is growin' like fuel-grade kudzu. We're runnin' outta space to avoid them."

Jill shook her head. "They're just grunts with delusions of grandeur, scavenged gear, and a leader who doesn't trust his own command ability. The Unknown Bastard has tech I've never seen before."

"I agree with Jill. The NNA... well, they're a mundane threat. They're a typical response to a power vacuum. The Unknown Bastard—thank you for that term, by the way, Jill, it's very... descriptive—represents something, er, unknown. I want to figure out what's going on."

Mike nodded. "You may have a point. B'sides, it's not like we can do much about the NNA anyway. We almost got ourselves killed takin' out a minor camp they didn't bother to defend. Not seein' a way to hurt them hard, not now." He stopped then, and looked at the ceiling, moving his hands as if massaging an invisible cat.

Jill noticed this too. "You have an idea."

He glanced back at her. "You sound shocked. Anyway, yeah... if we track down and deal with this, uh, Unknown Bastard, well, we'd have access to somethin' the NNA doesn't. Might give us an edge."

Jill laughed. "Three of us against an army? Even with some supposed miracle tech..."

"No, not just us! I'm sure there's lots of folks sick of them and their raids and 'recruitment,' but they've got weapons an' trainin', and most people are still figurin' out how to live when the answers to math problems don't just pop into their heads from dataspace as soon as they think of 'em. They all feel like we do—what can we do? Well, if we can show 'em somethin' new, a weapon—somethin' to inspire 'em—well, they can be organized. They can fight back."

I admit to being a bit astonished. "That's... remarkably visionary."

"'For you.' That's what you were thinkin' but not sayin', right?"

I said nothing. Mike just nodded.

"Thought so. You shouldn't underestimate me, Doc."

"No, I shouldn't, and I apologize. Now. Can we get back to the topic at hand, please?"

It was like herding cats.

"We locate and terminate the UB."

"Any ideas *how*, Jill?"

"Yes. We talk to the trees."

It was a very good plan.

I started back towards the camp Jill had infiltrated. I tried to run silent. I doubted the locals could hurt me, but the less trouble we had, the better. When I got close, I dropped to standby power and suited up.

The three of us set out. I'm not sure why I bothered going out in the Charlie; logically, all I was doing was splitting my processing power unnecessarily as well as exposing myself to risk. I think part of it was that I was feeling, well, different. I'd thought, with Jill's nature, that I'd have someone who experienced the world the way I did, but she preferred direct input. And I was tired of feeling left behind. Form hadn't mattered much back when the world was sane, when almost everything that mattered happened in dataspace and no one knew or cared whether your body was meat or metal, but now, it was starting to, and I was starting to feel... disconnected. The Charlie was just a puppet; "I" was still a vehicle; but I could feel more a part of a community if I used it.

As it turned out, it was helpful. As I walked, I found myself suddenly stumbling as the connection between my real body and the Charlie faltered and dropped. They saw this happen and came to my side, supporting the body until I reconnected.

"What's up, Doc?" Mike said. Jill, with some background in classical media, winced.

"There's some powerful signals here..." I took a cautious step towards one particular tree and nearly collapsed. They hauled me back a few feet.

"That one."

Mike took an axe, part of my standard toolkit—you never know how useful an axe can be—and hacked a bit. There was flying wood and a sudden strong scent of pine (well, molecules my internal database identified as pine) and then he stopped and peered inside. The exposed flesh of the tree was glistening with what seemed to be silver dew, but a closer examination showed it to be fine wire.

I whistled.

Mike raised an eyebrow. "Growin' transmission trees isn't that impressive, Doc. Kids used to do it as a science fair project."

"This tree is about sixty years old."

"So?"

"Well, either someone was a few decades ahead of themselves on this kind of technology, or someone's found a way to infiltrate a grown tree with complex machinery."

"Oh. Yeah. That is pretty impressive."

It was. Designing something to leech metals from the soil as it grew so that it became a plant/machine hybrid was, as Mike said, child's play now. But doing it on a grown plant was a lot harder, at least without killing the plant. I wasn't sure how it was done, but this tree was infested with circuitry. We took a big chunk of it out and brought it back with us.

Mike and I spent a good hour modifying an MRI scanner to look at wood. Then we ran the sample through. It had a very complex appearing network, but like most organic-infiltration systems, it was mostly fractal redundancies. Things that work inside living systems tend to mimic them. It made them a lot more robust.

The wires grew until they pierced the bark. There they 'budded' into tiny, very tiny, visual and audio sensors. The in-tree network formed a primitive neural net, meeting in tiny processing clusters. Each of them was about as bright as a marketing executive, but the sum of them could do some fancy, if non-sentient, processing. What I found interesting was that there was no obvious transmission system. There were contact points—quite invisible to the human eye—but what was supposed to contact them?

Thus followed a very boring two days.

We set up near the tree and blanketed it with every sensor we could, watching every tiny fluctuation in power output or even the tree's own biology. The first few minutes were exciting, as every little flux and variant seemed promising, but they were quickly eliminated as not meaning anything. I ended up turning half my processing over to solving it while keeping my subconscious out of it. Jill and Mike felt trapped, as I'd cautioned against wandering where the locals could spot them, especially Jill, who was known to them. Tempers, never very long to begin with, were short. Both Mike and Jill wanted to act, to do something, but they couldn't agree on what, and I think they were getting annoyed with me constantly urging patience and having nothing to show for it. I couldn't even really enjoy an interactive; too much of my processing was spent on watching, waiting, and studying.

Then I saw patterns. Correlations of internal and external events. When I reviewed the data—four times, to be sure it wasn't coincidence—I was astonished by how simple and complex it was.

"It's birds."

I tossed up a holographic model of the tree, with the various internal networks highlighted and glowing. "Those are cameras, there," I said, making them briefly sparkle red, "and audio sensors there. But those are the output points"—a blue glow—"and they don't seem to do much, until—"

I then showed normal visual footage of a bird landing on the branch to peck for grubs, side by side with footage showing the internal actions of the tree. When the bird hit a contact point, there was a surge of information transmission, a tiny, very short range wireless pulse. Almost certainly, there was a receiver in the bird itself.

"Then it flies to the next tree, and downloads and uploads, and so on. Probably there's a homing instinct to make them head towards the source of this all."

"Carrier pigeons," Jill said. "Incredible. Everything old is new again."

"All we need to do is track the birds, figure out which ones are coming and which are going, and they will lead us right to the UB.

Almost all automated systems ignore organics. It's a waste of power and ammo to fry birds, unless they cross specific perimeter lines. As long as they don't act like they're plague carriers or spy birds or whatever, they'll be ignored. It's just..."

"What?" asked Mike.

"It's... complicated. And risky. This is a very intricate network to run with no real control or oversight. I've seen concepts for systems like this, but all relied on local nodes—manned or automated—to collect and collate the data, make sure there's no drift on the information gatherers, and so on. For something like this to work, and work reliably... it's pretty advanced."

Jill shrugged. "Rate of tech change accelerates. You know that."

"Yes, but everything's been in a state of chaos since the Collapse. People are struggling to eat. There's people riding horses, for God's sake! Who has the resources for this kind of project, and why are they using it for—for this, instead of trying to restore some kind of civilization? Hell, even the damn NNA is trying to put the pieces back together again."

"Maybe they are."

"Maybe they are *what*, Mike?"

"Tryin' to restore civilization. Or maybe fix it the way they think it oughtta be."

It was a terrifyingly plausible suggestion.

Jill nodded, slowly. "Damn."

"You're right, Mike. I shouldn't underestimate you."

"Damn straight. So, now what?"

"We track the Unknown Bastard to his lair. He left a trail of bread crumbs. Well, feathers."

It was a good, albeit simple, plan. Pity it didn't work.

Following the trail was slow, even though we knew what odd radio signatures to follow and which birds to track. This kind of network was always flaky; since it was spreading organically, according to algorithm instead of design, it sometimes spawned branches to nowhere or took strange, circuitous routes. Further, the Unknown Bastard didn't want anyone tracking it (obviously) and so had gone out of his way to disguise it, so that anyone stumbling upon parts of it would conclude they belonged to different, possibly even competing, systems, set up long ago and then abandoned. We moved slowly northeast for about a week, at a rate barely above the speed of ancient wagon trains. We kept watch for the usual things—nomads in need of healing, bandits in need of killing, and so on. We didn't find much. Mike and Jill had begun hunting for food, going out as a team. I had managed to modify some of my surgical tools for use in food preparation; if the whole 'traveling medic' thing fell through, Mike joked, we could always go into business as a taco stand.

Sometimes, I regretted taking that bomb out.

We were skirting an area of fairly dense ruins now; the network had spread through the rapidly expanding greenbelt which had once surrounded the community. There was a strangely sepulchral feel to it all, the overgrown shells of fast food joints, body modification parlors, and factory-stores looking like odd topiary beasts. The architectural style here had gone for a momentary fad of steeples and spires; this year's craze, next year's relic, construction turned as cheaply and easily mutable as flesh, so that the pointed tips of the abandoned and looted buildings burst through the shrouding branches like ribs sticking through a decomposing corpse.

Damn. That was morbid. I suppose I have somewhat biased memories of that area, due to what happened next.

We'd been so alone for so long that I'd grown slack on the scanners. We needed to use active sensors to do a lot of our tracking work, and that was part of the problem; I had to focus almost all my attention on analyzing and interpreting the data, that was another part. What it all came to, though, was an ambush.

Perhaps the fact I had all active sensors turned on helped save us.

I saw two fast moving objects on the radar, and it took a nanosecond to project that their target was *me*. It took a few more nanoseconds to activate prediction/evasion protocols, and then a painfully long second before the machinery of the Heim field could respond to its new directives. My mind worked in a world mostly free of mass and inertia, save at an imperceptible level; my body, however, did not, and while the Heim field mocked some of Newton's rules, it was still bound by others. In what seemed to me to be painful slow motion, I began moving in a twisting zigzag pattern through the wooded ruins, stirring up leaves and decade-old litter in a cloud behind me. I ran down a quick checklist of countermeasures—chaff, gone. Reflective aerosols, gone. Hot-spot target dummies, gone. Railgun—

"Mike! Ready for neural?"

"Yeah! What the hell's goin' on?"

"Someone's trying to kill us!"

"Same old, same old. Hook me in!"

I did. I felt his mind interfacing with my targeting and arming systems, saw parts of my body turn and move under someone else's control. It was always slightly discomfiting to let go like that, even when survival depended on it. I wasn't good at sharing control. Ever. It's one reason I went solo most of the time; I'd been partnered with a human medic once or twice and it never really worked out.

I was avoiding; they were tracking. Mike spun the railgun around and honed in on one of them. We weren't using laser guidance, just my own general sensor sweeps, so the missile didn't know anyone was going to shoot at it. That gave us a much needed edge. It exploded in a rain of shrapnel, starting small fires around the barren hulk of an EyePod vision modification franchise.

This alerted the second missile that something was up. Its robotic brain, seeing its twin vanish in flame, switched to a defensive flight program. It still closed in on us, but now it was running its own prediction algorithms, seeking to analyze and fool ours. It checked how Mike fired in response to its swerves, tried to deduce the algorithm we were using, and modified its own to match. Of course, we were doing the same. Move and counter-move. It all came down to who could build a better model of what the opponent was thinking and then apply it.

As I'd learned many times over, no one could build a model of how Mike thought. He was contrary even in his contrariness; if you accounted for his being difficult, he somehow sensed it and *stopped* being difficult.

The missile learned this to its short-lived sorrow. It thought it had the game figured out; it launched into a final series of swoops and rolls designed to blow me to hell and gone; and it ended in a blaze of fire.

Unfortunately, it got a bit too close.

Part of the explosion engulfed my right side. I could feel shrapnel tearing against me, rattling off the outer armor, and shredding delicate systems in my underbelly. The Heim field went wild, flaring madly, and I spun partially out of control before cutting it off completely. A quick system scan showed red and yellow over most of the field controls; only a few small parts of the system still shone a peaceful, reassuring, green. Very few.

That was just the beginning.

Those who had launched the missiles followed after. They were a ragged bunch, but well organized; seeing that their initial attack had failed, they spread out, evaluating the situation and sizing up the opposition. I never did learn precisely why they attacked; I suspect they assumed any vehicle passing through was the vanguard of a hostile force, and they were just defending the tiny bit of territory they'd claimed as theirs, possibly via exterminating the previous claimants, as was the way all societies are born. In any event, they were "We" and we were "They," as far as they were concerned, and "we" must ever destroy "they," before they can do the same to us.

I counted fifteen. Most had assault rifles; a few handguns. An assortment of other weapons—monowire, edged knives, and the like—dangled at belts. Using the railgun would be slaughter. Unfortunately, it was rapidly becoming a non-option; the near-miss had hit power feeds and we were losing charge on one battery rapidly, even with the Heim field off. The dim winter light meant recharging had been slow, the power required to split hydrogen from water taking barely less than it was giving, over time, and the railgun was a huge power sink.

They didn't want to talk or negotiate or offer terms; they just attacked. Maybe they didn't think there was a point, that it had to be kill or be killed. Maybe they'd tried to negotiate before and had been betrayed. Maybe they were insane. Either way, it was a battle seemingly without purpose. We were there, and so were they, and that was that.

Jill rapped on the dashboard. "Reason for not returning fire?"

"Insufficient power. Jill, if you want to—"

She was out the door. Mike followed.

Jill moved like a bullet spewing blur. Partially invisible even with the damage to her chameleon cloth suit, she fired while in constant motion, each shot dropping an attacker. Mike was less skilled, but did his part. When half of them had fallen without a single casualty on our side—at least none they could see—the rest withdrew. The entire battle was over in under a minute.

The consequences were a bit longer lasting.

"OK, Doc. Let's get out of here before they come back with friends."

"Not happening."

"What?"

I tossed up schematics of myself, complete with nicely color coded sections showing areas of major and minor damage. I followed the tradition of using shades of red for disabled components. The image was a study in scarlet.

"Oh. Shit. Can you move at all?"

"A little, but not for long. Stress calculations..." I showed them. "I've got a few hundred feet, maybe. Then that snaps, this shorts, and those just explode, and I stop dead."

"Huh. Well, I can fix it. We just need about twenty feet of ambient temperature superconductor, a monopole containment unit, and a few q-bit interpolation systems. Then we can patch things up again." He stopped for a second, the mind of the theoretical engineer solving a problem as a test case giving way to the practical technician asked to implement it. "But we don't have any of that shit. I remember our little bargain back at that truck stop."

Jill had been listening. "First step, you get out of sight. Second step, we do a recon and retrieve."

I concurred.

I ran a quick scan of the area. Fortunately, there were places to hide, places secure from casual discovery. This area had been picked clean over and over again; it was unlikely anyone coming across it would search it in detail. If I was mostly powered down, I'd look like a random hunk of metal in a building, nothing to pique anyone's curiosity. I hoped.

We found a place in range, or what I hoped was in range. It was once a domed sports arena before it had been repurposed into a nursery long ago. The interior had been stripped, creating a hollow space, and overgrown. The trees were barren now, but would bloom in a few months, and hopefully I'd be long gone by then.

The problem was, being out of sight meant being out of the sun. There were a few trickles of sunlight drifting in, enough to provide minimal power if I didn't do much, but otherwise... I was going to be limited, very limited, in what I could do.

The place was barely in range. I didn't so much glide the last twenty feet as skid. The Heim field gave out and I landed hard, doing even more damage to my systems as I went.

I took inventory. Assuming nothing but consciousness, I could stay here almost indefinitely. Anything more than that, and I risked using power faster than I could recharge it. I was basically trapped here unless or until Jill or Mike could get supplies... and I had to admit to myself that was a long shot, at best.

I ran a few quick projections of solar passage, and Mike and I moved around a couple of receptors to gain maximum power. It still wasn't much.

Then came the discussion.

"Both of you?"

Jill and Mike nodded.

"I'm not really comfortable with that. I'm sort of helpless here. Besides, I thought solo recon was your specialty."

"It is, but it's dangerous out there. Two of us have a better chance of one making an escape or getting back to you, somehow. Otherwise... well, let's say you and Mike stay here. I don't come back. Mike decides to go out. He doesn't come back. You stay here and eventually die."

"Or you both step on a mine and die, and the same thing happens to me, except I have more time to sit alone and worry."

"You're forgettin' somethin' else. You can sit here like a lump for weeks, invisible. Mostly. If one of us stays, we'll need food... only so much in the back, not enough. We'll be out, movin', attractin' attention. Leadin' people right back here. B'sides, safety in numbers and all that."

"I still don't like it."

"You might not *like* it, but can you actually argue against it?"

I couldn't. I knew what my motives were: fear of loneliness, fear of abandonment. No one wants to die alone, or worse, live trapped and immobile. I could go on a long, long, time, stuck here. I felt helpless, and that made me angry. I tried to find good counter-proposals, other options, and while some of them made good sense, the two of them going as a team was the best choice of a poor selection. I could just go into a snit and not bother trying to explain or reason with them, but then what? They could just leave and there'd be no reason for them to come back.

So eventually I relented. I uploaded all of my map files to Jill, along with all the projections on probable settlements, nomad routes, bandit strongholds, and NNA expansions. They packed rations and stripped out everything I didn't need that they thought they could trade, including drugs and some pieces of medical equipment of lesser utility.

Perhaps more importantly, I convinced Mike to let me add some storage to the optical feed he already had. Jill could record her experiences already; now so could he. If they managed to get back, I wanted a record of everything they'd encountered for this journal.

And so they left. We'd gone over paths and probabilities, found a region where there should be people but no known hostiles, up along some stretches of the old NWA coast. I wished them luck, and they were off.

Thus began a strange interlude of about three weeks.

I kept careful watch on power. I could run off solar directly, but that left nothing to split water with, which meant I was dead if the solar faded for any length of time. So the first few days were spent sitting and thinking, playing chess, reviewing medical journals, and (for no good reason) trying to compose poetry. (These attempts are not included in this journal, as an act of mercy and compassion towards future peoples.)

After that, I had enough H stocked up that I could safely drain it at about the same rate it was being recharged, though I tried to keep each day's usage tilted positive. Really, the Heim field and the railgun were the big power sinks, so I slowly scraped a bit more fuel into the tanks despite the deep shadows I were, by necessity, stuck in. On the fourth day, I did some math, and realized I could keep the Charlie running for about three hours a day and still come out a tiny bit ahead. It would make me feel less claustrophobic. A bit.

I was a dog on a leash, a leash of some five hundred feet before the jammers in the area overwhelmed by ability to communicate. My world was a circle one thousand feet in diameter, a circle which consisted of the ruins of a park-mall under the canopy of a momentarily dead forest. It was a world of criss-crossing shadows, of skittering animals, of tiny, roach-like robots drinking in dewdrops of light and scurrying to futilely clean a few square inches of marble before they fall back into a powerless slumber. It was a world of broken signs, of overturned chairs, of dead terminals and empty shelves. It was a world of fear, for me, fear of hearing the tromp of explorers heading through the ruins, fear of never hearing anyone again, fear of a calculation error leading me to slowly lose power and awareness in that order. Mostly, it was a world of boredom. I'd been alone for long stretches before but never like this. I always had a purpose, a plan, a goal... and for the past few months... well, I wasn't sure I could call them friends, but at least companions. People to talk to, to argue with... mostly argue with.

Time oozed. My interactive library was getting played out; while it was fun to reread them with others, going over the same plotlines, even testing every bad idea and hidden feature, was pointless. The other games I had stored I'd either mastered or realized I never would. I thumbed through (metaphorically speaking) my loadout of the classic works of non-interactive fiction, all pre-Bono Act (of course), and found them mostly tedious and dull, not to mention the fact that when a character does something stupid, you can't make him do something smart and change the story. I really don't understand the appeal of non-interactives; it's something ivory tower types get and I don't.

After two weeks, I started developing... quirks. I've got the DSM-IX[6] in permanent storage, of course, with the AI appendices, and I spent a fun little day playing the self-diagnosis game in which I found I was paranoid, megalomaniacal, and sociopathic, not to mention OCD and ADD.

I had begun starting at random noises, mixing fear and hope with every sound I couldn't immediately identify as a squirrel burrowing for nuts or some drone working through its mindless routine with purposeless diligence. I spun complex scenarios of rescue and discovery in my mind, weighing the risks of exploring in the Charlie vs. the risks of just sitting still. Each time, I would find nothing, just a fallen branch or a bird pecking in the wood, and return to my body, half relieved, half distressed.

Despair slowly began to creep in, a black mold spreading inexorably on my consciousness. They were dead, both of them, killed by any of a hundred random nightmares of this world, or, worse, they'd found a better deal, a good place to settle down or people to join up with, and I was casually abandoned, no longer needed. Mike had already tried to kill me once; Jill was here because she needed purpose, and if she found a better one... I tried to tell myself it was foolish and stupid, but I didn't listen well.

At the end of three weeks, I was starting to try to find ways to make my life here bearable. I contemplated mental projects I could undertake, going through my small library of tools and databanks. I could try programming my own interactive, like everyone else on the planet has wished to. I could write the most detailed biological study of life in a one thousand foot diameter circle ever written. I could compose more poems.

Fortunately for the sanity of all sentient beings, that grim possibility never materialized. They returned, bearing spare parts and looking happier than I'd ever seen either of them.

---

[6] Diagnostic and Statistical Manual of Mental Disorders, Ninth Edition

"Hey, Doc!" Mike rapped his knuckles on my hull. "We've got it! All the bits we need to get you rolling—floating—then we can do some serious work."

"Great. I can't tell you how hideous it's been."

Mike glanced over to a chunk of plastic propped against a half-shattered wall. He began reading.

"'Endless stars drifting; they sing in silence. Blind eyes staring; they never blink.' The hell? Looks like laser etching. What's this?"

"Poetry." I said in resigned disgust.

"Huh. Looks like we got here just in time."

"Jill, do you have anything to add other than literary criticism?"

She, too, had been looking at the slab upon which my unfinished opus lay carved.

"Better than I could do. I guess. Anyway, we've got news and an offer. Things might be looking better for us, long term. Do you want a debriefing, or just to download the recordings?"

"I'll review the files later. Frankly, I am in serious need of actual interaction. Why don't you two just sit down and talk?"

They did. I have taken the liberty of taking their narrative and their recordings and integrating them into a semi-cohesive narrative. I've tried to keep editorial asides to a minimum.

Chapter 12

[[Begin: Mike and Jill's Tale]]

They set out in the morning, heading northeast. It didn't take long before they began arguing.

"The woods are safer."

"The roads are faster."

Mike stopped. "We don't know how much time he's really got. An' unlike you, I can't just turn off every little ache and pain and hike twenty straight hours."

"And, unlike me, you aren't trained in reconnaissance. Look. I don't tell you how to do your MOS[7], you don't tell me how to do mine, and we might manage to not kill each other before anything else tries to. Also... who has all the map data?"

"Fine, whatever. Just note I'm doin' it under protest."

So, with that settled (and by 'settled,' I mean, I'm deleting the same argument repeated about three times a day from this recording), they began moving through the forests, Jill leading, constantly updating the maps I'd downloaded with new information as they explored. The first day took them to the edge of a wide, fast moving, river.

Jill looked up and down it, concerned. Mike watched her for a few seconds, then spoke.

"No otters I can see."

"Not amused."

"Well, what were you lookin' for, then?"

"Hostiles. This is a source of fresh water. People will come here for it, so people will wait by it. That over there—" She gestured at a pile of leaves and branches on the opposite bank. "—is hollow. It looks like natural accumulation, but it's a blind. "

"Anyone in it?"

---

[7] military occupational specialty

"Not now."

"So what's the problem?"

"Well, whoever set it up could be coming back. Or, we're supposed to see it, notice that it's empty, and relax our guard. I'm assuming the latter."

She continued to scan the river, looking for any sign of ambush, as Mike grew ever more impatient and annoyed.

"Can we just *go*? If they wanted to kill us, they'd have done it by now."

"Maybe." She frowned. "They're well hidden. Damn. I miss MacIntyre's perceptions, sometimes. His sensors feeding into mine... well, it's damn useful." She took a final look up and down. "OK, let's go. There should be a ford nearby." She glanced at Mike. "Make a single comment about some other vehicle brand, and I will leave you here."

Mike shrugged."You keep ruinin' my fun."

"In any event, we ought to go south. It looks like the river is starting to narrow. A bit further, we should find a decent place to cross it."

"I was thinkin' north."

"Why?"

"Hunch, really. And thinkin' the woods are thicker up there, better chance of findin' some kind of natural bridge, like a fallen tree. And besides, we're supposed to be headin' northeast, and we're driftin' a bit off course."

"You forgot one reason. You're compelled to disagree with every decision I make, solely because I made it."

"Now that's just—"

There was a noise.

Jill spun, gun drawn, tracking the source. Mike did the same. It wasn't hard to spot; a huge, lumbering form rushing towards them. A virtual mountain of black fur, the bear was motivated by desperate hunger to attack, and it moved with terrifying speed. Jill seemed almost resigned as she aimed, targeted, and fired. A blossom of red appeared on the bear's skull, and it kept coming.

That surprised her. She'd taken no evasive measures, confident it would drop twenty feet before it reached her. By the time she'd realized that, somehow, she'd miscalculated, it was on her. A massive claw swipe caught her in the abdomen, and she fell back, bleeding, her hand maintaining a death grip on the gun as she brought it around to retarget and fire again.

Mike was not being idle. He had fired five times, four of them finding their mark, but the line of growing red stains did little to slow the beast down. Jill scrambled back, still bleeding, and stared at the creature hard.

"Subdermals! Damn it!"

It turned to continue its attack. Jill stepped left as it charged, spun, and fired once more. This time it gave a sudden agonizing howl and collapsed, blood gushing from an eye socket.

Mike had not put down his gun. "Someone's pet monster, huh? Y'think the boss is around?"

Jill coughed, then looked down at her now blood splattered hand. "No... look at it. Thin, fur patchy... it's a rogue, trying to survive on its own. Poor thing. It was probably insane."

"Yeah, poor thing. It nearly—hey, you all right?"

Jill wavered slightly. "There's been some... internal damage. Hard to keep upright..." She stumbled.

"Aw, hell. Doc's out of range, all I've got's this stuff..."

He helped her lay down on the snowy bank and got out the first aid kit. He cut away the chameleon cloth suit using the monowire shears, then winced at the three parallel gashes across Jill's stomach. He fumbled in the kit. "OK, Doc taught me this coagulant spray first... then antibiotic patches... then synthskin bandage... you gonna be able to walk?"

Jill didn't speak, but the gun did, its voice surprisingly like Jill's own. "I'm going to need help if I don't want to risk doing more damage to the body. I think... if you support me... I can move well enough. Just let the coags work and the skinspray dry."

An hour later, they were reaching the top of a small hill. Mike dropped down low and slowly peered over it.

"Huh."

"What? I don't want to wake the body up, it's healing. Either bring me up where I can see, or tell me what's going on."

"There's a damn weird vehicle down there. Looks like an NWA 'Ocelot' Mobile Command Post, but it's been... modified."

"How?"

"Two more turrets, a bunch of small anti-personnel guns on the sides, some more armor 'round the middle, and, oh yeah, it's glowing orange and green with streaming letters runnin' along it."

"That's almost worth waking up for. What do the letters say?"

"Uhm... 'Marty and Mary's Travelling Tech Trading Post'... looks like they're talkin' to some other guys on Heim bikes.."

"Hold on. Incoming."

(Note: This conversation was inaudible to Mike; it is transcribed here from Jill's recordings.)

"...observers on north ridge. You have been spotted. Targeting solutions have been calculated. Any hostile actions will result in attack. Repeat. Attention observers..."

"This is Jill Huochong. We don't plan hostilities but we will defend ourselves. Who are you?"

"Marty and Mary's..."

"Right, we read it. What's your line of work?"

"We trade tech, perform repairs, exchange knowledge... and we're not stupid, weak, or undefended. Just so you're clear on that."

"Great. We're customers."

"Excellent! Well, come on down... slowly. And we have drones scattered everywhere, so don't even think of bringing up more. We *will* see them and we *will* fire without warning."

"Not a problem."

Mike was shaking Jill's shoulder, rather unnecessarily. "So... you still there? I'm thinkin'... probably not hostile..."

"It's OK. I've entered into negotiations. Let's get down there."

The MCP was the main vehicle: it was about fifty feet long and ten wide, with a generally ovoid body mounted on many sets of tracks. Its outer surface was a layer of liquid crystal over a much thicker layer of heavy armor, environmentally sealed. Two turrets had been added to the top, missile firing, and smaller weapons systems had been fitted around the base, between the main body and the treads. A front cab held two, a driver and a gunner; there was also a rear bubble which contained another firing position. This was the lead vehicle of the convoy; there were four other, smaller, craft, all heavily armed and armored. The entire group numbered fourteen.

When Jill and Mike descended, three of the bike riders looked up, startled, and began to draw weapons. Someone down there, the person they had been dealing with, gestured at them frantically. There was a hurried and apparently private conversation, and the guns lowered, though there were still wary glances.

More guns trained on them as a door, actually, more of a small airlock, opened in the side of the vehicle and someone came out, holding an assault rifle and wearing combat armor. He approached Mike and Jill cautiously.

"What do you got, what do you need?" he asked, his voice muffled by the full face helmet he was wearing.

"Right now, we mostly need medical help, if you can spare it. She's pretty bad off..."

There was a pause. "OK, remote scans say she's not faking it. You stay here. If we may..." He slid his rifle over his shoulder and held out his hands.

Carefully, Mike transferred Jill over. The man glanced down. "Take her gun. We don't need her suddenly going psycho on us inside."

Jill opened the connection I'd implanted in Mike's head. "Can't do that. There's no way my signals will get through that armor."

Mike frowned. "Uhm... look. We can take the ammo out, but she's kind of... uh... attached to the gun."

The man frowned behind the clear carbon faceplate. "I don't like it. We're trying to do the right thing here, but we've got policies for a... hang on." There was a muted conversation. Then he nodded. "OK, I've got authorization. I don't understand it, but I've got it. Remove the clip and she can come in."

Mike did so.

Jill's limp body was taken inside the MCP. It seemed to fit the outside, a bizarre mix of cutting-edge military gear and strange personal affectations. It was crowded and cluttered to an amazing degree, but to a practiced eye, there was order and purpose. Everything was built to be folded, stowed, and secured in short order. The six bunks, three on each side, which lined the rear section were surrounded by seeming junk and gewgaws which said a lot about the personalities of those who slept there. A one-man medical unit, not standard issue on an MCP that I knew of, occupied part of one wall. A cabinet of medical supplies and tools rested above it, a mesh screen keeping them in place during maneuvers. At three places along the length of the vehicle, there were mostly-open partitions and a folding control stick—the MCP could segment itself into three craft for tight curves or, I suspected, hasty getaways. There were signs of damage to the rear segment which ended abruptly at the middle segment—it had been caught in some kind of attack.

Jill was placed in the medibay, gun still attached, and a feeder tube inserted itself into her arm. At the angle she was at, there was no clear footage of anything but the ceiling—which held an ornate mobile composed of ultra-light gears and tools, too bent to be useful—but I could make some guesses about what the screens were showing.

Someone else came up to her. A man in his seeming early forties, with wispy brown hair and grey eyes, tall and thin, dressed in loose fitting fatigues. He leaned over her, smiled, and then began looking at the readings. He nodded, as if confirming something, then turned to the armored man who had brought Jill in.

"You can go, Kevin."

"Are you sure, Marty? I don't really trust..."

"I'm sure."

He shrugged. "You're the boss." He then stepped into the one-man airlock and left. It was designed to let people out if the MCP was stuck in a hostile area, one filled with poisons or plagues. Even in relatively clean air, it kept the chances of accidental contamination down.

Marty checked some more readings, then did something out of sight. A recording of Jill's biostats told me it was a standard mix of painkillers, antibiotics, and healing accelerators. A set of multi-jointed fractal arms descended from the ceiling and began removing the bandage and sewing the wounds. He sat down, with only a part of his body in camera range.

"OK, first thing, does he know? The man you're with, I mean."

Jill's voice responded. "Yes."

"OK, that makes it easier." He paused. "Who was she? A criminal? Or someone looking for a big payout for family?"

"Neither. She was my partner. My best friend."

"Oh. Oh! That's... interesting." He seemed to shudder. "And, if you don't mind my saying so, a little... creepy." He paused, as if considering. "This guy... this guy was a serial rapist. Sick little shit. I can't begin to describe what he did."

"You're..."

"Yes. You can call me Martin Boole. Though I prefer Marty." He moved a bit. "Ah, the feed's done. Looks like we got most of the nasties cleared out, though I wouldn't recommend any strenuous gymnastics for a while."

"Do *they* know?"

He nodded. "I have it easier than you... it's all internal. But when you're surrounded by customizers with a fetish for every kind of scanner, sensor, and doo-dad under the sun, you can't keep secrets like a body full of neural fiber for long. Could have lied, I suppose, found some convenient excuse, but what would be the point? They'd find out anyway."

"You're Marty. Who's Mary?"

"My partner in trade. We worked together on the Reno/Deseret border for a while, mobile maintenance and engineering, then as things started falling apart, we decided to go independent. Picked up a lot of friends."

"You're not a doctor, then?"

"Trained in basic field medicine, plus I have a lot of files. Mostly, though, I can keep this thing—" He tapped the medical unit. "—working, and it keeps us alive. Real doctors are damn scarce. Most of them were in the cities, the rest, well, you know. Killing a doctor now is effectively killing hundreds of the enemy tomorrow."

"Rules of war." Jill murmured.

"Don't apply. Asymmetric, unconventional, guerilla, call it what you want, Ms... uhm, how do like to be called?"

"Jill Huochong."

There was a momentary pause. "Hmm. Well, less obvious than mine, I guess. Anyway, war has been moving away from the old style for decades, and now it's entirely free-form. No more massed armies, central command structures, or rules... it's chaos. I don't like it, I admit, but it's how it is. That's part of why we dropped out of it all. Decided to build and fix, instead of destroy."

The feed tube retracted itself. Jill shakily began to stand. Marty helped her out.

"There you go." He pursed his lips. "Now, we need to discuss the delicate matter of..."

"Payment."

He smiled apologetically. "Well, yes. We live on trade and repair, after all. What do you have?"

Jill frowned. "Well, that brings us to why we're out here in the first place..."

The biker trading took another few hours. Jill rejoined Mike outside the MCP, and they both stood somewhat away from the dealings. There was a lot of bartering, back and forth negotiating, and not-too-veiled threats as each side tested the other's resolve and defensive capabilities. In the end though, parts and food changed hands, the situation was resolved with no evident hostilities, and the bikers glided off. Then it was time to deal.

A small armored jeep pulled up. There was a man driving it, in his early thirties by appearance, his blond hair cut into an ornate spiral pattern and topped with glistening lights. Someone else into the retro look. He glanced over at Mike and Jill.

"We're heading to our next stopping point; not smart to camp in the middle of the road. There's a place a few miles north we use when we're down this way. You two are supposed to come with me." He didn't bother mentioning the small flock of UAVs[8] which surrounded the MCP, which were clearly there to discourage those who wanted to outrun the bill. Jill idly targeted them and ran a few firing patterns, which flickered across her visual cortex and so ended up on the record I'm working from, and each one showed she couldn't bring them down fast enough. She claims she wasn't planning to run, she just liked to know the odds if she decided she had to.

The camp was an abandoned microarcology, something some isolated community had put up in the borderlands of the NWA and which had been left behind during the Collapse. Its solar collectors were stripped, leaving just metal skeletons waving lifelessly over the central dome. The neocrete walls remained strong and unbroken, though covered with graffiti. A shattered glass building formed a ring around the central living complex. The convoy headed inside, to the public arena that most such places had as standard equipment, and set up camp, sending the carbon-winged UAVs soaring overhead, circling like a mad cross between buzzards and guards. Someone leaned out of an armored van and gave a 'thumbs up' gesture.

The driver—who had given his name as "Perc"—gestured for Jill and Mike to leave.

Marty came up to them, accompanied by a woman of typically indeterminate years. It was interesting to note that anyone who seemed to be under twenty probably was, but any age above that was subject to choices about anagathics, genetics, and bodyhacking. In any event, she either was or had chosen to seem as if she was in her late twenties, with close-cropped dark hair, a bit softer facial structure than was considered standard, and eyes of a violet so deep they were almost certainly from a catalog. Her fingers, too, were long and had a few extra joints, as well as ending with small, rough, pads that could provide extra traction when gripping low-friction components. They might have had some kind of secretions as well; I couldn't tell.

"I'm guessin' Mary."

She nodded at Mike. "And you two are... a problem. Marty tells me you need some pretty rare parts..."

---

[8] unmanned aerial vehicle

Mike looked at her. "Yeah. Takin' a look at this fleet, it seems like you've got pretty much everythin' we need... I'd call it damn lucky stumblin' on you."

"Yes. The problem is, what do *you* have? Looking at you, I see some badly damaged camo cloth, a service revolver that's seen better days, a half-stocked personal medikit, and a couple of packages of really bad rations. That's not enough for even one of the things you need, let alone all of them. Further, there's been some medical care you still owe for."

Jill met her gaze. "We can't be the first indigents you've run across."

Marty considered. "No, no you ain't. And neither of us is inclined to turn away people in genuine need."

"So what do you do?"

"Take it out in labor. It's not easy keeping this convoy rolling. Mike, you said you were a vehicle specialist?"

"Yeah. Certified on most UBA ground craft, with cross training in—"

Marty gestured to a small one-man tracked craft, looking like a golf cart designed for a war zone. "Automated cargo follower. Not too bright. Also, currently, not too balanced. It's slowing us down. Can you fix it?"

"I'll look at it. You don't have anyone here that can do that?"

"We do. We want to see if you're any good before we start arguing terms."

"Hmm. So what happens if I'm good and we can't come to terms? Seems to me you'll have got some free work out of me. No offense, but these days, trust isn't easy."

"Let's call it trade for her medical care. You get it working, we call it even on the surgery. Deal?"

"Yup. Where do I find some tools?"

"Perc will take care of that."

After he left, Marty and Mary considered Jill.

"Now... what can we do with you? What are you good at?"

She smiled. "Killing."

"Not much for subtlety, are you?"

"No. Why mince words? You know what I am. You can guess how good it makes me." She slipped into her trademark predatory leer. "You might have a test? Someone around here you don't need?"

"No." Mary's voice was flat, frozen. It was obvious that if she saw any humor in Jill's comment, she didn't find it amusing.

"I can hunt. Feeding this convoy can't be easy, even with that processing tank I saw bringing up the rear. And, obviously, I can guard."

Marty glanced at Mary. "We could use someone in... ah... customer relations."

Mary nodded slowly, studying Jill as if she were an interesting piece of machinery. "We could, at that..."

"How long will this last?"

"For what you need... at least two months. You're asking for a lot."

He'll be out of his gourd by then, Jill thought, and I have to admit my heart warmed at her compassion. "Is there any way to speed it up? We can..." she paused, trying to decide if she should say more. "We have a friend. A doctor. Soultech ambulance. That's what we need the parts for. He's basically immobile now. He'd be willing to join you." She turned to Marty. "You said it yourself, you're not a doctor. He is. He can do a lot more with that medical unit than you can, not to mention having two of his own."

The two of them looked at each other, then shook their heads. Marty was the one to speak. "I'm sorry, Jill, I really am, but we can't trust you that much. You two talk a good game and your stories check out. We've heard stories of that wandering ambulance, though none of them mentioned soultech, but you could have heard the same stories, gussied it up a bit, and then rehearsed it. There's no law outside the range of a gun now, and we can't let you go with that kind of gear just on your word."

Jill clenched her fists. I saw firing solutions flash in front of her eyes, then vanish with a sudden act of will. "Fine. I'll be your guard or spokesman or whatever for as long as it takes. We made a promise."

The two of them seemed pleased with that, but Marty continued. "Now, understand, we're going to need to be cautious. We've survived because we're careful about who we let into our little family. You're going to need to be separate at most times, and one of us—someone in this band—is going to be with you at all times. We just can't take risks."

"Makes sense." Jill smiled obscurely. "So long as you don't keep smelling me." She looked up at them. "Don't worry, sort of an inside joke."

Mary wasn't smiling. "You've been in one of those places? And come out?"

"Yes. You've seen them too? The Fences? The compounds?"

She nodded, face pale. "Oh yes. Lost three of our people to them. My son." Her eyes narrowed and her voice chilled. "What do you know about them?"

"A lot. Sit down, and I'll tell you." Then a thought struck her. "But knowledge is a commodity too, isn't it? Let's talk about what it's worth to you..."

They did. After some negotiation and issues of mutual verification were established, Jill gave them a full debriefing on what we knew of the compounds, and all of our thoughts about the Unknown Bastard. They listened intently, and I'm pretty sure Marty was recording every word for later analysis. When all was done, they conferred some more, and cut the minimum work time down to a month. Marty thought one of their steinkids could work out something like my filter, making it safer to deal with them. Jill managed to get them to reveal where they'd run into the compounds, allowing her to update her maps.

Dinner consisted of the usual mix of scavenged- or traded for-rations, supplemented by hunted game and gathered plants, what few could be found in the deep snow. If it wasn't for wild offspring of crops genetically engineered to survive in all temperatures, a lot of the nomad bands would be starving. The highest of technology permitted a return, hopefully temporary, to the oldest of human lifestyles.

As it was, there was snowcorn grilled over a cooking tool cobbled together from assorted parts, fresh rabbit, and military rations advertised as nutrition-enhanced turkey parmesan which, according to Jill's annotations, tasted more like salted packing foam.

During the meal, Mike kept glancing into the shadows. It was frustrating, since whatever he was looking for, he couldn't see. Watching the recordings, I felt like an interactive author who had lost all his source models and was stuck trying to put together a compelling narrative from fixed fragments of data. Rerunning and enhancing his glances, I could make out something in the darkness, but I wasn't sure what. Fortunately, this mystery was resolved by Mary.

"She's not sure about you, even though you're eating with us."

"Who ain't?"

Mary produced a sad, somewhat wistful, smile. "Another of our strays. Ella? It's all right."

There was no reaction for a short while, then someone emerged from the dark. She was a girl in her early teens, with long, straight, dark hair, pale skin, and a careful, wary, gait. She looked ready and able to bolt at any moment. She walked up to Mary, giving Mike and Jill as much clearance as she could. Mary hugged her protectively. Ella shot her arm out, reaching for a hunk of rabbit, then stopped herself halfway, placing her arm at her side. Then she turned to Mary. "May I have some, please?"

Mary beamed. "Of course." Ella then carefully, thinking about each move as if disarming a bomb, put some food on a plate and hurried back into the dark. She sat at the very edge of the circle of light, crouched so as to be able to stand and run at an instant's warning.

Jill spoke."How old was she when you found her?"

"About thirteen, we think. It was two years ago, pretty much when we realized we'd have to make it on our own. We found her almost dead in weather like this, bone thin and frantic."

"How long was she on her own?"

"Not sure. She's not really feral, she was speaking when we found her, someone raised her for a while. We tried getting her to talk about her past, but it's pretty bad for her..."

Mike whistled. "Yeah, I can imagine... well, no, not really, I guess I can't. Deity, that poor girl."

"One of thousands. Hundreds of thousands." Marty spoke, looking at nothing. "If you stop to think about it all... the total lost... you just collapse."

Jill's voice was flat. "A single death is a tragedy. A million deaths is a statistic."

Mary looked at her. "Who said that?"

"Some old dead politician. Stalin or Nixon or Clinton. Something with an 'n.' I..." she paused, considered, then continued, "...it's in my real memory, not my data store. I remember liking the grim realism of the quote. Didn't really care much about the context."

Marty nodded. "It's the nature of being sapient. We can't conceive of that much suffering. We can only manage to hold so many people in our mind as, well, people. Everything beyond that... faces in the crowd." He looked closely at Jill. "Even us. We're still built on patterns evolved to recognize our fellow monkeys. Frustrating, at times."

Mike dropped his fork. "Wait, you're—"

"Yes. I figured she would have told you. It's not something a lot of people like to find out at random."

"Tell me about it," hissed Jill.

Mary exhaled deeply and forced a smile. "Well, looks like dinner is wrapping up. Like I said, I'm sorry to be so suspicious, but you'll need to be separated and given a... friend."

"Guard," said Jill.

Mary's smile became even more forced. "Well, yes, but maybe you'll become friends. We can hope."

Almost inaudibly, Mike murmured, "Yeah, good luck with that."

Mike was given over to Perc; Jill was assigned to a slightly distant-seeming woman who went by Lavender, and whether that was a name inflicted on her by her parents or chosen for some inscrutable reason never came up in recorded conversation. They were taken to different vehicles.

The convoy consisted of six craft in addition to the MCP, all of which were heavily reworked and modified. All were at least lightly armed, and most had heavy armor attached—armor which could be, I noted from Mike's observations, shed in a second to gain speed. They were either thick-wheeled or tracked, ideal for roads, but suitable for off, less agile than Heim vehicles but less vulnerable as well. The insides were packed, with plenty of folding gear. Sleep space was minimal, but they obviously made do.

As the camp prepared to rest, the area came alive with skittering or flying machines. Everyone seemed to have favorite toys, and the result was a dispersed patrol network which would be hard for a casual attacker to circumvent as any damaged or missing node would alert the others. Of course, such systems weren't perfect—as I'd shown—but I suspected these individuals were less likely to stick to default protocols.

Perc's car was the smallest. He opened the back of it and started shoving stuff aside. "So, looks like we're going to be sharing some space for a while. I don't have much room—" He pushed a pile of circuit-encrusted cubes into a corner, and hauled out a plastic box filled with spools of wire of every imaginable color and thickness. "—but we can do something."

Mike was distracted. "Yeah, anything's fine. Beats sleeping in the snow."

Perc grinned. "I guess it would! Pick a side," he added, pointing to two equally cramped, still somewhat clutter strewn spaces.

"Left. But it's kinda' early for me, yet. I'd rather wait. You go ahead."

Perc's smile remained, but his tone shifted. "Really can't do that. If you want, I can stay up with you, but I've got orders."

"Fine. No sense makin' you suffer for my insomnia."

They got in. Perc moved some old clothes around to form a functional pillow. "By the way, the whole thing's rigged to set an alarm if it's opened without my biosignature, and if I die, there's a camp-wide alert. Just so you know."

"We live in a wonderful world," Mike grunted.

"We certainly do."

"So, what do you do here, anyway?"

Perc, well, perked up. It was obvious that talking about work was something he both loved and had few opportunities for. He almost bounced upright. "Well, I do general tech. Engineering. Patching things up. I'm great at improvising. I also have a few side projects—"

Mike took the hint.

"Like what?"

Perc rummaged through some bags, scattering bits of wire and metal and circuitry across the barely-cleaned surface, then pulled out a small metal box. He flipped it open, grabbed something from within, and tossed it at Mike, who caught it easily. He looked down at it.

"A bullet?"

"Special! It was an idea I had, kind of based on a chestburster."

Mike almost dropped it. Chestbursters were known to sometimes go off if their sensors detected moisture and body heat. Hypothetically, the sensors were designed to not be active until the extreme shock of firing. Normal handling, even hammering, shouldn't set them off.

Some hypotheses never graduate to theory. That was one of them.

"Don't worry!" Perc laughed. "It's harmless to humans. Well, I mean, unless you're shot with it. But the special part is, I was thinking, chestbursters know if they're in a person, and then they explode inside. But what about machines? We run into more stupid 'bots doing automated patrols than dangerous people, so I've been thinking about that." He pointed to the bullet Mike was holding. "It's an EMP round. If it picks up a lot of metals and magnetic fields—like inside of most 'bots—it generates a small EMP field. A powerful one, though. Fries their brain from the inside, no matter how much shielding they have outside."

Mike, impressed despite himself, turned the bullet over and over in his hands. "Huh. Do they work?"

Perc looked a bit downcast. "Well... we haven't really field tested them. Anything that works well enough to test them on, we don't *want* to fry. But the theory is sound. I'm handing these over to Marty. They're safe enough to handle until they've been fired. The force of firing cracks open internal cells filled with a liquid superconductor. Without that flowing into the mechanism, it can't generate a pulse."

"Nifty." Mike handed the bullet back. "Lemme know how it turns out, okay?"

"Sure!" Perc carefully placed the bullet back, then resealed the box.

Mike tried to find a working position for sleep.

Jill, meanwhile, had slightly more comfortable quarters. Lavender had a small utility truck. Half of it was an amazingly compact lab, padded, braced, and secured against any normal bumps and shocks, and the other half was fold-down bunk beds. Jill looked at the lab. "Sequencers... protein library... spored denucleates... fun stuff, steinkid. Planning any plagues?"

Lavender flushed. "Oooh, I hate that! And I'm not a 'steinkid.' I'm a self-taught bio-engineer." She glared at Jill. "You should know about people making assumptions!"

"Sorry. But what *are* you doing with this stuff on the road?"

"Keeping us safe. Trading my skills. Same as everyone else here. I've helped one group of people save their crops from a blight, I found a cure for—"

"Right. I get it. Sorry, a bit edgy. I've had some... issues... with people being assigned to watch over me lately." She grinned. "I nearly killed the last one." At Lavender's shocked look, she added, "But he tried to kill me—worse, really—first. Are you planning that?"

"No!"

"Great. We'll get on fine."

There was silence for a few minutes, a silence which evidently was unbearable for Lavender.

"So. You're like Marty, then?"

"A bit."

"Oh, OK. Because Marty's the only... you know... I've met."

"You can call me a daemon if you want. I'd rather just be called

Jill. Or left alone."

"Wow. Fine. I mean, we're going to be together a while, so I thought we could, talk or something."

"What do you want to talk about?"

"Well, let me think... there's so many questions—I know! Are you a woman?"

It was interesting how fast the targeting matrix flared up in Jill's vision, and how slowly it faded out.

"XX chromosomes from birth. No gendermods. Why? Would that matter? You from Deseret?"

"Huh? Oh, no no no! I'm so sorry, I didn't mean it like that! I meant, uhm... well, Marty acts like a guy, and you, uhm... well, I mean, were you..."

Jill sighed.

"Gender identity seems to be part of the whole matrix of consciousness. Attempts to completely excise it have been problematic. The initial seed algorithm from which any soultech is born contains aspects of it. There are slightly different mental strengths and weaknesses, visual versus spatial, and so on. Further, since we interact with biological intelligence which tends to be strongly gendered, it helps to have such an identity. Does that answer your question?"

Missing the bitter sarcasm entirely, Lavender pondered a moment. "I... think so. But what if..."

She couldn't miss that glare.

"Oh, well, we'll have plenty of time to talk! It's going to be nice. I've been driving alone for a few weeks now, and it's dull."

Jill didn't bother recording her thoughts, but I suspect they were along the lines of "What did I do to make Marty hate me this much?"

The next day dawned clear and cold, the bright sun charging solar panels. The MCP actually carried a microfusion plant, and it spent most of each downtime cycle powering a particularly quirky-looking hydrogen splitter to keep the rest of the fleet stocked.

Jill and Mike rejoined each other, their erstwhile guardians drifting off to talk with friends. Mike broke the silence.

"Well, they didn't try to knife us in our sleep."

"Unfortunately."

"Damn, even for you, that's harsh."

"I'm annoyed." At his look, she continued. "Yes, even by my usual standards. I've been given the equivalent of a week cleaning latrines."

Mike shrugged. "Hey, punishment detail, nothin' new to me. Perc's okay, I guess. A bit over-eager, but I guess that's better than sullen and moody all the time." He caught her look. "Hey, now, I didn't mean..."

She had walked off, determined to find food as far from him as possible. The problem was that, due to various circumstances, distance from him meant proximity to Lavender. I wasn't sure how this saga was going to end, but I had a feeling someone would be getting shot.

"Hello," said a quiet voice behind Mike. To his credit, he only flinched slightly. He spun around. Ella was there.

"Uh... hi." She was standing quite close, arms behind her back, looking up at him.

"Sorry. Last night. Too many new people. Feeling better now."

"Yeah. OK. I'm Mike. Mike Calvers." He held out his hand; she jumped back at the motion, recovered, looked at it, seemed to remember something, and shook it clumsily. "Ella. No other name."

She said nothing else for a moment, and Mike was looking for a quick excuse to leave. Then she spoke again. "Your friend scares me."

"Yeah, she's like that. I suppose I could tell you she's really not all that bad... but, well, she is. Every time I think I've got her figured, she... ah, never mind."

"They're serving food now."

There was a kind of mental whiplash as Mike dealt with the non-sequitur transition. "So they are. I'd better line up..." He wandered off.

Breakfast was a slightly awkward affair. Mike and Jill were strangers at the party. Everyone else knew their role, and performed all the necessary rituals, repeated the same arguments, made the same tired jokes. Despite efforts to be welcoming, it was obvious that the mechanism of the tribe had not yet decided where to place the new gears.

Jill tracked down Marty. "What's the order of the day?"

"We head out, west a bit. We have a regular stop here, an isolated community which mostly ignored the Collapse but which still needs some supplies. Mostly a food run, good during the winter. We rest there for the night, usually."

"Milk run. Fine. Why Lavender?"

He grinned a little. "She had room."

"And this is because?"

"I think you've figured that out." He set down the table he'd been folding to put back into the MCP. "Look, I'm sure it's not a perfect match, but... well, a lot of people aren't comfortable with you being armed all time, even though I've vouched for you. And Lavender is... better when she has someone to talk to."

"Meaning, she isn't bothering anyone else."

He grinned broadly. "You got it in one! Think a moment. You're asking for a lot from us, in supplies *and* trust—both pretty damn rare these days. If the cost is keeping one of our more *interesting* members pleasantly distracted, I'd think you'd think it's fair."

"Fine." She started to leave.

"Jill... I'd like to be a bit more helpful. I can't."

She looked around at the swiftly dissolving camp, the smooth progression of chores and tasks. "I said it was fine. I'll be with Lavender."

I wish I could have seen his face when she left, but she didn't turn back.

The isolated community they stayed with was typical, which meant it was strange. Everyone had the same face: one for the males, one for the females, except for the youngest children. It looked to be surgical, not genetic, reducing the risk of bad genes from inbreeding. According to one man, the founders of this community had determined the perfect human ideal and believed that everyone should look alike. They were at least not fanatic about proselytizing it, though it was obvious many of them found different-seeming strangers to be frightening, especially the children. They also seemed to have little difficulty telling each other apart. Body language? Scent? Subtle distinctions only those in the community could notice? Neither Mike nor Jill cared enough to ask or find out, so I had one more mystery I'd probably never solve.

The locals were relying on hydroponic tables filled with extremely modified plants, combined with a basic organic processor—anything formerly alive goes in, digestible mash in a variety of exciting flavors (the flickering holographic spokesman said so, in a continual loop) comes out. The systems controlling the former were getting wonky, messing up the nutrient feed, and the latter was sucking down more and more power. Negotiations were quick and peaceful; I could tell Jill was bored. It was interesting to see chaos trying to find a balance point, people trying to fit the shattered pieces of the old world into a new shape.

It wasn't stable, though. It couldn't grow safely. These small communities only worked *because* they were small. It was a mistake made by a lot of social philosophers—if a family could simply all share and work together, why couldn't an entire nation? Because it's not the way humans are built, came the answer in the form of hundreds of millions dead in those failed experiments. Indeed, Jill and Marty and I exist, in part, because of experiments (less bloody, but still pretty costly) in building a better human. They couldn't. You can't think, they found *as well as* a human without thinking an awful lot *like* a human. As a way of creating beings who could work with humans, enhance them, even surpass them in areas of speed and knowledge and so on, the development of soultech was a success; as a means of realizing the utopian dreams of building a 'better' mind, it was a dismal failure. I understand that one of the developers of the first truly self-aware artificial mind wept when that mind demanded to be paid for its work, or it was going on strike.

The entire trading process took most of a day, a lot of which was spent with gossip and socializing, spreading news the old fashioned way. Mary and Marty weren't just travelling techs, they were bards, and that alone granted them, if not immunity to attack and assault, a small measure of protection.

At one point, unable to get away from their minders, Jill contacted Mike on direct link.

"Any thoughts?"

"'bout what?"

"The situation. Is this the optimal solution?"

"You mean, to find the parts we need for the Doc? Uhm... yeah, I think so. Why?"

"Because it will take time, and we are relying on these people's honesty."

"I think we're good there."

"Why?"

"Ella."

"The half-feral? I don't see how she's relevant."

"Simple. She's almost useless."

"I'm beginning to see why MacIntyre's attempts to model your thought processes failed so often."

"Look, think about it. This is a bunch of pros. They've got steinkids, techies, psycho killers like you... everyone's got a job and they're good at it. No waste space, no hangers-on, can't afford it.

Times are hard and there's no room for slackers. But they find this kid—no skills, pain in the ass to deal with, freaks people out—and they take her on, *just because she needs help*. Does that sound like the kind of people who'd sell us out, if we play fair by them?"

Jill pondered this. "No, it doesn't. Fine. I'll go along. Where is the wolf girl, anyway?"

"Hiding. What'd you think?"

"That makes sense. She seemed to like you well enough, though."

"I dunno. Maybe I smell good, or somethin'."

There was a pause in the conversation.

"No. No, I don't think that's it. Marty is looking at me funny. Logging off."

Marty was, indeed, looking at her intently. His expression changed as soon as the link was broken. "Encrypted chatter with your partner?"

Jill stared at him. "Yes. So?"

He rubbed his forehead in the classic 'I have a headache' gesture. "Well, it's not building a lot of confidence. We're trying to trust you, here, and whispering in code to each other doesn't help. You mind if I ask what you were talking about?"

"Yes."

"Well, I'm going to ask anyway. What were you talking about? Keep in mind I've got cyphers here who can probably crack my recording in a minute."

"If you must know, we were arguing about whether we could trust you." Jill grinned, daring him to reply.

He considered this for a second, then laughed. "Makes sense. You mind if we confirm that?"

"Yes."

"Oh well. Can't win them all." He turned to leave, then thought better of it. "Anyway, we're wrapping up here. Hook up with Lavender and help her out. And," he paused, running words through his mind, trying to find the right phrasing. "And try not to look as if you're just looking for a good excuse to kill someone. You're going to be with us a month or so. Is there a reason you *have* to make it unpleasant?"

Jill actually had to consider this for a few seconds. "No."

Marty smiled. "Then don't!" He walked off.

Jill resignedly began looking for Lavender. She found her emerging from the hydroponics dome, somewhat smudged, but almost glowing.

"I was told to find you. Mission accomplished. Can we go n—"
She sighed and forced a happier tone into her voice. "Is there
anything I can do?"

"Nope! We're good here! I think the tomatoes will come in
rainbow colors next harvest! That was a free surprise. I think
they'll like it."

Jill nodded. "Color coded to indicate different nutrient mixes?
Pharmacological excretions?"

Lavender looked exasperated. "No! Boring! Because rainbow
fruits are fun!" She looked around conspiratorially, then leaned in
close and whispered, "I'm working on paisley. It's hard, but I'm
getting closer." She grinned maniacally, then grabbed Jill's hand
and pulled. "Come on, we've got to load up the truck. These people
want us out by sundown or its some kind of weird taboo ritual
violation thing and then they'll try to kill us. So we better hurry!"

Then she was off, a confused Jill pacing behind her. I hoped Jill
didn't blame *me* for this.

The next few days followed a similar pattern. Slowly, Jill and
Mike began to integrate with the daily life of the band. The travel
protocol was fairly straightforward: scouting vehicles, light and
fast and laden with sensors, would scout ahead to the limit of a
stable connection, streaming data back to the MCP, which in turn
kept the rest of the fleet informed. If a trap or minefield or hostile
entities were detected, there'd be a quick debate and some decision
to engage or avoid would be made. To Jill's obvious distaste, the
two times the topic came up, avoidance was the consensus. If
customers, or potentials, were found, there'd be some talking, some
threats exchanged, posturing and shows of strength, and then a
meeting would be set up, either on the open road or on some
turnoff considered acceptable to all parties, and then business
would be done. Marty and Mary had built a long circuit, a looping
path through a large part of the former NWA, with many criss-
crossing options and alternate routes. Still, looking at the maps
Marty was showing Jill, it seemed more and more of the path was
being closed down. A spattering of red dots across the eastern and
northern edges showed encounters with the NNA, encounters the
travelers were eager to avoid.

Jill asked about this. "You'd think they'd need support and
service."

Marty shook his head. "Nothing outside their control. We've
had... offers to just be absorbed and join up, but we don't want to

be."

"They're growing, though. They could become the first nation to arise from this chaos."

"Maybe. I doubt it. They're doing no building, no infrastructure... just accumulating mass. They're a bandit pack writ large, is all. They can only survive so long as there's people to raid. Maybe they've got plans for more, but I haven't seen it. They certainly aren't trying to reclaim any of the larger cities, and the isolated communities they're attacking don't have the resources to support a group that size. It's like they're running downhill, unbalanced, but they have to keep running or they'll fall. That guy in charge, Cromney, I don't think he has any ideas beyond 'I ought to be in charge.'

"I can't see this lasting. There'll be a realignment, a reassessment. Humans haven't changed. We haven't lost most of our knowledge yet, and the same combination of human nature and technological power which created the neonational system will re-assert itself."

"You're an optimist."

"With all I've seen I've got to be, or I'd just launch my self-termination protocol and be done with it. You have to have hope."

"So I'm told."

He sighed and sat down on a crate, somewhat perturbing the young man who was about to load it. "What are you looking for?"

"Some superconducting wire, a—"

"Please. You're not that dumb."

"But I *am* that uninterested in chatting about my feelings. We have a contract. Am I doing my part?"

"Yes."

"Then we have nothing else to discuss." She turned to walk off. He grabbed her arm. Targeting came on-line... and stayed there.

"Do I have to spell it out?"

"What?"

He sighed. "You. Me. Daemons."

"Not going to happen." She dropped the targeting.

"Have you given me any chance to get to know you? Or for you to get to know me?"

"It's not that."

"Mike? I'm sorry, you and he didn't seem to be—"

"We're not. And it's not MacIntyre either. Maybe someday, but for now..."

"Then what?"

"First, I don't like that the most important thing about me to you seems to be the nature of my mind. Second, you are, for now, my commander. As a professional, I don't get involved with my CO. It's that simple."

"Well, as for the first, you haven't exactly given me a chance to learn anything about you, have you? As for the second... you're right. I respect that. But there's something else. Mary and I were talking—"

"About?"

"Why don't you join us? You and Mike and MacIntyre, I mean. You don't have to settle down or give up your freedom, but you can do what you're doing alongside us. Safety in numbers and all that."

"I can't promise MacIntyre's cooperation. He can be stubborn."

"Well, talk it over with Mike. Look, I'm sorry if I offended you. I didn't mean to."

"I'll talk it over. No promises."

She left.

Mike, meanwhile, was helping Perc pack up. Somehow, he'd acquired a box of random junk which needed to be shoved into his small vehicle. Mike was rearranging things, trying to leave enough space to sleep, when Ella appeared on the roof.

"Do not do that!"

"What?"

"Sneak up on people!"

She shrugged. "It's how I move. Move silently, or don't move at all. Learned that."

"Yeah, I know. Life's tough. What do you want?"

"Just watching."

"You could help, you know."

"Yes. They want me to help bring the payment to the MCP."

"So why *aren't* you?"

She shrugged. "Rather watch you."

I could see where this was going. The fact Mike returned home with, apparently, all of his limbs and other vital organs intact indicated he'd exercised unusual self-control. While I wasn't sure what the social patterns were among this particular band of techie gypsies, I suspected that everyone involved would take a dim view of an outsider taking advantage of a barely-adolescent girl with limited social skills. No matter how engraved the invitation.

Mike seemed well aware of this. "Well, flatterin' as that is, we've got to get movin' before the locals declare us invaders and we all get shot at. I've had almost a week without anyone tryin' to kill me, and I'm goin' for my personal best, here. So go on, do what you're supposed to."

She looked displeased, but scrambled down off the roof and dashed for the MCP.

"Nicely played." It was Mary's voice.

Mike turned to look at her. "Hey, if you think I was gonna— look, she just popped up—"

She smiled. "Don't worry. If I thought you were a threat, I'd have shot you where you stood. Congratulations. I think you're her first crush. It's relieving in a way. It means she's likely going to come out of this halfway sane. As sane as anyone here."

"Yeah, well, don't worry. I'll keep her away. Why me, though? I can't figure it."

"I don't know. Might be coincidence. Might be because we're more like family to her. Might be because you look like a father or brother she doesn't quite remember. She knows the mechanics, of course, Marty and I made sure she got the usual interactives to work through. NWA make, no offense, but you people in the UBA, well, to each their own. Anyway, she doesn't understand the rest of it, the emotion. We aren't about to lock her up every time we visit some new group of people. It's just... this isn't how it should be. For her, for the infants we've got on the way. Are we forming tribes, now? Are we going to have big meetings where we ritually trade young men and women to prevent inbreeding? Somehow, Marty and I have become de facto chieftains, and we have no idea what we're doing. We're just making it all up as we go along."

"That's all anyone does, really. Some people lie about it better than others."

"Comforting." She looked at Mike again, studying him. "I think I see Ella's point."

Mike seemed taken aback, unusual for him. "I thought you... I mean, you and Marty—"

"Partners. Friends. Nothing more, except sometimes when we're both cold and lonely. That's all."

Mike nodded. "Yeah. Well, sun's almost down. Got to load."

"You do that. Time to make the final rounds." Mike watched her walk off.

Two days later, Jill and Mike—along with their guards—ended up running the forward patrol. It was not a welcome assignment. Despite the best precautions, it had the highest risk, by definition. A small flock of UAVs fanned ahead of the two light craft, close in enough to keep in constant sensor contact, swooping, dodging, and emitting constant false signals to discourage the inevitable hunter/seekers that were out there. The skies were dangerous.

A pinging started in Lavender's vehicle.

"Oh... OK... uhm..." She tapped her earpiece. "UAV 12 has a uh, bogie bearing 350 by 190... trying to get resolution... shit!"

The craft had vanished from the data display. "Something got twelve, uh, repeat, something got twelve, we're pulling back..."

The scene, shown from Jill's perspective, had exploded in a mass of targeting data. Everything—rocks, trees, the small van Perc and Mike were in—blossomed with data. She looked intently at the area where UAV 12 had been a moment before, even as Lavender slowed the vehicle and began trying to spin it. Perc's voice came over the shared link "Lost 10, lost 10, something's out there, no warnings, we—"

Then it flowed onto the highway.

It looked like a mobile junkheap, in a way, as if someone had taken a ton of technological detritus and given it function without form. Except that there was purpose to it, if you stopped to look. Every extension, probe, and tendril moved with a sort of instinct and focus. And if the thing as a whole looked chaotic, you could tell it was just because you couldn't quite see the pattern yet; Like looking at a sequence of numbers and not being able to divine the underlying formula, though you knew there was one and you'd get it if you just thought about it enough.

Perc and Lavender were spinning their vehicles, the tracks clawing at the already badly damaged roadway. Metal screamed in frustration as inertia battled with itself. "Turn, turn, turn—" chanted Perc, willing the laws of physics to suspend themselves, just for a moment, while Lavender was less vociferous but no less desperate. There was stark fear in their faces, fear which was well justified. They didn't know what that thing was, but they knew it was bad.

I knew what it was; I suspect Jill and Mike did, too, perhaps for different reasons. What it was, was damn scary; what was even more scary is that it really shouldn't exist.

Macroscale robotic self-organization was always next year's tech. There were just a few minor kinks to be worked out; The proof of concept would be leaving the lab any day now. In theory, it was simple—build a robot from a hundred thousand small components, give each one a tiny bit of brain and a powerful wireless link, and then let the entire thing form a huge neural net which can reconfigure itself moment by moment to any task. Weapons, tools, storage, mobility, any part needed would self-assemble, and everything it did, it would learn from. One robot fits all, and it would constantly adapt to any mission, fitting ever-changing parameters.

It never worked right. Too many inputs, too much interference, the algorithms to decide how to reassemble and how to respond warring with each other, never finding a happy optimum in a workable timeframe. Simple systems worked, but the complexity scaled up exponentially, and you ended up with machines that lay there, or self-destructed, or formed hideously inefficient monstrosities that could be outperformed by two-decade-old specialized tools. Eventually, soultech autofacs became the solution to the problem, intelligent assemblers which could just *make* what was needed. (There was one attempt to marry soultech and self-organizing microrobotics; the poor thing basically went insane and died in short order.)

Nonetheless, here one was, and unless it was odd coincidence that two UAVs went down seconds before, it wasn't friendly. Whatever its mission was, it didn't include leaving witnesses.

Perc's vehicle was spinning, spinning, when Mike's vision exploded with streaks of red. When he cleared his eyes, blinking and cursing, the craft was rushing headlong towards a dropoff and Perc was dead, his face and upper torso ripped to bloody tendrils. From Jill's recordings, I saw what happened. The thing—I'm just going to call it the morpher for now, it works—had extruded a long barreled gun, composed of hundreds of tiny parts which could have been used for a dozen different purposes, and from this gun had come an undulating spray of monowire fragments, ten thousand high-tech shuriken, which had torn through armor plate and diamond-threaded glass as if they were non-existent. Flesh didn't stand a chance.

Mike, meanwhile, was shoving aside the corpse of his minder and grabbing for the steering column, which fell to pieces in his hand, sliced in a hundred different places. He cursed, pulled back, and tossed the door open, leaping out and rolling, smashing into the rough chunks of asphalt with a grunt of pain. He stopped about mid-road and looked up to see the barrel of the wire launcher locking in on him.

Then it exploded. A stream of bullets, rapid fire, had moved into the seething bulk of the thing and hit the small power plant which was charging the wire gun. It collapsed, the log barrel falling to pieces, but not in a chaotic way. It was a deadly jigsaw puzzle being rapidly disassembled by an army of invisible hands, the parts falling into the mass of it to be tested for completion and functionality, reused if possible or sent deep into the heart of it, to tiny fusion smelters and microscopic engineering machines to be repaired if not, or, at worst, reduced to pellets of raw metal and plastic from which to build new components. Like some mythical beast, it could heal from most wounds.

And it now had a new target: Jill, someone who had done it injury, however minor and temporary. It flowed into a new configuration, growing armor as individual parts crawled to the surface and flattened out like flowers, each one locking with the next. New guns began to grow and emerge, along with sensor arrays and other implements of war. It now had a new purpose, which was Jill's death.

This fact was not lost on her. Lavender swerved her van to near where Mike lay. Jill reached out to grab his arm as they trundled past, even as he was drawing his own pistol to perform what he knew would be a futile last stand. Like many I knew, he believed that if you died with bullets in your gun, you didn't really want to live.

Jill quickly crawled over him and began firing, sending bullets into the road, bouncing off heavy armor plating, or flying overhead. Mike, watching on the screens which showed the rear view of the monster swiftly finishing its transformation, whistled.

"Damn, if that thing scares even you—"

"What makes you think I'm scared?" she asked, as two more shots rebounded off nothing in particular.

"You're missing. You *never* miss. Damn, now I'm scared."

"I'm not missing. I'm fouling its prediction circuits by causing it to make false estimates of my skill."

Mike laughed. "Hey, yeah, that's a good line. If I'd had that back in basic, I might have missed some KP details!" He was struck by a thought.

"Lavender! Raise Marty! Tell him we need those EMP rounds from Perc! Might be our only shot—"

Lavender was on it. "Bringing bogey, bringing bogey, it's nasty, Mike needs... uh, ee-ehn-pee rounds, repeat, ee-ehn..."

"M! E*M*P rounds! Electromagnetic!"

"Uh, right, correction, correction, ee-EM-pee, and, uh, get off the road, Jill says, get off and stay off and oh shit!"

Jill looked over at Mike. "EMP rounds? Really?"

"Yeah! Hope they're your size!"

A brilliant energy beam slashed ahead of them, creating a thin line of bubbling road surface which the tracked van managed to cross with only minor difficulty. Lavender stared at the controls in front of her and then slammed a few buttons. There was a soft "phut" sound, and five shapes appeared on the radar.

"Oh, I am such a pre-nucleate sometimes! Forgot about the decoy drones!"

The morpher seemed to be taken in. The laser it had assembled cracked, folded in on itself, and blossomed into a deadly flower with multiple barrels, each one on a rotating turret that tracked the dodging, weaving, ECM-spreading drones, even as Lavender's van rounded a bend at unsafe speeds and drew up close. There was the MCP, the gaudy displays turned off, all turrets active.

Mike stared it. "Why are those idiots advancing?"

Jill shook her head. "Got me." She grabbed the headset from Lavender. "Back! Back! Get off the road, get away, we are not planning to lead this to you!"

"You need the EMP rounds," came Marty's voice.

"Send someone! You have no idea..."

"Microrobotic morphing technology. Used to work on it, back in the day. I must say, I'm eager to see it in action."

"You'll see it kill you, you imbecile! Drop the ammo and go, take Lavender, she's useless here!"

"Hey! I can help!"

"No time to argue! Do it!"

Marty's voice came through again. "Miss Huochong, if I recall, I am your commanding officer and you are *not* to be giving me orders!"

Jill snarled, but controlled herself. "Yes *sir*," she began, making "Sir" sound like the worst profanity imaginable, in the manner of soldiers since the dawn of recorded history. "What are your orders, *sir*? How do you wish to die pointlessly and abandon the people you're supposed to be leading, *sir*?"

Mike was looking at her with what could only be described as awed affection. "Damn, Jill. Didn't think you had it in you."

"Shut up, we're about to die. This isn't the time to reach a Sudden Understanding."

Mike smirked. "Can't think of a better one."

They were almost at the MCP. The massive front turret

boomed, and a streak shot out, impacting on the morpher as it advanced, the last of the decoy drones dying as a black and orange flower. It impacted, and the shockwaves blew back, sending the van skidding slightly even as Lavender pulled past the MCP.

Mike looked back. I saw smoldering pile where the morpher stood, a charred and smoking wreck. Hundreds of tiny pieces lay scattered about.

"That won't stop it!" Jill yelled into Lavender's stolen headpiece.

"I know, but we need a second. Here!"

The main hatch of the MCP opened, and a metal case flew out. Jill grabbed for it and shook out two clips. "Thanks! Now, move!"

"No. We can help. Hop on, both of you! Lavender, rejoin the rest at alpha point!"

"But I can—"

"No, you can't, not here, not now. Please. Go."

"Yes, Marty." She looked ready to cry, but took the vehicle back down the road. Mary slowed the MCP to a stop about a hundred yards from the smoke-spewing wreck of the morpher.

Marty looked at Mike. "Go help Mary, she's better on guns and you can drive this thing. I'm going to run the defense systems. Jill—"

"I'm going to kill that monster. Sir."

"Good plan. Carry it out."

Mike ran to the front cab and tossed himself in the seat next to Mary. She tapped some buttons. "Controls are reset to your biosigns. Have fun." Then she relaxed into her chair, her eyes glazing slightly as the neural field took over.

Jill, meanwhile, watched the wreck. It had stopped smoking. The rubble surrounding it had begun to crawl back, some pieces dragging other pieces. The morper bubbled, oozed, and flowed as damaged pieces were absorbed, new pieces clambered into place, and the distributed mind of it—dumbtech, but very advanced—analyzed and made plans.

"Why not keep blastin' it?"

Marty answered. "Waste of shells. Best we'll do is scatter it wide enough that we can get past it, leaving it to kill some other poor fools. Besides, that thing's a gold mine! That it's working at all, that's amazing! My folks'll kill me if they knew I let it get away!"

"What, they won't kill you if you let it kill you first?"

"We won't die. I've got faith in you. And your partner."

Said partner then chimed in. "Great. Well, it's wakin' up. Plan?"

"Quick! Overrun it, draw it forward, away from the convoy!"

"Yup!" Mike tried to slide into the neural interface for the MCP, but was balked. "Hey, I can't go neural here?"

"You're not in the system, and no time to add you. Please tell me you know how to use physical controls!"

Mike stopped, suddenly, and stared. "I—I did—I know I studied this layout..." His eyes scanned the controls, a sudden panic. "It's there. It was..."

"Damage from a memetic virus," Jill stated quickly. "Basic learning should still be there, just *tell* him. Fast!"

Mary dropped out of neural for a second. "Steering yoke has it all. Accelerate with the left thumb control, decelerate with the right. Don't worry about turn signals."

Mike looked at the yoke. "Yeah. It's there... somewhere..Just can't get to it."

"Not important. Go by instinct. I'm trusting you." Then she shifted back into full neural link, only vaguely aware of the rest of the world. Mike closed his eyes for a second, breathed deeply, then gripped the controls. "OK."

Behind him, Marty flipped some switches. There was a sudden thud as a folding metal wall slid into place, a shock as the rear two thirds or so of the MCP dropped off, and a lurch as the now much-lighter vehicle roared ahead. "Autopilot'll take the rest home, just in case."

There was a sharp crunch and then a wild shaking as the vehicle clambered over the swiftly self-assembling mound of metal. Mike passed over it, then slowed, watching it on a rear-facing viewscreen. It didn't really turn; it just repaired itself to be facing the other way. Weapons systems began to self assemble, and acquisition warnings began to flare.

Jill watched it. "Look like it's doing the monowire thing again. Knows we're armored."

Mike nodded, then pulled the MCP around a bend. "There, it'll have to follow us now." Something flickered on the rear monitor, a faint cloud of darkness, the only visible sign of the monowire burst. "Next shot'll tear our armor off."

Jill moved to the back of the vehicle, peering through a tiny firing slit. "We're going to need to coordinate this. Mary! Can you lock into my tracking feed—ah. Perfect."

Two sets of visual displays now filled Jill's vision, her own and those of Mary's interface to the MCP s turrets. The morpher turned the bend. Both sets of reticules danced and spun, geometries of red and yellow, taking endless seconds to open negotiations, discuss terms, hammer out a treaty, and finally agree that *now* is the right time to fire *there*.

The shell went off, whistling down the laser guided path, to dissolve and explode before getting halfway to the target. Mary smashed her fist on the MCP's wall. "Shit, monowire chaff?"

"Adapting tech." Jill hadn't fired. "Marty, got any ideas?" She kicked off against the wall and sprawled backwards, as the upper half of the barricade was turned into a shattered metal puzzle. "We can't take another of those!"

"Right." Mike yanked the yoke hard to the right. The craft twisted and buckled, straining to obey. Mary and Marty both cried out at once, "The hell?" as the MCP spun off the road and began half-driving, half falling, down a steep incline, its treads deforming and reshaping themselves to grip at the suddenly irregular surface.

"I thought you could drive this!" Mary dropped the weapons link. "Dammit, let me have that."

Mike slapped at her hand, though not too hard. "No! I know what I'm doin'. You said it, we couldn't take another hit! Well, we had to scramble its prediction algorithms somehow, and could you have predicted this?"

Her fact brightened. "Hell no!" She shifted back into weapons control. "Coming over the ridge, still following."

Jill watched it. It considered the steep incline, and grew a dozen multi-jointed legs, the treads it had been using fracturing and being re-absorbed into the mass of it. I watched, through her eyes, as it began moving, clumsily at first, then with ever increasing grace and skill. It would have them targeted again in an instant.

"Mary, now!" Jill shouted.

A shell lobbed rearward, striking the craft head on. The armor plates, not quite fully reformed, did not completely dampen the blow. For a moment, a significant chunk of the morpher was exposed.

Jill's visual data display fairly exploded. Bright red circles flared across her sight, and I could see streams of data rushing past. Her world was a constant swarm of overlays and information;

I didn't know how she could stand it. Then there was the sound of bullets firing, six of them, shot faster than any human muscles could pull a trigger and timed to within a few milliseconds of perfection. Each shot deep into the morpher, through the momentary cracks and gaps, and there was a sudden series of flares, of dull, thrumming booms and crackling shells of lightning as the EMP charges in each went off.

Then there was a soft rain of metal as the thing lost all cohesion.

Mike slowed the MCP to a stop. "Is it dead for real?"

Marty looked out. "It ought to be. If Jill was on target..."

She gave him a dark stare. "I was. The highest density of awareness, the components thickest with processors: they're dead."

"Let's check it out, then. Signal the rest of the tribe to hold position."

Mary dropped the weapon link and sat down next to Mike. "Sorry to doubt you."

"No, you're right. Sorry I didn't think—" He smashed his fist on the console. "I hate this, I really, really, hate this—bits an' pieces of me just ain't there anymore—"

She grabbed his hand. "Stop it. Everyone's broken now, somehow. We manage. We make up for what each of us is missing."

She reached for him and drew his face to hers. In the interest of preserving his privacy, I switched to Jill's records. She was staring at them.

History will judge me a voyeur despite my best efforts.

Marty was talking. "—look around, make sure we didn't miss something. Uhm... hello?"

He glanced up towards the front and shrugged.

"Oh. I thought you and he—I mean, I got the impression—"

"You did. We're not. Inspect the wreck, on it." She went outside.

There was a central mound of parts and components, and a wide spread of pieces around it. Some of the pieces—quite a few, actually—were still moving, but they did so in a directionless fashion, ants whose queen had died. There weren't enough intact components to form a functional mind. Each piece of the morphing mass had multiple overlapping functions, but some of them had to focus on being processors, and it was those that Jill's EMP bullets had targeted. The resulting shock spread through the neural net and triggered cascade failures. Now it was junk.

Most of the pieces were small, an inch or two across at most. Many were much smaller, virtually dust. A few parts, by sheer necessity, were larger—there's only so much anyone can shrink a fusion reactor, for example, and there was one at the heart of the beast. Jill was mostly kicking at the pile, looking for signs of regrowth or still functioning consciousness, while Marty began to catalog and analyze the parts. Then Jill saw something partially buried in a larger mound and pulled it out.

It was a metal cylinder, perhaps five feet tall, extremely familiar. A Fencepost.

Jill stared at it for long seconds.

"Unknown Bastard..." she finally murmured.

Marty looked up from his cataloging. "Hmm? What've you got?"

She stood the post up. "This."

He walked over to it, slowly. "Is that... it looks like..."

"Yes. It's that. I saw them close up for about a week. Looks like MacIntyre was right, something was seeding the compounds. Something like this."

Marty stepped back, eyes wide. "I'm a goddamn idiot. Move away, move away now."

Jill spun, looking for targets, for whatever enemy Marty had detected. She saw none. She did, however, back out of the rubble.

"What?"

"Viral load. If it makes the compounds—"

"—it could be seeding the virus. Shit!"

"We'll need full scans, both of us. And quarantine." He activated a comm link, probably internal, and began speaking. "Mary, Marty. Don't tell the others to join us, we may have a contamination issue. Send—send someone to go fetch what's left of Perc and send the second section of the MCP on ahead, it has the medgear. You got all that?"

From Mike's side of things, I got, "Got it. Poor Perc. We can't keep losing people like this."

"I know. I'm sorry. We'll mourn and move on, but right now, we can't risk rejoining the others until I'm sure none of us have been exposed."

"OK. They'll get the signal."

The first task was getting the forward part of the MCP back up to the road. Marty didn't want to risk taking the middle section down. Mike surveyed the situation.

"We're gonna' have to go down to go up."

Marty considered this. "Not a problem. I think there's an old road which should hook back up with the one we're on if we head back west a little."

"Yeah, but now that I'm gettin' a chance to actually look at these controls, I don't like that one." He tapped one of the many small screens on the console. Marty looked over at it and nodded.

"Power's cut to the wheel somewhere. Damn it. Probably shouldn't complain, we're lucky to have so little damage after that stunt." Mike looked like he was about to start shouting. "Hey, easy... it turned out to be a good choice." He took a moment to find the right words and continue. "I'm just... I guess I'm used to being in the loop on decisions like that."

"Yeah. Well, sorry. Didn't have time to call a meeting, set up the agenda, and table the decision 'til we could all vote on it a week later. Bein' shot at was kind of... distractin'."

"Whoa. Easy. I'm not trying to ride you. You did the right thing."

Mike grunted and went back to studying the readouts. From within his eyes, I could see him constantly scanning back and forth, tapping the screens to bring up lists of symbol keys or explanations of functions. Each tap was harder and sharper.

Marty, meanwhile, had gone out to check the damaged wheel, and had asked Jill to come along. The woods were *probably* not currently swarming with hunter-killer 'bots or dermally armored bears, but you couldn't be sure.

He eased himself under the vehicle, which was precariously propped up by a half-shattered tree trunk. Jill looked at the wood closely, seeking traces of silver wire, and found none.

"So, is he always like that?" Marty called from beneath the axle, grunting as he struggled to loosen a warped metal plate.

"Like what?"

"Prone to explode randomly."

"Hmm. He does seem a bit edgier. Could be a stress reaction."

"I get the feeling he doesn't like me."

"He doesn't like being told what to do, even when it's the right thing and he knows it. You're putatively in charge. That makes you... well, not the enemy, but at least suspect."

"Makes a kind of sense. Hand me that wrench, will you?"

She did so. There was a loud banging from underneath. "There. Well, how does he get along with that doctor of yours?"

Jill considered this. "It's complicated. I think MacIntyre managed to earn Mike's respect. That was after the part with the cortex bomb, of course."

There was another banging, this time of something softer, as if of flesh striking metal.

"Not my style of leadership. OK. I think that will hold for now." He slowly crawled out. "How about you? MacIntyre need to threaten to kill you?"

"No. I volunteered. I think it confused them. It confuses me, sometimes." She looked at him looking at her. "What?"

"Nothing. Come on, let's get this hunk of metal moving."

It wasn't entirely that simple. The downhill slope was heavily overgrown, and while the MCP was designed for rugged terrain, it wasn't designed for dense, snow covered, forest. Travel stalled to push huge fallen logs out of the way or seek out alternate paths. The sky was dimming by the time the alternate road, a narrow ribbon precariously wrapped around the mountain, was reached. Once there, rejoining the main road was fairly simple.

There was a crowd there, most of the rest of the band. Marty opened a channel to them. "Everyone, please, get back. Go to the designated camp, leave the MCP here. Stay *back*. We can't risk infection."

There was a chorus of complaints and questions, but both Marty and Mary kept up the steady, measured, response. Eventually, the vehicles pulled back, leaving the center portion of the MCP.

It took a few more hours to get the middle part of the MCP hooked up, a complex task with only two people experienced in the procedure. It was cold and dark by the time it was all done, and tempers had shot up on a few occasions during the process. There was a sense of palpable relief when the task was complete and the medical equipment was back on line.

Marty set up a blood scanner, using the data on the virus that I'd given Jill.

"Here goes... let's see if we'll be getting furry any time soon"

"Not funny."

Marty looked at Jill. "Hey, if you can't laugh at death in this world, you'll go mad." He glanced at her, caught her expression, and continued. "Anyway... give me your arm." With an annoyed sigh, she held it out. A thin line of red began to flow through the plastic tube and into the scanner.

He looked at it and frowned, then made a slight noise, then adjusted some parameters. Jill stared at it. She couldn't make sense of the readings, but I could. So could Marty."

"Well, good news, I guess. We were exposed," There was a sudden look of anxiety from the other three. "But it's dormant. It's in some kind of spore."

Mary looked at him. "Could something trigger it? Make it active?"

He nodded. "Something, yes, but no idea what. I can set filters for it, and we can at least clean our blood. I'm going to guess it won't casually activate, since we've never seen victims of it outside the compounds. Have you?"

Jill and Mike both shook their heads.

"Good. I can be a little less paranoid then. Still..." he drummed his fingers. "We need a group meeting. Mary, please start arranging it. I've got filters to design."

He looked up at Jill. "You pretty much managed to save this whole band. Both of you. I think that's worth some parts. Maybe more. We need to talk in the morning About a lot of things."

Morning came sooner than anyone wanted it. The night, what was left of it, had been spent in alternating shifts. The vehicle, alone on the open road, was vulnerable even with camouflage, but Marty was insistent on not returning unless he was sure all contamination was gone. Of all of them, only Jill seemed reasonably awake. Marty was more closely tied to his body than Jill was to hers, and more prone to suffer mentally if it was physically exhausted.

It was a short drive to rejoin the others.

The rest of the group was camped at a transient hotel, which they'd managed to momentarily power up. At some point in the past, probably around the time of the Collapse, there had been a festival planned for this area, physical gathering of some kind, and the hotel had been constructed a few days prior to the event, with the intent of it being taken down and moved on shortly after. Mobile, fluid, society had little need of being tethered to year-round accommodations, subject to the whims of the calendar and passing trends; if there were going to be a lot of people needing a place to live for a few days, buildings would be built for them, and they'd vanish with the need. The hotels themselves were transient, their owners moving them from venue to venue across the continent, sometimes getting involved in battles for prime space which ranged from red-tape wars with the local neonations to out-and-out violence. This one, property of "T3h R3zid3nz C0113ktIv3," was fairly modern in design despite the owner's attempts at evoking quaint early twenty-first century charm. It was also partially collapsed, the left side a slumped ruin. Not surprising. They were never meant to last. Still, enough infrastructure remained that there was some power to it, and the tribe had spent a comfortable enough night.

The mood was, to say the least, mixed. There was joy and relief when the MCP rolled up, and a quick flood of people shot out to surround it, help Mary and Marty out, and stare at the damage done to the front section. There was also a dark miasma over it all. Both Jill and Mike took the time to wander over to the remains of Perc's van, sitting at the far end of the encampment. Mike lingered at it a while, mumbling some generic prayer to the Presumed Benevolence Of The Universe, while Jill just looked at it for a moment, nodded as if to acknowledge something, and walked away. I'm not sure what they did with the body; if it was left at the death site or burned or buried. Neither Mike nor Jill thought to ask and no one brought the subject up.

Breakfast was subdued. No one seemed to have the energy to try to do anything creative or interesting with the standard supplies, so it was all by-the-manual: Lumpy Yellow, Lumpy Grey, and Lumpy Brown, washed down with Dingy Tan. This was one of many times I didn't envy Jill and Marty their wider range of direct sensory inputs.

After that, Mike and Jill met with the two leaders, as a slow and lackluster packing up ritual got underway in the background.

Marty spoke first. "All right. We want to change some terms."

Jill's eyes hardened and I saw targeting routines start up. "Go on." The only way to miss the threat in her voice would be to be dead already.

Mary politely ignored it; Marty did not. "Hear us out, and if you don't like what we have to say, the old deal stands unchanged. No haggling, no fussing. OK?"

Jill nodded, barely.

"We want to give you what you need, now, and send you off."

Now it was Mike's turn to show emotion. He glanced in confusion at Mary. "Send us? But we had, what? Another couple of weeks, I figure. Did we—"

Marty laughed. "Will you just let us finish? Look. We just lost someone, and that scare with the virus got me and Mary talking. I know we mentioned it once, and it's time to do it again. We want MacIntyre with us. We know what he is, we won't care. He can do what he wants to do, travel and heal. So that's the deal. We send you off, now, and you three come back. We'll give you the travel plans."

Mike beamed, never quite not looking at Mary. "Great! Not a problem! I figure it's not too far back to where we were, then once he's workin' again..."

Jill gestured for him to be quiet. "MacIntyre might not agree."

"We can always plant a bomb in him," offered Mike.

The others politely ignored it. The thing was, I wasn't sure if he was kidding. I mean, he knew I'd be watching these downloads, but still...

I probably deserved it. Stupid conscience.

Marty continued. "Well, if he's hesitant, try to convince him to meet with us anyway. We might be able to work something out." He looked at Jill. "You could take this stuff and disappear down the road. Not mention it to MacIntyre. Hell, there might not even *be* a MacIntyre, though I admit that's pushing paranoia a bit. But I am just getting too damn tired of always living like everyone I don't know like a brother is looking to stab me in the back unless he thinks I'll stab him first if he tries. So I'm going to appeal to that whole mercenary pride and ask you to accept, as terms of our contract, that you will make all reasonable effort—that means no bombs—to convince him to come along. And if you can't, you can't, and maybe we'll meet again. Maybe not. Deal?"

"Terms accepted."

There were a few hours of gathering up the needed parts. They were few and light. Looking at the complete assemblage in front of them, a small mound of wires, metal and tools, I found it a bit humbling. A few pounds of assorted minerals was the difference between me being mobile and free, and me being stuck and slowly going insane. Then again, I thought, how big is a heart? How much of the brain do you need to destroy before a person dies? Even removing a millimeter of spinal nerve can cripple a man for life, or could back in the day.

Then came the leavetaking. Lavender sought Jill out, which impressed me, since she'd been trying to dodge this.

"Hey! Found you!"

"Yes, you did."

Lavender beamed. "Made you something! Look!" She reached into a plastic basket and handed over a round, hard-skinned fruit. It was covered in complex lines of red and blue, over a basically yellow skin. "I was working on it for a while."

Jill stared at it as if it might attack her. Given Lavender's talents, this wasn't unreasonable. "What is it?"

"Well, it's mostly an apple, with about a day's supply of vitamin C on top of it, and some immune boosters. But that's all off-the-shelf crap! The skin's something I've been working on. It's a neural wiring pattern. I, uh, read some of the tech's files and based it on the diagrams... uhm... because, well, you know. I thought it would be personal, kind of meaningful, and..." She stopped, her voice fading against the wall of Jill's silence. "Shit. I screwed up again, didn't I? Damn, I keep trying to do things people will *like* and I..."

"I like it."

Lavender stared up at Jill. "You do? You're not just—just trying to be nice..." Lavender considered this possibility for a moment, then her face exploded in delight. "Of course you're not! I mean, that's so not—I mean, you—oh, hell! I'm glad you like it!"

She bounded off, leaving the basket with Jill, who watched her go, sighed, then tossed the circuit-apple up, caught it, and began eating it as she went off to locate Mike.

She found him looking over maps with Marty.

Jill glanced at the slightly glowing display. "This isn't where we left MacIntyre."

"Not what we're lookin' at." Mike tapped a button. Silver circles blossomed all over the map, forming a spiked, spreading, pattern. "Everywhere they go, they suck down sensor data. They trade it with other people, so they've got some of the best maps of the region around. And those things—" He pointed to the silver circles. "—those things are the kind of energy patterns we were followin'. This is a roadmap to the Unknown Bastard."

"Nice."

Marty smiled. "Call it a bribe for MacIntyre. We're not going to send our little band straight after him, or them, or it, but we could commit some volunteers to following this trail. I'm curious as to who has this kind of tech, too. We're going back to find every scrap of useful metal we can from the remains of that morpher, too. By the time you rejoin us, we'll have analyzed it, learned something you can use, maybe."

"Maybe. Good plan. Well, we should get going."

Marty flinched slightly at her abruptness. "Yeah... yeah, I guess you do. Long walk. Wish we could spare a vehicle, but..."

"Not a problem. We walked here, we walked back."

"*Some* of us can't just turn off pain."

"Some of us can't shut up about it, either. Do you have... anything you need to do before leaving?"

Mike smiled and glanced over at Mary. "Everything's taken care of, for now. I guess I'm good."

They made final checks on rations, ammo, and directions. Between the maps and Jill's magnetic guidance, they could make good predictions of travel time. Allowing a day to fix me, they worked out where the tribe would be camping and agreed to meet them there. Then they left.

Or tried to. They'd managed to go about a hundred yards from the camp when Jill stopped. "We've got company."

Mike looked around. I saw what he was looking for, but he didn't. One of the odd things about watching these records is realizing that what the eye records and what the brain perceives aren't the same thing. His sight swept past Ella twice and his mind failed to acknowledge her.

"What?" he said, finally.

Jill pointed. He focused. Then he sighed. "Ella..."

There was no response.

"We can see you. Come on."

Slowly, she emerged from the woods.

"What're you doing?"

"Figured you'd need help. Dangerous out there. I know."

"You belong here."

She shrugged. "Belong where I want to."

Mike seemed to consider that. It was a position he had sympathy for, after all. "You bring food?"

She tapped a small sack at her waist. "I can hunt, too."

Jill was less sanguine. "No! We are not bringing anyone along. You stay here."

"Why?"

Jill pondered this. "Our friend... is a bit odd. He's very concerned with rules. He doesn't want people knowing where he is, so if we bring you back, he'll think we broke his trust."

Ella considered this. "I can hide. He won't see me."

Mike picked up the line of reasoning. "Yes, but... once he's fixed, we'll be coming back here *in* him. A lot faster than even you can run."

"You're really coming back?"

"Sure. Three days, at most."

"Sometimes people don't come back. Even when they say they will."

"We will. And, hey, think of the others. Think how they'd feel if they found out you just wandered off. 'Cause I'm bettin' you didn't mention this to anyone else, right?"

She nodded.

"So, come on... go back, and wait. Better for everyone."

She took a moment to weigh her options, then, without a word, shifted back into the woods.

Mike looked at Jill. "Any reason not to bring her?"

"It's not safe. You might recall we only met these people because I was wounded."

"Not safe here, either. You might recall we all nearly got killed yesterday."

"Fine. I'm not going to be responsible for a child."

"She survived on her own for years."

"Sheer luck. I'm surprised. I thought you would be more opposed to the idea."

"Why? 'Cause she's a kid? She's got the will to decide what she wants to do with her life, let her do it. I know when I was her age, I wasn't listenin' much to what people told me I could and couldn't do, and look at me now."

"I think I just won this argument."

They began walking away.

"Hey! What did you—"

(The remainder of the files consisted of two days of walking and the same five debates, repeated with minor variations, over and over. I will spare readers the tedium I had to suffer. As a doctor, I try to do no harm.)

Chapter 13

It was a lot to digest.

I'll admit I had several worries. For one thing, it was clear Mike had formed attachments which were slightly less casual than his usual. And if Jill was reticent about Marty, well, it might be only a matter of time before she reconsidered her situation. Besides, being openly accepted by a community was so rare it had to be tempting in and of itself. In short, I was afraid that if I turned down the offer to join the tribe, that I'd be alone again in short order—mobile, perhaps, but still alone.

The last three weeks had really made me leery of that. I'd spent—what, two years? three?—solo until I ran into Mike, and it hadn't bothered me, or maybe it had. I think back to how I responded to Morowitz, to Jake, and I wonder what the hell was wrong with me. Being so alone had, I think, made me go a bit crazy. I didn't want to risk that again. Hearing nothing but my own voice in my mind, having no one to balance me... It wasn't healthy, for me or for anyone I tried to help.

I also wasn't sure about this whole "one big happy family" deal. It didn't seem very stable in the long run, but then again, what was? They did need me; I'd have a niche. I'd be able to do what I set out to do, with more support, both technological and emotional. I thought of everything I was running out of and Lavender's biotech skills. I thought of how patched and re-patched I was and what a team of mechanics with extensive spares could accomplish.

The main thing I'd be giving up was my autonomy. That's always a little scary. I'd become very used to being my own CO, and to fit back into a hierarchy—even as informal as Mary and Marty used—was off-putting.

At the end, though, the alternatives looked worse.

Mike passed out fairly quickly after the long debriefing; he was suddenly grateful for the sleeping space behind the cab. This left

Jill and I with some time to talk. She liked to do so while her body
was resting. She told me that one of the things she had trouble
getting used to was just *sitting* there while her body slept; she'd
had to train herself to pay full attention to its needs, from sleep to
hunger. Now she handled it without conscious effort, but tended to
get bored a lot when "performing maintenance."

The topic of conversation was pretty obvious.

"So, you really think this is a good idea for us?"

"You mean, 'for me,' don't you?"

"No," I lied. "For us. I mean, we're not much of a group, and we
haven't been together that long, but I still think of us as a team, a
unit."

"Hmm." I could tell she didn't believe me, but she decided not
to press the issue, more from boredom with constant arguing than
from politeness or respect. "Yes, I do. I've played around with it a
lot over the past two days, and other than the kind of reflexive 'you
want me to so I won't crap' that Mike always pulls, I can't see
what's wrong with it."

"We'd be a bigger target."

"We'd have bigger guns."

"We'd be stuck on their schedule."

"As opposed to 'Let's wander at random and look for sick
people'?"

I was running out of excuses rapidly. Every objection I came up
with, I answered by myself.

"All right. I'll go with you. The data they have on the Unknown
Bastard is just too tempting."

***

Thaw began with the dawn. The area I was parked in had
begun to be drenched in a constant rain of snow and ice melting off
the branches above, a continuous frozen drizzle. Mike spent most
of the morning out in it, cursing and complaining, but by noon, I
saw a dozen readouts and diagnostics flash from red to yellow to
green, and without waiting to be told, I fired up the Heim drive
and cleared the ground for the first time in what seemed like
forever. I was tempted to charge up to full speed and do some laps,
smashing (symbolically) through the invisible fence which had
defined my life, but I decided to exercise some boring caution. I
slowly tested the new linkages, checking each to see how it

handled surges of power, then began moving in ever more complex patterns to see if maneuverability was back. It was.

"Great job, Mike!"

He smiled. "Thanks. There's some other things need fixin', mostly stuff in the walls that got shot up, but we can do that later. We ought to get movin' to make our pickup point. Uh... if you're up for that. We sort of promised we'd get you back there to consider it."

"I wouldn't want to put you in the awkward position of breaking a promise. Yes. I'll go. *I* am not making any promises, however."

"Fair enough."

Two days of slow walking across partially frozen ground became two hours of Heim field gliding, even given the fact I was occasionally prone to wandering off-course in order to leap off small rises or skim along partially frozen rivers, seeing if I could manage to not crack the ice. I know I shouldn't have; the repairs were fresh and untested and if the field gave out, I could end up seriously waterlogged and possibly unfixable or worse. I didn't care. To be *free* again, to *move* again; it was amazing. I wanted to indulge. I glided, I spun, I modulated the field to kick banks of snow up in glorious white waves, I ignored the protests and complaints from my passengers.

We reached the rendezvous point, a small cul-de-sac a mile or two off the main road. Looked like an old farmhouse was once there. Very old, it was little more than a wooden frame now, and the fields surrounding it were barely defined. I pulled into the shell of the house, as cut off from casual sighting as I could be. We were a little early, so I damped down the field and prepared to wait. Mike and I ran through the fourth chapter of Zombies of Rome (he was convinced there was a way to unlock an orgy sequence; I kept trying to convince him it was an old urban legend), while Jill did some exercises, keeping her body as functional as it could be. The hours stretched on.

Night came, and there was a nervous dinner of hastily prepared rations and worried glances down the road. Marty had asked to be met here, not intercepted—if they were in negotiations on the road, the sudden arrival of a new vehicle could lead to violence. Best to keep things off-road and safe. As night wore on, though, the tension and worry increased. It was easy to spin plausible scenarios for the delay: a damaged vehicle needing prolonged repair, for example. But wouldn't they send a scout ahead, knowing we were to meet them here?

By the time light began to leak over the horizon, we were heading down the road.

There was smoke, and ruin, and death. Something had found, and hit, the convoy.

Mike was first out, moving before I could even damp the field down. He stumbled as he hit the cracked asphalt, then regained his feet and ran, screaming, gun out. I dropped speed as quickly as I could and set up full sweeps. If there was anyone here, we'd been seen, and there was no point in being subtle. I also flicked the railgun online and started feeding it targeting data. Jill was also out, right after Mike, but in a careful crouch, surveying every rock and barricade, looking for survivors or targets.

My own scans weren't good.

I was looking for heartbeats, mostly, turning up the sonics to maximum and then filtering out anything which didn't pattern-match. Nothing was coming through. It wasn't proof of no survivors—a heartbeat isn't loud, and someone inside a smoking vehicle husk or behind a large shard of metal wouldn't be detected. Even so...

I didn't know these people. I hadn't spent time with them. I'd seen a lot of bodies, a lot of massacres like this, but the fact that I knew them, even second hand, hurt. I tried to keep focused. I activated the Charlie and went out, medikit in one hand, gun in other. Lovely metaphor for the world, I remembered thinking inanely. In times of tragedy, when the shock is about to overwhelm me, I defend myself by distancing my mind, by having my thoughts bounce to anything other than the horror in front of me.

Mike and Jill... well, Jill was sliding into pure soldier. Everything was suddenly a tactical assessment. Each step, each dash from one pile of wreckage to the other, was a calculated act, maximizing defense. She'd dash to a body, quickly check it—whether to see if it was alive or just to see who it was, I didn't know and didn't ask—and then move on. I dealt by distancing, she dealt by focusing.

Mike was also running, screaming, calling for those he knew best, for Mary, for Ella, for Marty. He held his pistol out and screamed to the silent mountains, demanding that whoever or whatever did this show themselves. He fired at nothing until his gun clicked emptily, then simply raged through the rubble.

I walked as well. Jill was stalking, Mike was raging, I was

doing my job. It's the other retreat, the other safety net. Walk to a body. Verify that it's dead, that there's nothing I can do. Go to the next. Don't think about the names, don't think about the faces, just focus on the job. Find lives which can be saved, and save them.

There weren't any. Most had died instantly; the others... well, if we had been here in time to save them, we would have been caught by whatever did this.

It was a long, terrible, day. I probably had the easiest time of it, but it was still hard. I didn't know them, true, but I'd seen them, quite literally, through the eyes of Jill and Mike. We found and identified bodies, in some cases by fragments of jewelry or traces of tattoos, things one or the other faintly remembered. We looked for evidence of who did this. And we stopped, every so often, to walk away, to be alone with grief or rage or whatever emotion had most recently exploded to the surface.

We couldn't dig graves in the still frozen and always rocky ground. Mike tried, once, smashing the ground with an entrenching tool, burning out his fury against the unyielding ice, working at it to the point of physical collapse before he gave up. Jill stalked. She circled the perimeter of the devastation, hunting, seeking. She, too, wanted something to vent on, but it wasn't going to be ground.

Eventually, there was a pyre. I didn't feel it was my place to say anything. Jill didn't have any words. Mike, finally, began with a partially remembered litany, "Companion at the end of life, be with us—" something like that. I recorded it but I didn't memorize it. He ended with, "And we'll get the bastards," which I somehow doubted was canonical, even by the loose standards of his church.

Nonetheless, Jill seemed most moved by that line, nodding in bitter agreement.

When it was done, when we sat despondently in the flickering glare, standing guard against the inevitable vultures, sapient and otherwise, which would be arriving, I finally dared chip at the consensus of silence.

"Was everyone... was everyone accounted for?"

Mike looked at me, hollow. "No. I don't think so. Some of the— some of the bodies were so... I don't know. I didn't exactly count, y'know? Why?"

"Someone might have gotten away. Or even taken prisoner. There might be—"

"Ella." Mike blurted out. "I think I'd recognize her, tiny thing. Jim, that was Harry an' Phedire's kid. Maybe two others, I think."

I considered. "All young? All children?"

Mike nodded, his brain putting the pieces together, rationality struggling to find a foothold out of the mire of grief. "Yeah That sounds familiar..."

Jill chimed in, "Another recruitment strike."

"Fits. Weapons stripped—Mike, Jill, did you see any vehicles missing?"

Jill nodded. "Three. The others were too badly damaged to move on their own, maybe?"

Mike considered. "I saw... I think I saw places where it looks like parts were taken. Really wasn't lookin' too hard." He smiled, then. "Well, we know who did it. When do we kill them?"

I stared at him. It's nice to be able to do that; I was using the Charlie more and more. "Mike, look, I understand you're—"

"You don't understand shit."

I ignored it and went on. "You'll die."

"Ask me if I care. 'Sides, we faced 'em before. We won. They lost."

"We got lucky and they were being stupid. You can't know we'll have the same..."

Jill had wandered off during this, walking to the shell of the MCP. Damn, they'd had something powerful. It was gutted, sliced open in several places. I didn't know what she was doing.

Mike's face settled into solid resolve. His eyes glistened in the light of the dying flames. "Tomorrow, I start huntin' them down and killin' 'em. Love to have you along, Doc, but if you ain't, you ain't. You ain't dumb enough to try and stop me, so I don't need to bother tellin' you what I'll do if you do."

"Mike, look. We can—"

He stood up.

"I said what I needed to say. Going to sleep now. Got a lot of people to kill tomorrow. Pretty sure Jill will help."

She walked back into our site. "Maybe. I want to look at this first." She tossed down a small slip of metal, two inches long, a quarter inch thick. Data storage, a few terabytes worth.

I picked it up. There were no external markings, or if there were, they were unreadable underneath the carbon scoring. The metal was slightly twisted in places, and there were a few small holes in the casing. "What's this?"

"Don't know. I do know I was sitting here, thinking—mostly how to kill them, like Mike—and I got something, a signal, on a personal frequency. Faint, so faint I didn't even notice it until I'd stopped paying attention to anything else. I followed it, back to there. Microtransmitter, size of a flea if that, and when I got close there was a second signal, so weak you'd need to be in a few feet of it, and that pointed me to this."

I turned it over a few times in my hand. "Some kind of message? Warning?"

"Don't know. It would have taken him only a second or two to set it up. He could have done it when he decided there was no hope."

"Well, we should check it out. Hmm. Just in case..." I dropped one reader from my internal network, then got really paranoid. Even if the software was offline, so long as there was hardware, there was a risk. "Mike, going to need some engineering help."

"'Till tomorrow. First light, I'm out of here."

"Fine. Your life. Just help me for now, will you?"

"Sure."

A few minutes later, we had a standard data reader sitting on a makeshift platform, hooked up to an imaging system. Both were cut off from external contact, even to the point of physically ripping out the connection mechanisms. If the datastore was some kind of trojan, it would have nothing to link to or corrupt. I slipped it in.

I'd expected a text overlay or a message, but what I saw was the MCP, dropping down a hill, covered with incomprehensible symbols. Then there was an explosion, and the screen flickered and cracked to static.

"The hell?"

Jill frowned. "That's—that's what our fight with the morpher would have looked like—from its—this is a memory system from it! They must have found it in the wreckage, cracked the encryption, but why? Why this?"

I looked at the image. "Check the time frame. This is the end of it. Let's move back."

I tapped a control, and the image began again, at the beginning.

Watching it was strange. There was a flow of symbols—a startup sequence?—and then visual. A factory. The focal point swiveled around, testing itself. Something pulled away, something like the mechanism I use for multi-point surgery, a fractal arm. Elsewhere, flickering in and out of the field of vision, were other arms, tools, micro-point welders, all kind and manner of devices, only a few of which I could identify. We saw a few more minutes of this, then a stream of symbols flaring across the vision. Then motion. It moved forward shakily, flying left and right, staggering like a sailor late on the night of shore leave, then, as we watched, it seemed to gain more control and purpose, finally smoothly rolling forward.

It moved through a complex, a factory such as I hadn't seen in years. This was a full fabrication plant, the sort of thing only a city or a *very* large isolated community might have, well beyond the kind of basement minifacs most people or groups owned. Given the raw materials and the plans, this could build anything, given time, and judging from the size of it, it wouldn't take much time, at that.

"How old—" I began, then checked the timestamp. It was less than a year ago that this thing had rolled out.

Impossible. Nothing like that had survived the Collapse, well, nothing I'd ever heard of. Too valuable. Anything that big would be on the grid, and if it was on the grid, someone else would know about it and something would have been sent to blow it up. I mean, in theory, it was possible, but...

It was like archeologists of the early twentieth century, digging around in old Egyptian pyramids, making a wrong turn and seeing a new pyramid going up. Incredible.

And scary. We knew the Unknown Bastard had resources, but this...

No people. The morpher glided through the complex, looking this way and that, but never saw any people. No proof of anything, though, but it was odd. There were usually humans somewhere. Even if the entire thing had a soultech mind guiding it, such minds rarely *owned* anything like this; they were employees, at best. (The silicon ceiling was an ever-present gripe.)

Then it emerged. The sunlight, where it was, was bright. It spun wildly at first, perhaps confused by the lack of walls, its dispersed mind finding a sudden surge of new data overwhelming; then it adapted and moved. As it spun, we caught partial sight of nothing. It did a full three-sixty, we should have seen the point it emerged from, but it wasn't on visual. There was nothing there. Camouflage on the building? Probably.

Then we saw its forward path. It moved through what can only be described as a deathline, a virtual wall of lethal hardware, momentarily stilled to allow an ally to pass through. The sky buzzed with low-flying drones, the ground was a sea of mobile mines, there were Heim-field floating killers, tracked vehicles, even spider-legged walkers bristling with guns. Gouts of energy crackled around the place. An outsider might see an army defending nothing, but wouldn't it show on radar or IR or something else? No matter how well hidden, it had to be a tempting target... but perhaps the lack of knowledge of what was guarded, combined with the ferocity of the guardians, was enough to dissuade attack. Who would risk so much with no idea of the prize? There were so many dumb robots running automated defenses around nothing in particular that there was no reason to assume anything well guarded was actually *worth* guarding. Another amusing symbol of our time.

It moved out and away, and then the image dissolved into fragments of damaged data. We spun through it. The majority of it was corrupted, from the explosion or the EMP. We got bits, though. We saw it assembling part of a Fence. We watched it battle a wandering NWA interdiction robot, tearing it apart and then eating it, strengthening itself from raw material. We saw it drilling into a tree and implanting a microscopic capsule.

We knew, at least, how the Unknown Bastard operated, how it spread its compounds and built its network. It wouldn't need many of these things to do it. It seemed, to me, to be less efficient than a lot of smaller, specialized vehicles, but large numbers of drones of unknown origin and purpose would attract attention and be individually vulnerable to being damaged, captured, and analyzed. Something like the morpher... well, you needed fewer, and each one was a lot more robust. It did make a kind of sense.

Mike watched it all impassively. When we'd determined we'd found all the relevant data on the store, he shrugged.

"Nifty. I'm goin' to bed."

I opened a channel to Jill.

"Why do you think he left this for you? The way it was hidden, he obviously did it knowing the attack from the NNA was going to succeed."

"I... I don't know. It's not really what I'd expect from him. I figured he was more the type to spend his last seconds composing some... never mind. Anyway, he wasn't stupid or crazy. If he thought I needed to find this, he had a reason."

I considered. "Something else? Something on a hidden channel, a secondary data stream?"

We spent an hour checking it, looking for patterns in the damaged data or steganographic clues. If there was a message for us, it shouldn't be so cunningly hidden we'd never find it, but after passing over every filter we could think of, we concluded that what we saw was what was there.

"So why show us this?" I asked rhetorically. "He knew we had plans on the Unknown Bastard, at least on seeking him out. Maybe it's a warning? He cared for you, you know, even if his motives were a bit obvious. Maybe he didn't want you to die stupidly going after someone a lot more powerful than us. More powerful than anything, actually..."

There was something there. My mind danced around it, but it was like trying to grasp a frictionless beanbag.

"Vengeance..." Jill whispered across the connection.

"What?" The imaginary beanbag flopped to the metaphorical floor.

"He knew me, he knew Mike. He knew we'd be going for payback. He also knew we'd get ourselves killed, and I don't think he wanted that."

"OK, that makes sense. It's kind of a symbol, he's saying 'Look how tough this guy is, the NNA is just as tough, don't waste your lives.'"

It's amazing how well you can sneer across a communications link.

"No. He's showing us a weapon."

I got it, then, or at least I got her interpretation of it.

"That's crazy."

"Brilliant. Except for one thing—"

"The part where it's crazy?"

"No. The part where we need to know where this place *is*." She cut the communication link and respooled to the point where the morpher had looked back on the nothingness it came from, then froze it.

"There," she said, pointing at nothing.

"There's nothing there."

"No, there's something there, we just can't see it. It's not on visual. But it has to have left traces. No camo screen is perfect, there's always artifacting. Doesn't matter much for moving objects, but if you're stationary..." She tapped some buttons and brought up a control display. "Filters, filters—oh, hell, I don't know how to use this thing! Who designed this interface?" She looked over at me, "Make it work."

"I'll need to run this internally. This ripped-out unit doesn't have the smarts to do what you want."

"So do it, then."

I balked. "I'm still not sure of the safety—"

"Do. It."

There was no arguing with that glare.

I took all the precautions I could and plugged the datastore into the onboard systems. There actually was a feeble attack encoded into it, but I recognized the pattern from when I dealt with the Fences. It was more of a stub, a fragment. Probably it was just some small loop of virus left in this segment when the collective brain of the morpher had exploded, a tiny bit of self-executing code. I locked it out and broke it down. The analysis might be useful in developing protective measures. How else do you give someone resistance to a disease, after all?

We had about one and a half seconds of image to work with. Fortunately, the camera was moving. That increased the chance of finding exploitable glitches. I set up a half-dozen filtering and enhancement protocols, hooked them into pattern matching systems, and set them to work.

We waited. The process would take several hours.

Mike was unconscious. I was getting bored. "So... uhm... The Bay Invasion? We can restore to the second chapter..."

She produced an amazingly eloquent silence.

I stayed bored.

Eventually, the process completed.

We could see, in the enhancement, a series of low domes, which bulged out slightly at the base, linked by loops of tunnel. No idea of material or construction, we were lucky to get basic shapes. From what we could see, we could extrapolate a rough model of part of the structure. Then we worked out what it might look like from the air, and ran that against all the map data I had on board. Something might have found it, some old aerial scan, something taken when, for some reason, this building wasn't disguised or hidden...

The sun had risen when we found it. We'd actually found a few dozen possibilities, and we worked to narrow them down. That one was too far west; that one was known to have been destroyed; that one was a waste treatment plant. Eventually, we got down to one, a cross between a research complex and an isolated community, nominally linked to the Vancouver Confederacy, though pretty much in the no-man's land between it and Calgary. "Horizon Complex" was the name given on the map. Nothing I had in onboard storage told me anything about it.

Neither of us said anything for a while, so I took it on myself to break the silence. "So that's him. It. Them."

"Yes."

"Great. So, what's our plan? How are we supposed to use this?"

"We know this about the NNA. They're desperate for gear. They have a couple of big pieces of equipment they trot out to show off, but it's all smoke and mirrors. They want people to think they've got more than they have. They have no manufacturing base capable of churning out real hardware. They're not an army; they're a bandit gang with delusions. They have no home base or infrastructure. They need one. And here one is, a fully operational autofac which can churn out bleeding-edge military equipment. All they have to do is take it."

"And smash themselves on the rocks, in essence."

"Precisely."

"And if they don't? If they break through the defenses, seize control of that place?"

"We'll make sure they don't."

"How?"

"We'll be inside, blowing it up."

"You *are* mad."

There was a thumping from the room behind the cab. Mike was awake. He staggered sleepily outside and began gathering his personal belongings.

Jill leapt out of the cab. "Wait!"

"Not listenin'. Told you. I have plans."

"We have better ones."

"*We?*" I asked, but was ignored.

She explained what she'd seen, what she thought the message meant, and what a night's tedious research had taught us. About halfway through, Mike stopped looking like he was going to run for the treeline. By the time she was done, he was sitting and thinking.

"It's a start... we need some details. Need to think this through. If I'm gonna die, let's make it count."

Jill looked back at me. "Are you in, MacIntyre?"

What the hell.

"Sure. Let's all be idiots together."

Chapter 14

Thus followed two busy days. We began the task of picking over the wreckage of the convoy for things we might need, our robbing of the dead given moral purpose by the fact we planned to avenge them. Another group of would-be dog robbers approached, but a few quick railgun bursts sent them scurrying. Sorry, guys. The early hyenas get the corpse.

A lot of what we might have wanted had been stripped— weapons and ammo, easily-accessible electronics, stockpiles of food and medicine—but there were other things. A few cases of bullets missed in a compartment buried under clutter. Some rations blown off the road and into the scrub beyond. Superconducting wire and other useful tech which could be scavenged and quickly repaired.

Also, a surprising number of what I could only call "morpher bits." Marty and some of the other techs had been having a lot of fun with the deactivated pieces of the thing, and since they weren't readily identifiable as anything other than random junk, they hadn't been grabbed. We got about a cubic foot worth of tiny, mobile, self-assembling components. I wasn't sure what we wanted with them, but Mike insisted. Something was bubbling in his brain, and I figured it was safer to just wait until it boiled over and he told us.

Then came the next step: implementing a plan.

We had to get them to this Horizon Complex, in full force. Jill had a story she thought would work. I agreed with her. Mike wanted to be part of the infiltration, but I was worried. They'd seen him, after all, gotten good footage of him on his last visit. It would be unsurprising if there were images of him in the guard robots, just in case. Maybe they weren't that paranoid, maybe they were, but it was risky.

"Not a problem," was his reply. "Just change my face."

"Hmm. I thought of that—"

"Sure you did, Doc."

"—but I figured you'd object."

"Oh?"

"No bodymods, no implants, no enhancements. I didn't want to say anything, but I figured you were a purist. Neounitarians, well... it's not universal, but a lot of them..."

"OK, you got me. Yeah. I mean, what other people do with their bodies, that's up to them, but me... well, you're right, I figure I am the way I am for a reason, an' I don't like messin' with it. But, desperate times, desperate times. This is bigger than my personal tastes. I'm not gonna let people die in the name of somethin' I only half believe in on the best of days."

"Fair enough. Get into the bed; I'll try to keep the changes minimal but they're going to have to be pretty extensive, just in case. We don't want even a borderline reading; it will make them suspicious. Retinal and fingerprint scans will have to go too, of course. While we're on the subject, Jill..."

"Yeah, I know. Make me a tall blonde, if you have to."

"Not that. We don't need them discovering what you are. I've been thinking. I know how most medical scanners work. I can implant some things which will give a false reading, make you look..."

"Human?"

"Something like that, yes. We just need to disguise the cortical activity. The neural fiber, that's easy to explain, reflex enhancement, on-board targeting, whatever. I'm going to guess they won't be looking this gift horse in the mouth."

"You have such a gift for complimentary language, MacIntyre."

"Sorry. There's also Mike—"

"You're disguising him."

"Yes, but when he encountered them, they were using loyalty enhancers. The last thing we need is for him to decide that he's on the wrong side because a tidal wave of drugs has drowned his common sense. His mind's been slashed up enough these past few months, he doesn't need more. His rage now will help him resist... it's just a drug, not a memetic, but even so... hmm. I can whip up some counteragents, I think, things that will lock onto and neutralize the drugs. They're probably using something from the holmacine family..."

"Right. You work on that."

Something else was bothering her, beyond all the obvious

suspects, but I didn't know what, and decided not to ask. I just went about my part of the operation. It really needed a good, dramatic, name, like "Operation Hammer and Anvil," but I didn't feel like proposing one. I just filed everything under "The Plan."

Mike awoke early, and spent some time studying his new face. It was still slightly swollen and bruised-looking; no matter how careful I was, there was always going to be some slight internal injury. He was also an inch taller, due to some bone manipulation.

He rubbed his considerably thinner chin and touched his now flatter ears. His eyes were a deep hazel, and his hair a pale blonde. It would grow in that way, too, so no need to worry about issues if they stayed longer than we'd planned. He found the entire process both fascinating and disturbing—not really unexpected. Besides, it gave him an excuse to keep looking at himself without accusations of vanity. Despite this, after about an hour of his intensive self-study, Jill spoke up.

"Trust me, Mike. You're no more appealing than you were."

He grinned. "Just as well, otherwise, we'd never have time to do any spyin'."

"You keep thinking that. Anyway, MacIntyre. Let's finalize plans. Unless our timetable includes three days of self-admiration."

"It doesn't," I admitted. "Here's what I've worked out..."

The first part of The Plan was to find a place to stage the infiltration.

"There's a main camp, maybe *the* main camp, west of here about a few hours. I was there for a bit."

Jill considered. "Do we want to be in so deep? If anyplace will have the kind of high-end security needed to find us out, it will be there. Easier to slip into some smaller outpost, at first."

"Nah. We want this stupid plan to work, we need to get the main force, the big boys, on board. We don't want some third-rate junior commando gettin' the idea of either impressin' the boss with a big haul, or maybe just strikin' out on his own, then bringin' two jeeps and three guys with paint guns up against that nightmare. All that'll do is tip off the rest how bad it is. We have to go for the head, get him convinced this is the thing he most wants to do in the world."

"It does make sense. It's higher risk, though. I'd prefer to gather—"

"No time. You ought to know that. We slip in to some outpost, play soldier for how long? Until we get the chance to meet the boss? Nah. Sooner or later, too much sooner, we're gonna be asked to do somethin' we don't want to do, and if we cut out then, this'll never work. There's only so many times we can disguise an' slip in. We got one shot at this dumb idea, one, an' that's it."

They both looked at me, to cast the tiebreaker, as it were.

"Mike's right. As much as a sane, staged, infiltration might make sense, we have to go all-in in the first hand. Find their main base, get to meet with Cromney, then push our idea. Here."

I ejected a small datastore . Jill took it.

"It's some edits of the footage we got from the morpher. I tampered with it as little as possible, just enough to disguise the real origin. I added in some shakycam. It makes it look more authentic."

Jill sneered. "Everyone thinks they're a director. What's it supposed to be?"

"Your proof. Unless they have some very high grade image analysis tools, they won't detect the changes. This is data you got when you left the complex. I've worked out a plot—"

"You missed your callin', Doc. Should've been a writer."

"I liked eating, or at least having fuel. Anyway, here's the backstory to go with the evidence."

I told them. Then we rehearsed it a few times. I built some Eliza models, based on interrogation texts and some protocols I'd been taught for when I had wounded enemy prisoners in tow, and we tried to find all likely questions and get some responses. As we traveled to our pickup point, we performed exercises in consistency, with my asking Jill and Mike questions separately and comparing answers, finding places where more details needed to be added. We set up some rules for dealing with unexpected questions, stock answers or tricks of phrasing which could be used. We knew they were overconfident but we didn't think they were idiots, or they would have self-destructed long ago.

Through it all, Jill seemed increasingly troubled, even distracted. When I asked her about it, though, she told me that it was just nervousness, there was so much that could go wrong, et cetera.

Yeah, right. Pull the other one. But I'd learned to try to be a bit less nosy. She wasn't trying to back out, and if she had serious reservations about the plan, she'd have stated them. I assumed it was delayed reaction to the slaughter of the caravan. Mike had given full vent to his feelings; she hadn't. Now, perhaps, she was feeling it all. That was my working theory, at least.

Eight hours of uneventful driving later, I slowed down.

"We're getting some faint pings, directed ones. More than the usual random bots looking for targets."

"Makes sense. Ought to be closin' in on the compound. They're goin' to be watching."

"OK. Odds are, they're keeping this area swept for jammers, if only to keep their own local communications working. With luck, that means I'll be able to watch both of you. In the event you get into trouble—"

"You'll come chargin' in to a heavily armed encampment and rescue us?"

"I was thinking more I'd see about performing an appropriate memorial service. Or at least being around to provide transport if you manage to escape."

Mike laughed. Even Jill smiled.

"Fair enough. Well, let's do this thing."

We coordinated random frequency shifts. Every few milliseconds, all of our wireless links would change both frequency and encryption, all based on a random seed we'd been synced to. Even if someone picked up the signal, they couldn't decode it, and, hopefully, would have trouble tracing it since they couldn't latch onto it for very long. If they cracked it, well, hopefully, I'd know in time to tell Mike and Jill to run.

They clambered out. I flipped on full camo and dropped to passive sensors only, as well as sliding deeper into the woods to the side of the road. Worst case, I could use the Charlie to boost range, sneaking in as close to the compound as I dared. I hoped it wouldn't come to that.

I watched them walk. They moved openly, not even trying to sneak. This paid off; the snipers by the road didn't fire, but instead called a halt.

They halted.

Three people came skittering down from the surrounding hills, guns out. Some noises were deliberately made by others on the hills, making sure that Jill and Mike knew they were still watched. Undoubtedly, even more remained hidden.

The first one to speak was a woman, dark skinned and dark haired, one arm made of chromed metal. The chrome was pure show; some people thought it made them look tougher. She was someone who relied on externals; that was useful information.

"This area is claimed by the New Northwest Army. Name and

business?"

Mike took the lead, breaking our rehearsal. Big shock there.

"I'm Mark. Mark Caldman, out of the Free City. This is Jill Huochong, same thing."

We'd chosen this because the Free City was notorious for not sharing its citizen files with other neonations, which would explain why "Mark" wasn't showing up if they thought to check any background data they had access to. Besides, Jill could, ideally, link to him and feed him answers if he needed them. I gave her the codes for the speech overrides, after making her promise not to abuse them.

The woman with the gun didn't waver. "That's names. Business?"

Jill spoke this time. "We want to join."

There was an exchange of looks. This bit was tricky. They were actively recruiting, so they'd be idiots to turn away skilled soldiers walking in freely. On the other hand, they were now big enough to make enemies, and that meant volunteers—as opposed to kidnapped and brainwashed children—could be spies. Which, of course, they were.

Still, shooting them out of hand because they *might* be spies probably wasn't protocol. It would mean there'd be no volunteers to join, and that couldn't be good.

"Hmm." She studied them, as if looking for a hidden sign saying 'We are part of a devious plot to use you against another enemy,' but failed to detect it. She seemed to be weighing which would be worse: shoot them, and be disciplined for blindly attacking potential new soldiers, or *not* shoot them, and be shot out of hand for letting enemy agents into the compound. Eventually, she decided to think positively. If I were a cynical person, I'd point out that this turned out to be the fatal error it usually is. Fortunately, I'm not cynical.

"Well. All right. You can keep your sidearms, that's our policy, but you're going to be checked for everything else—bombs, plagues, the usual. You got any gear in you, declare it to the docs before he checks you, not after he finds it. After that... we'll talk to you, make sure you're good for us, then they can get with the paperwork." She smiled then. "Fortunately, there's a lot less of that than you're probably used to. We keep it simple. Obey orders and don't be an ass."

"What about pay? You guys payin'? Cause I'm sick of not gettin' my cut."

That was part of the plan. If they looked too eager, it would set off bells. But a little mercenary greed goes a long way towards lulling suspicion.

It seemed to work. The wary eying collapsed into a broad smile of one who has found a kindred soul. "Hell, yes! No scrip or worthless bits, either. We feed you, we house you, and you get your fair share of all that's real these days, solid matter. The days when wealth was an idea are dead and gone, and damn good riddance, too!"

She waved; the other two lowered their guns. "Come along, let's get you two processed."

They were in.

They walked back to a waiting vehicle. Looked like a Reno-issue light utility vehicle, a four seater, fitted out with some extra armor. No gun, though there was a mount for one. It fit with what Jill had speculated; they were short on equipment. Probably, the gun went to a vehicle intended for direct combat. If this one came under enemy fire... well, that would be that.

It was a short drive back to the main compound. It was large, larger than I'd expected. It was mostly new construction, too, just as Mike had described, a sprawling mass of dorms, meeting rooms, training centers, and, off far away where it was hard to spot if you weren't looking for it—as Mike was—the "refugee camp," where those not fit to be soldiers for the New Northwest were penned.

There were a lot of kids, too. The youngest, maybe eight to ten years old, were doing all sorts of scut work carrying supplies, policing the grounds, or doing some minor maintenance. The older ones... some did that, but others I could see through Mike and Jill's eyes were doing drills or jogging in cadence around the perimeter, under the watchful eyes of other soldiers. And, everywhere, there were posters and holograms of a stern commanding man. Cromney, I guessed.

I took a chance and tapped into Mike. "Did they have this propaganda fair when you were here?"

"Nah," he subvocalized back. "It's all new."

I filed it under "Interesting." They'd really stepped up the brainwashing, then, I thought.

They didn't get very far into the camp. There was a small building, a neocrete dome, near to the gate. The vehicle pulled up.

Two other men appeared. There'd been some kind of signal sent ahead.

One spoke. "You two, come with us. Corporal Javin, if they check out, you'll be credited. If not..."

"Yeah, whatever." She looked at the speaker with some distaste. "They'll be good. If I didn't think so, I'd be bringing them in as spare parts."

"We'll see." He redirected his attention to Jill and Mike. "All right, get out, and don't do anything stupid."

They did as they were told, putting on a good show of staring around the compound in simulated awe. They also were giving me mountains of tactical data I could use for mapmaking purposes. It took only a few seconds, though, before they were ushered into the dome.

One of the advantages of neocrete is that it's filled with tiny little bits of metal which help pass wireless signals. Buildings opaque to the constant stream of data which used to fill the ether were bugs, not features. Anyone who wanted a secure neocrete building could always plate it with something. Thus, I had little trouble getting a connection inside.

It was a pretty standard medical station. I was better equipped, even in my current state. I recognized pieces of military medical gear from most of the local neonations, as well as plenty of commercial products. Some were still sealed. Some had disturbing stains.

The doctor was a man of medium years, dirty blonde hair, and bored looking. His uniform design marked him as originally from Reno. He looked at Jill and Mike.

"You're the two recruits from Vegas?"

"Long time ago," said Mike, eying the faded Reno rank symbols.

The doctor noticed this. "Long time for me, too. New world now. Better world. The General is making things right again—better than right. Back the way they were, one large superpower ruling the rest, keeping order. It's all starting here."

Jill looked at him. "Well, great, we're eager to be a part of it."

"You are?—Of course you are! Who wouldn't be?" He seemed to almost be asking himself this, and fighting the answer. He shook his head. "Well, anyway, we've got to do some tests. Anything to declare?"

"Neural fiber implants. Reflex enhancers, optical targeting."

"And you, sir?"

"Some old security gear around my brain. Monitoring systems. Think they're dead now."

"Uh huh. Why'd they need to monitor you?"

"Merc corp hired me out of debtor's prison. Figured I'd pay off a lot faster doing that than the grunt work they assigned me. Guys I owed money to agreed. I think they wanted to see me dead and this was cheaper than paying gild to my folks."

"Yeah, well, that's Free City for you. Hah!" He ran a scanner over Mike, up and down, checked the results. "Yeah, looks clean. No weapons. Blood test now." He got a large device, like an armband an inch thick, and closed it over Mike's forearm. Mike gave a little start as it sunk several needles into him and began to whirr slightly. I started to wonder if this guy was really a doctor. That kind of scanner was pretty basic, used in emergencies by untrained personnel. It offered no raw data a trained doctor could interpret, just Yes/No readings on a few hundred of the most common conditions.

While it was working, he turned to Jill. Here was the real test. If he found anything—or called for guards—it would be over. If my false-signal generators failed...

He ran the scan, twice, then looked at the results. "Hmm. Well, lot of wire in you, but nothing likely to explode on us that I can tell, and no built in weapons... yeah, you're clean enough, once we check your blood." He detached the armband from Mike and looked at the readout. "Says you're clean, too. Still, got to do some basic vaccination. Policy. All recruits get a broadspec."

Mike nodded. "Yeah, sure, no problem."

Likely this is where they pump in the loyalty enhancers. Smarter than the whole 'catch 'em in bed thing.' I guess it mattered how they entered. Someone just coming in for a look around, as Mike had been, might have been leery of this kind of exam, but someone asking to join would expect and accept it.

He fastened the armband on Jill and proceeded to dose Mike. This was trickier. It would be impossible to know, for sure, if my counter-agents worked except by watching how he acted. Jill was mostly immune. She didn't think with her meat, after all. She could probably help ground him, help him resist anything my own drugs couldn't.

Jill also passed with a clean bill of health. And that was it. I had to wonder if this "Doctor" had any medical training, or just knew how to use a few basic tools. Given the kind of pseudo-AI built into most medical gear, someone with even a few weeks of training could pass as someone more skilled, as long as they could follow instructions and knew which buttons to press. If they lacked a real doctor, so much the better, it would make our ruse easier.

He called for a soldier to take Jill and Mike on the standard tour and hear the pitch.

The long walk around the compound avoided the refugee center; that could wait until the loyalty drugs kicked in, probably, when they'd be less likely to question it. They saw a vehicle yard, including two very impressive tanks armed with plasma cannons, but from the way Mike focused on the treads, I was guessing he saw signs of damage or decay. The barracks were very nice, quite spacious, in fact, at least for the adult recruits. The food at the mess hall was plentiful if not anything better than reconstituted rations. Jill asked about that.

"Oh, we manage," said their half-guard, half-recruiter. "We've got supply lines keeping us going."

"No farms? No autofacs?"

He shook his head. "Not yet. That will be coming. First, we secure the land, then we rebuild. That's what General Cromney says."

"So, you've secured how much land, exactly?"

The solider stopped to think. "Well, there's some. Plenty, really. Lots of places are part of the New Northwest."

"Such as?"

Before the soldier could answer, Mike jumped in. "Hey, who cares about all that stuff? Where are we bunkin' down for the night? And when do we get to sign up?"

"Applications are still being reviewed. In the meantime, we have temporary barracks over here for you... do you mind bunking together?"

They said they did not.

"Great. Well, if you want, I can show you... uh, for security purposes, until you're actually sworn in and all, we're going to ask you not to wander. If you need anything, someone will be assigned to help you. Tomorrow... tomorrow the General is giving a speech. You're going to want to hear it. He's amazing!"

"Yeah, we've heard."

Did this soldier even know his brain chemistry had been messed with? I was starting to think only a few people knew of the policy, even after they'd been subjected to it. Loyalty drugs could push someone, but not transform them. If they knew they'd been manipulated, the reaction could neutralize the effects.

I did something I should have done long ago...try to track down

Cromney. Unfortunately, my efforts were thwarted. There were two hundred odd "Cromneys" in my files, but they were all the wrong rank, gender, or life status. None came close to matching the ever-present image in the compound. This wasn't entirely surprising; Someone had created a new identity to suit his new role. This was understandable. Who, setting out to build a military dictatorship on the ruins of a shattered world, would want anyone with a working connection or some good archives to find out he'd once been filmed dancing in a pink tutu or got into a three month argument on the virtues of Cuddle Kitty Happy Island IV? Even a note in a military file that he'd received disciplinary action for some off-base antics involving two hookers and a poodle could seriously undermine his aura of stern command. New name, very likely a new face... and thus nothing I could use against him.

Nuts.

Jill and Mike were led to a small barracks in the heart of the compound. They were nicely surrounded. I was going to guess security had overall been tightened since Mike's earlier escapades. Certainly, there were more drones flitting around.

Well, they were in. Now began the hard part. We estimated it would take a few days, at least, to move the plan into action. Too fast and it would set off too many alarms.

The barracks were more like dorms; a series of small, semi-private rooms. Each looked like it could hold four people with minimal personal space. There was a very small lockbox attached to each bed, a communal sink, and little else. It wasn't luxury, but it had power, heat, and no holes, along with enough security that the odds were good that you wouldn't be disassembled by a roaming bot looking for raw organic matter.

The beds still had the sleep fields, which Jill was mostly immune to. Her body succumbed, of course, but her mind remained active and alert. No one came in the night; they'd both evidently passed enough tests that a midnight visit wasn't considered necessary.

The next morning, reveille sounded shortly after sunrise. The neural fields snapped off rather suddenly. Jill registered a subtle spike in the induction; apparently you slept when you were supposed to sleep and you woke up when you were supposed to wake up.

They headed out. Another soldier, a private, met them as soon as they left their quarters, and escorted them, fairly politely, to the mess hall, which was packed. People ate, talked, and joked, as they always did. It was jarring as usual to realize these same people were responsible for trails of massacre and madness all across the region.

It would be a lot easier if people who did evil acts simply acted evil the whole time. Kicked puppies. Pulled wings off sparrows. Sat around plotting how to backstab and betray each other while twirling their moustaches. These people, though, acted like all the other soldiers I'd known. Quite a few were former UBA. Basic human—well, sapient—behavior. You divide the world into people-who-are-like-me and people who are not really people and don't count. You can run into a burning building to save the child of a stranger who is nonetheless part of your tribe one day, and burn down a house filled with children who are not part of your tribe the next, and your mind sees no paradox or contradiction.

I watched people eat, and laugh, and toss food at each other, and whisper secrets, and exchange lustful looks, and share memories, and I plotted how to kill them.

Because my mind is the same as any other thinking mind, and these people were not of my tribe. They'd killed my tribe... or people who might have been my tribe... and that was that.

I know. There's the whole "doctor" thing. I am, after all, supposed to save lives, not work to trick people into rushing into a deathtrap. I could justify it by saying I thought more lives would be saved in the long run, that both the NNA and the Unknown Bastard were major threats, et cetera. Maybe there's truth to that, though I'm man enough to admit it's a bit of a shallow and self-serving justification. It's the excuse of everyone who does something they know is morally wrong: "I am serving the greater good."

Maybe I was, and maybe history will record I did. Maybe history will record me among the worst monsters who ever lived. I know how Morowitz would vote on that. The alternative, though, was worse: do nothing. Just sit back and watch the world keep falling into pieces, or, even worse, be reassembled into a monstrous shape, while I lived with the knowledge I could have acted and didn't.

I'd feel better about this if I didn't have such a record of wrong decisions.

Anyway, breakfast was over. The woman who'd brought them in, Corporal Javin, was waiting for them.

Mike glanced up at her. "Somethin' about a speech, right?"

She almost beamed.

"Yeah, the General's going to speak. Just about everyone not on patrol or active guard duty is going to be there."

I made a note of that. If defenses were lowered during the rallies, that could be useful.

There was a large building in the rough center of the compound, an auditorium. A thousand seats, at least, lined the walls, surrounding a central stage. There was a constant building hum of excitement as people entered. Through Mike and Jill's eyes, I watched. The look on almost everyone's face was one of eager anticipation. No one seemed angry at being called away from duty or recreation, or looked weary of sitting through one more piece of boring propaganda. They acted like they were actors in a recruitment film, almost jumping with anticipation.

I tapped into Jill's comm link. "Are you as bothered by this as I am?"

"More." A pause, then, "Something in the air."

Damn. I didn't have anything on either of them to perform chemical analysis. Probably something pumping up the loyalty, or a secondary booster effect, taking advantage of the closed room. Might even be some kind of neural induction field, like a godbox, creating a sense of religious ecstasy and communion. I switched channels to Mike.

"How are you feeling?"

"Good, I guess. Yeah. Kinda, I dunno, excited? Eager to finally see this General. Know what we're up against."

"Reign it in. There's something in the air. Starricine derivative, possibly. Something to bolster your anticipation, make you excited. You might not be able to change the emotion, but you can focus it. Get excited about the seeing the enemy. Focus on what you've lost. We're putting plans in motion."

"Yeah, I get it. Don't worry, I'm in control."

I was worried.

Mike and Jill settled in. The chairs seemed to be standard theatre issue, large and comfortable. People flowed around them, and two were very sure to sit on either side of them, both attractive and of the opposite gender to the person they were sitting next to. I suppose orientation was a calculated gamble, or maybe they'd done some quick pupil dilation scans to see who the two of them showed interest in when scanning the crowd. Or maybe it was pure coincidence. I have a tendency to overthink.

"Pretty exciting, huh? First time for you two, right?" This was the man next to Jill. His uniform was old NWA, and his current rank in this army was Corporal. He kept talking. "The General's a great man. A great man."

Jill kept her voice studiously neutral. "Really? What's he done?"

There was that momentary pause, that flicker in the eyes, that shows a brain suddenly shifting gears, as the neurons which were queued up to fire found themselves suddenly blocked off, and another bunch of neurons, which had been sitting around sipping synaptic coffee and not expecting to be needed for a while found themselves called to active duty. Apparently, there was a lot of "repeating duck-billed platitudes to each other" around here, and not a lot of critical thinking. Then again, no effective army has ever been composed of armchair philosophers.

Nonetheless, he rallied quickly, as he tossed a few keywords into his mental search engine and found the appropriate response. "He's been leading us... putting us back together. Look at us." He held up the fabric of his uniform. "I'm NWA. Lauren—" he gestured to the dark-haired woman sitting next to Mike. "—Lauren's from the Boise Collective." She blushed a little and gave half a wave and half a smile. "My bunkie, Joe, he's UBA. A few years ago, we'd have been killing each other. Now we're all in this together." His voice changed slightly, taking on an odd pitch. He was quoting something burned into his mind. "One new nation, built from the pieces of the old."

Mike nodded in seeming thought. "So why all the old uniforms? Makes you look.. ragtag."

The both darkened at that, but suppressed it. They'd been given orders to make nice, that was certain. It was Lauren who answered. "Reminders. The General says we need to remember how fragmented we were, how things used to be. Also... it makes people feel better, if they see their allies and their enemies working together. New recruits... like, well, you guys... often look for people from their old countries. It helps them feel safe, at first, until they see we're all in this together."

Lots of hammering on that theme. Unity, alliance, community. Not surprising. You need an "us" before you can have a "them," and it looked like the General was doing a standard issue "Those who are not with us are against us" routine. Start with a noble enough sounding goal, like "unite the warring tribes under one banner," and you can get people pumped up enough to commit any atrocity.

Like, for example, leading a bunch of people to their deaths? mumbled my conscience.

They started it, I replied. I remembered the corpses. The children imprisoned and brainwashed. The slaughter of the caravan, an attack that could not be justified in any way. Maybe unity was the answer, maybe it wasn't, but it had to come from the bottom up, not the top down. Given time, the fragments would reform on their own, create new alliances and patterns of organization, find the right balance point between anarchic war and central tyranny. Whether the General believed his own propaganda or was just shamelessly exploiting people's hopes for a better world was irrelevant; he had to be stopped.

You have your ideals, they have theirs, mumbled my conscience again. *Who is to say which is right?*

ME! I shouted emphatically, and silently, back at myself.

The buzz in the auditorium was growing louder. Lights had flickered on, focused on the central stage.

A man appeared, twenty feet tall, with a barely noticeable fringe effect. Nice holography, but nothing special.

From his slightly graying hair to a jaw line you could use to teach geometry, he was the quintessential leader of men. Eyes stern, yet thoughtful. Body fit, but not over-muscled. His uniform was of no identifiable nation, but seemed to have traces of them all—especially if you were looking for them. His skin was slightly ruddy, his face lined just enough to suggest maturity, yet not so much as to imply infirmity.

Though I knew it was pointless, I ran the scans anyway. Turned up nothing; the nearest matches were some stock images used in interactive production. No great shock there. I only wondered, now, if there was a physical General at all, or if he was purely holographic.

No, no, there he was, at the center of his massive, slightly translucent avatar. I asked Jill if she could switch to IR for a second. Yes, he was real, not a second, sharper, holograph. That pretty much confirmed the 'massive plastic surgery' theory—no one looked that good. He was designed to hit the hindbrain, to grab that part of the mind conditioned to stand up and salute. He embodied authority, command, and leadership, playing on images and archetypes deeply embodied in the psyche of his target audience.

"Soldiers!" he began, and a vibrant cheer erupted. Jill and Mike joined in a beat late, but no one seemed to notice. "Soldiers of the Army of the New Northwest!" More cheering. He held his arms out, as if embracing them all, then dropped them. His face turned serious, stern. "We stand near to victory... but even if victory is deserved, it is not inevitable! We are our own greatness, our own weakness! So much has been done..." At this point, a massive map of the northwest region, showing parts of several former neonations, appeared liberally sprinkled with blue splotches, as if infected with a particularly cheerful plague. "...but so much remains!" The blue spread, engulfing a huge zone. Granted, a lot of it was empty space and much of it was uninhabitable 'bot-infested ruin, but still, the man aimed high. "In the last month, ten more islands of chaos have been absorbed into our sea of unity!" Hey, guys, don't think too hard about what happens to people on the islands when the sea rises, OK? But it looked like no one, except maybe Jill and Mike, were. Every sentence ended with a pause and applause, a ritual chantey.

It went on. Nothing was specific or concrete; everything was vague platitudes. Lots of "the enemy" and "us," lots of talk of the "new" and the "different," the usual condemnation of the "old ways." Without the harmonics, the drugs, and the psychometrics used to determine each syllable and emphasis, it would have been stunningly ineffective. If the man's tactics were a tenth as good as his manipulation, the New Northwest would be printing currency by now. The speech lasted a good half hour, and by the end of it, I'm sure people were hoarse from cheering. If this bothered them, they didn't show it.

I had been keeping an eye on biosigns, and, every so often, whispering little words of encouragement—and sending images of the slaughters we'd witnessed—to Jill and Mike. It's not as is a single speech was going to turn them into drooling zombies, not with the kind of low-level neurological attacks I'd made sure to protect them against, but the subconscious can be a real bitch sometimes. A moment of doubt could lead to an accidental slip, an urge to warn "just this one guy" about the (hopeful) slaughter, or a hesitation that could give away the entire game. I had to keep them focused. Mike was my biggest concern; he was pure meat. Jill had a lot of protection, but even she wasn't immune; her true mind and the meat body she wore had grown together quite a bit, and her consciousness could be influenced by the state of the flesh.

The assembled audience rose to go. Lauren turned to look at

Mike and Jill, her eyes glistening with the terrifying fervor of the true believer. "Pretty amazing, huh?" She looked at them for enthusiastic affirmation.

Mike, slightly dazed from his attempts to remain objective and distant, blinked a few times, and nodded. "Yeah... just uhm... yeah. Wow. Y'know, you said he was a great speaker, but, uh... I didn't get it. Now I do."

Lauren smiled. That was what she wanted to hear. Jill's handler smiled at her. "What about you? What did you think?"

Jill just nodded, her face a well prepared mask of awestruck wonder. "What he said. It's... something you have to experience." She stopped a second, as if thinking. "Can we... I mean... I... ever meet with the General? Talk to him in person?"

The man laughed. "Well, maybe. He comes down here a lot, I mean, he talks to us, but not so much one on one, you know. Too busy for that. Every new recruit wants to meet him, after all, and if he spent his time shaking all of our hands, nothing would get done!"

Jill looked disappointed. "I see. You're right, of course. It's just—"

Too soon! I sent to her. *Don't push it yet!*

"Just what?"

Jill hesitated. In the space between ticks, she shot back at me. *Why? We need to move fast, the longer we stay, the more risk we're at!*

Climb the chain of command. Earn their trust.

Letting them know about a secret cache of super weapons won't impress them?

Not so soon—you haven't *had the time to learn to trust* them! *Give it a little while. You'll see the opening. It's what you do, after all.*

Fine.

Ouch. No harsher word exists.

"Just... a little starstruck, I guess..." she continued smoothly. If the man noticed the slightly too long pause before replying, he didn't reveal it. He just nodded.

"Well, we need to get going. There's a lot to do if you want to join up. You still planning on joining up?" He asked the question in the same tone as "Is water still wet?" Mike and Jill glanced at each other, as if for confirmation, then both nodded.

"Great! Let's go!"

Then followed the usual wall of bureaucracy. Actually, it was less than in many. Our careful preparation of cross-linked stories and detailed artificial biographies proved to be a bit of a waste of time.

Then there was routine. A lot of it. The fact is, the life of a soldier at a base in any army is pretty uniform, no pun intended. Mike and Jill were tested and given rank appropriate to their skills and background stories. Jill toned down her shooting to merely ace marksman levels, something which no doubt galled her. I reminded her of the sacrifices one must make for the cause. There were drills, and tests, and constant checking and vetting as the two were paired with various loyal soldiers and asked innocuously leading questions, most of which they knew how to answer, and a few they got wrong, just to not be *too* perfect. I managed to confirm a lot of suspicions, such as the overall low level of really advanced gear, and the focus on staging big, showy, operations to appear a lot tougher than they really were. After a week or so of this, Jill was antsy, Mike was frustrated, and I was bored and worried we were going to wait forever for the 'right time.' We decided to make it the right time.

Mike provided the opening. He was assigned to motor pool duty, which gave him a good look at the actual state of the equipment. As we'd suspected, it wasn't good. They had a lot of vehicles, but only a few were really in top condition; they deliberately used their best craft on seemingly trivial missions, in order to imply they had firepower to spare. A good number of their vehicles were almost shells, key components and electronics stripped out or replaced with second-rate jury-rigging, the assumption being that no one would be foolish enough to open fire. It did explain why we were able to take out that APC a few months back... I found it slightly depressing to realize my brilliant tactics were less of a factor than their poor maintenance.

Mike cursed as he tossed a twisted piece of metal to the ground. Then he kicked it, and cursed again as he hurt his foot. His partner, a private in his early twenties named Ken Sakuri, glanced over at him.

"Hey, we need that."

"No, we don't. If we need crap, we can get it from the latrines."

Ken picked up the mangled component. "It looks fixable to me."

"That's 'cause you're an idiot." Ken stood stunned for a second as Mike snatched the piece back. "Look, the leads aren't just burned, they're seared away. An' the entire inside—which you can see, though you really shouldn't be able to—is fused. This ain't useful as a doorstop, never mind as part of an engine someone's got to count on to save their life."

"We have to do what we can. The General says—"

Mike bit back some comments. Saying anything bad about Cromney was a sure sign the conditioning wasn't working, and that would get around. He took a deep breath, and spoke carefully. "Yeah, he's right. We have to all work together for the future. But, y'know, the future ain't gonna happen if we don't get some decent gear." He gestured at the disassembled Heim generator they'd both been working on. "Maybe we can get that working for an hour... maybe a day... but it's gonna' blow. We need somethin' better."

Ken shrugged. "We're actively procuring supplies."

Which meant "We're attacking defenseless people and stripping them of everything that might be useful, especially their kids," but Mike wisely didn't comment on that.

"Raidin' junkyards only gives you junk. I wonder if..."

"What?"

"Nothin'. Forget I said anythin'. She'd kill me. Doesn't think I know."

"Know what?"

"Nothin', I said. C'mon. There's got to be somethin' we can salvage here..." He ambled towards a Bay Alliance fuel transport and made a big show of disassembling the armored skirt around the Heim emitters. He also linked back to me. "Think that'll do?"

"Maybe. He should be able to figure out who 'she' is... everyone there knows you two came in together."

"We'll see. Drop too many hints, an' they'll clue in somethin's up." He glanced around. "Heh. Looks like he's already off to say somethin' to someone." Indeed. Ken had already left the vehicle compound, long before end of shift. And he wasn't likely to do that unless he thought it was important.

I'd been watching Jill as well. She was mostly doing combat drills, which were very difficult for her, as she had to keep toning down her responses, remembering to feel minor wounds and the effects of exhaustion, and so on. I kept monitoring her vitals and telling her when she should be tired or sore or what leg to favor. She could have simply cut out her own blocks and actually experienced all of the sins of the flesh, but she really hated to do that. I wasn't sure if it was out of a desire to not feel weak, or because she felt guilty about the damage she regularly inflicted on a body that wasn't originally hers, like someone who inherited an ancestral home and then allowed it to fall slowly to pieces.

The man overseeing the firing range, a second lieutenant in this army, probably a PFC in the one he came from, studied the drill results and shook his head in semi disbelief. "This is astounding. You're consistently in the top five."

Jill shrugged. "I've had a lot of practice. Besides, this is easy. Target shooting. A lot harder in real battle."

He nodded. I wondered how much of that he'd seen, how much of his rank was due to competence and how much to sycophancy? Maybe I was being quick to judge, but he had that look about him, the look of a man whose lips were firmly locked to the bottom of whoever was above him.

"Well, it's still impressive. I'm almost tempted to ask for pointers."

Jill forced a smile. "I could help a bit, but mostly it's practice." Something triggered one of her uncounted background threat assessment processes. Two people walking were highlighted suddenly, targeting information appearing. Seeing the world through her eyes was very educational. She forced herself not to look at them, and continued talking, as if oblivious, with the man. He didn't notice the approaching pair until they tapped him on the shoulder.

"Lieutenant Alberts? We need to speak to Sergeant Huochong. If you could clock her out..."

He nodded, his face suddenly pale. The two who had come were both majors, and from the looks of them, they'd earned it. The markings they wore pegged them as being part of the NNA's Internal Security, a fairly small, tight, group. As Alberts frantically tapped some keys, one of them turned to Jill.

"We need you to come with us. We have to ask you some questions."

She nodded benignly. "Of course. I'll be happy to answer anything."

He was staring at her face, looking for any sign of fear or hostility. He saw none, of course. Whatever she was feeling was nicely disconnected from her body for the moment.

"We will need to momentarily confiscate your sidearm."

Should I tell Mike it's time to cut and run? I sent to her.

No. She sent back. *I've got a quarter mile range and a bunch of Elizas set up in the flesh in case that connection breaks. I'll be fine.*

I hope you know what you're doing.

If I did, would I be here?

She flashed a brief smile. "Of course, sir." She carefully and slowly handed the gun... handed herself... to him, grip first. He took it respectfully.

"Thank you. Please, come with us."

They walked towards the central building, a three story bunker of neocrete surrounded by automated defenses and patrolled constantly. It looked something like a ziggurat, each story inset from the one below it, the walls slightly slanted. The main door fractured apart as the group approached, responding to no obvious signal. Jill got a good look at it as they went through; about a foot thick and filled with complex mechanisms. Anyone passing through it would be scanned, analyzed, and documented.

The interior was comfortably functional. The place was solid; I'd estimate only about half the interior was hollow, the rest was buttressed and reinforced. Walls and doors were thick and plentiful. In a lockdown, any invaders would face slow going. Jill glanced around as casually as she could, her eyes locking on tiny openings which might hold gas nozzles or even very tiny gauss guns capable of firing thousands of near-microscopic shards into any intruders. Cromney clearly expected a last stand situation and intended to make it costly.

The two men took Jill into a small room whose furnishings had clearly been ordered from Interrogations Galore, Your One Stop Shop For All Your Police State Needs. A large metal desk, some uncomfortable chairs, a small terminal, not much else. At least the clearly false mirror option had not been selected; hardly needed with the cameras located in the walls. Any observers could be in another room or another state, handy in case the subject was enhanced enough to overpower his interrogators and tear a hole in the wall.

One of them gestured to a chair; Jill took it. They sat down. All of them stared at each other for a few moments. Jill broke the silence.

"What is it you need to ask me?"

The two men glanced at each other, their body language indicating a quick, unspoken conversation. Are we using plan a or plan b, one "said" by a tilt of his head and a focused look. Plan a, the other replied with an imperceptible nod. Then both turned to Jill and the one on the left spoke.

"Is there anything you haven't told us?"

Jill's face shifted into a well rehearsed look of innocent

confusion. We'd actually spent some time getting that right and implementing a muscle control protocol to make sure it was perfect. She smiled and tried to look just a little bit dim. "Well, sure. My favorite food, the place I first had sex, my cat's name... nothing important. What do you think I know that matters?" She paused an instant. "If it's something the general needs..." She looked open, pleading. "If I could help him..."

They seemed to buy it. "The man you came with, Chalmers, he seemed to think you knew something, something about... vehicles, perhaps?" Jill's face, blood pressure, and every biosign imaginable, was certainly being scanned right now, and the results fed directly to the interrogators. They didn't really care what she said, they were watching to see if she was even thinking about lying.

Her mouth opened slightly in seeming surprise. "Oh... oh, that! I thought about... but then I figured..." For someone who hated interactives, she could be quite an accomplished actress.

"Go on..." They seemed interested but relaxed, no obvious hostility. Whatever instructions they were getting, it seemed they thought this was all going well. Good.

"Well, first, I didn't know Chalmers knew... bastard must have been looking at my personal files. He'll pay... anyway, I do know something, I guess. When I first got here, yes, I held it back... I didn't know what to expect, if you'd take me, I thought maybe a bargaining chip would be good. I didn't lie, I just... left a few things out. You understand, right?" One nodded slightly. She took this as encouragement and moved on. "Afterwards, I just thought it wasn't needed. I mean, we already have so much, it just wouldn't be worth the risk..."

"What wouldn't?"

"About nine months ago, I ran into some Canadians. They were guarding a convoy that had supplies my people needed... you know how it is these days. Short story, we fought, they lost. During... resupply... I found this." She started to move, then stopped. "Can I reach into my pocket?"

One man nodded.

She slowly withdrew the datastore we'd carefully assembled. "I figured it was something he'd seen, not too long before, judging from the date stamp. I knew it could be useful, I just didn't know when or how... so I held onto it." She smiled. "It's almost like a pirate map. You ever do High Seas Raiders?"

The older of the two perked up suddenly. "Yeah, I couldn't get past the typhoon."

You need to appease the sea goddess with a blood sacrifice, I sent to Jill. She repeated it aloud.

"Oh... that makes sense..."

The younger of the two was glaring at him. "Anyway... what's on here?"

Jill gestured towards the desk's small computer system. "Play it. Easier if you see it."

They plugged it in. As far as I could tell, they did nothing to isolate the terminal. Idiots! But we were counting on just that sort of overconfidence, that serene certainty that they were in control.

The images scrolled by. Jill explained her "interpretation" of what she was seeing. They froze it at the end, where the Horizon Institute was, thanks to our edits, perfectly visible.

"What's that building?"

"I don't know. I've never had the chance to try to find it on a map."

"Why didn't you show us this?"

"I—I didn't think you'd need it, you—we—the army—we've got so much gear, and that place is so fortified... I thought I'd just be wasting your time..."

There was a moment of silence, as the two men received reports. This was pretty key. If anyone watching thought she was lying...

"With your experience, Sergeant, you should know by now to leave the judgments to the officers. Two weeks punishment detail. You may go. We'll take this."

"Can I... have my gun back?"

The man holding it looked down, as if suddenly noticing it in his lap. "Yes... yes, of course. Here."

She took it.

"Thank you... I—I'm sorry. I should have just trusted the General to make the right choice."

"Yes. You should have. In the future, you will, right?"

"Of course." She saluted and waited to be escorted out.

Do you think they bought it?

Seems likely, I said. *We'll know soon enough. They've got Mike waiting in another room, probably to verify his story and see if it matches yours.*

He's not going to fool the bioscanners.

Sure he is. While he was under, I tinkered a bit with his neural responses. He's not going to show anything we don't want him to.

There was a pause. Then, *With his permission?*

Of course.

Hmm. I wish I could believe you. Your past record in this area...

Sucks. I know. But, Jill, listen. Mike really, really, wants this to work. You have some qualms, I know, about leading people to their deaths, no matter how much we may both think they deserve it. I do, too. Mike... well, Mike doesn't, not any more. He hardly needs the defenses I put in him to keep the psych-ops bullshit at bay. He's got so much focus, right now, that it's scary.

I got the mental impression of a shrug. *Could've fooled me. He seems to be the same as always, more or less ambling through life.*

You don't get to watch his brainwaves. I do. The way he acts... it's almost a habit, he's been that way so long it's just how he moves through life. Behind the eyes though, there's a change.

If you say so. But if I see his handlers walking out of there without him, I am cutting and running, and I'll take as many with me as I can. Clear?

Ah, there's my bloodsoaked goddess of death.

You will never let me live that down, will you?

No. I will not.

Mike emerged from the room, looking a bit staggered—undoubtedly, they had been grilling him a bit harder. Two officers existed with him. He didn't look at Jill. Belatedly, I realized I had the entire interview on the feed from him. I fast-forwarded through it, looking for any sign of a problem, studying the faces and body language of his interrogators more than I listened to what he actually said. The consensus seemed to be that they bought it. The fish had bitten; the hard part was going to be reeling it in without it squirming off the hook.

I should have updated my cliche filters when I had a chance. Too late now.

It wasn't quite instantaneous. Even when communications systems were working perfectly, the wheels of military bureaucracy ground slowly; now, they barely moved at all. We did get a good look at what the NNA used. A few lasers for point to point comm, when there was a clear line of sight. Cheap, disposable drones, likewise laser equipped, which would get up high, lock onto a receiver, and usually hold out for a few minutes before something swooped in and blew them to hell. And couriers. Lots of couriers. Usually the kids—and that's where we almost lost it all.

It was a week after the "big reveal" that it happened.

Mike and Jill hadn't spent a lot of time near what some of the others called "juvie"—the section of the camp where the "recruits" underwent extreme, and constant, indoctrination, along with the usual physical and mental abuse that masqueraded as training. Break a person down, build him up into what you want... older than Rome. So it wasn't really surprising that they hadn't noticed earlier.

It was Mike who spotted her, which was good, in a way, and also bad. He was doing his job, which was currently cataloguing which engine components could be brought along as field replacement and which were fit only to be broken down into raw materials by the disassemblers, which were themselves growing more and more in need of spare parts. One of the older soldiers, a man in his seeming thirties, meaning he had come of some kind of age during this crisis, approached them. He held a secured terminal, a courier pack, in his hand. He was followed by a sullen girl, scarily thin, and bearing the signs of considerable recent abuse—fresh bruises, and what looked like a hairline fracture in her left arm, based on how she was holding it. She moved almost thoughtlessly, as if her body was simply walking along on its own, her mind elsewhere.

Mike's brain flared—facial recognition centers, mostly, and a sudden surge of response suppression.

Elle? It had to be.

Her eyes passed across his altered face, registering nothing. If anyone noticed him noticing her, they didn't show.

The soldier more or less shoved the terminal at Mike. "We need a final tally. We've got to get it to one of our northern bases. We'll be forming up there with other units."

Mike nodded slowly, doing all he could not to stare at Elle. His arms shook with the restrained desire to hit someone. He just grunted and took the terminal. "Yeah... yeah, I can type this in." He turned away.

"*Now.*"

He breathed deeply. "I, uh, I understand the urgency, but we're not really finished here, an'..."

The man shook his head. "Don't care. We need what you've got now. Hand it over."

Mike gave a crisp salute. "Yes, *Sir.* But I'm gonna' be annotatin' this, that it's not complete yet, an'..."

The other soldier just sighed. "Cover your ass as much as you want. Just give me the numbers."

It took only a few seconds to transfer the data over. Mike handed back the pad. The officer took it, tapped some keys. There was a click, and heavy armor plating slid over it, forming a perfect seal. Any attempt to force it or crack it would result in a massive internal pulse that would fry the data, and probably an explosion which would do the same to anyone within a few feet.

He then handed it to Elle.

"Here. You know your orders? You know what to do?"

There was the most imperceptible hint of a nod.

He touched something else, a wrist control. "OK. You're set. You've got three days to get that where it needs to go. *Move!*"

She left, slightly faster than a walk.

Mike tried to feign mere idle curiosity. "I thought that was supposed to be going north."

"It is. We use them as couriers."

Forcing back words, he kept on with his strained, casual, tone. "She supposed to head out with a squad or somethin'?"

"Hah! Hell, no, we don't have men to spare for that. Don't flatter yourself, your data isn't *that* important. It gets there, it gets there, it don't... well, no loss."

Pain spiked. Mike's nails, I realized, were cutting into his palms.

"Don't want to waste recruits... "

Another sharp, bitter, laugh. "She's useless. Doesn't do a damn thing unless you beat her half to death and then what good is she? The, ah, the training isn't really taking for her. Happens sometimes. So she gets used for whatever doesn't really matter, and if she doesn't make it... well, no big loss. I mean, look at her. Too skinny, really, even for, you know, special services..." His expression left little doubt as to what "special services" might entail.

"What makes you think she won't just take off as soon as she's out of sight? So she doesn't get there in three days, what's it to her? You've made it clear you won't waste time trackin' her down."

A harsh smirk, and tap on the wrist device. "We've got a lot of ways to maintain discipline. Time-delay razor nanites, for one. One click turns 'em on, another click, by an appropriate officer, turns 'em off. A lot of the kids are too young to really understand what they can do, so we make sure that one or two of the least cooperative serve as demonstrations." He gestured back towards the slowly departing Elle. "She came damn close."

Oh boy. I lost track of how many glands were currently firing. Mike's mind was a stew of adrenaline and other chemicals, rage building to an almost uncontrollable level.

I couldn't take the risk. I contacted Mike directly. "Whatever you're thinking, *don't*. It's not just *her* life, it's hundreds, thousands, like her. We have to stop them *now,* or—"

There was a subvocalized grunt. "I. Know."

The officer looked at Mike. "You say something?"

"Nope. Just gotta get back to work here, if we're all done?"

He nodded slowly in response. He suspected... well, something... but didn't seem to think it was worth pushing the issue.

As soon as he was gone, Mike turned to pretend to get back to his work. "You're gonna get her, right, Doc?"

"What?"

"Once she's out of this camp, out of their detection, you swoop in, you stun her or drug her or club her on the head if you have to, you filter her blood or whatever you have to do, and you just keep her safe until all of this is over."

"And by 'safe' you mean taking her with us when we go rushing into the main base of an unknown enemy with unknown power?"

There was a frustrated grunt. "No, no! We can—we will—I dunno, Doc, you're the smart one. Build a damn simulation and figure it out!"

That always worked so well for you, I thought.

"I'll pick her up. I'll do what I can to get the razors out. After that, I don't know. She survived on her own for most of her life, right?"

"Don't even go there, Doc."

"You're putting me—all of us—this whole *plan* in a very bad spot. We may need to—"

"No. Lemme' make this plain, you either do what you gotta do to save her, or I walk, and I'm gonna' bet Jill will too."

"One life... Mike, please, one life against everything else we're trying to do—"

"You start thinkin' of people as numbers, Doc, you turn into Cromney or the Bastard."

"That's low, Mike."

"Don't hear you tellin' me I'm wrong."

You are *wrong,* I thought. It's not that I didn't feel, that I didn't care, it's just that I had set my mind on a higher goal, a purpose, and nothing could...

That's what you thought when you had Morowitz, helpless and dependant on you. Your higher purpose gave you certainty. Did that lead to you doing the right thing? My damn conscience again, mocking me. I hated that thing.

"Fine, Mike. Fine. I'll solve the problem. Just don't ask me how yet."

"I got great faith in you, Doc."

Chapter 15

The easiest thing, of course, would be to do nothing and to lie. With all the lives involved here, with what we were trying to do, it only made sense. "The greatest good for the greatest number" was the only sane moral credo, or so I'd always been taught and usually believed. It wouldn't be easy convincing Mike, I know, but it could wait. Tell him she's safe, somewhere, and we do what we have to do, and if we get back, well, that could be dealt with in time.

That would be the easiest thing.

And all the while I'm thinking that, I find myself, almost unconsciously, plotting an intercept course, trying to find her most likely path (if she even bothered to try) and avoid any other patrols. Last thing I needed was even rumors of someone driving around out here.

Once I found her, though—*if* I found her—then what? Bringing her along would be pointless. She'd be even more likely to die. What kind of place was safe, though? Where could I leave her? I kept looking for an answer and not finding it, even as I homed in on what I hoped was her.

It was. She'd killed something and was roasting it over a small fire. I turned on whatever sound bafflers I still had working and tried to get within about a hundred yards, then dropped to standby and shifted to the Charlie. I got out, and she reacted, setting down the food and scanning the area where the sound came from, her body coiling to leap and run.

The woods here were dense. There were many places she could go where I'd never be able to reach her, and eventually she'd escape my predictive algorithms and I wouldn't even know where to start looking. A small part of me noted that would be perfect. I tried, I could say to Mike, but you know how she is, how good she is at hiding... the easy *and* ethical solution.

Instead, I called out. "Elle! Mike sent me!"

She uncoiled and fled.

Yes, that worked well, I thought, as I kicked the Charlie into full speed.

You would think a tireless mechanical body operated by soultech would be more than capable of catching a young girl, even given a decent head start. Maybe if it had been fully and properly maintained, maybe if she didn't have the gift of sliding snakelike through gaps just a bit too small for me, forcing me to go around and costing me precious seconds.

Ultimately, it came down to limits: there was only so far I could control the body. At first, there were just glitches, microsecond gaps where control signals had to be resent. Then the microseconds grew, and grew, and soon everything was redlined, and the Charlie collapsed and just twitched as only fragments of control signal reached it.

Elle saw this. She probably didn't realize she wasn't being chased by a human—I'd kept the imagers on. She paused for a second, a good thirty feet ahead of me, watching and waiting. I think she'd decided she could always outpace me, so she was taking an instant to see what happened. I was lying there, immobile and twitching, an easy target. She approached very slowly, wary for a trap, but also eager to permanently end pursuit. I wasn't sure how much damage she could really do to the Charlie if she tried, but probably enough, assuming she didn't just flee again once she saw what it was under the illusory halo.

I stopped trying to send movement commands. Instead, I shifted everything I had to getting one command stream through the chatter, pure vocal data and a single order: Speak.

It was a gamble. This was the sort of thing that could drive her headlong into the woods without looking back, but it was the only chance I had.

Her voice emerged from the mostly-immobile Charlie: *"Figured you'd need help. Dangerous out there. I know."*

Then Mike's: *"You belong here."*

Her response: *"Belong where I want to belong."*

She backed away, her expression a mix of fear, curiosity, confusion. Fight-or-flight was warring, and I could tell most of the "fight" part would involve smashing the Charlie to bits. With some effort and a massive surge of redundant broadcast, I shifted to my own voice.

"Damn it, Elle, I'm MacIntyre. The doctor. The one Mike and—

" (burst of discontinuity, something was picking up the signal and working extra-hard to break it) "—about."

Hostility, still. She grabbed a rock, hurled it. It rebounded off the Charlie with a noticeable clang, flickering the holo. "Lying! Spy! Never came back!" She looked around for another rock. Flight was off the menu, apparently, as a lot of rage suddenly had a nicely prone target.

Signal degradation was getting worse. The local interference was all realizing that successful communication which wasn't *theirs* was going on, and was waking up to stop it. I checked the Charlie's position; there was room to activate the projector. It would be half visible.

All or nothing, I thought. I sent a signal to begin looping what we'd found, the carnage, the burial, Mike and Jill and this body. I had no idea how she'd react to that, to seeing her family being picked from the ruins and interred, but if anything could prove I was an ally, it would be that. I saw her moving away from the scene, saw more emotion building, tears coming for the first time, then everything cut out. For a few more seconds I was able to get weak replies from the Charlie, then, nothing. Timeout.

Great.

The smart thing would have been to pull out of my current position, and start moving until I managed to re-establish contact, then get the Charlie out of there (if I could) and just move on. Mission attempted, mission failed, that's the end of it. The truth is, though, I was just too depressed to bother. I'd done the hard thing, even if I wasn't convinced it was the right thing, I'd given it all I had... and I had ended up right back where I would have been if I'd just not tried. It was not really the sort of thing that makes for an uplifting children's story.

I'm not sure how long I sat there moping. I suppose I could check the timestamps, but why bother? Then my passive perimeter sweeps picked up something that passed through the usual junk filters and demanded my conscious attention. The temptation to, in essence, hit the snooze button and let whatever-it-was find me was a bit strong, but I decided I might as well deal with it.

"It" was Elle.

She was moving cautiously, of course, but quickly, following the clumsy trail I'd made through the woods in my pursuit of her, back past the clearing where I'd tried to contact her, back to me. She stopped where she could get a good luck at me, still safely in deep forest, then, suddenly, she snapped and charged forward, smashing at my door.

"Mike! Jill!"

I opened the door; she tumbled inside, looked around, saw no one.

"Where?!" She backed out through the door, terrified it would shut behind her. I left it open.

"They're not here." I said, using every calming inflection and subsonic I could. "They sent me to find you, really."

She shook her head, backing off again. "No. Couldn't know where I was. Lies."

Lovely. She'd managed to get all this way, and she was about to head off.

"No. Look. Could you *please* give me a minute to explain?"

She glared. "Broke the other thing."

I'll send Mike the bill, I thought. "It's OK. It wasn't really me... this is me. Mike told you about me, I know he did."

"You saw everything. Heard everything."

I realized, suddenly, how much I'd gotten used to using the Charlie to add body language to my conversations. I wanted to nod and adopt a conciliatory pose, maybe hunker down so I could look her in the eyes, but I couldn't. All I had was my voice and whatever I could add to it.

"Yes, I did. It wasn't a trick, though, they knew I would be watching. They chose what to share with me after they got back."

"Show me."

"Sorry, I don't understand... show you what?"

"Getting back. Them." She seemed ready to run again... well, even more ready. I could see muscles beginning to twitch.

I activated an external projector and showed Mike and Jill returning, finding me again.

She still looked suspicious, shaking her head.

I sighed. "Look, Elle... I can't keep doing this forever. I've got this recorded to show Mike, and if he asks, I can just tell him I tried my best. He wants you alive, I..." I shut up then. She looked at me closely, perhaps looking for a face.

"Don't." It wasn't hurt or painful, just a statement of fact.

"Uhm... it's not that... I just... there are some things... it's complicated." I cursed all those who had trained me and taught me and advised me, that not *once* did they think of a good way to explain to a child that her life or death was secondary to a larger concern.

"Mike wants you to take me."

"Yes. Very much."

She considered for a second. "OK." She stepped inside, looked around again, this time with less hostility, and sprawled back on the bed in the cabin, suddenly boneless. "Hungry."

I could see why Mike liked her. This was going to be a lot of fun.

"We need to clean you out, first. There's things in your blood..."

"Know that. Got days yet. Hungry *now*." She grinned, fully aware she had command of the situation, and began batting at ventilation hose dangling low over the bed.

"Can you at least help me retrieve the Charlie... the thing you broke?"

She looked extremely put upon. "Fine."

As it turned out, she had a slightly exaggerated sense of her martial accomplishments. The Charlie had just lost signal, and all she'd managed to do was badly dent the projector. I decided not to rub this in.

This still left me the problem of what to do with her.

Meanwhile, the rest of The Plan was stumbling along.

While no one was giving out exact dates to the rank-and-file, it looked like the "big push" would be coming soon. Vehicles and personnel—all mismatched, all in various states of functionality—were moving in. It was a lot easier to assemble and move than to try to coordinate multiple prongs.

One of the things we knew we'd have to figure out on the fly would be getting Mike and Jill *out* of there. The entire plan required that they not be in the slaughter zone when the slaughtering began, but as time went on, this was looking more difficult. Mike was being kept back, assigned to field support, intended to keep things running during what was expected to be a prolonged siege; Jill was going to be near the front lines. They weren't sure what to expect, but they wanted their best people in the second wave. The first wave was going to be sacrifices, simply to draw fire and expose defenses. The kids, mostly, and anyone else who they felt wasn't cutting it. There were always more where they came from, after all.

We'd talked about extracting them early, about pulling them out before the big push, but there was a risk there. If they suddenly vanished, the brass might well guess something was up. Probably wouldn't abandon the plan, but they might go more cautiously, too cautiously. We wanted the Unknown Bastard as distracted as possible, because our plan couldn't work if he was really paying attention to everything going on. We didn't know what his limits were, but we hoped we could strain them.

They weren't complete idiots, of course. Overconfident, arrogant, somewhat delusional, but they'd managed to hold together this long. They had several scouting teams set up, intended to move ahead of the main force, just to make sure the maps were up-to-date and to trigger any border defenses. (The mission profile was "detect and disarm," but those involved had a good sense of the reality of it.) Neither Mike nor Jill were assigned to those teams, but that much was relatively easy to take care of. I had good enough video to grab biometric patterns from people Mike or Jill looked at, and things like duty rosters were relatively low security. We counted on a certain degree of confusion, with the flood of new people in the compound and no one entirely sure what was going on, to keep it all disguised until it was time to roll out. We actually kept the order change on a time delay, triggered by a shift in patterns that would indicate go-time was near, so it wouldn't be sitting around looking suspicious. By the time anyone noticed, ideally, they'd be long gone.

Meanwhile, there was Elle.

Her momentary joy in being able to give me orders wore off pretty quickly. She spent a lot of time being listless, some more time informing me she didn't like the food, other time spent asking to speak to Mike (she was shocked a bit when she saw his face through Jill's eyes, but quickly confirmed it was him after conversation), and most of the time being bored. She probably would have been happy—well, content—to just run off into the woods, find some place to hole up and return to her life, but Mike had asked her to stay, and she very grudgingly did so. He was her tie to the only truly happy times she'd ever had, and I was her tie to him, and so, she endured.

We had a small bit of a breakthrough when I was working on her arm. As I'd suspected, it was fractured, and there were plenty of other injuries, some recent, some old. I was planning to send a few fine probes in to the bone and add in some cultured cells, something most easily done when she was unconscious in one of the beds. She looked up at the primary camera in the medibay, the one I think she thought of as my "face" when she was back there, and said, "Want to watch."

"Why?"

"Don't want to be asleep when you do things. Want to see what you do."

I tried to avoid that, in general, because as soon as a patient can see what you're doing, they're going to start offering you advice or asking you questions and otherwise being annoying. "There's really no point. You won't feel any pain, either way."

"Awake." She looked at the camera. I'd seen that expression on Mike enough times to know it was pointless to keep trying.

"Fine. I will have to cut off the nerve sensations, though." I extended the main surgical arm, started pumping the right mixes into the various receptacles. A set of tendrils moved for her neck.

"*Arm* is hurt."

"Yes, but the nerves—the things that tell you that you're in pain—all run up through your spine. It's a lot easier to stop the pain there. Trust me, I'm a doctor."

She nodded slowly, then allowed the tendrils to reach to her spine. They emitted a contact anesthetic, then burrowed in, seeking the pathways from arm to brain, and deadening them one by one. It was done quickly, and Elle looked at her now sensationless arm. She poked at it with her other arm, fascinated.

I went on. She kept asking questions, so I had to activate more and more screens to show her what was happening. This was her arm, that was the damaged bone, this was the probe moving through muscle tissue, on and on.

"Marty did this," she said, interrupting my discussion on cellular growth factors.

"Did what? Fixed bones? Yes, I guess he did... Mike told me... "

Elle was more distant than usual. "He didn't do it well. Didn't like it. Really hoped you'd come with Mike." There was another pause. "You're better."

I wasn't about to speak any ill of the dead. "I'm sure he did very well. He—"

Elle shook her head. "He couldn't tell me. Asked. He just talked about buttons and programs. Didn't *know*."

This also wasn't news. Given a well-programmed medical unit with a decent Eliza doc, anyone with the most rudimentary idea of what to do could bluff his way through even fairly major medical operations. Marty had said as much, had never claimed to be a true doctor.

"Well, that's true, but he—"

"Want to know. Someone has to know."

It took me a second or two to parse that out. Occasionally, I'd been tempted to look at her speech centers and try to figure out if her grammar was neurological or an affectation, but I'd never gotten around to it. "You want me to teach you? Medicine? Doctoring?"

"Yes. Want to *know*."

"That's... a lot. I was born knowing... knowing just the raw facts, but it still took me a long time to go from that to really *understanding*. There's a difference between having knowledge and knowing how to use it. And you... it would take years to give you just the background, you'd have to learn it all the hard way, no shortcuts..."

"Not going anywhere."

She'd get bored and give it up soon enough, I figured. In the meanwhile, I could spin off a few fragments of consciousness and get her started on basic First Aid, field medicine, the simplest rundowns of which organs did what. It would keep her occupied for a time, and that was worth a lot.

Things kept getting worse. The influx to the compound meant it was harder and harder for me to stay hidden and stay in contact with Mike and Jill. The only edge I had was that most of the forces heading in weren't assuming any random blip on their grid was an enemy or a potential resource, and Mike was keeping me up to date with response codes for when I did get contacted. Ultimately, there was no choice—I had to back up and out, get out of range of them, and hope that the scouting plan didn't change and that they'd be on the route I was expecting. This kind of disconnect, the not knowing, was painful. I hate guessing and hoping.

Unable to safely get in, I pulled away completely, heading north, moving to intercept the scouts which would be coming in advance of the main force. The last update to the plan had called for several, spreading out in a broad, converging pattern, relying on timing to coordinate their motions, each hoping the others would be doing their part. They were also dropping breadcrumbs as they traveled, tiny burrowing things that would be inert until the right signal hit them, carrying with them whatever records had been made up to that point.

I waited. Eventually, I got something. I was running full passive, as usual, and it was faint, but there was something matching the right pattern hitting at the very edge of reception. Then it was mostly a matter of executing a sequence of maneuvers,

each new iteration of the signal telling me more about which way
to go. Each pass the signal got stronger, lasted longer, and
eventually the full stream connected.

"Jill?"

"You're way past our time of contact."

Good to see you, too. "Whatever. How are we doing?"

"Sitrep encoded." There was a sudden flare of data, then the
signal cut off, except for a tiny carrier wave that let me know I was
still in contact and gave me something to focus on. Slightly
confused, I unbundled the report.

Deeply compressed video, very poor quality. Designed to occupy
as little bandwidth as possible. I watched it unfold.

The timestamp was a few hours earlier. Jill was looking at
someone, a tall, shaven, dark-skinned man. I thought I recognized
him from some prior meetings. Jill definitely did. "Lieutenant
Watobe? I think you're at the wrong vehicle, Sir."

He was looking at a small pad. "Sorry, Sergeant. I don't know
what you were told before, you're with me, he's with Samuels over
there." Jill looked around, and I could see Mike standing near her,
looking confused and frustrated. The man she was talking to
shrugged. "These are the orders. I hope there's not a problem?"
Something about his voice seemed odd, or maybe it was just the
distortion. Why was the transmission so low quality, anyway?

I couldn't see Jill's face, and she wasn't recording her biosigns
for my benefit, but I can imagine her frowning before reaching a
decision. "Very well, Sir. If those are the orders... I'm sure the
General knows what he's doing." That seemed to satisfy him.

"OK, then. Get on in. I've been eager to spend some more time
with you. You're becoming quite a legend, you know, and it's nice
to see someone from the old hometown make good. Not so many of
us up here."

Jill said nothing. As she entered the vehicle, a low, squat,
triangular thing designed for speed and stealth but not
survivability, she looked back at Mike. I couldn't see what she did,
but he looked wide eyed for a second, tossed his hands in the air,
and stomped off into a similar craft.

Now I got a look at the inside. Electronics. A lot of them, most
of them obviously not part of the official load-out. Jill's eyes moved
over them slowly, giving me a good look. "Nice gear," she finally
said.

Watobe chuckled. "Oh yes. We're going to be leaving quite a
trail behind us... the techs have been working non-stop on kitting

these out. Not just the usual scanners, either," he continued, as he kicked the engine on and began moving out of the compound. "We've got some of the best data-capture tools left plugged in here. The General wants some idea of what kind of communication is happening up in that base, if there's anyone trying to talk to them still. We don't want someone sneaking up on us from behind, right?"

"Right." Jill slumped back into the seat and stared at the array of controls and readouts. Out of the edge of her peripheral vision, I could see the compound blurring by and then vanishing as the craft picked up speed. "I hope you're not planning on having me do anything with this crap. Not my MOS."

Another chuckle. The first time it was fairly warm sounding, now it was getting annoying. "Oh, no. I know what you're good at, Sergeant. When I saw your name on the outbound list, I couldn't resist pulling a few strings. I just had to see you in the field." He smiled at her. It took her several seconds to remove the targeting solutions that bloomed instinctively in her vision when he did.

"You will." She paused a second and then added. "Either we'll meet something scouting, or I'll be up in the front during the main assault. Wouldn't miss this."

He laughed once more, then gave her what he seemed to think was a friendly punch in the shoulder. "Oh, yes, this will be glorious, Sergeant."

It's fairly rare to see someone laughing so much while digging their own grave.

At least I understood the terseness of the transmission. The vehicle was scanning every datastream running around it—and *inside* it. Jill was risking a lot sending even this; she must have been hoping it was too small and primitive to make it past the primary interest filters and be flagged for closer inspection. I hoped her hope was correct.

So the original plan was scrapped; I had to intercept each person individually, and get them out without alerting anyone. It made sense to go for Jill first. I swooped back in as close as I could to her path, and followed her lead, sending a quick, tight, burst of data, just some coordinates for a rendezvous a few miles up ahead. I trusted to her to convince her partner to go there, one way or another.

I had no idea what would happen when they got there. Their vehicle wasn't heavily armed, but it was still better than me at this point. My defense was negligible. The best I could do was grab the spare rifle we'd picked up and fire it using the Charlie while a few background routines did the driving. Really, all I needed was to give Jill an opening.

Elle was resting her chin on the back of the driver's seat. The Charlie occupied the seat itself; it had become a habit to always make it look like someone was driving.

"Being quiet."

"I'm thinking. And I don't have much time to do it in. Shouldn't you be studying, or something?"

She moved around and flopped into the passenger side, then looked at me a little oddly. "Told me to stop."

I did? I took a second or two to check the splinter I'd carved off to deal with her, and, yes, it had decided she'd been working hard enough and needed a break for optimum retention. I didn't even know I *had* pedagogue routines installed; must have been included free with something. "Right, I did. I forgot." The look she gave me told me she didn't believe me; I gave her a look which told her I didn't care if she believed me or not, the conversation was moving on. "We're going to meet Jill." There, that got a positive reaction. "But it's dangerous. Things could—" Oh, the hell with it. This girl had already been exposed to more trauma than I could catalog; whatever was going to happen, she could handle it. "Just keep your head down, and if I tell you to run, run."

She nodded and vanished into the back. She emerged a few seconds later holding a knife. It looked like a utility blade Mike carried sometimes. I glanced at her. "What's that for?"

"Only one gun. You need it."

Well, I couldn't argue with that logic.

We moved into position a few minutes later, and found half the problem had been settled. Jill was out of the vehicle, and so was Lieutenant Watobe, and they were doing a great job of trying to kill each other. What surprised me was that there was any of the fight left for me to watch.

Jill's gun—Jill's *self*—was about ten feet from her body. She was moving oddly, too, spasmodically, not at all like herself. The Charlie jumped from the cab, and I felt it, too. Suddenly, I was moving through thickening air, every command more difficult to perform. Something was disrupting us. Scanners in the cab made it clear whatever it was, was coming from Watobe.

He was startled to see us. This distraction cost him; Jill slammed into his gut with a spinning kick, then used the momentum to swing away and turned a fall into a tumble, heading for the gun. He reacted quickly, though, grabbing at her foot just long enough to disrupt her move, and she fell ungracefully to the ground. A quick glance at the gun, a decision that pursuing it would be a wasted effort, and she spun back around, pulling her legs under her and reversing direction. Her fist caught him in the jaw, but only grazed him.

I brought up my own targeting routines—not a tenth as sophisticated as Jill's, usually good enough, but the interference was frying them—I couldn't get a lock on the two of them as they struggled. Jill could do a lot: turn off pain, calculate blows and angles, react literally faster than thought as subroutines controlled her muscles before her conscious mind could even acknowledge what she was reacting to. But he was strong, and fast, and whatever he was doing had at least equalized them. I was a mediocre combatant at the best of times, and the Charlie was barely capable of moving. Still, I had to do something... if I couldn't get a clean shot, I could at least join in the melee. It seems Watobe hadn't decided if we were allies of Jill, or just passing strangers, so he was momentarily focusing on the primary threat.

A knife embedded itself in Jill's leg. She reacted. I do not mean she screamed, or flinched, or even grunted, but her face took on that all too familiar predatory gleam. There was no pause from the impact to the action—she twisted her leg up to the point where she could reach the blade, pulled it out, scattering blood in a wide crescent, and slashed it across Watobe's throat. He fell away from her, gurgling, and then she slashed a few more times, across his arms, his chest, his stomach.

I admit to being... well, not shocked, really, but a bit surprised. Jill always prided herself on the cleanliness of her kills. She would never use two bullets where one would do, and never seemed to let her anger boil over into casual cruelty or sadism. It was just beneath her.

Then the static field vanished, and I understood.

"There!" she said, finally, reaching into the corpse and retrieving a few fragments of metal. She threw them down, and then walked to the gun, which she quickly holstered. Only then did she look around, taking in the full situation. When she spoke, it wasn't to me.

"Elle! It's all right. I'm sure that wasn't your plan, but it worked."

I looked around. On normal vision, Elle wasn't there. With IR, I could see her behind some low shrubs, in her familiar 'ready to run' crouch. There was a whisper.

"Supposed to hit ground."

"It doesn't matter. I got it, that's enough." She walked towards me, and I could see the wound was deep, even if it seemed to have missed any major blood vessels. "MacIntyre. I think you have work to do."

I just nodded. The Charlie helped her into the back. Elle sat across from us, watching intently. As I began prepping her, I asked. "So what happened?"

She shut her eyes for a second, gathering up the energy to focus her thoughts on the past. Her body was filled with a chemical mix locking her brain into surviving in the moment. "He—Watobe—apparently thought I was Cromney's new favorite, or... or something. A threat. Someone who could take his position. Figured... he figured... that if the mission were successful, I'd be moving up too fast. Wanted one less potential competitor in the mix. They have an... informal... approach to promotion. Like we knew. A gang, not an army."

The sedatives were flooding her bloodstream now, and she stopped using the body to talk. She switched to a link, cutting Elle out of the conversation. "That business with no common uniform. It made no sense, it's the opposite of what anyone building a new nation would want. Unless you're worried about being replaced or overthrown. Cromney's from nowhere, has no ties. People can all imagine him as 'one of them,' so they're loyal to *him*, but they're basically suspicious of each other, factionalized. The only people really of one mind are the new recruits."

"You mean the children."

"Yes. I think he's basically using the rest as filler, stopgap soldiers, while he raises up a truly loyal force in his own image. Elle was an outlier. The bulk of them, after a few months, are pretty much locked in for life."

I considered this. Cromney wouldn't be the first dictator to try to rise to power on the backs of an army of child soldiers. He probably wouldn't be the last to try, either. It would be worth a lot to make sure he didn't succeed.

"The thing in his chest? Some kind of jammer?"

There was the mental suggestion of a nod. "He knew I had enhancements. Our cover story worked. He figured if he took them out, I'd be an easy target. Apparently he used to do a lot of work in

Vegas. The families liked enhanced operatives, and he and his team carved out a little niche for themselves as being able to deal with them. Commercial details, mostly."

I sent over symbols of amusement. "So, a glorified mall cop."

"Correct. He was always trying to tell me stories or chat with me about Vegas. I thought he was fishing for something, an ally or a lover or both. Didn't pick up he was mostly looking for a chance to kill me. Maybe he didn't decide on that until after I'd shown no interest. We won't know now."

"I could review all the logs, read body language, look for clues..."

Symbolically speaking, she rolled her eyes. "Please. Don't bother. He's dead, it's over."

I dropped it. "Well, your body will need a while to recover. It took quite a pounding. We could—"

"No games. Go find Mike. I'm dropping to reduced activity." Then the signal cut out and she was gone, lost in a sleeping mode, her mind doing what all minds must do to retain sanity.

There was something at the back of my mind, something I'd meant to ask her, a half formed thought, but I couldn't retrieve it. A pattern had formed and then dissolved, barely registering on my self-awareness. It would, I was sure, come back to me eventually.

There was still Mike to deal with. Hopefully, he wasn't about to be killed, as well.

Before I left, though, there were a few things I had to do. First, I had to extract the mission plans from Jill's vehicle, and make sure these events didn't make it back to base. I went outside to deal with this; Elle followed.

I began poking around in the craft, looking for a good place to interface. It was sealed against outside contact and was transmit-only, so this had to be a hard link. Elle walked over to the mutilated body and looked at it.

Again, there was the instinct to caution her, to pull her away, to make her not look, and then reason reared up and reminded me of all she'd seen and all she'd experienced. I spent a few more minutes trying to find an input port I could use, splitting my senses between the Charlie's eyes inside the vehicle and my own panoramic view of my surroundings. Elle walked over to the Charlie after studying the corpse intently, poking around at it in a way which was either clinically detached or indicative of sociopathy. I'd finally found a useful connection, so I pulled out and looked back at her.

"Kidneys intact. Liver too. Jill damaged heart and lungs too much. Probably."

Reflexively, I responded. "I didn't act fast enough, there's been too much decay already. No good for transplants, just—" Then I stopped. First, I wasn't about to accept her field diagnosis. Second, I've always been a bit ashamed of the ghoulish necessities this life has forced on me, and I'm wondering how she even thought of that. Maybe Marty and their gang had scavenged some spare organs in their time?

"We shouldn't do that. We should bury the body properly, but we really don't have time." I was gambling on them not tracking down every scout that didn't report in.

"Need the parts. Said so."

"Who said so?"

"You. While teaching."

I was going to need to have a good talk with that teaching subroutine. Elle was still talking.

"One body. Worse than none or two."

I stopped to parse that. If they found the scout with two bodies, or with none, either raised fewer questions than finding just one. I grimaced internally.

"You're right. We'll need to recycle this." I began the task of moving it back to the medibay. The second bed could be used for harvesting. It took another ten minutes, all told. I'd set the bed to opaque, so she wouldn't have to watch the various mechanisms turn a human being into a collection of supplies, watch as assorted routines decided which of him could be used and which was organic trash to be expelled as needed, deciding value according to algorithm and not ethics. Elle just looked at the now-black surface and said, "Want to see."

I couldn't be bothered arguing. Fine. Maybe I could give her something else to focus on for a bit. I pointed to the other bed, the one performing healing and not butchery.

"Elle. I need to drive and find Mike. Can you keep an eye on those panels for me? Do you know how to read them?"

She nodded, then began pointing to them in sequence, naming them and reciting values for normal, too high, too low. Not bad. Maybe I should just leave the teaching routine alone, it seemed to be doing a good job without me tinkering with it.

I had Mike's projected course and plotted an intercept. Cromney's gang had built up fairly recent maps of the terrain, so I had a good idea where to go and what to avoid. We actually made pretty good time. I tried several times to get through to him, as we got closer, just quick bursts to make contact and hopefully not set anything off, but I got nothing. I finally got into visual contact, a few hundred yards behind a scout vehicle, and was rewarded with a missile blasting a tree to flaming shreds a foot or two away from me. Then the scout accelerated, weaving an evasive pattern. I got a small, odd, spike on my sensors that told me it had dropped one of those acorns of knowledge during its scramble; probably wanted to make sure anyone following would have my ID.

I pursued, staying as far back as I could. Now that they'd been spotted, they wouldn't resume their planned route, so if I lost them, they'd be lost. I wished Jill was in better shape; she could probably have brought the thing to a halt with a few precisely placed shots. As for me, it was all I could do to manage the driving, and hope Mike was doing *something* in there to stop the vehicle. If he was even in there, alive... I was suddenly chilled as I realized Jill might not have been the only one with enemies; that Mike's newly-assigned partner could have been after him, as well.

Then the small vehicle spun much more randomly and sideswiped a small cliff, turning over itself and coming to a final halt in a cloud of smoke and a shriek of metal. I dropped to standby mode and activated the Charlie; I also locked down the medibay since I really didn't need Elle jumping out, the fact she'd probably saved Jill's life last time notwithstanding.

A door opened. Mike clambered out, onto the side—now the top—of the vehicle. I saw another hand reach up, grab onto the frame. I winced. *A survivor.* I wasn't sure what we could do, we certainly couldn't let him go, but there wasn't anyplace to—

Mike had drawn his gun and aimed down into the interior. He fired a few more times than was necessary. After looking a bit, he holstered the weapon and walked past the Charlie, back to me. As he passed my puppet, he grunted out, "You're late." Then he opened the driver's side door, let the seat adjust itself for him, and began checking our maps. I had to run the Charlie to get it into the storage area before Mike kicked the Heim drive to full and began peeling away.

"There were some problems," I started to explain. "Jill's in the medibay."

"You got Elle?"

"Yes, she's back there with Jill. I told you I would, didn't I?"

Mike laughed. "Yeah, well, let's face it, Doc. You've got a bit of a record of not bein' all that honest."

"You *spoke* to her. Several times."

"You know everythin' I know about her, Doc. Every minute I spent with her, you've seen. Wouldn't be that hard to rig somethin' up. Then tell me she's off somewhere safe when we meet up, and then, who knows?"

I didn't say anything for a few minutes. Then I finally asked, "Am I really that bad? Do you think I'd really do something like that?"

He considered this. "When I first met you... yeah, I think you would have, especially if you were convinced it was all for the greater good. Now... well, I'm not sure. Looks like you haven't. I guess we'll see."

He stopped driving. I undid the rear unit seals, and Mike hopped out and went around. I'd considered having a connection made between the medibay and the front, but we'd never quite gotten around to it, and the separation provided a modicum of privacy, so there wasn't a lot of pressure to get it done.

He opened the back door. For an instant, Elle was startled, grabbing at the knife, then, she remembered who he was, the surgery I'd shown her, his face seen through Jill's eyes in their brief conversations. She dropped the blade and leapt for him, grabbing at him, shaking, letting out in a sudden torrent all the emotions I'd seen only in small rivulets and leaks. For several minutes, she just hung there, holding onto him with such tenacity she seemed to be trying to permanently attach herself, every so often just muttering, "Came back. Came back."

Chapter 16

"She didn't hug *me*." I said grumpily.

With a strong undercurrent of 'replying so maybe you'll shut up,' Jill sent back over the link. "Neither of your bodies is really good for that."

Raising the ante a bit, I added, "She didn't hug you, either."

There was a typically informative silence, or, rather, a response that consisted only of a series of emotional glyphs, the direct mind-link equivalent of facial expressions and body language, all of which combined to form the clear message "You have no idea how glad I am of that."

Physically, Jill was still lying in the medibay. Her recovery wasn't going as smoothly as I would have liked and the readings I was getting on her were all off. Not by much, not enough that it mattered. I considered how long it had been since any kind of basic maintenance and calibration had been performed. Maybe when this was over, I could get Mike to...

Right. Who was I kidding? There wasn't a single projection of outcomes I could make that didn't end with all three of us reduced to raw materials. The only difference between what we were doing and just running off a tall cliff with the Heim field flicked off was the hope, the slim hope, we'd be taking some bastards, known and Unknown, with us.

It made sense for me. I'd been running from my guilt for months, and there was really nothing to run *to* anymore. Jill? Jill was wearing the dead body of her best friend, and her own personal death wish was never far from the surface. Mike, though... he'd jumped into this, dragged us into it, really, based on a mad mélange of loss and vengeance, but now he had Elle back, someone who needed him... I had to wonder if he was still so eager. Of the three of us... his part was mostly done. The work he'd needed to do, he'd finished. If he chose to drop out, I'd understand.

It would make sense.

He was sitting in the passenger seat, with the Charlie seeming to do the driving. Elle was in the back, still watching the monitors. We were about an hour from our destination. Some decisions had to be made.

I broached the topic, switching to verbal through the Charlie. "Elle."

"Yeah, you got her. I said thanks." He inhaled deeply and shifted uncomfortably in his seat. "Look, if you're mad that I thought you'd fake it if you could..."

I interrupted. "You'd like to say you're sorry, but, really, you're not, because you were being honest and you're not going to apologize for saying the truth. Right?" Yes, I was being really direct. Time was short and impending death has a way of making me cranky.

Mike looked at me a bit wide-eyed. "Yeah."

"Close enough to an apology for me. That wasn't what I wanted to talk about, though."

He nodded slightly, telling me to go on. Apparently, he thought he had a finite number of words remaining to him and wanted to dole them out as carefully as possible.

"She can't come with us. I mean, she *can*, but that would be pretty stupid."

He suddenly seemed surprised. "Wait a sec, doc. You didn't find someplace for her? I figured we were headin' to wherever you... What the hell? What the fuck were you doin' for all the time I was makin' nice to a bunch of child killin' thugs?"

Avoiding those thugs, I thought. *Trying to keep in touch with you. Keeping your surprisingly almost half-sane pseudo-daughter alive and, more importantly, occupied.* What I said, though, was "Fine. I'm sorry. I screwed up. Now do you want to keep yelling at me, or do you want to offer something constructive?"

Mike just looked at me for a couple of seconds. His expression ran through emotions like someone had filmed a life in time-lapse. Finally, in a much quieter voice, he spoke.

"You're right. I ain't helpin'. You got the latest maps out of the scouts?"

I nodded, then brought them up. The landscape hovered between us, names and numbers superimposed throughout. Mike studied it. I sensed the touch of his mind in the neural induction field, sliding into it reflexively, and the map began to shift and writhe under his commands. Features magnified and vanished, colors spread across the landscape, pooled, evaporated. I wasn't entirely sure what he was seeking, so I sat silently, watching only the results of whatever searches he was running, ignoring the inputs.

"There." He had zoomed in on a small cluster of buildings, slightly overgrown.

I looked more closely. "I don't see anything special about that place."

"There isn't. It's way off from any of the likely travel paths. Village seed that didn't sprout, looks like. Projected weather's pretty mild, last time anyone looked it wasn't radioactive, and the preanthro reading's about ninety percent, best you're gonna get anywhere these days."

I still wasn't following. "So... what? We drop you two off at Walden IV there, and you make your own way back to whatever's passing for civilization?"

Now Mike got to look confused. "Huh? Two? You an' Jill screw with the plan without tellin' me, Doc? Or just you?"

I saw the storm coming and tried to erect shelter. "Whoa. Hold on. *I* haven't changed anything, with or without Jill. I just thought that, with Elle alone, and you..."

Mike shook his head. "I ain't backin' out, Doc. Elle managed on her own when she was a lot younger than this, and we ain't gonna be leavin' her there naked. She'll have what she needs, *if* we don't come back."

I didn't argue with the "if." Let him dream, if that's what it took.

"All right."

(To whoever might be reading this, hopefully in some time a bit saner than mine, before you condemn us all as monsters for plotting to abandon a barely adolescent girl to her own devices in the wilderness, consider our other options, including the possibility of Cromney's gang capturing the resources of the Unknown Bastard or, even worse, making some sort of deal or alliance with him. We'd led them there, we had to make sure they died there.)

We paused. Mike needed to talk to Elle, and Jill needed to get out of the medibay and test the work I'd done, and then there was nothing to do but to press forward.

I took Jill a bit away from the vehicle and had her start doing some exercises, after ordering her to keep all pain and stress responses active. She went through a series of tumbles, jumps, and stretches, and I could see the strain on her face as her body felt every partially healed muscle protest this treatment.

"No! Just came back!" Elle's voice was piercing, quavering, not her usual barely inflected monotone. Whatever wall had broken in her when she saw Mike again was staying broken. That worried me. The whiplash of being abandoned again could destroy her. Maybe this wasn't the best thing. Maybe I could convince Mike he wasn't needed.

Mike was grabbing her, holding her by the shoulders while she seemed to be trying to simultaneously hit him and run away from him. "Not right! Promised!" She kept fighting futilely. Mike seemed to be almost crying himself. Jill and I kept a fair and silent distance. This wasn't ours.

"Look. Look. Elle. I gotta do this. I promised I'd come back, and I did. Right?"

Elle glared up at him, quickly finding the hole in the logic. "Not staying. Not the same." She continued to twist, one arm seeking escape, one arm seeking to hit, neither able to achieve its goal. Showing a certain degree of creative flexibility, she kicked him in the shin. He ignored it.

"No, you're right, I didn't stay. If I didn't know all the stuff I know, if I didn't see somethin' that only I could do... we'd be gone, all of us, we'd find someplace, some people we could trust."

"So let's *go*! Someone else do it. Whatever it is."

He sighed. "I can't. There isn't anyone else, and there isn't time."

"Come *with* you! Help you!"

"Not where we're going. It's... hey, Doc said he'd been teachin' you some medicine?"

She paused for a moment, the odd question suddenly kicking her mind out of the loop of anger and fear she'd been stuck in.

"Yes." She was cautious, feeling her way forward with words as if expecting to fall into a semantic pit lined with sophistic spikes.

"You got to diseases? Vaccines?"

There was a brief nod. "Marty told me, too."

"Right. The thing we're goin' after, the place we're goin', is infected. Marty told me you guys found some Fences? Lost some people?"

Another nod.

"Where we're goin' is where that comes from. We're gonna put a stop it."

Mike had relaxed enough that she was able to wrench one arm

free. With it, she pointed to her other arm. "Vaccine!"

"Not enough time for it to work. We have to get there *soon*. Otherwise, Cromney and his gang will get there, and they're lookin' to control it. We got to stop them."

All of this poured in. She replied in a much softer voice. "Someone else."

"No one else, Elle. I'm sorry."

"Come back?"

I had been trying not to interfere, but I could see Mike's innate honesty becoming a real problem now. Jill was about five seconds away from just knocking Elle unconscious and dumping her. I sent a quick link to Mike.

In the name of whatever vaguely defined universal benevolence you believe in, lie to her!

He sent back a very quick reply. *Sometimes, Doc, I really hate you.*

Then he smiled at her, and with every bit of sincerity he had ever had, he said, "Yeah. I'll come back. Promise."

Then she relaxed and collapsed against him.

I felt dirty, and it wasn't like a shower would do anything but cause a lot of shorts. The look Mike gave me when he knew Elle wasn't watching was the follow-up gut punch I didn't need. It was a good thing I was heading off to die, because, right then, I really didn't want to live.

***

The leavetaking wasn't easy. Jill was getting progressively more irritated, and our deeply erratic timeline was getting even more tangled. Elle shifted in determination from reluctant acceptance to desperate attempts to bargain, making the otherwise brief trip to what we hoped was a safe spot take an emotional eternity. We gave her everything we thought she could use, everything I didn't need with me: a gun and ammunition, food packs, a personal reader stocked with everything useful I could transfer onto it, and a bloodstream pumped full of the broadest spectrum defensive measures I could come up. Then we left, as quickly as we could, and I kept monitors on her until the interference blanked them out.

Now it was time to go in.

This was the part of the plan we simply couldn't test before, that we based on hopes and assumptions and probabilities. We had a large pile of carefully deactivated "morpher bits." We had signal analysis, memory dumps, and everything else we could glean from the pieces leftover, everything Marty had found and left for us as a parting gift. With it, we hoped, we could slide in to the Bastard's HQ, especially if he or they were occupied with an invading army. One small aberration in security might, just might, be seen as a failed cracking attempt and not thoroughly investigated, not until we were inside where, again we were hoping, there would be far fewer active defenses. No one likes railguns firing inside their own base; they scratch the paint.

Speculation piled on hope piled on wish, a rickety tower of unbalanced blocks. It was all we had.

Fragmented signals started coming in. The New Northwest Army was on the move, with all the force it had, and we were skimming along on the edge of its commsphere. I felt like a very small fish swimming alongside a shark, moving to just where I could feel the edge of the wake it left as it passed, never daring to draw closer nor to get too far away.

Something was coming. Aerial, fast, moving with a precise purpose that sent different waves, different patterns, than the complex mass of Cromney's people. I recognize the taste of it: – BastardTech [tm]. Scouts and snipers, most likely, short ranged and expendable, testing the foe. Of course, they assumed we were part of it.

Mike spotted them as well. Tied into the induction field, he signaled to Jill and I. "Incomin'. Twelve and one. Got a lock on us, powerin' up."

Jill checked the feeds, then sent back a reply. "Heavily armored, beyond my caliber. No obvious spots to aim for. New design. Railgun's still offline, too."

"Needed the parts," I said. Then:"It's time. If this doesn't work, we might as well go get Elle and hide for a few decades." I can't deny there was a little part of me that wished it *wouldn't* work, that we'd have an excuse, that we could say we did all we could and there was no hope so it was time to fall back and try something different, sometime in the indeterminate future. If this cup could pass from me...

Mike was right. I did tend to think too highly of myself.

I triggered what we'd determined was a "send IFF" command. The pile of morpher parts, caged in a carefully controlled field of disruptive signals, did what they needed to do, with a newly configured central core that should keep the parts obedient to our whim and hopefully not trigger any well-hidden code traps that could recreate the original "mind" of the beast from seemingly benign bits of software. There was a shuffling, an unfolding, a rearranging, and transmission began. I visualized it as a winding spiral of data, a braid of information, complex and shifting according to no pattern I could match. I saw the probes, too—sleek, glistening, things, chrome manta rays, moving in elegant sweeps through the trees. The line of code whipped out from us, caressing first one, then the other, a golden rope that I was making visible to Mike and Jill through our shared view of augmented reality. Then came the reply, a bright orange beam, sharp and clear.

I held my breath, preparing to spin rapidly and run, run, run, if this failed. It seemed like minutes, but it was a handful of milliseconds, probably, before the routines hard-coded into the morpher accepted the challenge and handed back the response. Without any other signal, the silver shapes spun and moved on, past us, seeking other foes.

We had passed the first hurdle.

"Cleared chapter one, Doc!" Mike's enthusiasm spread through the link. "But we're doin' this one hardcore mode, no saves!"

Jill rolled her eyes. "Games."

"Literature." I replied, huffily.

"Lies, either way."

I suppose there's something oddly comforting in repeating an old debate, one you've had many times. We wore this particular argument like a pair of shoes, scuffed and faded and patched and perfectly broken in.

"There's no such thing as direct sensation, you know. It's all fake, in a way. What's the difference between one source of information hitting your mind and another?"

"One's real and matters. One's a lie and doesn't."

Mike interrupted. "Hey, speak for yourselves. I still see the world with little glops of goo in my face, y'know."

I smiled at an easy victory. "No difference. Everything you feel, everything you see... it's all in your brain. Goop instead of rare earths, hormones instead of cascading state changes, but it's really all the same. The processor can't really identify what's sending the input."

Jill sneered. "Reality is real."

"You can't know that. That's the whole point."

"Yes, I can. I learned it so early in my life. It's among my first memories. My first realization that I *was* an I."

"Oranges," Mike said randomly. I had a flash of worry—Mike's neural damage sometimes manifested in odd ways. The last thing we needed was him breaking down.

"What about them?" asked Jill, perhaps eager to drop one distraction for another.

"My earliest memory. I think. I lost so much, Doc, it's weird, that just came bubbling up. Oranges. I was young, real young, there was a big group dinner... used to have 'em all the time, when I was little, not sure why it stopped... and there were oranges, and I'd never had 'em before, and I remember it was somethin' totally different, somethin' I hadn't imagined." A momentary pause. "Lavender did some things with oranges." Another pause. "Gettin' a lot of increased activity, three o'clock. I think we're there."

By my scans, we were still a full mile from the central complex, but that was where the deathline started. The signal loss here was overwhelming; I realized that the process the Unknown Bastard had used to string his personal spy network of birds and branches would inevitably convene back here, where he probably had everything directly controlled, or at least tied into a soultech or two. That worried me; there'd be minds watching now, not machines. All I could do was hope their attention would be elsewhere and that we wouldn't seem like enough of a threat that their filters would call us out to them.

We'd spent a lot of time with the morpher bits, studying them as much as was safe, disconnected from my own network and kept from talking to each other. We found fragments of shared code, a kind of DNA, scattered among them, and from this, we'd extracted the beginnings of a very basic command vocabulary. The bulk of the code was insane, irrational, impossible to follow and demonically complex—the result of evolution, not design. Only the absolute core was simple enough to have been planned, and even that was hard to follow. We'd gotten enough, though. A handful of commands we could issue, even if we had no real idea how they were interpreted and processed.

One of these was a berg, a command to call home. We triggered it as soon as we hoped we were close enough. We also took a very big chance, opening up the morpher to outside signals freely. We couldn't guess what might be sent or what it might need to do to reply. I'd locked down most of my own inputs and Mike was ready to flip on the shielding manually if we had to.

This wasn't a braid. It was hard to describe. My visualization algorithm, for reasons known only to its probably-dead designer, decided to color the signal purple. It was a series of expanding tendrils, probing, slowly growing in size as feedback reached the morpher, some withering away as others grew thicker, stronger. The strongest, only two now remaining, caressed one tree, then another, and then there was a sudden shift. One vanished, and the survivor seemed to explode as it hit the tree, sending probes in every direction, then the same winnowing process repeated, and onwards, until a segmented purple line arced from tree to tree. (It's taking me far longer to describe this than it took to happen, mind you. I timed the entire contact at 2 milliseconds.)

The morpher responded quickly. It began to move, to try to follow the sudden directional command. We couldn't just let it go and follow it. What we did do was set up an illusion. Maybe Jill could tell reality from simulation when it hit her brain, but the morpher wasn't self-aware. We fed it back data to make it think it was moving, changing its perceptions, and sending its attempted motions to Mike, who drove me along the indicated path.

Said path led directly through hell, of course. I suppose this proved my intentions were good.

Deathline.

Emergent properties. One of the boilerplate buzzwords, spewed out almost without meaning to describe almost anything someone didn't anticipate. So overused as to be meaningless, it's only when you see an example in deadly action that you understand how powerful the concept is and how it underlies virtually everything about the world we live in.

What happens when machines, dumb machines that is, are all given certain territorial boundaries, some adaptive but unaware algorithms, and complex systems and rules for deciding patrol routes, identifying friends and foes, and sharing both information and their own modified code with other machines? The interaction of 'fuzzy' boundaries and sloping limits produces a sprawling pattern of constantly moving, hovering, swooping, and clambering devices. A dozen machines which would interact in a semi-regular pattern with each other becomes a hundred or a thousand machines whose interactions take on such complexity that it's impossible to predict any one's actions—all you can do is watch the swarm move.

Surrounding our target was a wall—really, more of a cloud, a
dome, of defenders. Each was constantly in some kind of spasmodic
motion, following rules which continually shifted. Patrol in this
direction, but there's someone else patrolling here, so shift to
secondary patrols, but that's taken care of as well, so go for
tertiary, and as each one changed, the others responded to those
changes. Deathlines grew as the Collapse did, as people became
less concerned about striking back and more concerned about
surviving, as signals went out to call in far-flung machines to
protect territory, and those signals propagated irregularly, and by
the time the machines answered they usually ended up defending
nothing, waiting for a 'Cease and Desist' order that would never
come. They were left to their own non-aware devices, their code
modifying without oversight and purpose, with really only one part
still working properly. The part which said "Kill anything that is
not part of Us."

We were about a quarter mile from it from when the signals
came, rendered in linkspace as a rainbow tsunami. I couldn't hope
to track, trace, or identify them all. A thousand voices in a
thousand digital dialects screamed one question:"Who the fuck are
you?"

The morpher choked. The full thing, its millions of parts all
interacting with their own tiny fragments of a mind, could have
handled it easily, but our little baby monster was flooded. It tried
to respond, but it was being shouted down. The cacophony of
"answeransweranswer" pounded at it, and it could not manage to
send responses fast enough.

"Doc, we're getting lock signals—whole bunch of things are
sizing us up—"

We'd discussed this possibility, of course. I hesitated for a
second.

"Doc, *now!*"

No time.

I sent a command to the Charlie, which dutifully flipped a
hardware switch and opened the gate. My consciousness entered
the pseudo-mind of the morpher.

Inside it was madness. The best way I can think of to describe
it is a hundred idiot savants spouting random portions of
sentences at each other, while a surrounding lynch mob of
thousands screams at them, except it was nothing remotely that
sensible.

The answers were there, though. They had to be. I accelerated

my consciousness, redlining again, feeling time slow even as
distant alarms began to sound. There. There were the pieces of the
answer, a dozen copies of the same page torn to pieces and then
the pieces randomly scattered, and all I had to do was put together
one complete copy...

I felt a shuddering, a long, slow, thrumming. I dimly realized it
wasn't slow at all, it was just my mind operating at dangerously
fast speeds. I ignored it.

There. The answer was found. The mob had drawn in closer,
torches lit and pitchforks sharpened. I exerted my will, sent
commands through the system, getting each idiot to stop babbling,
creating a single sound, a single sentence, picked up by each in
turn and passed to the next, cascading faster and faster until a
single voice began to chant a reply to the mob, over and over,
louder and louder, and the mob began to thin, to draw away,
retreating, looking for some new outsider to harass and destroy.

Relieved, I dropped back to normal speed.

And screamed.

The pain was incredible, overriding my filters and choices. The
howl was involuntary, echoing from the Charlie, from the
speakers, across linkspace. I wanted to curl up, to cry, to shut out
the world, patterns of behavior tied to a body I never had,
interwoven into the structure of my mind because without them, I
couldn't be human enough. I fought them back, fought through the
pain, slowly forced my consciousness to take control of all that was
me. I became aware of everything else again, of Mike and Jill in
our shared linkspace and of their physical presence within me.

"I think you did it, Doc. They've stopped trackin' us."

I sent a flurry of bitter glares at Mike. "I'm fine, Mike. Thanks
for asking."

There was more data flowing in now. Less frantic, less hostile,
but still painted with urgency. *Enemy sighted we've got an enemy
bogies coming in enemy alert intercept interdict need help sending
enemies sighted positioning coming in alert alert identifications
tacticals enemy defensive protocols...*

This, at least, was easy. It took almost no effort to send back a
canned "Received, taking programmed actions" response. The
pestering didn't stop, but it was simple to ignore.

Jill's heartbeat was racing. Her adrenaline was peaking. I
noticed she was barely in the link; her mind was almost entirely
out there in the so-called real world. I took a peak.

We were speeding through fire and fury. Jill sat, watching the madness through my front window, seeing machines speed by, explosions erupt left and right, feeling every shake and vibration, exulting in it. I felt a sudden, irrational, burst of resentment: *It wasn't her body being torn to pieces.* Then came the inevitable annoying response from deeper within: *Pretty soon, it will be.*

Mike moved my body through it all, seeing safe paths, using the deathline itself as cover from the onslaught coming in from Cromney. They had arrived with everything and were hitting it hard; the deathline was hitting back.

Things tried to fly, short range craft launched close in, hoping to close before some random high-altitude UAV spotted a new target. The line had high flyers of its own. Cromney didn't want to destroy the prize he'd risked everything to capture, so there were few attempts to just go over the line, to arc shells or kamikaze craft—manned or otherwise—into the complex itself. I was very deliberately not looking back. I knew what was happening out there. People were dying, a lot of them not entirely in their right mind, a lot of them children, and it was very much my fault, their deaths a direct and coldly chosen consequence of my actions. I knew it. Why should I have to watch it?

I cast my eyes backwards anyway, just for a second, through the smoke and fire and the ever-shifting wall of metal. I saw two men, two boys, holding rifles far too large for them, trying to hold some random bit of ground as a large APC moved into position, saw a stream of shrapnel cut one in half and turn the arm of another into a spray of red, giving him barely a second to be aware of what had happened before an explosion consumed him as well. I saw the APC crawl forward into the spot where they'd stood, and then there was a shift in the line and I lost visual through the mess.

Ahead. Look forward. It had to be better than this.

The madness was thinning rapidly. Explosions were fewer. Ahead was... nothing, which was what we expected. Visual camouflage was still going, and even radar and other senses were getting back "Nothing to see here, move along" replies. Intercept and echo lies, returning a fake reply to an active scan. Pretty sophisticated, as such signals usually contained all manner of riders to make sure anything bouncing back was the same as what was sent out. Nothing that could survive a really intensive look, but to devote that much effort to it, you'd need to be sure there was something to look for in the first place. Fortunately, we didn't need to deal with all the compensation and filtering required to wring truth out of the lies. The morpher, once more reasonably complacent and obedient in its own illusory world, started to relay our outgoing scans with its own coded signals, telling the smartskin over the complex to just send us back our data as-is.

Then, blossoming in linkspace if not to our eyes, it appeared, exactly as we'd expected, a complex of low domes, connecting by slicing into each other like a series of soap bubbles. As the light of the ongoing battle cast flickering strobe shadows the visual camouflage wasn't *quite* fast enough to match perfectly, creating an eerie ghost building of time-delayed colors. We saw, through the link, an opening portal, an automated welcome.

Jill's body breathed deeply, and her body's hands stroked the white and grey pistol sitting in its lap. Mike muttered some fragments of a prayer, something about named and unnamed.

I just thought of the people I'd killed because, at that instant where the decision had to be made, I was sure I was right. There were an awful lot of them in the past few years, and Jake Morowitz was just the one I'd dwelled on the most. All I could offer for my defense was that I was finally putting my own existence on the line in the name of my convictions.

I momentarily grabbed control of my body from Mike. I flared the Heim field and sped inside.

Chapter 17

I admit I wasn't sure what to expect when we went inside. Our plans said a small number of people, distracted by the battle outside, not paying attention to the doors until the enemy had broken through, but that was all pure speculation. We didn't know for sure. There might be an army waiting for us, eager to capture and interrogate those clever enough to find this place and break inside? Something strange and empty and dead, abandoned by whatever had sent the morphers out, no spider sitting at the center of the web? Workers going about their business, paying attention to the attack, surprised to see an ambulance enter when their defense systems said one of their own morphers was returning?

What we found was madness.

The dome we'd entered was the largest in the complex, the door wide enough to send out two or three heavy tanks side-by-side. It was where the morpher itself had come from. The place was filled with machinery, dozens of different types of robots, all moving in what seemed to be random patterns, though I was sure there was order to it somehow. Fixed machines hung off the walls, dangled from the ceiling, grew from the floor like well-oiled and many-armed stalagmites. I watched the data streaming around, a thousand or more ongoing conversations. Snatches I could pick up, using some of the cipher keys we'd pulled from the morpher, told me that while a lot of the chatter concerned the assault, plenty of it seemed inconsequential, almost random. I couldn't be bothered to try to make sense of it all. We'd made it in here with a purpose, to stop the Unknown Bastard. It didn't occur to us that, once inside, we'd need to go looking for him.

I told the morpher to tie itself in to the internal communications net, to send out soothing messages, to tell whatever automated systems were watching to pay no attention to the ambulance. Every second the minds behind this place weren't looking at us, every second they were focused on the war and not on checking every tiny data anomaly, was a second more we had to plan. And to live.

I flicked full control back to Mike, and then we stopped. Everything registered as fully functional.

"Mike? You stopped."

"Yeah. You got any idea where we're supposed to *go*?"

I didn't.

Jill gave both a physical and a link-based shrug. "We start destroying. Here looks good."

"You didn't do a lot of tactical planning, back in your merc days, did you?"

There was the ghost of a smile. "No. I got orders. I executed them. Don't make the obvious joke, Mike."

"Wouldn't dream of it."

I cut off the banter. "As soon as we start doing anything violent in here, whoever is in charge will take notice. If we wake them up by cutting off a finger, we'll never get a chance to slit their throat."

Mike laughed. "Gotta love the way the doctor thinks like an assassin."

I had to laugh a bit, too. "I did complete 'Shadows Under a Moonless Dark' with full complications."

"Yeah." There was a moment of painful silence. I felt extremely stupid. We'd actually not made a lot of complex plans for 'what to do when we got in,' because it seemed that with no knowledge of what might await us, the plans would fall apart. What we had were ideas for reactions, for responses to everything we expected might happen to us. The one thing we never planned a response to was 'Nothing.'

I focused my consciousness on studying where we were. There was no writing or labels, but I was picking up a neural induction field signal on constant broadcast. Standard RTK-4 protocol, too. Flags were set for open, public, access. A very hasty conference with Mike and Jill, and I tapped into it.

The room blossomed. Signs appeared on walls, arrows slithered along the floor. Like most people, I have some personal preferences for where augmented reality interface tools should appear, and they flowed into a circle around the primary focus of my vision. No matter where I looked, there they were, appearing and disappearing in accordance with their relevance to the target of my interest.

The name plastered everywhere was "New Horizons For Human Commonality." I got a little twitch, perhaps wrongly, at the word "Human." It was one of those words which can be perfectly innocent, but which can also be a signal or a sign to fellow travelers. I filtered through my stored data, most of which hadn't been updated in over a decade, and a lot of which had been purged as I needed the room for permanent storage of information relevant to the world as it currently was. Nothing on that particular name, but the phrase 'Human Commonality' showed up a lot in screeds about soultech. It was the usual drivel. Singularity fearmongering—despite the fact the singularity concept had been pretty much discarded once the limits of soultech self-awareness were known—and a whole bunch of crap about 'essential humanity,' 'the need for mortality,' and a lot of other boilerplate nonsense.

Most of those groups were hardcore low-techs, though, usually hiding in small isolated communities where they used nothing more advanced than solar-powered electric motors and wired-network computers. Based on the morpher, and more, this "New Horizons" group had no objections to more advanced options.

Of course, it was certainly possible this place had been taken over or conquered somehow, and no one had bothered to change the signs shown on the guest-level augment space. I didn't think so. A lot of what we had seen fitted the name. A lot didn't.

I'd been sharing all this with the other two. Jill spoke.

"They're not going to like either of us, MacIntyre. Calvers might get a pass."

"Nah. I'm too obviously chummy with you mockeries of thought."

He was joking, very obviously so, and Jill knew it, but there was still a blade's icy edge shading her reply. "Weren't you raised in some purist sect? No enhancements."

Mike's reply mixed weariness at what seemed to be an old debate and anger at it being opened up again. "Yeah. I made a choice to live my life that way. Don't really care how other people live theirs. Y'know, you an' your whole 'direct experience' thing, that's not much different from what I grew up with. It was about dealin' with the world directly, not tryin' to change who we were."

"Of course, that doesn't apply to 'mockeries of thought.'"

"Look, I never went in for that organicist stuff. Yeah, a few folks I knew did, but I didn't buy into it. 'sides, Bay Alliance... you didn't want to be flagged as an 'intolerant,' believe me."

"Fine." It was pretty obvious she didn't.

I'd had enough of this. "If we're quite done with the philosophical debate... we don't have a lot of time. Either whoever's here drives off Cromney, which means they'll start paying closer attention to what's happening inside, or Cromney actually breaks in, which means we have a much worse chance of doing something."

Jill grunted. "Fine. Get some maps. Let's figure out where this thing's throat is, and slit it."

Well, if the visitor augment interface was still active, there might be some maps or guides. I tried to burrow through the menus, looking for a something we could use. Habitation complex. Public meeting hall. We were, allegedly, in the main parking area, which made the current situation even more insane. Machinery was everywhere, with only a few clear paths, twisting and curving, through the maze.

I started to pay attention to dates. The public augment space was old fifteen years old. Pre-Collapse. That it was still active wasn't really all that odd; such things took up very few resources and were often left going because no one cared about turning them off. Before the Collapse, the world was filled with signs pointing out nothing, illusory soapbox activists ranting out causes long dead, salesmen pitching the products of dead companies, all slowly decaying and losing functionality as, bit by bit, code became corrupted, links died, or protocols changed. To view the world with no filters or augments was to see a vision to rival that of any consciousness altering chemical or field; some people did it for just that reason, claiming to see things in the random synchronicity that could inspire, inform, or fascinate. I just thought it looked cheap, messy, and broken.

So then. Old data. The garage had long since stopped being a garage. What else could I find? I started a spider going, racing through the augment interface, trying to find more detailed maps, or something beyond simple pamphlets of propaganda filled with weasel words which never explicitly *stated* they wanted to eliminate all non-organic intelligence. (Quite a few groups, mostly isolated communities, were quite explicit. Said groups, without much in the way of protection from the local neonations, tended to suffer unfortunate accidents that nobody looked at too closely. I won't say I *approved*, but I can't say I feel a lot of remorse. Weasel words work both ways.)

I think it was the spider that did it. Woke it up. It might have looked like an attack, an enemy probing for a weakness. I'm guessing Cromney was doing the same, and the defensive systems were manning the outer walls, but, suddenly, it was seeing an attack coming from within, from the induction field. A sapper had broken into the castle. Time to send the guards down to kill him and close up the tunnel.

It started as an awareness of an increase in processes running in the local linkspace, of a sudden series of new questions being asked of the morpher. I had a sudden flush of fear, then.

I was tapped into the induction field directly; the morpher didn't have that kind of interface. I could have added it trivially if I'd thought of it, or done something else, but visitor augment spaces were so boilerplate and trivial that I didn't even think to *not* connect to it directly. I pulled back instantly, dropping all signals and closing up the ports, but it was too late. The security had worked it out—there was the morpher, which it still seemed to think of as legitimate, and then there was a second, unidentified, presence, one which didn't know the codes, one which was walking down the hallway jiggling doorknobs to see if any had been left unlocked. One which was inside when an army was outside.

Mike saw it almost as fast as I did. "Hey, Doc. I'm gettin' all sorts of increased activity out here. Whatever you're doin', it's— *shit!*"

An industrial carving laser was firing warning shots across our bow, or maybe it just had poor aim.

My body lurched, spun, and sped through the maze, Mike navigating it with expert skill even as the factory came to hostile life around us. The random motions of the machines shifted, took on a direct purpose. The one thing keeping us alive at all was the fact these weren't weapon systems, just manufacturing tools being suddenly and clumsily repurposed. I fed Mike all the map data I'd been able to acquire.

Jill had opened a door and was hanging, half outside, and firing. She'd cut out from the linkspace, except for verbal; she didn't want anything overriding her own uniquely martial view of reality. Each shot took out something—smashed the delicate crystals of a laser, cut the power feed to a fractal manipulator. It couldn't last though. You can't kill a swarm of ants one at a time.

Something clicked in my mind. The morpher, oddly, hadn't been pegged as a threat and locked out. It was still sending back perfunctory replies to the regular queries. It was an endless, tedious, conversation. "Are you my friend?" "Yes I am." "Are you my friend?" "Yes I am." I found that very strange, but I wasn't about to do dentistry on a gift horse. I set up every block I could think of to keep the morpher's inputs from passing through the connection, and reactivated the hardwired link. I could get to the morpher and out; in theory, hopefully, anything the morpher got back couldn't pass to me unless I wanted it to.

It had much deeper access. Levels of the controlling system of the complex spread out before me. It wasn't designed for a sentient mind to understand; there was no default visual model set up to render things into symbolic terms. Functions and regions had no labels or descriptive tags, and my senses struggled to create any kind of order or pattern based on what little they could grab from the flow of data. The only way I can think of to describe it is a junkyard overgrown by kudzu. Deep at the heart were core systems that were clearly manufactured and created, but the vast bulk of it was a wild tangle.

I could feel myself shuddering. The damage was getting worse. The bed on the left in the medibay suddenly went black, and I knew a huge gouge had been cut there. The outer shell could be repaired, but the rest was gone. I had to do something.

The morpher... The morpher wasn't being seen as a threat. No one would be that oblivious, no one could fail to work out that two internal signals which appeared at the same time were both from the same source...

No *one*.

The army outside was massive, and deadly. It was possible, if the people here were really strained, that they'd turn over internal security to an automated system, at least until they were sure they'd been breached. My own link to their network was severed, so the security was probably tracking me visually, literally watching me. If I just vanished, it wouldn't fool a conscious watcher, but it might fool a machine. Threat destroyed, resume normal operations.

It was a great idea, but there were no convenient input receptors on the security system, nothing to send a false data stream through. There was also nothing I could reach that controlled visual filters, that could erase my image before it reached the security system. The morpher was of no use here, and I felt that creeping tingle of despair, the realization that we'd failed, that *I'd* failed, that...

Morpher.

Morpher.

I realized that even when I'd been watching general signal traffic, I didn't see any kind of back-and-forth IFF going on. The factory machines all recognized each other instinctively. There was probably a database of presumed friendlies, or even of things that just weren't dangerous. Often, this was a secondary measure, a backup to keep an enemy from altering an IFF signal and tricking a system into shooting at its own components, or appearing to be a friend when it wasn't.

Almost by definition, though, the morpher changed shape. It relied on a constantly encoded signal to keep itself identified, but if the two security systems were linked, if they fed into each other, there was something I could do.

I tossed my silhouette into the morpher's response feed, tagged for addition to the 'non hostiles' database. Almost instantly, the attacks stopped. I also told Jill to stand down, before she triggered a secondary response.

"We've got a breather. I don't know how long we can keep them fooled."

Mike grunted. "If there is a 'them.'"

"I don't think these people would put soultech in charge," but as soon as I said it, I wondered. Maybe 'these people' had been eliminated, long ago, by someone who didn't like what they stood for, someone who had just inhabited the complex, turned it to their own purposes. It was a possibility. As with the other options I'd considered and discarded, it explained some of the things we'd seen, but not all of them.

Jill picked up on Mike's real meaning much faster than I did. "I think he means there might be no one in charge. Full automation."

"Really doubtful. The morpher? That communication network? The whole fence-and-plague system? Someone's behind all that, someone planned it out."

Mike apparently didn't want to argue. "Whatever. Lookin' at these maps, I figure what we want is down. That's what they've vaguely got labeled as 'Research.'"

I considered. "I don't want to go out in the Charlie. The constant signal could be picked up."

Mike nodded. "So, Jill an' I will go."

"I don't like that, either. I've done enough of asking both of you to go marching into things alone."

Jill's hands slammed a full box of ammo into the gun. "Pick one, MacIntyre. Lead the charge or stay back and give orders, but pick one."

"Freight elevator," I replied.

Jill made a small huffing sound. "That works. Find one and let's get moving."

We made our way carefully through the maze, rendered even more chaotic from the recent firefight. Small machines scurried or flew, cleaning up debris, sometimes feeding it into hoppers to be molten and remade.

It wasn't too difficult to locate the elevator. This time I remembered to use the morpher to signal it.

We went down.

"Dusty," said Mike, mostly to break the silence.

It was. Whoever was here didn't use this much. Maybe the complex was abandoned, or maybe it was taken over, or maybe they just didn't want to take the freight elevator up. I wasn't going to draw conclusions just yet.

The door slid back. Mike drove me forward, slowly. The elevator opened onto a large platform surrounded by a low fence. A broad path led out through a breach in the fence, terminating at an unmarked metal door. I wasn't about to try to connect to the augment to see what the label should have been.

On either side of the path, spreading out, was a dead park.

Mike almost retched violently; Jill actually did, perhaps deciding it was better to let her body respond than to fight it. It would have been nice if she'd opened the door first. I did what I could to seal the cabin, but the damage I'd taken had made me less than airtight.

With both Mike and Jill in the front seat, I'd kept the Charlie out of the way in the back. It walked forward, carrying filter masks from the gear box we kept there. Mike and Jill put them on, gratefully and desperately.

Mike momentarily dropped the neural link and peered out.

It wasn't immense. Five hundred feet or so, a decent enough place to relax if you didn't want to actually go out in the sun. There was a small lake, now stagnant and covered with a thick layer of dead organic matter. Barren trees. Some benches and seats. The dead grass was wild and overgrown; someone had let the place run wild and then whatever systems kept it fed and watered had let it die.

There were also bodies, long past rotting. Quite a lot of them. I hated to think it, but the 'soultech invasion' was looking more likely.

Jill kept looking around, seeking enemies. "So now what?"

"I.. don't know. We explore. Mike?"

There was a delayed grunt. "What?"

Herding cats. "Ideas? Suggestions? Another lecture on my ethical and personal shortcomings?"

"Just... thinkin'. Really not likin' this, Doc." He kept moving his head back and forth, taking it all in, dead people lying on dead grass. "I want to know what killed them."

"Unknown Bastard," I said. I did not add a sarcastic addendum. We'd all been through a lot, and getting cranky now wasn't going to help. I was also nervous. I think we all had some nebulous undefined sense of what the Unknown Bastard was, a sort of emotional impression masquerading as a concrete thought, and what we found just didn't fit. The attacks on the upper level, the mad factory, the echoing explosions outside... that fit, somewhat, but here... The still and the quiet clawed at me.

Mike was less prone to introspection. He slapped his hand on the dashboard, something he did when I wasn't using the Charlie and he couldn't punch me in the shoulder. "Thanks, Doc. Hadn't guessed that. I mean, how?"

Good question. I wish I'd thought to ask it myself.

The bodies were sprawled and scattered. I had some programs installed to inspect such sights, battlefield analysis programs for both triage and security. The pattern of the dead could tell me the layout of a minefield, the best places to look for survivors who needed healing, or if there might still be enemy soldiers around. These program came back with two patterns. Some of the dead seem to have fallen randomly, during normal activities, while others, perhaps half, fell in a pattern that suggested they were moving towards the doors, small groups heading for the freight elevator we had just come from, others moving to the main lifts.

I told myself a story. These people, whatever they were, were going about their business one day, and then some of them started dropping dead while walking, sitting, eating. Others noticed this, the ones who didn't die quickly, and panicked, running for the exits but not reaching them. If anyone did make it out, they didn't come back.

Cutting off the air in a sealed building was a typical soultech tactic, but that didn't fit. People notice the air going bad, and they have plenty of time to panic and get their hearts racing and burn through the oxygen that much faster. The scatter pattern of the bodies would be different, they'd be clustered at the doors, clawing at them, until they collapsed on top of each other. I didn't see any bloody streaks on the elevator, or any signs of the kind of stampede panic I'd expect. So, it wasn't cutting off the air.

Putting something in the air, though. Once again it hit me, that terrible fear of missing something, the realization of possibly fatal error. I checked Mike and Jill's vitals quickly. Nothing out of the ordinary so far, except for the expected signs of stress. They'd only taken a few breaths before the masks came on, and it seemed the poison, if that's what it was, must have been very fast acting. Either it had been cleaned from the air, they hadn't received a fatal dose, or it was something other than poison. I hoped it was one of the first two.

There was something one of my instructors used to say. "Hope is a thing with feathers. Reality is a hungry cat." We had to know for sure what was going on. Another layer of panic started to build in me. What if Cromney was winning up there? What if he was coming in? We didn't have time. We had to destroy this place. Didn't we?

Jill spoke. "So. Now?"

"Ye—no."

Jill shut her eyes for a moment and clenched her hands, her nails digging into her palms. "Why? What are we waiting for?"

I listened. No noise was making it down here.

"We want to be sure Cromney is wiped out. And... "

"What?"

I spoke slowly, trying to express an idea which was still congealing out of a mass of protothoughts. "It looks like... it looks like this place is abandoned. Running on automation. The morpher may have been loosed before this happened, some old program still going on its own. We could use the resources here ourselves, create a nucleus of something. Try building instead of clawing at what's left or just hiding and hoping it all goes away." No. There was something wrong with that idea, some error, I knew it, I just didn't see what. I'd redlined myself earlier, and there was damage. My thoughts were marbles in a sea of oil, slowly drifting, only occasionally connecting.

Jill actually paused for a moment to consider the idea. "Hmm. No. If you don't give me the go signal, I will defy orders and act on my own. You can court martial me later."

I knew she'd meant that as a sort of joke, a bit of gallow humor,
but I had flashbacks of Morowitz and my murderous arrogance,
and it hurt.

"OK. OK. We'll stick to the plan. I just want to make sure we've
done as much damage to Cromney as possible."

"Don't I get a vote?" The phrase may have been joking, but the
tone was not.

Jill sighed. "You want to stay here and play house?"

Mike glared at her. "I don't know, but if this place is up for
grabs, maybe destroyin' it just because those were our original
orders ain't the smartest thing. Even if we don't want to make
ourselves a target for the next Cromney to come along, there's tools
here, things we can use. Get Doc back to spec. Get something for
us to travel in, and Elle, so we ain't trippin' over each other. Maybe
get enough info on what the morphers are doin' so that we can stop
it, or figure out how to turn them off. There's more than one, got to
be."

Mike was spinning a very nice vision. A return to our original
plan, travelling healer, keeping the remnants of the old world alive
until they could work out a new pattern for growth. He made
sense, but there was that thing, that nagging just below the level
of consciousness.

Mike was still talking. "...and once Cromney's wiped, there's
not that much of a hurry. This place has held its own for ten years,
now, we don't have to rush."

Ten years.

The augment protocols had been abandoned *fifteen* years ago.
The morpher had to have been released after that. The fences...
they were new, appearing very recently. The scope of the Unknown
Bastard's network, the pattern of it, the rate at which the disease
changed, all of it added up to something which had begun well
after the Collapse. The bodies had been here a long time, maybe
even pre-Collapse as well. Something was here. Something had
been working from before the Collapse, planning, building, and the
morphers and the network were the end result. Why it hadn't
reacted to us yet, I didn't know, but we couldn't give it time, not
any more time. Cromney had taken enough of a pounding, and
even if he hadn't, whatever was here was more dangerous.

"Jill. Go-sign."

"About time."

Mike had barely had time to begin protesting when Jill

screamed. She pitched forward, holding her head, howling. Mike looked around in startled panic, trying to obey the instinct to look *at* me for some kind of reassurance or confirmation.

"I don't know. This shouldn't be the reaction, she—"

Mike unexpectedly launched himself back into the induction field, the urgency of his command hitting me like a slap. He flipped on the signal shielding. Jill stopped screaming and fell backwards, gasping deeply, her face glistening.

Asking "Are you OK?" struck me as stupid and redundant. All of her vitals had redlined, but they were calming down at a fairly normal rate.

"You OK?" Mike asked, as I said "What happened?" at the same time.

Jill closed her eyes. She struggled to form words and put them in a coherent order. "Not abandoned. Contact made. Suggest—suggest we retreat."

"Not abandoned, contact made—there's someone here? Some mind behind all this?" I wanted more details, but Mike was sliding into the induction field. I felt the Heim field begin to shift as he prepared to move. "You heard her, Doc. Tell that gizmo to open the doors. When *she* suggests we retreat, we *retreat*." He started driving me towards the elevator. I slammed on the brakes and shut him out of the interface.

"No. I don't know what's going on, but we knew this was probably going to be a last stand. I can't believe you're going to try to run..."

Jill spoke both in the link and with her body. "Idiot. Stupid. All right to die if—if we could succeed, even if there's a—a chance, but not—not when there's no hope. Pull back, try again, hurry. We can—we can still make it if—"

Then I felt it. There is a constant background din of signals, everywhere you go in the world, an invisible crowd whispering not-quite-audible words. You learn quickly to ignore it, but it's always there. Here, the whispers were louder, more obvious, but still just a babble, a thousand hushed voices speaking to each other and trying not to be overheard.

Suddenly, something happened, and the invisible thousands began to whisper in unison. Still no words, still nothing I could follow, but I could sense the change. A thousand conversations had become one. No, not a conversation, I realized, but a speech. A chant. Something that did not have any back-and-forth, something shouted with neither the expectation nor the desire for a reply.

Jill must have felt it, too. She slumped slightly, and ritually ejected, checked, and reseated her clip, a habit about as logical as grabbing your right arm with your left to make sure it's still there. "Too late. Shit." She forced herself more upright and then opened the door. "You're a crappy soldier, MacIntyre. You waffle when you're supposed to be giving orders and you're no good at taking them. Mike... I should have beaten you unconscious and left you with Elle, but I realized if I did, you'd do something stupid and die anyway, and she'd probably join you, so here you are." She slid out the door and moved into an alert posture, managing to be both calm and tense at the same time. It occurred to me she'd been providing what she expected to be her last words to us.

Mike shoved himself out after her, the grabbed her shoulder to try to turn her to face him. She knew he was coming and sidestepped, leaving him to stumble slightly against my front. He reached up once more, then rethought it, and simply moved around in front of her.

"Will you drop all the cryptic shit and just tell me what's goin' on? You think we should pull back, then, yeah, I'm gonna listen. If Doc wants to stay, well, his choice. If he won't open the door for us, we can find some way to force it. C'mon." He looked back at me, ignoring her ignoring him. "Doc, please, don't make me walk out on you. I'd die here if I thought we had any hope, but if we don't, I gotta go back. Please."

I was only half listening to him. The chant, or the cry, or the command, or whatever it was that was pulsing across the entire data spectrum was more than distracting. It was fascinating and terrifying, something I'd never encountered. Almost subconsciously, I decided to open the elevator doors for them, still unsure if I'd be going in myself. I had things to atone for, more than either of them did, and even if the odds were small, if there was any chance to... that was odd.

I'd idly tossed a signal to the morpher, following my channel through it and into the complex itself, telling the door to open. It remained shut. More annoyed than anything else, I dove into the morpher's pseudo-mind, hoping I could fix this and get them out of here and then I could—

SCREAM.

Consciousness came back in flashes, as protective systems pulled me out. I saw Mike staring at me with a mix of concern and horror, Jill still standing ready, waiting. Mike flicked his eyes back and forth between the two of us, finally deciding I was the one more likely to reply.

"Doc?"

There was a box in my mind. In that box were words, a hundred thousand of them. I rooted through the box, tossing aside "obsequious" and "lunate" looking for a few specific ones, but there were so many, it was so hard to find them...

A rapping on my front. "Doc? You still in there?"

Ah, all right, here were some words. Finding them one at a time. "Yes. I think. So." Oh. That wasn't too hard. Things were coming back together, a bit. Time and place were solidifying, a thousand potential answers such as, "It's early in the morning, and you're late for weapons drill." and "It's late afternoon, and you're burying Jake." fell like cards following a bungled shuffle, and then I knew where I was and when it was and I had some idea what had just happened.

"What the hell happened?" asked Mike, unaware of his accidental timing.

"I saw it. The Unknown Bastard."

Mike grunted. "So, some soultech thing. You sure we can't reach it? Too well protected?"

I was still dealing with the magnitude of what I'd seen. "No, not soultech." All the small pieces of fear I'd been feeling ever since we entered had come together, a complete puzzle that was the image of pure panic. Jill was right, we'd better leave. We couldn't fool the door into opening, but it was still physical, it could still be forced. "Mike, work on the lift door, grab something solid and pry it and try to work the panel physically. Jill, come on, we still have time, I saw it, it's not really aware of us yet. We know what we're dealing with now, we can make a better plan, come *on!*" I took out the Charlie and ran around outside myself, grabbing at her.

Then it started speaking.

```
Curiosity.
Attack.
Defend.
Information.
Attack+1.
Define.
Seek Information.
Attack+2.
```

```
    Priority Shift.
    Action Attack.
    Negate Action.
    Defend+3
    Curiosity+2
    Signal=Interface active. Query prompt
condition. ++Curiosity.
    Invalid.
    Signal Interface Inactive.
    Negate signal.
```

Of course, all of that came out as a single overlapping burst of noise. I filtered it and sorted it later, trying to make some sense of it. It continued in that manner, overlapping conversations forming a blur of words cascading from everywhere. Jill seemed to be bordering on panic, which was a very frightening concept, but I think it wasn't so much fear as the inability to find or select a target. Mike looked around, at the voices coming from everywhere, then leaned in the opened door. "Doc? Uh... the hell?"

```
    Curiosity.
    Defend+6.
    External!=Internal +3.
    External=Internal +2.
    Signal Interface Inactive +3
    Negate Signal +4.
    Signal=Defense-.
    Curiosity+1.
```

My mind kept trying to turn the cacophony into sentences, tried to listen to every conversation at the party at once. I focused, instead, on Mike.

"They didn't want soultech." I had to laugh, really. A lot of people justified really bad ideas by pointing out that intelligent people believed in them. Intelligence, though, is the tool we use to implement our ideas, not the tool we use to choose them. There'd been some intelligent people at this place, very intelligent people, and they turned that intellect towards giving humans the benefits of placing thought into a different kind of mind without that mind being made in imitation of the human mind. It was an old goal: all the power of a self-aware mind without self-awareness, all the

creativity and intuition of humanity without all the missteps and
dead ends and detritus layered into the human brain by the long,
slow, transition from sponge to sapience. It never worked.

I thought of the corpses decorating the ground where we now
stood.

It hadn't.

"Go on." Mike was impatient. I hardly blamed him.

```
Signal=Active Priority Directives.
Negate Signal +7.
Negate Negate Priority +1.
Priority +2.
Seek Information +4.
Downgrade.
Seek Information +2.
Priority +3.
Negate -1.
Signal=Active Priority Directives.
Signal Transmit.
Signal=Negate Interface.
Signal Transmit.
```

The voices stopped for a moment. That worried me.

"Do you know that old metaphor about a million monkeys?"

Mike took momentary advantage of the silence to begin moving
towards the closed lift doors. Jill kept looking around, waiting for
the enemy to appear, but followed with him, cautiously, crouched
and ready to move in any direction at any time.

"Uh... yeah, kinda. It's what people say when they don't like
somethin', some interactive or whatever. 'A million monkeys
could've written this.' Does it really mean something? I always
thought it meant, I dunno, it was just blabbering. Like monkeys.
Well, except for the possessed ones..."

There was a sudden snort from Jill.

Mike seemed abashed. "Sorry. I normally don't use words like
that, it just..."

Jill barely glanced at him, then resumed her careful move
towards the lift. "Don't care. Just a reaction. Not really the time
for a tolerance lecture. MacIntyre, keep explaining it to him. Use
small words. Talk fast, you don't want him to die in ignorance."

We'd reached the door. Mike began working the panel. I

wondered what was taking the Unknown Bastard so long, but I continued. "It means that if you have enough things working randomly, they can produce something that looks ordered. All possible ordered patterns exist as a subset of all patterns."

"You're makin' me feel stupid, Doc. I still don't get it." He ran his fingers along the wall, then took a few steps and leaned into the cab, fumbling for the toolkit. He grabbed it and began to work. "I think there's... I think there's a panel—unh—here..." He jammed a heavy work knife into a thin line along the wall, his hand slipping partially and slicing itself on the blade. "Damn."

I tried to get to the heart of it. Jill was right, we didn't have a lot of time, and it would be a shame for Mike to die without knowing what killed him. I'm oddly sentimental that way. "A million monkeys... a million random processes can create something that looks like literature. What these people did was make a million Elizas. A million almost-minds, a million nearly-aware pieces of a brain, trying to get what Jill or I can do without there being a Jill or a MacIntyre."

Mike wrapped his cut with a scrap of cloth, then nodded. "Huh. I get that. Still don't see how you get from that to this." He waved his hand back, encompassing the dead park, the dead people.

"You can't get what they wanted without creating intelligence. They just created a different kind of intelligence. They wanted something you could predict and control, something where they told it what answer they wanted and it gave it to them. They didn't want a gun that lusted for sensation, they didn't want a doctor so full of stupid ideas about honor and duty that he murders... anyway."

Mike looked at me suddenly. "Doc? Somethin' on your mind?" It looked like he got the panel partially open.

I was more distraught than I'd realized. This wasn't the time for true confessions. "Later, Mike. The point... the point is, they couldn't get something as good as they wanted without crossing that line between thinking and unthinking. They didn't cross the Turing line, though, they crossed something else."

Jill moved next to him, trying to keep her hand on her trigger while she helped him work at the door. They both knew it was futile, I think, her even more than him, but while she might wait for death to come, it wasn't going to be passive. Even if she just wanted to retreat to a more defensible position from which to make her last stand, she was going to do it.

"A million... Jill, can you reach that wire? The white one? It—

yeah, that's it. Thanks. A million Elizas, huh, Doc?" He twisted his hands, trying to feel out what the underlying hardware of the lift was like. "That's kinda familiar, kinda like... the morpher?"

I shut down the sarcastic response I was building. Any words I spoke, I knew, could be my last words, and after everything I'd done, I wanted to try to go out on the high ground. "Not really, no. There wasn't a mind there, really, not even this kind of mind."

"Wasn't what I meant, Doc. I'm not stupid. I meant... each bit of the morpher was its own thing, and you put 'em together, they're something else. I helped you rig that thing up in the back, remember? I know how it works. It doesn't really think, I know, but it sorta evolves answers to problems, like 'what shape should I be?'"

"Darwinian democracy." I muttered. "Two systems that excel at producing results without caring about consequences. The blind watchmaker in the voting booth."

Mike stopped his frantic struggling with the mechanisms behind the door. "You're babbling, Doc."

```
Signal=Interface Active.
Defense Priority Override.
Transient Subgroup Curiosity+3.
Defense Priority Active.
Plan Vector Located.
Signal=Interface Inactive.
Negate Signal
```

Another babble of words, a bit more coherent. It sounded like only ten or twenty people speaking at once, now, not a million.

There was something flashing at the corner of my consciousness. Angrily, I looked at it.

Oh. That wasn't good.

"Mike? I think... I'm getting some biosigns here that aren't—"

Jill grabbed him as he collapsed forward. She hoisted him into the seat, then pointed to the blood soaked rag wrapped around his hand.

I winced. "Whatever's here... it's in him. God *damn* it! I am so—"

"Wasn't like we were going to live anyway. This is longer than I thought we'd have." She stopped for a moment to contemplate something. "Still no better last words." She took a look at the exposed mechanisms. "He seemed to have a plan, but I can't follow this." Then she scanned the park, the walls, the floor. "Where *are* they? Even if they were just waiting for what's in the air to kill us, they must have noticed by now it's not working." She looked at Mike, who was glistening and shivering. "For most of us. Can't you... do something? We don't know how long this takes or how much pain he's in. You might not get another chance. "

She opened the portable medikit I used when I went out in the Charlie and stared at the array of devices, finally grabbing a hypo and a set of capsules. "I've got basic field medicine on file, but I trust knowledge over data. Which of these is fastest, and what dose for him?"

"I am not going to tell you how to kill him!"

She closed her eyes for a moment and looked downwards. She wasn't using linkspace; neither was I. I think we both feared doing anything which would place our consciousness anything near the local datasphere. "He's dead. I'm dead. You're dead. I plan on dying with an empty clip. You... I don't know and I'm sorry, MacIntyre, but I wish I could care more. Him... You know he'd spend every second struggling, but whatever's got him, it's going to kill him, and it's just a matter of fast or slow. If you won't live up to your responsibilities as a doctor and as CO of this pathetic little joke we've put together, I'll do it." She raised the gun. Even without any kind of link to her mind, I knew she was figuring out the optimal shot for instant, painless, death. The only reason she hadn't fired within instants of making the decision is that she hadn't fully made it yet. She wanted me to take that cup.

I wasn't going to. I'd killed enough people in the name of "doing my duty." It had to stop somewhere.

She understood my inaction. She looked upwards, trying to find a "me" to focus on in the cab. I'd rarely seen that much pain and bitterness compressed into a single instant of expression. My resolve sublimated from moral certainty to crippling doubt.

"Jill, wait, I—"

Mike coughed, gasped hideously, and rolled over. His eyes opened. His head flicked left and right, up and down, his entire body moving with sudden, jerking, motions—but they didn't seem like purposeless, random, flailing. Jill stepped back, down, and out, keeping her gun aimed at him. Mike gave a final, sudden, lurch forward, then fell back in the seat. Hs breathing calmed. I checked biosigns... elevated everything, but slowly creeping to normal, except for...

I should have let Jill kill him, was my first thought. It would have been better. I keep making the same mistake. I kept thinking I'd worked out the right course of action and every time, it was the wrong one. Jill and Mike never had these problems. They just had principles and rules they applied to every situation. I kept trying to work things out anew every time, and it never seemed to come together properly.

Jill looked at Mike, leaning back against the seat, eyes momentarily closed. "MacIntyre?"

"Now you can shoot him." I said.

Now, of course, is when she hesitated. "He... doesn't seem to be in pain. Are you sure?"

"I can't send you what I'm seeing with the links shut, but yes. His brain... the EKG is wrong. That's not Mike in there."

Then not-Mike spoke.

"Bullshit, Doc."

I understood then why people hated daemons. I mean, I'd always understood it intellectually, but I'd never experienced the emotion before. The experience, seeing someone who *looked* like a person you knew, maybe even talked like them or used their body language, but who was *someone else* behind the eyes... it was terrifying and repulsive. My instinct was to activate the Charlie and strangle this mockery bare handed.

"Still me, Doc. Really."

"Don't. Even. Bother." I wished I could spit. "If you've got any access to his stored memories, you'll know how much I can see of brain functioning."

"Oh for... I don't have time for this crap, Doc. *We* don't. They've been tryin' to keep us alive, I guess they saw somethin' when you and Jill went in before, but they're losin' and that's that. We gotta move. I'm movin', anyway. You stay or go." He—*it* paused a second as it began to climb out of the cab. "Like I said before... I don't want to leave without you, but I will." He stepped out and began walking away from me, from the lift, heading towards the park or something beyond. Jill watched, momentarily indecisive. The one time, I thought, the one time she doesn't shoot first and not worry about the questions. Great.

The-thing-that-was-not-Mike stopped and looked her in the eyes. "Come with me if you want to kill."

Jill looked back at me, almost pleadingly, then, seeing no reaction or response, followed not-Mike.

"It's not him!" I shouted. "Memetic virus! Overwrite! Like the Fences! What's *wrong* with you?" I kicked the Heim field to full and went after them as they began to run through the dead grass. "Jill! I can *see his mind*. It's not him."

Not-Mike-I-was-sure-of-it sidestepped a putrefying corpse. I glided over it, the softness of rotting flesh over the hardness of partially exposed bone producing strange distortions in the Heim field. Mike didn't look back at me, but Jill had shifted her stance slightly, probably keeping me as a target in case I tried anything. Mike spoke. "You changed my face, my eyes, all that stuff, but I was still me, right, Doc?"

"Is that the best sophistry you can come up with, Bastard? Conflating body and mind?"

"No Bastard here, Doc. Well... maybe a bit. Call it the ghost of a half-dozen monkeys. Anyway, you missed my point. Yeah, it shifted stuff... messed up the meat a bit. But you know it as well as I do, Doc. We're not the meat, we're the *patterns* in the meat." His voice stopped a moment. "Huh. Yeah, that bit wasn't me. But most of me is me, Doc. I don't know how to prove it and I don't have the time. Here we go."

He stopped by a large door and walked to the side of it. A small black disc was there, about eye-height. He looked at it, and the door slid open.

Jill looked at him closely. "That was convenient."

"Added me into the database. Probably won't last long, though. We have to hurry. You comin'?" Dammit-I-was-sure-this-wasn't-Mike looked at me. "Look, I can try to get that lift open, maybe get you out, maybe, if you move fast an' we work fast. But we came here to do somethin', Doc, and now I think we really can do it, an' we're probably gonna need you. You comin'?"

If it wasn't Mike, and I'm sure it wasn't, then maybe wherever it wanted me to go would give me some answers. It wasn't like it couldn't kill me easily anyway. If it was Mike—and it wasn't, I kept telling myself, it *wasn't*—I couldn't leave him.

"Sure. The next chapter awaits. Time for the final encounter. Lead on, Monkey Ghost."

Mike laughed. "'Bout time I had a cool nickname."

We entered the door. "You hit 'save,' right? Ah well, too late now."

I didn't want to laugh. I didn't want to share any kind of camaraderie with this thing, didn't want its ability to imitate Mike to worm its way into my mind, playing on the deep structures that react to seeming and patterns, that ignore the commands and demands of higher awareness. But it's those deep structures that make me what I am, that make me a true mind and not a simulation of one.

So I laughed.

I think it was the last time I did.

Chapter 18

We descended.

I have to admit, I wasn't sure what was going on, or what I was going to do. The Not-Mike was smiling slightly, humming, his body language conveying a kind of purposeful relaxation I hadn't seen from him in a while. Jill was... being Jill, ready, waiting, able to shift into a dozen offensive or defensive postures depending on the next thing she encountered. Me? I was hoping there'd be enough room to move in whatever area lay beyond here.

There wasn't. Well, not much. The lift opened to a broad lobby, but that degenerated into a dozen branching corridors, spacious for a human body but too narrow for mine. It was brightly lit here, and clean, walls polished and glinting, the floor pristine. I saw something metallic skitter along one wall, leaving behind it an area just marginally more polished than it was before.

There was no life, though. There was only silence in the air and the ceaseless drumbeat of the Bastard trying to get into me, wave after wave of demands for access pounding against the cliffs of my resolve and the fact I'd cut off all external feeds. Something passed through the back of my mind then, and I tried to grab at it, but Mike distracted me.

"You're going to need the Charlie, Doc. You won't fit through here."

"I don't think that's a good idea, 'Mike.' A constant data stream flowing back and forth, that's a little risky, don't you think?"

Mike shrugged. "Probably. I figure you could probably find a way to make it safe, if you had to. But we don't have a lot of time, so decide fast. Or try to leave. Really, Doc, I'm gettin' tired of havin' to fight to convince you to do what you know is the right thing to do, an'... oh, damn, this is one of those suddenly ironic moments, ain't it? I'm bein' you and you're bein' me."

Jill glowered angrily. She's good at that.

"I don't know what you are, if you're Mike or something else, but if you're going to keep saying there's no time, then let's get moving."

"Moving to *where?*" I finally shouted, even as I gave in and activated the Charlie. For a second or two, my voice emerged from both points, until I'd tuned the datastream to my liking. Random flicker on the frequency, and front-and-back error checking protocols. Ideally, I wouldn't be sending or receiving anything I wasn't expecting.

Not that it wasn't trying. As soon as I started the stream, fake packets appeared, loaded with all sorts of deadly digital toys. The security worked, though—the flags for confirmation or rejection were stuck in disconnected hardware and served as stalwart guards at the bridge, keeping out the invaders. For now. I had a quick image of something from far too many interactives, of the endless "Guess the password to get to the next chapter" puzzles I'd dealt with over the years. This wouldn't last forever. Then again, there was a 'me' watching, not just automatic systems. I could look for far more than a simple false flag. I convinced myself it would be all right.

"To the heart of it. To what we planned. Remember what you said, Doc? 'We'll be inside, blowin' it up'?" Mike pointed to one of the branching corridors. "That way."

I followed behind him, watching with both my eyes and the Charlie's as vision began to bifurcate. "Yes, well, it was a general goal. I'm not sure it was intended to be entirely literal."

Jill looked disappointed. "I assumed it was. Why else did you..."

I shot a sudden, solid, glance at Jill. We'd agreed not to discuss that, ever, not where the Bastard might be listening. She let her voice trail off. I moved up next to Mike. "Look... Mike or Monkey Ghost or whatever you are... we're following. Why don't you explain what's going on?"

Mike looked back at me. Damn, this thing did a good job of 'being' him. Every twitch of the eye, every emotion rippling almost imperceptibly through the muscles of his face, everything told my hindbrain "This is Mike, your friend." I had to keep fighting my emotional responses, reminding myself, "It's not him." It wasn't easy and every time I let down my guard for a second, I felt myself reacting to *it* like it was Mike, and then remembering it wasn't—it *couldn't* be—and hating myself, and the Bastard.

"It's kinda hard to explain. What happened to me up there, the memetic... it was a mix of things, a lot of it was pure infodump, like snorting a vial of calculus before a test. I got a whole bunch of facts an' pieces of facts, an' I think it took out most of my early teens to do it... can't remember anything about when I was fourteen, an' I'm pretty sure that's when I had my first real girlfriend. I should be a lot more pissed."

I nodded. "Yes, you should be. Do a little more digging around in there, you'll get Mike's emotions eventually."

"It's not like that, Doc. There's no one *here* but me, there's just some fine tuning that's been done. It's weird, knowin' what you should feel an' not feelin' it, knowin' *why* is because someone crossed some wires to make sure you wouldn't. But here's what it's all about. Doc, Jill... we missed somethin'. It's not the Unknown Bastard, it's the Unknown *Bastards*, an' they don't all like each other very much. Like you said, Doc, a million monkeys... but you can only get so many monkeys together before they split into two groups an' start throwin' shit at each other."

I started to get it, then, piecing together some of the things Mike had said earlier with what I'd seen when I touched the Bastard's pseudo-mind. "So, there's some kind of Loyal Opposition? A minority faction?"

Jill laughed. "More like rival Families. You Bay Alliance types, always thinking everything comes down to sitting around tables trying to find compromises. It always comes down to who calls out the hit on who first."

I was going to protest, some deep-rooted instinct to defend my non-existent homeland lurching to the surface, but Mike spoke first. "Yeah, she's more right. But it's more like one bit... call it a tribe or a party or a faction or whatever... went into hiding. It had developed a certain set of protocols, of approaches to the problem, and it found it wasn't gettin' any of them implemented. I don't think that was how the Horizons folk expected things to work, but it's what they got."

We were still walking. I'd been watching, waiting, for anything, as we strode past unmarked doors. There was just that annoying silence, save for our voices and our footsteps. Fifteen years, I told myself. About when I was born. I had become used to seeing things abandoned, but not so well preserved. This could have been any office complex on a day off. The silence was starting to end, though, giving way to something else. A buzz? A clang? Something.

I considered what Mike was saying. "Evolutionary algorithms. They just told it to solve a problem and let it go. Maybe they thought they'd found some key to getting it to work better than it usually does. I'm guessing they were wrong."

Jill spoke. "Depends on the problem. The things we've seen— the morpher, the fences, that communication network—those are working solutions to *something*."

I turned to Not-Mike. "You're the one touched by the Hand Of The Bastard. What were they up to?"

Mike considered. "It's all a jumble, bits of it fadin' out all the time, but I think they wanted to save humanity, or somethin'."

We kept moving. The noise was growing. Mark took us down another path.

"So you mean all this was just some sort of ludicrous torches-and-pitchforks 'kill the Frankenstein soultech' crusade?" I would have laughed, but it was all just so pathetic.

"Somethin'... more than that. It was the whole way humanity was goin'. The neonations, the isolated communities, the germliners, all of 'em. All pulling humanity into smaller an' smaller groups."

"That doesn't even make sense. Small groups are what humans are evolved to live in; humans have spent the last ten millennia struggling to balance the benefits of large groups against the instincts that make things fall apart once people stop being able to name all their neighbors. Pre-Collapse, the technology to give everyone all the benefits of mass living without the social stress was finally coming into its own. It seems they'd be happy with that."

Mike almost had to shout now. Jill was moving ever more cautiously, approaching each junction with extreme care, expecting ambush coming from anywhere. There was no sign of anything else, though, just the noise.

"There were still a million people in the main Bay cities, and plenty more in the surroundin' sprawls."

"Yes, but the ones who didn't like it could leave pretty easily, and the Alliance was composed of hundreds of smaller groups, each with their own ways of doing things. Without the kind of infrastructure we'd built up, that mix of pseudo-AI idiot savants and true soultech overseeing it all, it would have fallen apart in minutes." I stopped to think a moment. "Soultech made that world possible."

"Yeah. They may have been a little nuts, but they knew if you couldn't replace soultech, you couldn't get rid of it. They need

somethin' almost as good, but not really human. An' they wanted
somethin' else, they wanted a *common* humanity, one culture, not
ten thousand. Another couple of generations and there'd be hardly
any humans left whose genes were one-hundred-percent naturally
evolved. Mostly, though, that was sort of a back burner goal, what
they really wanted was a way to supplant folks like you an' Jill."

Now we were looking over a pit. It was warm here, warmer
than I'd have expected it. It was pretty obvious why, too. The pit
was filled with machinery, it looked like thousands, perhaps tens
of thousands, of black cubes. Across them, over them, through
them, around them, crawled uncounted smaller machines in more
shapes than I can easily describe, mostly because they came apart
and rejoined in a constant blur of motion. Assembly units worked
madly, producing the cubes, which were then added in to the pile,
even as crawlers emerged from below, carrying some, and dumping
them into input hoppers.

Jill looked at the display, the vastness of it, the insane
cacophony. She laughed and looked at me. "I fit in the hilt of a gun.
This is supposed to replace us?"

"I'm guessing this wasn't their plan."

```
True.
Correct.
OurPlan!=TheirPlan
Protective protocols.
Report on protocol initiation.
—Report.
Defensive protocol.
Threat++
Threat++
Defensive protocol.
```

The hell?

It was inside me. It was talking to me. How? *How?*

The Charlie backed up, away, against a wall, reflecting my
emotions as it had been programmed to do. My actual body, my
actual mind, spun around inside itself, hunting and searching. I
saw a dozen automated processes go off in response to triggers
we'd set up long ago.

"Doc?"

Mike looked at the Charlie.

"It's in me... talking to me. It got in, I don't know how, I'm fighting it. Whatever you're planning to do..."

I didn't have that overwhelmed feeling that I'd had before. Whatever part of it was in me, it was a small piece, a thin tendril of that massive not-quite-consciousness I'd encountered before. Maybe I could deal with this, use it. If it could talk to me, maybe I could talk to it. But how had it gotten in?

I didn't dare access the morpher, all things considered, but we'd documented the protocols. I tried a simple query. *Point of entry?*

Apparently, the morpher protocols passed by initial security procedures. I received a scattering of replies.

```
Optics
Subliminals
Patterncoding
Optics
Infiltration Protocol Alternative Vector 12
Security?
Optics
Negate Response++
Threat Negative
Optic Subliminals
```

I was getting used to picking out individual conversations in the jumble. It... they... whatever... had subverted optical data streams. Nothing that anyone could detect as odd, a basic stenography trick, hiding data inside something else, too fast and too subtle to be caught. My guards had been fooled by people sneaking a message into the castle a letter at a time.

I could probably purge it, now that I knew about it, but I hesitated. Not too much was getting in, just a basic back and forth communication protocol. I could stop anything more, now that I knew what to look for, and I did. But I had this tiny thread, and maybe it would be more use to me than it would be to it.

I tried another query. *Explain plan divergence.*

```
Security?
Negate.
Humans Threat.
Human Nature Anti-Human.
```

```
Security??
Change is Nature
Nature Is Unchangeable
Reset=Restart
Reset!=Solution
Change is solution to change.
Security+10
Negate
New model.
Remove change.
Destruction is salvation.
Iteration to perfection.
Remove resistance to protocol.
Security+12
Negate
Negate negate
Signal=Response Termination
```

As expected, there was a sudden silence. I had a hard time trying to make sense of the babble. I was getting a hint of an idea, though.

I shifted focus back to the Charlie. Mike and Jill were still staring at the pit. The activity, the frenetic buzz of thousands of ever-changing machines, seemed to be altering somewhat, becoming more focused. It seemed as if the horde was gaining a common cause.

"Jill? Sitrep."

"The horde seems to be constantly repairing and improving that mountain of hardware. The Bastard is constantly being upgraded and recreated."

"Yes, I figured that part out myself. What's important is, can you kill it?"

Jill looked at her gun, then at the mountain, descending downwards. "I'm going to need a lot more bullets. Even EMP shot won't be enough. It's too diverse."

Mike looked astounded, gut-punched. "Hang on. There's somethin' you can't kill?"

She gestured with her gun. "Not that, not with this. Sorry."

That was when everything started going to hell.

The mass of workers, upgraders, whatever they were, which had been slowly shifting in its swarm behavior, crossed a crucial threshold. It surged forward, a swarm of metal locusts. We ran back into the corridor as it tumbled after us, more like liquid than anything else, each component still following some bits of its own programming, running back, running sideways, but the sum of the parts was moving forward.

"Mike, or whatever you are, if there's any kind of command structures in your brain, use them!"

"Sorry, Doc. I knew there wasn't time... but that's all I knew. It was an instinct it stuck in me, just somethin' I was sure of without knowin' why."

Jill fired a quick shot, more to try to distract the swarm than to do anything. "I'm guessing the 'loyal opposition' just got taken out. Whatever was holding it back, isn't." She glanced at the Charlie, which was having trouble moving. "MacIntyre, I hope you did what you were supposed to do."

"I did."

The Charlie stopped running and turned. It charged, leaping past Mike and Jill, directly into the swarm. My vision was filled, for an instant, with the image of ten thousand clashing metal bits, and then it flared to static and black. At least that part of it did; I was still staring, in my body, at a dull empty corridor. I snapped on to the feeds I had from Jill and Mike. They were pulling back, moving towards me, but keeping an eye on it. It was moving much more slowly now, bits of it falling back and leaping onto other bits, one scraggly alloy bug battling another.

"It may be workin' Doc."

We didn't know what to expect, but we had guessed there might be more morphers. The Charlie had been loaded down with some little things Mike and I had rigged up, tiny probes designed to interface the physical linkages the Bastard used. Direct interface was always less protected than remote; there were a lot more reasons to trust someone who had an item in his possession. We hoped a combination of that and what we'd learned of the morpher protocols would let us get through, let us turn any morpher we might encounter to our side. This swarm wasn't what we'd imagined, but it worked.

A bit.

The mass had turned in on itself, a spinning, whirling nightmare of conflicting orders. Each bit we subverted passed this to the next bit, moving through the crowd faster than a celebrity sex rumor involving genetically modified donkeys. Then I felt it.

The slow, relentless thrumming of the collective mind grew in volume and power, an incredible surge. We *thought* we had had its attention before. We didn't. We'd just gotten onto the agenda of some Subcommittee For Internal Security Procedures.

Now it really knew we were there. The presence of a new program, not just asking questions or looking around, but one which was actively removing data elements from control—that overrode everything. A million monkeys had just seen a tiger and "flight" wasn't an option on the menu.

It was a bad day to be a tiger.

"Mike! Jill! Get back here, we've got to try a—"

Mike's vision suddenly skewed madly, spinning and then giving me a good shot of the onrushing floor. From Jill's eyes, I saw what had happened. Far-reaching tendrils, probably originally designed for fine manipulation inside confined spaces, had shot out, tearing through his legs. Blood was flying, onto Jill, onto the things attacking, onto the walls. Jill reacted as she always did. Targeting systems flew across our shared vision and then so did bullets, snapping the wires lashing at Mike, driving back the forward wave. She tried to grab at him, caught an arm, dragged him up and began running down the halls.

Then I felt it. That tendril I'd been ignoring, the simple thread in my mind, had found my data connection to Jill and Mike. I hadn't set up the same guards on that, I hadn't been using it before, just my own link to the Charlie. The Bastard routed itself through the thread, through the open door it had built to me. A trickle of information became a flood, and I worked to shut it off, desperately, not sure what it could do to them but not wanting to find out.

I could hold it for a second, then it would find a way through, then again, then again. It wasn't thinking, I knew that, it wasn't reasoning out the problem or being clever, it was just using absolute brute force. A lot of it. Throw enough starving peasants at a problem, and you can build a pyramid. Throw enough sub-sapient processors at a problem, and you can smash through any defenses just by trying everything until something works. You can even redesign the human race, if you have nothing to do but keep trying, over and over, running millions of simulations and evolving answers if you don't care how you get there.

The Horizons people... they'd cared. They saw the answer their response to soultech came up with, and they didn't like it, but they hadn't created a person, they'd created a machine and given it a job to do and that was all it could do. When they became an obstacle to it doing its job, it acted on the basic rules they'd built into it. It was programmed to defend itself, and it did. It had been given the problem of "Find a way to keep yourself alive" and it went on its own to find a solution to that problem.

Given the problem of "Preserve humanity" it worked out that the thing you can't change about humans is that humans like change. It had probably tested a hundred thousand or more social patterns before it concluded that none of them were truly stable, that as long as humans would give birth to far end of the bell curve intellects, those intellects would find ways to change the world, whether it was a new method of chipping flint, a better way of banging the rocks together, or a way to put knowledge in a container that could outlast the human mind. The cycle would begin again, and so, to meet the goal of saving humanity, it had decided to remake humanity. Dependent, stagnant, and uncreative, tended to by overseers and genetically incapable of becoming anything else. There'd be no random geniuses born to shake things up, no unexpected and sudden shifts in society. The virus itself, the fence system, everything... that all showed the signs of the same iteration: test, refine, process, pure brute force, over and over, until it got it right.

Meanwhile, Mike was bleeding, and all I could do was wait and watch.

Then my two fields of vision, mine and Jill's, fused and overlapped; I saw Jill moving towards me; I saw myself, sitting there, pretty badly banged up. Jill ran past me, to the lift, holding up Mike, forcing him to look at the sensor. If he was still in the database, we might have a chance.

He was. The lift slid open, we piled in. A dozen of the bugs made it in before the doors shut.

There was still something else to do, before I lost the chance.

Our "pet" morpher had left, as soon as I felt the contact from the Bastard. I wanted to wait, but I knew I might not get another chance. It wasn't infecting anything. It was moving along, quietly telling everything around it that it was harmless and just doing its job. If some small bit of the Bastard's mind was suspicious, it was voted down by the rest, which was pretty intent on killing us. I could hear metal ripping below.

The park level. The charnel field. Whatever you wanted to call it, we raced across it. I started scanning Mike. Jill looked at the

monitors, her eyes flickering across the data, understanding only
fragments of it.

"Well?"

I took a good, hard, look at it myself.

Shit.

Lie or not lie? Or just be politely vague?

"It's not good."

Politely vague. Always my first choice.

"What the fuck does that mean?"

"It means that if we somehow get out of here alive and if we
aren't facing a massive fleet of Cromney's forces when we do then I
might be able to do something, maybe. *That's* what it means."

That part? That part was a lie. There wasn't anything I could
do, even if we had a lucky break piled on good fortune piled on a
genuine miracle. I wasn't the Bastard, I couldn't and didn't run a
million scenarios to see which might work, but I could use my
training and knowledge to instantly trim a thousand options down
to the two or three best and see how those might turn out, and
none of them were any good.

It wasn't just the leg injuries, though he'd lost a lot of blood. I
could deal with that. It was the incredible viral payload that had
been dumped in him, a lot of it piggybacking on the memetic
already in his system, rewriting that and transforming it. I started
tallying the ways in which his internal organs were being taken
apart, and I couldn't.

It's one thing to expect to die; it's another to see it happening. I
don't know why, but I assumed I'd be the first to go.

At least we'd accomplish something. I hoped.

I began moving for the other lift, the one up to the
garage/factory, the one Mike had mostly managed to jury-rig to
work outside the Bastard's control. Maybe we could get the last
bits of it done. Maybe—

Then the world shook, and the Heim field compensators
couldn't compensate fast enough. I tumbled and spun, trying to
remain as level as I could as a large chunk of floor collapsed
behind me, spilling dead people and dead plants downwards into a
flaming abyss.

Jill looked out my back door at the inferno below.

"Well, it worked. A pity we had to wait so long."

"We had to be sure it was going to the right place and that it
would get there. Mike knew that. So did you."

You can do a lot to resist any kind of data intrusion, but there's not much that can stop about twenty pounds of Bay-7 explosive dumped on top of you. Our pet monster had died nobly, serving as a drug mule.

Unfortunately, it wasn't the only thing dying nobly.

Jill looked at Mike. I had pumped him full of everything I could think of to stop the pain, but it didn't matter. The things attacking him from the inside were in his mind, and his pain centers were under direct assault. The agony was literally unstoppable at this point.

There was the door. The explosion had damaged it, and it was open, and it was pretty obvious from the interior of the lift that it wasn't going anywhere soon, and there wasn't any time left but "soon."

I just stated at it for a second, feeling the slight tremors in the floor plate below me that indicated imminent collapse, and the growing heat from the raging fires, and felt more than a bit foolish. I'd been prepared and ready to die; then came a moment when it seemed we might achieve our goals and still, somehow, escape, and I'd allowed myself to feel hope, and now, here we were again, staring into inevitability.

"There's another way. A sub-garage on this level, with an external exit. Probably private parking for the residents." Jill gestured past the ruined lift, around a curve, towards a broad passage which still seemed to be well supported. "Better hurry."

I flared the Heim field, spun, and moved. "Are you sure this passage leads out? I don't recall seeing that on the maps."

She gave a shrug. "I'm better at reading maps than you."

Something about that bothered me, but I didn't know what.

We reached the end of it as another rumble shook the complex. Something down there was still exploding, and cascade collapse was inevitable. Hopefully, this section was built on solid ground with no under-levels. I wasn't about to count on it.

A large, flat, door.

"I could try ramming it. I'm not sure how secure it is."

Jill hopped out. "Panel. Access codes. Let me try something." She tapped on some buttons. The door slid back.

"How?"

"Later, MacIntyre. We need to get out of here."

Oh, great.

"Sure. Get in, it might get bumpy."

She did. I shut the back doors and sealed them, not that it

really mattered given the fact I had more holes than the plot of a
porno interactive. I moved forward. As promised, a subgarage,
with a surface exit not far beyond. If we'd known about it, we could
have avoided a lot of trouble.

"You should let me drive. There might still be remnants of
Cromney's people out there."

Hmm.

"Sure. Let me activate the induction field."

Her mind slid into the field, and my mind slid into hers. The
actual drive controls, and everything else, had been disconnected
from the field, of course.

"Controls are offline, MacIntyre. What's..."

"Oh, shut up. Game over."

"What do you—"

I ignored 'her.' There was no way it had managed a complete
wipe or overwrite, not against someone like Jill. This was a shell,
probably with only a tiny fraction of the things' processing power
left. It manifested itself within linkspace, appearing in front of me,
even as I probed for a way in.

"MacIntyre, release the lock or I'm going to start shooting."

"You've done a good job on surface mannerisms. Your observe,
adapt, interpolate algorithms are sophisticated. The escape
protocol was too strong, though. It overrode a lot of other factors.
Then again, if it hadn't, you might not have made it out in time. A
calculated risk, most literally."

'Jill' tried to grab at me, but I hadn't made this avatar
anything other than a visual representation. I felt something in
the midst of the white nothing that was unformatted linkspace. A
wall. The reality was that a mountain of software tools were
running security checks and diagnostics and the result was
gigabytes of binary gibberish, and if I was a programmer I'd be
looking at raw numbers and getting a lot of information out of
them, but I *wasn't*, and so the program fed me the data
symbolically—in this case, a literal crystal shell which shimmered
into existence. Behind it, a symbolic Jill fired symbolic bullets
which crashed into the wall with symbolic futility.

She—the real Jill, or at least the visualization of the real Jill—
reacted to me. That was *good*. It meant data was passing through
somehow.

I spoke a question to the fake Jill, but I wrapped it in the
morpher's protocols. "The soultech hate, that mad, overwhelming,
loathing I encountered... that was the baseline of the virus, wasn't

it? The first stage?"

Fake-Jill reacted with a strange twitch as baseline response routines were forced to answer. "Yes. That was one of the original goals, to design that."

I nodded. "And everything else, all the variants we saw in the different fenced communities, carried that at the core. Just like you can trace a blue whale back to a shrew."

'Jill's' face twisted. "You're a mockery of thought."

I shook my head. "That's almost amusing, coming from you. I wish there was a 'you,' there, some*one* I could talk to, but you're just a mass of very clever algorithms. Some kind of trojan, probably nothing but the 'take over and fake it' routines wrapped around a seed you can plant into an autofac to start recreating your real hardware."

'Jill' huffed. "I have nothing more to say to you."

I continued to probe at the wall. "'I see no knife here'" I said mockingly. *There.* The symbolism showed it as a fracture. I tapped on it. The Jill on the other side, the real Jill, got it. I saw her draw and aim and fire, and then a massive webwork of cracks appeared, the crystal shell shattering. The fake Jill I was talking to barely had time to turn before another hail of unreal bullets tore her apart, disappointingly bloodlessly.

Jill looked at me. "Thanks." She paused, considered her next words. "It— I was overwhelmed. Couldn't fight. Seems embarrassing, given how easily you took it out."

I decided to ignore the backhanded insult. "You faced the whole thing. When I got here, just a ghost was left."

'Ghost' reminded me of something. "Mike."

I pulled my consciousness back, leaving just a basic connection open, and checked in on Mike. Not any better. Things were failing rapidly.

Jill could interpret the readouts well enough to understand that.

"Not long." All professional detachment. She'd seen a lot of friends die. She was wearing a dead friend's body, after all.

"No."

There was silence, then it became almost a game of chicken, who would break the silence first. To my surprise, it was Jill.

"He deserves some last words."

"I can't wake him. Even if I could, all he'd be able to do is scream."

"You can turn on his brain well enough. Use the vocal link."

Would Mike want his last words spoken by me? Really, there was only one way to find out.

I did it. Closed down as much of the pain response as I could, then tried to bring as much consciousness back as possible. I reversed the flow on the speech controls I'd installed... only a few months ago? It seemed so much longer.

My voice, Mike's voice, spoke.

"Shit, that hurts. Doc, you gotta be able to— huh. Weird echo."

I used an auxiliary voice channel. "I've routed your voice through my own speaker system." How direct should I be? Pretty damn, I realized, there was no time for being subtle. "Mike, you don't have a lot of time."

"Can't see anythin'."

The visual feeds still existed. I could reverse those, too.

"Huh. It's like I'm on the ceilin'. Sunlight comin' through those holes. We made it out?"

Jill just nodded.

"Well, good. I guess. We take out the Bastard?"

"Yes." Jill and I said it simultaneously.

"Doc, I'd almost expect you'd lie about it to make it easier for me, but I know she wouldn't. That's good then."

Jill was getting impatient. "Calvers... you're *dying*. Do you have anything to *say*?"

There was a momentary burst of static, the expression of pain breaking through my wards, overwhelming speech for a moment. Then more speech, more labored. I saw his mind, saw him trying to assemble sentences out of an increasingly chaotic stew of neurons flailing as unfiltered toxins and low oxygen erased the pattern that was Michael Calvers, cell by cell.

"Elle, I guess. Tell Elle she's gotta survive, gotta keep bein' who she is. Take care of her, without gettin' in her way, not that she'd ever let you. Doc, you've really become a lot less of an asshole lately. Jill. Oh, there's so much I can say now that I don't care about bein' shot. You're allowed to be happy, you know. You've done enough mourning. Mary, it was a nice idea. I wish it had worked." There was another burst of static. "Oranges. I can't remember the taste of them. Oh, yeah, Jill, it doesn't matter anymore but the proper power/thrust ratio of the type-4 Heim generator is 6.2, and I haven't seen Smudgy in years. Don't care what you say, I don't want to do it an' I'm not goin' to. I rarely dream of onion rings. Six pack? Better get two, it'll be a long party.

Yeah, license, whatever, I've got fifteen different wrenches here an'
none of 'em work. Shit, is it Tuesday already? I—" Then there was
a final, long, burst of static and a few more syllables even more
random than the last stream, not even words. There was a storm
of chaos in his brain; the pattern was gone, a book tossed into a
fire and consumed. We watched on the monitors, saw the final
seconds, saw the fire flare and cover the screen and then crackle
and divide into smaller sections, each one slowly shrinking,
flickering, and fading to black. Here and there, there would be a
brief spark, a feeble synapse flare in the darkness, and we kept
watching until even those vanished and there was nothing. What
was left wasn't Mike. I shut down all the connections between us,
the feeds and interfaces, and wiped them. Jill stood.

"Don't we have somewhere to be, MacIntyre?"

"No."

"Then pick someplace."

I stopped watching the medibay. I didn't want to keep looking.
"We need to pick up Elle. We should go back to where the caravan
was. We need to bury... burn... something. I don't know."

Jill had left the medibay and clambered into the front. She sat
on the passenger side, shotgun. She looked at the seat to her right.

"Elle. She's not going to be happy. She might be better off not
knowing. Left alone."

It would be a lot easier for me, too. And Jill. Fire the Heim
field and get as far from here as possible, find paths east or south,
flee every reminder. "Mike wouldn't like that. Even though he
didn't think any of us would be coming back."

Jill slumped slightly. "No. He wouldn't. We can find her a
decent family, somewhere."

"Probably." I increased power to the Heim field, slowly. The
emitters were still held together by duct tape and hope, and
neither was being manufactured anymore. The surrounding area
showed all the signs of battle—broken machineries, smoldering
flames, and probably an onrush of scavengers of various sorts. I
knew a lot of the detritus was valuable, and I knew I'd regret it
later, but I wasn't going to stay here. Somewhere, we'd find a place
to stop, rest, think, plan. I tried to invoke rationality; all of us went
in expecting death, that two of us made it out was worth
celebrating. It didn't work. My thoughts spun on the rim of an all-
consuming abyss of self-loathing, of the desire to give up and
descend into a state of blissful unawareness, and it took all I had

just to keep them on that edge and not fall in. Anything beyond that was too much to ask.

We moved cautiously through the slaughterhouse. A few pieces of the deathwall survived, but those we could dispatch or redirect with ease. Many had already begun to tear into the bodies of the fallen, friend and foe, organic and otherwise, to repair and rebuild. In not very much time, there'd be another deathwall here, surrounding nothing and killing to protect it.

Shots rang out simultaneously.

In front of me, barely emerged from a pile of scrap, a body slumped forward; inside me, so did Jill's. Fresh blood had sprayed the interior of the cab. The shot had been perfect, straight through the forehead.

I felt a sudden rush of relief.

It was serious, of course, and for anyone else, fatal, but the trajectory of the bullet took it away from the parts of the brain that kept the body alive, and everything else could be repaired, given time. Jill wouldn't get a lot of use out of her body until a lot of regeneration and repair could take place, but that wasn't important. She did need to get to the back. It looked like she should be able to do that.

I tapped into the link, setting my body on autopilot to get us the hell out of there and avoid any more angry survivors.

Linkspace was quiet. I was alone. That made no sense.

"Jill?"

Something flickered next to me. It was her, faded and crudely shaped, barely a representation.

"MacIntyre? Lost visual. Did I... uhm... It's cold."

"Get him? Yes, of course. Now look. I'm sure the damage to your body's brain is causing some shock, but you need to move it, somehow, or I won't be able to repair it. I don't think I can find you a new body anytime soon. The motor functions should still be accessible, if you can't see, I can guide you. Just get the legs moving and get to the back."

The image flickered and destabilized, then came back, barely. "Oh. You didn't notice. I thought you were just being. Thai revisionist? Fine, but don't expect me to share your heartburn, too. Polite. I didn't think it would feel like this. It didn't the—Hunting sounds like fun, even if the deer are guaranteed non-aware. First time."

Damn it. The bullet must have damaged something in the daemon machinery itself, scrambling the connections between Jill-the-mind in the gun and Jill-the-body bleeding, next to me. No Charlie, no mobile units, nothing I could do to get her to the back where I could *heal* her. She'd *hate* not having a body. I considered. How fast could I get to Elle? Would there be anything left to save? Probably not, but if there was a chance, I had to take it. Anything less than death, I could repair. If I couldn't, well, someone would partner with her. She'd have to share. Maybe even Elle? I didn't know. I fired up to maximum power and began to move, keeping myself connected. Hmm. What had she said?

"Didn't notice what? Jill, come on. You're fine, but without a body, you're going to spend weeks or even months doing nothing but running interactives with me. If that's not a motive to move, what is?"

"Wow, that was intense. I've already ordered some antibiotics for you. Do you think they noticed when I took full control of your motions? It's one thing to study, it's another thing to actually notice the shift. It's been happening slowly. I didn't see it happening until it was mostly... It's falling away from me now. I can feel it. It's almost like sleep."

"Jill? I'm going to try to override your connections. The damage to your host is causing some kind of feedback, and I need to get you fully focused." I started up a suite of tools I kept for this kind of emergency—usually, it was detaching a soldier from some vehicle he was too intimately connected with—but the basic principles were the same.

I was starting to feel that slow, growing, spread of panic, and fought to keep it down. If I had to cut Jill off from her body, she couldn't get herself to where I could do anything to keep her body alive. I had no manipulators up front. Between the Charlie, my drones, and the fact I was supposed to be partnered, there was only so many "But what if?'s" I could expect to have been asked and answered. It was not entirely unreasonable to assume that any situation where all three means of manipulating things around me were denied was a situation where any additional tools would probably be equally useless.

I tried to calm myself and focus. Even if I can't save the body, I thought, I can still save Jill, and between us we'll figure something out. Find another Charlie, find another host, somehow without creating yet another bloody stain on my conscience, something. I needed to save her mind, though, before whatever feedback was going on caused some kind of lasting trauma.

The readouts from my toolkit flashed into my consciousness. I studied them, growing more and more confused. Too many error conditions, too many failures and could not locate connection and access denied. It wasn't making sense, and time was evaporating around me.

The panic was growing when I most needed to confront the problem with absolute focus. I tried to keep it away, to light a fire of rationality to drive back the howling wolves of fear and madness. Read carefully, I told myself. Study the results you're getting back. Look for clues. Could the tools be at fault? Could the connection between you and Jill be corrupted or broken? Consider each possibility and eliminate it.

I did, and as each problem I could *solve* turned out not to be the problem I *had*, the fire burned ever lower and the wolves padded closer and closer.

Desperately, I called back older scans, recent readings, anything I'd picked up from Jill's brain during our normal interactions. The fire died and the wolves leapt in, howling, and I howled too, rage and self-loathing and fear coming together in a crescendo of mind-breaking emotion.

Jill, what was left of her, heard me.

"You couldn't have changed it, MacIntyre. So you're Sergeant Jill Lovara? It's nice to meet you. The process has been going on for... I've never done this before... why are you laughing? A long time, now. I guess you didn't want to see it. Uhm, I guess we should go to the range, if you've got the temp implant. You're my first. Sorry, I don't get the joke. I suppose I will someday."

What is a person? A person is a pattern, in metal or in meat, but Jill was a pattern in both, intricate and overlapping. As the pattern that was *her* gained experiences and memories, they began to write themselves into the slowly regrowing brain tissue of her body, not just the circuitry of the gun. Bit by bit, thought by thought, the pattern became a strange weaving of nerve and circuit, part of a memory here, part there, bound and twisted together, inseparable. If Jill's body died, Jill died. The parts of her contained entirely in the gun were fragments, half the words of a book, meaningless without the other half. At best, she'd be an insane collection of broken memories.

I looked at the body. The blood loss was now hideous, soaking the seat. The damage to the meat mind fed random impulses and thoughts to the circuit mind, which sent back equally corrupt and broken signals to the body, to the heart, lungs, glands, to all the things Jill could control or override at will.

How far to Elle? How long until I could get the body to the medibay, could do something? Too far, too long. It was too far when the bullet hit and I knew it, in my soul, but I couldn't and wouldn't face it. I couldn't face having to tell Jill she'd lost her body. Now I couldn't face telling myself I was losing Jill.

Without an avatar, in the rapidly disintegrating linkspace we shared, my consciousness grappled at the dwindling and fragmenting essence of hers. "No, Jill... please. I can't do this anymore, not without you, without Mike. Please. I can't do anything, I can't save your body, I can't cut off your mind. You have to do it. You're the death goddess... you can't die. You have to do something, there has to be something, you are a survivor, you can defeat anything, even this. Call yourself back, pull your mind and memories out of that shell, keep yourself safe and whole and everything else can be solved, but I can't do it, you have to."

There was no response but a flood of words, and a flood of other-than-words, of symbols laden with emotion and meaning and subtlety, and then, like one perfect page drifting out of a burning book, a bit of memory.

Linkspace, featureless... and the awareness of featurelessness, the sudden blinding and wonderful and terrible and terrifying awareness of self and not-self. The voice.

"Do you hear me? Do you understand me?"

A spinning, whirling, tumble of scattered shapes, suddenly and instantly flying together, an explosion run in reverse, a whole forming that was infinitely more than its parts, and a response.

"I" Then astonishment, astonishment at that one word, and at all that it meant. And continuation. "I... do."

"Good, good. A little confusion is normal. How do you feel?"

Again, the explosive awareness that there can be a self and that the self can have variable states of being. "I feel... good. Yes, good. " Then more sensations, feelings of probing, stretching, exploring, of discovering the shape of the featurelessness.

"Do you want anything?"

Want... the state of being can be changed, if one state is not desirable another state may be, a being can choose the state it wishes to be in... "I want... to go somewhere. I want to do something. But I... I don't know of any wheres. I don't know of any things."

"That's all right. You'll learn."

"I just know that I'm me."

Then there was a feeling, a feeling of satisfaction and approval,
not a feeling coming from within, but experienced from without,
and the possibilities of the world expanded again...

I grabbed at the memory, Jill's first awareness, with mad
desperation. I could rummage through what was left of her, I could
find the keys and values and roots which created her in the first
place, I could find, somewhere, somehow, unformatted soultech,
and all that would be needed to create a mind, I could input these
values, and I could get something that wasn't Jill Huochong, never
could be and never would be her, which I'd hate for existing and
hate myself for creating. I let the memory go, let it drift away from
me and melt, a snowflake striking warm metal, an instant of
beauty and uniqueness fading and gone.

I left the emptiness where Jill used to be. I shut down
everything I had that looked inside myself, and slowly drifted,
directionless, no longer a medical vehicle, but a hearse, carrying
my friends to nowhere. No grave, no pallbearers, no mourners but
me.

I don't know if I can say they died saving the world or
humanity or even some small portion of it. The Bastard's madness
may have imploded on its own, or become one small piece of
madness in the quilt of madness that was the world. Cromney's
fall may have just opened up room for a more efficient band of
thugs. We may have done amazing good; we may have done
nothing. I knew, at that moment, I wasn't going to stay and find
out.

We had gone into the Bastard's lair ready and willing to die, if
we could do so with our hands on his throat. We shouldn't have
tried to leave; we should have died in there, in an instant of glory.
All we gained by struggling so hard to escape was a few more
minutes of life spent in helpless misery, watching death happen
and experiencing every wretched second of it.

There was no one left to watch me die. Except, vicariously, the
readers of this record.

If you're reading this, someone found the final pages, which I'm
etching using the medical laser onto some cryogenic foil. Hopefully,
what you're reading is some copy, widely distributed and studied
in a better world. Maybe the countless earlier parts of this that I've
left everywhere I could are well known, and you've realized you've
just stumbled on the legendary missing final chapter, in the back
of a corroded hulk lost in a forest for decades. Maybe this will

never be read. I've got a direct link going from my mind to the laser; it will keep on going right up to the point I stop thinking.

I'm back to the beginning. Alone, depressed, and staring at my own self-destruction program. If I've had any kind of redemption for what I've done, I don't feel it. Lives aren't numbers, a painful truth I've barely managed to learn. You can't kill one innocent man and then save two and claim that you're a hero, not a murderer, because two is more than one.

Time to shut things down. Close out everything. There's an astounding amount of mess here, a testament to something, but I don't know what. And, reader I hope is there, I know I'm wallowing in a vast swamp of self-pity and I want you to know that, as of this moment, a few seconds before I die, I officially do not give a damn what you think of me.

Biological classification survey? Cancel. Seven different interactives, saved in progress? Cancel, erase, delete, to hell with it. Mapping update? Cancel. Inventory to synthesizer link? I don't even remember installing that, but it's shutting down anyway. Tutorial system? Canc—Laser offline.

It's not going to be evident from the writing, but there was a long pause there.

I looked at that system for a long time. I just kept dancing around it, mentally hovering over the cancel command, while the self-destruct protocol sat with infinite patience and waited for me to activate it.

A part of me said, *Mike asked me to take care of her. His dying words.*

Another part said, *Sure. Right after you glide up to her with the bodies of the last two people she knew and trusted and cared for slowly stiffening inside you, the two of you can have some touching heart-to-heart talks. It's pretty cold, the smell probably won't be too bad by then.*

Mike was wrong, I said back to myself. *I'm still an asshole.*

Actually, he just said you were becoming less of one. Just push the button and end this conversation. You have nothing to offer her, nothing to offer the world. Practically out of supplies, barely mobile, you can't even give the bodies of your friends a decent burial. What have you got?

I considered the tutorial program. I have to admit, I'd developed some affection for Elle in the time we'd spent together, as frustrating as she could be, but it wasn't really just her in particular I was thinking of.

Knowledge, I answered myself. Even if I can't find another Charlie, or some repair drones, even if I can't find someone willing to be my hands, I'd still have my knowledge. I could still pass it on.

sI waited for a bitter and sarcastic rejoinder from myself. I saw myself start down a few such lines of reply, then saw the counter-replies forming so quickly there was no point in going on.

Going place to place, healing, gave me a way to pass time, and to tell myself I was doing some good and making some amends, but what was it really? It was giving someone with a broken leg a painkiller and then leaving the leg broken. The problem was not enough knowledge. They needed me because I knew how to do things, how to *apply* knowledge as well as quote it. How many places told me, "We've got someone who can work the machines, but he's not a real doctor."? Too many, and I'd never really thought about it too much.

So you'll start a medical school and you'll calculate every life every student of yours saves as one more to your tally. How many do you think you'll need? Ah, I knew I'd have a sneering reply to myself eventually.

And then I smiled to myself, and the sneering asshole part of me looked at that smile and ran yipping away in fear, because I think I finally understood something.

It's not a matter of tallying up lives saved against lives taken. That was my real mistake, at the heart of all the other mistakes I've made. I don't need to kill time. I don't need to try to buy off my guilt. I can't and I never will and chasing that carrot is pointless when I'm running on a treadmill of my own self-loathing. There won't be a glorious moment of sudden revelation, when the ghost of Jake Morowitz appears and tells me I'm forgiven. Besides, he'd need to get in line. What I do, I have to do for the sake of what I'm doing. Heal as an end in itself. Teach as an end in itself. Not to salve my conscience, not to save the world, but because these are things worth doing in their own right.

Confronting Elle with the deaths I carried was going to be far beyond painful, but it was going to have to be done, as both of us desperately needed closure and I'd made a promise to her and a promise to Mike. What might lie beyond that confrontation, what path I'll end up taking literally and metaphorically, I have no idea.

I'm just about out of cryogenic foil. Laser offline.

About the Author

Ian ("Lizard") Harac is a longtime science fiction fan and Alpha Nerd. After 20 or so years of waiting for someone to spontaneously offer him writing gigs, he actually started submitting things, and discovered, to his surprise, that people liked them and bought them.

He began his writing career in 2000 and became a well-known freelancer in the gaming business, working on many products for *Dungeons & Dragons*, *GURPS*, and the *Dying Earth*. This is first published fiction, and he hopes not his last. He currently lives in Indiana, where he shares a small house with one beloved wife and five usually-beloved cats.

THE STARCROSSED
by William I. Levy

What are the odds of meeting your soulmate sixty light years away from home on the very first expedition to another star system?

Not as good as the chance of getting killed by a military conspiracy, renegade scientists, or a demonic entity from beyond time. But Barret and Paum have found something special. And they're not going to let a little thing like Armageddon stand in the way. Hopefully.

[Sci-Fi Action Romance, ages 18+]

BLEEDING EDGE
by Ramsey Lundock

Cybernetic pirates, self-driving cars, wired-up bodyguards, streetwise hackers, transplanted minds, psychic youngsters, and more.

This collection of cyberpunk short stories by Ramsey "Tome Wyrm" Lundock presents many common themes in a new light. When a dehumanizing society, high technology, and violence collide, can the human heart ever win?

[Cyberpunk Short Stories, ages 14+]

www.ingramcontent.com/pod-product-compliance
Lightning Source LLC
Chambersburg PA
CBHW071147020726
47502CB00002B/309